Previous selections of the
Universal Book Club

CAPER SAUCE
by S. P. B. MAIS

THINE ENEMY
by SIR PHILIP GIBBS

MARY OF DELIGHT
by NAOMI JACOB

WEB OF DAYS
by EDNA LEE

A FLOWER FOR CATHERINE
by FRANK SWINNERTON

THE BEND OF THE RIVER
by GODFREY WINN

AT SUNDOWN, THE TIGER
by ETHEL MANNIN

HONEY FOR THE GHOST
by LOUIS GOLDING

MART OF NATIONS
by WINIFRED DUKE

THE DANGEROUS PLACES
by LOUIS GOLDING

Subscibers may receive, as additional books, any or all
of the Club's previous selections that are still in print.
PLEASE WRITE FOR ORDER FORM AND CURRENT
LIST OF PAST SELECTIONS STILL OBTAINABLE

BY THE SAME AUTHOR

The Rajah's Guests
Cantonment
Government House
Take My Youth
The Man He Was
They Went to Karathia
The Promotion of Fools
North from Bombay
Himalayan View
Clash By Night

CARILLON
IN
BRUGES

by
SUSAN GILLESPIE

5 & 6 ST. ANDREW'S HILL, CARTER LANE
LONDON, E.C.4

First Published *February* 1952
Univeral Book Club Edition *March* 1953

Made and Printed in Great Britain by
GREYCAINES
Taylor Garnett Evans & Co. Ltd.)
Watford, Herts.

To

EVE and ERNEST BENOIDT
in Gratitude and Affection

"*The real beauty of the carillon was only achieved by the contrast of the deeper with the lighter tones—so it was with a man's life. The lightness and the sweetness and the merriment alone left but a memory of tinkling cymbals. The savour of existence was in the blend of the grave and the gay; in memories not only lit by laughter and song but by trials faced and disaster and loss met with courage, of love that cast fear from the soul.*"—ANON.

BALDWIN OF CONSTANTINOPLE

THE room was in darkness save for one small reading lamp to the left of a glowing wood fire, and the flames of the fire itself, which on that winter evening roared up the tall stone cavern of the chimney-piece and cast dancing flashes of brightness on the sombre walls lined with books, and gave colour to the bindings, gold and brown and scarlet here and there. Outside a bitter north wind lashed the shutters and tore at the trees, which bent before its fury, as it rushed across the Flanders plain. It would be spent before morning; but, with the barometer falling, the Countess de Fermandois knew she would wake to a still and perhaps white-rimed world, and the elms and poplars would be etched stark and black against the cold brilliance of the sky. If the cold weather continued there might soon be a thin coating of ice on the lake, which, with the surrounding bare trees and the brown sails of the windmill motionless against the sky, would resemble a Ruysdael painting. But that scene, when the ice hardened and thickened, would be filled with figures Bruegel might have known and portrayed, for they would come from the village and frozen fields to gambol and sport and slide and skate, as children among children, muffled in scarves, with skates and wooden sledges.

She spoke of this to her husband, who was sitting across the hearth from her, as she watched the clock anxiously lest the moment for which they were waiting should arrive before they were aware of it. She watched it in fear and impatience and excitement, as they continued to talk, not of the event for which they were waiting—he, as well as she, in excitement ringed by an unusual nervousness—but of the prospect of skating at Christmas and of the plans they had already made. The stillness in that room, when eager for the moment that was yet delayed by the slow movement of the clock they had fallen into silence again, was of the peace that was in their hearts, but which might, in an unguarded instant, he thought, be disturbed, though not destroyed, by memories.

So to fill those last empty and dragging minutes and to prepare her for what was coming, so that she would meet it with courage and delight and pride and happiness, the Count de Fermandois said to his wife, "Read me Miss King's letter again." And she rose from her chair by the lamp and found the letter in her writing-case on a table. She came back to the fire again, and still standing bent her head to read.

"Really, she says very little. It is only to thank us. She says, 'It is so good of you to have sent me two tickets. I don't know how to thank you. I am taking a friend who is very musical, for whom it will be such a great treat. Although after I had invited her—she is old, like myself— I thought I should have taken someone younger, who would be able to say in after years, "I was present at the first performance of *Baldwin of Constantinople*. And what a scene of splendour that gala night was!" When I learned how much your dear husband was connected with it all, I hoped you would both be present. But as you say you will be listening to it I know you will be there in spirit. Whoever would have thought it, the summer before last? Because Adrian seemed so young and carried his talents so modestly.'" The voice did not falter, it was low but even. "'I fear this will revive memories for both of you, as it will, in a much lesser degree, for me.' . . . That is all. Except the messages to all of us at the end—and her love and more thanks."

There was a pause, in which he knew there had been another glance at the clock. "It is time. Nearly time, now." There was the sound of her footsteps moving away from the fire, and when she had returned to his side, after she had bent down to add another log to the fire, he felt her hand touch his and close upon it.

Into the silence a clear voice spoke.

"This evening from the Royal Opera House, Covent Garden, we are broadcasting the first performance of a new opera, *Baldwin of Constantinople*, by the Belgian composer, Michel de Castelberg, with libretto by Adrian Morbeigh. This performance is being given in the presence of His Excellency, the Belgian Ambassador and the Foreign Ministers of Belgium, Holland, and Luxembourg, who are attending the London Conference of Foreign Ministers of the Benelux Countries. The performance is also being heard by listeners in Belgium to the B.B.C.'s European Service."

She had dropped on her knees beside him.

"*Ici Londres, le Service Européen de la B.B.C. vous présente ce soir une émission relayée depuis l'Opéra Royal de Covent Garden. Cette émission diffusée à l'intention spéciale de nos auditeurs Belges, vous permettra d'entendre la première exécution de l'opera du compositeur Belge. . . .*"

Following that introduction the voice in English spoke again. For listeners unacquainted with the story of the opera there was time to recount it briefly, to tell how in the year 1199 Count Baldwin of Flanders and his wife, Marie of Champagne, received the emblem of the Cross in the cathedral of Saint Donatian in Bruges, and to describe the opening scene set in the cathedral. To tell, also, of the death of Marie in Syria, in the scene which followed.

The Countess de Fermandois laid her head against her husband's knee, and turned her face from the fire into the caress of his hand. The voice was still speaking, telling of Baldwin's adventures after his wife's death. The intrigue in Bulgaria; his betrothal to the princess; her murder, and his escape. His life as a nameless hermit, a poor Christian doing penance for his sins in the great forest of Tournai, when Flanders believed he was dead; his renunciation of his worldly conquests, his throne and his name. Then his weakening beneath persuasion and flattery and his admission of his identity. His return to Bruges, to be received not as a crusader and conqueror, as Prince of Flanders, but as an outcast by his daughter and condemned to death.

A*

This libretto, the voice ended by saying, was written by a young Englishman, Adrian Morbeigh, while on a holiday in Belgium.

"Ladies and gentlemen—*Baldwin of Constantinople*.

"*Mesdames et Messieurs, veuillez écouter—Baudouin de Constantinople, de Michel de Castelberg, livret d'Adrian Morbeigh.*"

Into the room and into their memories there came the solemn music of the overture. . . .

CHAPTER I

PIERRE DE FERMANDOIS had been told his sister-in-law, Julie, was in the rose garden; and he went slowly along the path in that direction, with his left hand curled inside a leather loop attached to an Alsatian's collar, and his right hand closed upon the knob of a walking-stick. It was midday of an early September morning and the sun was hot.

Beyond his brother's garden and farm the Flanders plain stretching northwards to the sea and westwards to France was dwarfed by the sky. Under the immensity of that sky, in cloud or in sunshine, the farms and fields and the sheep and cattle, the windmills, rivers and canals, and the villages all assumed toy-like proportions. The roads, new, arrow-straight *autostrades*, or ancient tracks paved with cobble-stones, and the cream-coloured trams that trundled from the coast to Bruges were Lilliputian under a sky that had always filled three-quarters of a canvas that any artist had ever painted of that country. To Pierre de Fermandois the *Flandre* was his home; and long ago as a young man—when life held a promise he never questioned— he had wondered if that all-enveloping majesty of sky had given the Flemings—tenacious, thrifty, often dour and suspicious, ill-disposed throughout their history to accept a foreigner on equal terms—their unwavering faith in God. In the little wayside shrines and calvaries they brought Him close to their lives. From there had sprung the art of the country, in simplicity and integrity, rooted in the soil, the hearth and the home.

As he walked along the path in the hot sunshine a bell was ringing in the distance, and in the single, unmusical strident clang there was a significance, rarely forgotten by those who heard it, because that particular village church had been renowned for its peal when he was a boy, and all but one bell had been removed by an enemy, which twice in his lifetime had invaded his country. Hearing it break upon the warm air in the silence he did not think of its

solitary reminder of those two invasions, but of a deeper
and more lasting significance, as Verhaeren's oft-remembered
lines beat in his heart to that accompaniment, temporarily
filling that placid, now hidden landscape with light brilliant
enough to piece his darkness.

> *Pays de fruste orgeuil ou de rage mordante,*
> *Dès qu'on barre ta vie, ou qu'on touche à ton sort.*
> *Pays de poings lourds et de fronts redoutés*
> *Pays de patient et de sourde volonté.*

"Oh, Pierre!" Julie cried. "I never heard you arrive.
Jean is somewhere around, I expect. Fiorelle had her calf
this morning. Is that what's brought you over?"

In Julie's speech, although her father had been English,
and she had been educated in England, there was a pro-
nounced American accent inherited from her mother and
the early years of her childhood spent over forty years ago
in Connecticut. She was a big woman, white-haired, plump,
and handsome, with a laugh that in boisterous gusts could
break upon any gathering of dullness and correctness and
be infectious. She paused, with a half-filled basket of roses
in one hand and a pair of secateurs in the other, to tilt
back the cart-wheel, coolie straw hat that covered her head.
She wore no make-up in the mornings when pottering about
the garden, and perspiration was running down the sides of
her nose from underneath the enormous white frames of
her sun glasses.

"Darling, I'm much too sweaty to kiss you." She laughed.
But Pierre kissed her cheek all the same. He was fond of
her. She had a heart to match her laugh, big and unre-
strained. But she could be interfering and managing, and
she possessed a trait common to many women of her
mother's nationality, a desire to improve men in small
ways, to which her husband, Jean, and her two sons, when
they were home for the holidays from Ampleforth, submitted
philosophically.

"They are about over," she said. "All the roses. It is
this drought. Last year they were still quite a show at this
time."

The rose garden had been his own present to her, when he knew she wanted to make one, for step by step, outside and in, she had asked for his guidance and advice, so that in his imagination he saw the growth of an old farmhouse into a home of more sophisticated tastes. He gave her the rose garden in gratitude for giving him an interest, and for their having come back to settle, when the war was over, in the country of Jean's birth.

"I've been cutting what there are," Julie said, "to welcome Olive Fulmer. If you are going back through Bruges, could you leave them at the hotel for me? The Dierick d'Alsace. And ask for them to be put in her room, and in water?"

"I'll do that," he agreed. And then, musingly: "Lady Fulmer, the mother-in-law to be of our young friend, and his fiancée, Elizabeth. Tell me something about her."

He had often thought, regarding Julie, that only a woman of the Anglo-Saxon race would still retain in her middle forties such a tenacious interest in her old boarding-school. A trait he had never found very much among convent-educated Belgians, not to that extent, or expressed in quite the same spirit. Julie regularly attended old girls' reunions, as far as he and his wife, Ghislaine, had ever been able to discover before the war, more out of curiosity than sentiment. And, indeed, she had confessed to him before flying over to England in the summer of 1945 that she was anxious to see the effects of time and war on all of them. On that occasion she was to be the guest of honour, being the only one of their number to have had first-hand experience of an invasion. She was worried about her own appearance, particularly her hair, which had once been chestnut-brown, curly, and luxuriant. But with a blue rinse and the attentions of a hairdresser, milliner, and dress-maker she was ready to face what she imagined might be either a too sympathetic or too critical world. It had been disappointing, she had recounted on her return, to find no one there she knew, no one, in fact, of her own time, except Olive Gilbart. And Olive, she had repeated to Jean and Pierre—particularly to Pierre, because he took an amused interest in all Julie's goings-on and he encouraged her more at that time than at any other period of his life, in order to take his mind off other things—had never been a particular friend of hers. In fact, the reverse. And if Olive hadn't come up to her and said who she was, she might never had recognized her again. Never, no never, would she have recognized in a gracious Lady Fulmer the former Olive Gilbart of Grace Darling House, Saint Ursula's School, if she hadn't come up like a long-lost friend. Well, there she was, with a welcoming hand thrust out. And that did the trick. They travelled back to London together and kissed on parting at Paddington Station.

As a result Julie acquired a new friend. She thrived on such relationships, which multiplied, Pierre thought, year by year, whereby she would be the confidante, the adviser and the helper in time of need. As she had been the friend, he never wished to forget, of the unfortunate and abandoned, hungry and penniless British nationals in Brussels during the war. Old governesses, former coachmen and grooms to great families, pensioned before the first war, when a franc bought an undevalued franc's worth, in their poor hiding-places they knew Julie, a friend to all the destitute in those years.

"You mean, tell you about Elizabeth?" Julie asked. "I should have thought Adrian would have——? I hardly know her because I only saw her once, on that day, and no girl looks her best in English school clothes at that age. And last time I was over, and lunched with Olive and Sir Frederick, Elizabeth was finishing in Switzerland."

She held out her arm and Pierre took it, after he had let the dog go free. They went along the path and up some steps on to a parched lawn, and the heat made the scent of the roses she carried in the basket sweet and strong.

"But she had the makings of a very pretty girl, I could see that. Lovely hair and good features. A sweet child. Adrian is lucky."

"And her mother?" Pierre asked. "Lady Fulmer?"

The steps that led up to the little stone-flagged terrace, which ran the whole length of the south side of the farmhouse, were before them, so Julie did not answer immediately.

The steps, which were fairly new to Pierre, had to be negotiated without too much emphasis on her guidance. The white walls of the house, relieved by green shutters, were dazzling in the brilliant sun. Would this weather never break? she wondered. For over two months the country had sweltered and gasped under a burning sky, with never a breeze, not even on the coast, to relieve the heat.

They entered the house by a centre door, which opened straight into the long *salon*. Curtains were drawn across the windows, shading the room from the glare outside, and the pale green walls reflected a coolness, emphasized by the big square chequer-board tiles with which the floor was paved. Julie put the basket of roses down on the grand piano and pulled off her hat. When she had removed her sun glasses her eyes were as brown and as bright and as inquisitive as a bird's, but with a child-like candour in their depths. She took a comb out of her skirt pocket and ran it through her blue-white bubble curls. In the mirror on the wall she watched her brother-in-law sitting down behind her, and her bright, inquisitive eyes softened.

"I could do with a drink, couldn't you? Martini? Or just a plain, long drink with gin and lime? Or beer? It's fattening. But that need not worry you. It doesn't me, any longer. Should it, Pierre?"

He laughed. "I am not Jean, to answer that one for you. How much more do you weigh, these days?"

"Than before? I daren't tell you. Jean's getting that way too. Terrible. The harder he works outside, the more he eats. I've always said Belgians eat too much."

"Where are the boys today?" Pierre asked.

"Gone to Zoute with their two English friends. It is more exciting for them than swimming in the pool here. And I can't provide the attractions of the *plage*, either." She laughed. "They are growing up. Oh, dear! What's the news of Robert?"

"Washington is having a heat-wave too. He still seems to be enjoying himself."

"One of these days," she said, "you'll be having an American daughter-in-law. He was safer in Paris." She turned from the mirror and faced him. "Would you hate that?"

"Why should I hate that, Julie? In those matters I hope Robert feels he is his own master."

"But it wouldn't be conforming."

"To what, Julie?"

"The custom of your family, which Jean didn't follow." But one, she knew, Pierre himself would follow, if he ever married again. "You will stay to lunch?" she went on. And when Pierre said he had hoped he might, she said, "Good. We don't seem to have seen much of you lately," but a little reproachfully. He knew by the tone of her voice, and the shades of reproach in it, that he was in for an interrogation. He had not long to wait.

Drinks were brought and the flowers were taken away to be put in water. And when the door was closed again on the servant's departure Julie said, "What was it you asked me, just now, outside, about Olive Fulmer? Were you wondering what kind of a mother-in-law she will be? Of *our* young friend, you said. And that he certainly is not, if you are thinking to include Jean and me. For since that day Adrian came here on Olive's introduction and happened to meet you here we haven't set eyes on him. He's your young friend, maybe, but hardly ours."

She laughed gently, but she had been feeling a little put out because she had wanted to vet the young man at her leisure, and she had not had an opportunity because Pierre had snatched him away from her, right from under her nose. Reading between the lines of Olive's letter after the engagement was announced Julie had understood that it was not all going to be plain sailing, since the young couple could not hope to marry for some time. She knew that after that first meeting Adrian had been constantly out at the château, and had, indeed, until a few days ago, been staying there. She had, herself, only been over there occasionally, owing to the constant stream of her own summer visitors, but every time Jean had been he had found Adrian there. In spite of all that hospitality, and that before then Adrian had been stopping in a cheap little inn in Bruges, she wondered how he had managed to stay in Belgium all that time, since the end of May, when the longest holiday English visitors usually enjoyed on their legitimate allowance of currency was four or five weeks.

Thinking of this she said, "I expect you've helped Adrian with francs, haven't you?" And when Pierre smiled, but did not answer, she went on, "Well, my dear, it is very sweet of you." But for some reason she felt annoyed. She was tired of the way English people were behaving abroad—from what she heard. And it was being overdone. He might, she reflected, have asked her, if he wanted help, since she was Olive's friend. "Very sweet of you," she repeated. "Because I don't suppose you want to go to England and eat their awful food and be cold in their houses, do you?"

"Actually, Julie," Pierre said, "I have been promising myself a visit there for a very long time, if only to order some suits. I should like to—*feel* the air of London again. In the war one thought of it so often. Do you remember the words Roosevelt quoted in a message to Churchill, 'the world hangs breathless on their fate'?"

"Oh, darling," Julie cried. "Sometimes I think you can be more English than the English when anyone criticizes!" She put down her empty glass and was thoughtful. In those days was there more kindness, more good faith, more sympathy? She said slowly, "I'm sorry I sounded peevish. But what made Adrian come here, to Bruges, I mean, in the first place? It is not what a young Englishman entirely on his own would normally choose for a holiday, is it? And to stay so long, all summer, especially when he had got himself engaged."

"He wanted," Pierre replied, "to live there quietly and write. He had planned to do that a long time ago. But he did not, it is true, intend to stay so long. Not originally."

"And write?" Julie repeated. "Well, yes, Olive told me he'd had some poems published. But that won't keep them."

"He doesn't expect it to."

"That's a good thing," Julie said. "I think Olive is a bit worried. She said Sir Frederick could have found him a job in Civil Aviation, but Adrian wouldn't take it. Neither would he apply for a permanent commission in the Air Force, but was absolutely set on going up to Oxford."

"He is twenty-four," Pierre said. "And his education, like that of all young men of his age, was stopped when he was seventeen and a half. The war caught him as it caught thousands, and as he has survived, naturally he wants to recapture what he lost—especially as his release from the service was considerably delayed through one thing and another."

"I can understand that, in a way. Or I could understand it better, perhaps, if he hadn't asked Elizabeth to marry him. A man like Sir Frederick could pull all sorts of strings."

"I expect he could, Julie. But some young men don't like strings being pulled for them, especially in the wrong direction."

She was about to answer sharply, but checked herself. It was the heat, she thought. She used to enjoy it. That was what getting stout did to you. And, anyway, why was she ranging herself in this matter on the side of Olive and Olive's girl, when she didn't really know if there was any difference of opinion to argue over? Once, early on in the war, Pierre, who was reckless enough of his own danger and the danger to which his activities were exposing those whom he loved, had said to her, "You are a born partisan, Julie. But, take care!" She knew then, at a time when critical faculties regarding one's own shortcomings were exposed and naked, that he was afraid of her tactlessness, her impetuousness. To be of any real help in those days, to live according to one's conscience and faith, those faults were fatal. She knew, now, that she could turn from this subject—which, after all, was none of her business—and talk of other things till Jean appeared. But she could no more turn from it than she could have from the warmth of a fire on a cold day. Her curiosity was roused. What had the young man been doing at the château all that time? And why had Pierre taken an interest in him?

Julie looked again at her brother-in-law. He had kept his figure better than any of them in middle age, far better than Jean, who although younger, was round and corpulent and growing bald. Pierre's hair was as thick as it had ever been. A little grey now, but he had been growing grey ten years ago. How strange that was after all he had been through, when only worry and anxiety had turned her own white! The lines that had covered the skeleton of his face when he came back had vanished. There were only the creases of laughter round his eyes, and the deep ones near his mouth in serious repose. He still had the figure of a young man, lean and hard and fit. The shrunken stoop had gone from his back, except very occasionally when he was tired, or off his guard. That erectness was a measure of his self-discipline, his total immunity, she thought, from pity. In his dark colouring, the deep-set, once humorous, sparkling eyes, the high cheek-bones and the acquiline nose he bore—where the fair-haired, ruddy-complexioned Jean did not—traces of the mixed blood in their ancestry. Yet of the two, Pierre was the more passionately Flemish, with his almost mystical—opposed to Jean's practical love of the soil.

She thought of his loneliness since the death of his wife, Ghislaine, with his son, Robert—an attractive monkey with all his mother's looks and his father's charm—away in America. Robert ought to come home and marry according to the custom of the family and gradually take over all the business of the estate. But did Pierre want that? Jean had said, when he came back, that the last thing Pierre would do would be to abdicate. In the loneliness of that big and now somewhat neglected house, with only the garrulous company of his old English manservant—who had been her own ally in her work in Brussels in the war, so she knew the extent of his garrulousness, as well as his Yorkshire tenacity and courage—pottering anxiously behind him, watching in fear and affection all his movements, Pierre had probably welcomed the companionship of Adrian, in the way he often had Michel de Castelberg, the young composer, who had been one of his lieutenants in the *armée blanche*, staying with him. And not unnaturally Adrian had fallen under his spell, because Pierre had always had that gift of

attracting men and woman to him. Young men with their
lives before them, attracted by his wit and scholarship
and his conversation full of strange ideas and theories,
which were strange to those who knew how devout he was
and on hob-nobbing terms with all the clergy in Bruges,
saw in him perhaps something of a leader, a Master? And
they'd be attracted by his worldliness too—his former
worldliness, for he loved life once, for all it gave him. And
once it had been bountiful, extravagant and gay, but
redeemed—if one was critical and envious and considered
redemption necessary, though God, no!—by that simplicity
in his character that was so Flemish and home-loving.

But what was there in Adrian, she wondered, to have
earned him this notice, that she had not discovered the day
he came to tea? His appearance had been pleasing—that
almost Viking fairness—and his manners had been all
they should be. He had been self-possessed but not presump-
tive. She remembered his eyes had seemed both older and
wiser than his years, but that was not uncommon among
his generation. She had, perhaps, had a picture of him in
her mind before he came and he had adequately filled it;
and that picture concerned his short Air Force career, so
that she saw him personifying a gallant band of young men,
many of whom she had entertained in Brussels after the
liberation. Remembering them, for two pins she would
have kissed him on arrival, but those days were over; she
was a middle-aged woman, the friend of his future mother-
in-law, holding out her hand to him, saying how-do-you-do,
when he got off his bicycle in the yard.

"Has he been writing anything here this summer?"
she asked.

"That is what has kept him here," Pierre answered.
"Kept him with me. He became interested in an episode of
our medieval history, and has been working on that."

"Goodness," Julie commented. "That would need a
lot of imagination, if you mean something out of the very
early times."

"He has imagination, and so far he has interpreted
the thoughts—the motives behind men's actions of that

period extremely well. They don't change much," Pierre went on, after a pause. "At least I don't think they do."

"And you've been helping him?"

"I can say my library has."

As his hand groped for the edge of the little table near his chair, in order to put down his empty glass, Pierre wondered if this conversation would be repeated to Lady Fulmer, and if what he had said, under the pressure of Julie's curiosity and questioning, would assure a woman very rightly concerned with her daughter's happiness of sufficient stability of purpose, which was, no doubt, what she and Sir Frederick wished to be assured of in a future son-in-law who had stood out against their advice and refused to consider their suggestions. He had not, up to the announcement of the imminent arrival of Lady Fulmer and Elizabeth, given much thought to that part of Adrian's life—a most important part as it was, and without doubt the mainspring of his endeavour. He had been interested in his talents, looking on, as it were, from the distance of his own middle age at the aspirations and dreams which were driving youth forward as with the force of a gale. But then, again, he was committing the common fault of a man whose personal aspirations and dreams had long since fallen from him—some realized, some discarded—of laying too much stress on the quality of youth, in this case in one on whose shoulders manhood had set its firm seal. Because it was the mind of a man, not a boy, that could look beyond the confines of the present and with philosophy and penetration and understanding bring one scene out of the past to live again with all the splendour and pageantry, faith, and treachery. It was a quite unusual talent, the ability to take the story written by the last of the monastic historians, Mathew Paris, of a prince and conqueror, whose military and civil achievements paled before the weird legend of love and crime and solitude and Nemesis, and translate it with poetic feeling into a modern medium.

In the beginning, when in Julie's drawing-room he had given him a casual invitation, "Come out whenever you like. Don't bother to telephone first, as I am rarely away," he had known nothing about him. The young man had come, and on his second visit, early in the morning when he, himself, was about to go unexpectedly to Brussel's, he had told him the library was his for the day. "Amuse yourself in it!" And he had returned late at night to find him still there. When asked what he had been doing, Adrian had told him and said, "But it is stupendous, this saga of Baldwin of Constantinople! Hasn't anyone thought of its possibilities?" Before he had asked him what possibilities he had in mind he had said, "So it was this kind of thing that brought you to Bruges?"

"Yes, this kind of thing, sir. A long time ago, I thought if I lived I would go into this subject—the Crusades, and fasten on one individual and try and interpret his actions, and all the motives. But it was not, actually, that particular subject that brought me here. After all, I could have sat in a library anywhere and read. I just wanted to come to Bruges because I'd seen pictures of it and knew some of its history, wanted, also, to see its pictures. I thought I'd write —whatever came to me, while I was here. But about something right away from the present."

"Is the present, then, not good, not inspiring?" Pierre had ventured, "that you want to escape from it?"

The boy had laughed his young laugh. "My present is very good indeed. I have survived the war and I am engaged to be married. I have Oxford in front of me." Then seriously, "But I wanted to explore another age, even if it held just as much cruelty and barbarism and fear."

Cruelty, barbarism, and fear! Was that, then, how youth summed up the world today?

"It would hold, also, love and sacrifice. And it is here, isn't it, in the story of a man eaten with—— Dare I say it to you? Ambition, a desire for conquest, and a wish to stand well with his contemporaries? And his wife——" Then, because he knew, the boy had stopped. Did he, in that instant, know how much was close in that story? Of how one of them had seen in the work on that story—in whatever form it would take—the emptying of all confusion, perplexities, sorrow, and remorse from the mind? No, he had not known. Adrian had been told why there was no mistress in that house—not by Julie, there would not have been time, but by Prendergast, shuffling in with the tea-tray, or waiting on him at lunch. "Dare I say it to you?" meaning only the fear that a Catholic would take offence at attributing a mixture of motives in the mind of a Crusader!

So from that day it grew, in study and concentration, as it took shape and the characters and scenes came alive, with, of course, the inevitable set-backs and disappointments, with inspiration and stagnation, hope and despair—until one of them knew it was made for music as well. And he, himself, had not been so happy for years. During the last weeks there had been a noticeable slowing up, as though the spring of Adrian's inspiration had ceased to rise— and there was one scene he could not finish, nor could one help him there. One knew there were other things in his mind. He was restless and silent in turn. "They are coming over," he announced. "Elizabeth and her mother." After that he shed his seriousness, forgot the medieval past, opened his eyes, perhaps, and saw evidence of the passing of summer in the parched grass, the ripening apples, and became eager and excited, concerned with the reservation of rooms in a hotel and plans for a holiday and for feminine entertainment. Ceased, also, to worry over the elusive scene, and to confess his ignorance of women, which, he said, hampered his being able to interpret the thoughts of the Crusader's wife.

Pierre heard Julie sigh. "It doesn't sound at all practical for the future to me. And I fear it won't to Olive."

He could tell her more, which might perhaps sound more practical, although he wouldn't know for certain until he had seen de Castelberg.

"But what is Adrian intending to do, later on?"

"When he leaves Oxford, you mean? That is a long way ahead, my dear. Today is much more important to him, because today Elizabeth arrives."

Pierre turned his head on hearing his brother in heavy farm boots thumping across the tiled floor behind him.

"Ah, Pierre! Come to see the calf? She's a beauty. There is just time before lunch."

Jean gave his arm to his brother; and when they had gone outside Julie sat down and began a letter of welcome to her friend, Lady Fulmer.

·   ·   ·   ·   ·   ·

The Hôtel Dierick d'Alsace stood in a little square where there was a fountain that no longer played, facing a row of uneven, colour-washed houses with gabled roofs. The back of the hotel, three storeys high, rose straight out of a canal, casting a black shadow over the brackish-green water.

In the early afternoon the square was empty and quiet. No children congregated round the fountain and no stray dogs played in the gutters. Only a stout blonde padded painfully homewards over the hot cobble-stones, carrying a red plastic hand-bag and a string-bag bursting with groceries, observed by Rene De Jonkheere, who had just escaped from the eye of his mother to take the tram to Knocke, with boredom and disinterest. Twenty-one years old, dark and handsome in a flashy way, he was too fat for his age, as were many of his generation who had suffered malnutrition in adolescence, increased in his case by an appetite for sweet pastries at any hour of the day. His mother had wanted him to remain in the hotel that afternoon to await the arrival of important visitors, to assist Jules, the quarter-witted youth who stoked the furnace and cleaned shoes, in carrying up their luggage, which would be of the expensive kind, and heavy. But he could think of better ways of employing himself on a hot afternoon.

Madame De Jonkheere heard her son depart, watched him from the office sneak quietly through the door, and shrugged her shoulders. In the little private sitting-room behind the office her mother had settled down to mend the linen. All was quiet and hushed and would be so until the expected guests arrived. The summer season, strictly speaking, had yet one more month to run, but she could say it had been a most successful one, as she could look back on the last three years of her enterprise as being fruitful. They had earned it. With God's help they had earned it. God had restored her husband and son to her from the horrors of the camp at Breendonck, and He had watched over their business affairs with equal care. Still uncertain as to her loved ones' survival, although her faith had never wavered, on the night of 2 September, 1944, she had watched the performance of Louis Beyaert, the black traitor, former seller of missals and rosaries, being made to jump round the Grand' Place in a sack before the hairs of his beard were torn out one by one. What a night that was to look back upon! When Monsieur Nauwelaerts, the *carillonneur*, caused to be rung out such improvised airs from the belfry and a few bars of the 'Brabançonne'! That night, in serious consultation with a relative, who had money to invest, she had decided to buy an old house that would shortly—now the hated enemy had gone and business would be restored to normal—be on sale, and, if they could obtain the necessary permits, to turn it into a hotel with modern comforts that would attract the best class of tourist. She imagined that English ones would want to eat well after such long years of fasting, like everyone else. She had not bargained for the apparent poverty of England after the war, and the restrictions imposed on foreign travel. But there had been compensation in the sudden riches in her own country, which brought those who had made money—she sometimes felt by questionable means— out every fine day and every week-end in shiny new cars to acquire culture amidst the antiquity of Bruges and to enjoy good food and wine.

It was of English guests expected that afternoon she was thinking, as she flicked over the pages of the book of room reservations. They were friends of Monsieur Morbeigh, and he had engaged the best rooms for them on the first floor facing the water, which had a connecting private bathroom. Those rooms had been vacated that morning by an American party who had spent a lot of money on Scotch whisky every day, of which—although it was profitable—she did not approve, especially as it was the best season for Zeeland oysters. But then one should not complain about Americans' habits, since the English—with the Canadians, blessed liberators!—did not always show the good taste one was accustomed to think was theirs in the past. Lady Fulmer, she instinctively felt, would show good taste, and would not, within the allowance of Belgian currency that ogre of a controller, Monsieur Cripps, would permit them to bring, be too careful or mean.

Expected also today were two children and their mother with an automobile. It would be quite a little colony of them up there on the second floor, with Monsieur Morbeigh and Mademoiselle King. They would all have to use the same bathroom, and she hoped the children would be well-behaved and would not slop water everywhere because Marie Berlearts could not be expected to run upstairs to mop up after everyone. Not that Mademoiselle King would ever complain. She was one of those quiet, old-fashioned English ladies who made no trouble, but who, alas! were always too poor to drink anything except a bottle of Spa water they made last a week. One of those elderly English ladies who spoke excellent French and knew Bruges inside out, and had no friends and never made any.

Madame De Jonkheere closed the book and popped her lacquer-smooth dark head round the corner of the office door. The *salon*, which lay between the dining-room and the little entrance hall was empty and she could see that no one had emptied the ash-trays or smacked the cushions in place, nor had they drawn the curtains to shield the carpet from the afternoon sun that was pouring in. She retreated back into the office and put her finger on a bell.

So much rested on her own shoulders, Madame De Jonkheere thought. Always, always must she be for ever watching her staff, in the kitchen, in the dining-room, upstairs, everywhere. Her husband had never been the same since his internment; although none was better than he at marketing and choosing the best cuts of veal and beef steak, the plumpest chickens, the freshest lobsters and sole and vegetables. None better than he in judging wine. But he would not use his authority with the servants. Not watched, they would make a monkey of him. His memory, too! He continually forgot things unless they were written down. She had sent her son, Rene, to a commercial college to learn book-keeping, and he was smart and quick at figures, but, alas, he was lazy and vain and was too fond of getting the tram to Knocke and strutting along the *plage* eyeing painted hussies from Brussels, whose displays of nakedness were a scandal to behold. He was idle and he was spoilt, and for him his father had suffered so cruelly. In the camp men and women had denied themselves for the young Rene, with his pretty face and winning ways; they had sheltered him, starved that he might eat more than his share of the pitiable ration of turnip soup. He was taken with his father in order that his father would talk. But old soldiers did not talk. Though afterwards they were never the same. It did no good to remember those things. God was merciful. Business was excellent. And next month, when the last visitors of the season would have gone she and her husband would take their annual holiday. This year, since the exchange was so favourable, in a good hotel in Nice.

Upstairs in a room on the first floor Marie Berlearts, who came from the village of Donk, stood in front of the dressing-table, on which had been put a large vase filled with hot-house carnations, white and pink and crimson. She knew they had been bought at the most expensive florists and she fingered the petals of one flower as though she were afraid they would dissolve at her touch. Such blooms! Such extravagance! But then they had been bought by Monsieur Morbeigh because he was in love. The room having been done to Marie's satisfaction she turned away from further contemplation of such expensive emblems of affection and climbed the stairs to the next floor. One door on that landing was open and she saw the occupant of the room sitting, as was usual, and in Marie's eyes, unhappily, alone in a chair by the window. Mademoiselle King was elderly, and for those ladies, when they were unmarried,

what was there? If she were Belgian and Catholic there
would be the numerous churches for her devotions, and
saints' days never to be neglected, and perhaps days of
feastings never to be neglected either. It was far too beautiful
a day, although hot, for anyone with leisure, on a holiday,
to be wasting it indoors. As she stood on the threshold,
Marie said so.

Miss King put down her book and smiled. She would
take a little walk later on. But she liked sitting there because
the view was so nice. It was her first holiday for many years,
and no one could really understand what a treat it was to
be waited on and have her room done and not have to
worry about the rations. If it were going to prove a little
lonely on her own, when she wasn't going to Knocke to
see her cousins, she must not mind that.

"It would be nice," Marie suggested, "to take your
book to the Lac d'Amour."

Miss King laughed gently. What names they did give
to places abroad! But it was not new to her because she
had sat there long ago; long before this flaxen-haired little
Flemish girl was born, before the first war. She had watched
children playing there, the funnily-dressed little Continental
children of those days, with button boots and lots of petti-
coats, very sedately. It had never occurred to her that but
for the first war she might have married and had children.
If it had done so she would have said, in her modesty, that
was by no means a certainty. But she had often thought
if her brothers had not been killed in that war she might
have had nieces and nephews.

"Perhaps I will," she said, "presently, when it is a
little cooler," and she picked up her book again and heard
Marie walk away and knock on the door of the next room.

.   .   .   .   .   .

Adrian Morbeigh heard the knock, but he did not
immediately answer. He was standing by a table putting
papers together, and he had just written on the top sheet
of a manuscript: To Elizabeth. The bright sunlight gave a

smooth patina to the age-darkened bricks and tiled roofs of the houses on the opposite bank, and below the tiny, iron-railed balcony the olive-green brackish water was only disturbed when a little motor-boat filled with tourists chug-chugged past. He had chosen that room, small as it was—with a bed, although pushed up against the wall under the slope of the ceiling, taking up most of the floor space—because of the view of the roof tops, out of which rose the belfry tower, from where at intervals the sweet, tremulous carillon shook the air.

To Elizabeth, he thought, and for her, although it was not yet complete. He turned over the pages of the opening scene, which was set in the church of Saint Donatian on the morrow of Ash Wednesday in the year 1199. All the burghers of Bruges were assembled there to see Count Baldwin take the Cross, the whole élite of Flanders, the very flower of Flemish chivalry. Ranged each side of the altar were the canons in their white linen rochets and purple veils. In front of them the choir from Saint Donatian's school. The great bell tolled—the bell that five centuries later fell from its lofty tower and lay buried for fifty years, and which now sent forth its melodious voice from the steeple of Nôtre Dame. "Receive this symbol," cried the Archbishop of Tournai, as he fastened on Baldwin's breast the white linen cross embroidered with threads of gold. "Receive this symbol in memory of the Passion of Jesus Christ and of the cross on which he died." Then Baldwin's wife, Marie of Champagne, rose, and as she knelt before the prelate and besought him to place the cross upon her also, a shout of admiration and dismay burst from the crowd. She was so tender, so beautiful, and the way of the Cross was steep and hard.

He had asked Pierre, who had known the love of women —of one woman, as possibly few men had known it in all its entirety, "What were her motives? What manner of love was her sacrifice? When she lay in the tent in Syria waiting for Baldwin and he did not come, what were her thoughts? And did she ever see through him, see him as he was?" Even her face, Adrian thought, was hidden.

He had wandered through picture galleries, and the faces of women had looked down from their frames and given no answer. In Baldwin's later hermit years was she the mainspring of his remorse, behind his abandonment of all his conquests? Or had he forgotten her? How often had they thrashed that out, in the library of the château! No, he had not forgotten her. She would be beautiful, Adrian thought, and she would be a woman from whom a warrior had drawn strength, a woman who by that warrior had been selfishly ill-used because at times he would have had much in his mind that did not concern her. She would have purity and innocence of heart—and humour too, enjoying music and gaiety because a princely warrior would not love dullness made a virtue of.

Adrian heard the second knock, more insistent this time, on the panel of the door, and in answering it he turned from the past to face another Marie: Marie Berlearts from the village of Donk, with flaxen hair and pink cheeks and the thick legs of a peasant, whose mother had toiled from infancy in the fields. But dressed in mantle and coif, he thought, she might easily have been an attendant of Saint Ursula in Memlinc's triptych.

"You refused to let me dust the room this morning," she said. "And I shall get into trouble if it is not done. In fact," she continued in the thick, atrocious Flemish accent of her spoken French, "I am already in trouble with Madame and do not want to add to it." She laughed, showing a row of small, even white teeth and pink gums.

"It is all yours," Adrian said, "except the table."

She advanced with a duster in her hand towards the balcony. How beautiful was the view from there! It made her heart swell with devotion and pride and local patriotism. There could be no city in the world to compare with it. She had never been to Brussels, but Ghent, the farthest point of her travels, she considered to be inferior in every way to Bruges. How pleasant it would be to take a chair and place it on this small balcony as Monsieur Morbeigh had done yesterday, and sit and dream the afternoon away. Poor Mademoiselle King had no balcony. If she wished to see the traffic passing below she would have to lean out. Monsieur Morbeigh had sat with his feet up on the iron rail, with his arms folded and his eyes closed, and he looked like an effigy carved in stone. Like a knight on a tomb, and instead of a dog to rest his feet on there was the balcony rail. She looked down at the iron railing against which his feet had rested, when his long legs had been stretched out and his chair tipped back, balancing his weight so. She stared at it closely, and bent down and touched it.

"Come and regard this," she cried. "Look! It is unsafe. It is dangerous. These stakes are loose. Madame should be informed."

"Yes, I know," Adrian said. He was standing before the dressing-table putting on a tie. "I noticed it this morning. It is probably the heat. I told Monsieur De Jonkheere."

"You should have told Madame, not him. He remembers nothing. He suffered greatly in the camp at Breendonck. Since then his memory is bad. It is not the heat. It is old age. All these houses are very old."

As she spoke the sound of bells filled the air, and she saw Adrian push back the cuff of his shirt-sleeve and glance at his watch. "My God!" he cried. "I shall only just make it." He picked up a jacket that was on the bed. "You can do the room now, Marie; but please don't touch anything on the table."

He ran from the room and down the two flights of stairs into the hall, which was curtained against the afternoon sun. In the doorway he saw a uniformed chauffeur, whom he recognized, holding a bunch of roses and a letter in his hand. Adrian took them from him and raced back upstairs, and in the room that was to be Lady Fulmer's he searched hurriedly for something to put the roses in. He found a tooth glass in the bathroom and filled it with water. The roses were drooping and he propped the heads up against the dressing-table mirror and put Julie's letter against the tooth glass, and ran downstairs again.

In the dazzling brightness of the square a large black limousine was parked by the hotel entrance, and Pierre's voice called out to him, "That you, Adrian? James said you'd taken care of Julie's offering. What are you doing here when you ought to be in Ostend?"

"I'm going to catch the train now," Adrian said.

"Get in," Pierre commanded him.

Adrian did so, and when they had rounded the corner of the square Pierre said, "You had better take the car all the way. I can be dropped first. And keep the car to come back in. I wish I had thought of it sooner, then you might not have been so out of breath. You cut it fine. What were you doing to forget the time?"

"Oh, just tidying up and putting the whole thing away. Then I suppose I began thinking about it and forgot the time."

"A good idea to put it all away for a while," Pierre said. "The hotel is comfortable?"

"Oh, very."

"The usual run of visitors, I suppose?"

"Very much the usual run. Americans—two lots since I arrived. They rush in and out and the guides are busy. An English spinster on my floor, looks like a school marm, but I don't think is one. She knows Bruges well. Had an uncle living here before the first war. She seems awfully lonely, though she tells me she has some cousins at Knocke. I think loneliness must be an awful thing, especially on a holiday abroad. Fancy watching people all the time, watching their fun. And being too old to join in, even if they asked you."

"One doesn't mind that so much," Pierre said, "when one is old, you know."

"But, good lord! You are not——"

"I'm forty-nine. Fifty very soon."

"That isn't——" Adrian began, and did not know how to finish. "But I knew you must be round about that, as Robert is my age. I never can think of you as a father, though. Probably because you are such an awful lot younger than mine."

"Anyone else of interest in the hotel?" Pierre asked.

"No. There's another English woman coming today,

with two children. They'll be on my floor. It's a funny thing about other guests in any hotel. There they are, sleeping so near one, and they might be a thousand miles away usually for all the impression they make."

The car came to a standstill behind a tram. The narrow street was crowded with cyclists and cars and priests and nuns and children. The sun beat down on striped awnings outside confectioners' and drapers' and souvenir shops. The heat was suddenly stifling, and the Alsatian dog, which was on the front seat next to the chauffeur, rested his muzzle on the ledge of the open window, and saliva dribbled down the panel of the door.

"For all the impression they make on one's mind, I meant. For all the influence, I suppose, on one's life."

So spoke, Pierre thought, one who was highly impressionable, with the sublime confidence of youth. And with that very special English brand of confidence. Yet he had never returned from a walk without some encounter, some incident to relate. That very eager mind missed little that came his way.

As Adrian spoke—impatient now at the delay caused by the traffic in that narrow street, beginning to fret inwardly lest the boat arrived at Ostend before he was there to meet it—he wondered if it had always been like that, or if he were growing old suddenly. No, it hadn't. But he had been sent across half the world, west and east, lived cheek by jowl with all types and conditions of men and found some of them very curious oddities, when he had indeed been very young. He had been in many countries and in some had lived in communal conditions, which was the way men had to live in war; and for relaxation he had glanced at comic-strips—that was in Canada, when he was being trained—and at the taste of his immediate neighbours in pin-up girls, and had listened and taken part in conversations that covered only one topic at night in the huts. For what were they, most of them, but curious adolescents and correspondingly crude in either conjecture or claims to experience? One of them once—older than the rest—had said, "Think you're all a lot of —— little

B*

crusaders, don't you?" They had all rolled over in their bunks laughing. But he had stared at the ceiling thinking that among men centuries back the talk was probably much the same. When some of them, far from their homes, cried at night in nostalgic sickness for what they feared they might never see again, for the familiar—above all for the familiar—he had felt a strange sense of detachment because he couldn't feel that way, and hadn't been able to feel that way since his father had come down to see him in the late autumn of 1940 and when they were walking past the school chapel, told him what had happened the previous night in London to his mother.

He never spoke of that to anyone for a very long time. In that very physical life that followed quickly on his school days the mind was closed to confidence. Survival was problematical and wise chaps had their fingers crossed and did not speak much out of their secret hearts. If they had private loyalties and beliefs they, also, were hidden. If they had time to remember earlier ideals, boyhood heroes, they knew how far short they had fallen in their own deeds. It was an existence that was full of contradictions, sometimes exciting, often boring, filled with ugliness and harshness. The ugliness was in the colourless surroundings, everything camouflaged to a uniform drabness and darkness. They endured strain and fatigue—and ceased to think; ceased to notice the ugliness and came to be like ants, drilled but obedient. A good many drank to ease the strain and fatigue, dim the memory of what they wanted to forget. And each one found his reality, or his escape from it, in his individual way. The trouble was to know where either was to be found. If it were in the searchlights that, blinding you, seemed to tear out your entrails as well as your eyes; in the mess or a pub afterwards; or at home listening to Beethoven and drinking father's port. Or in the act of love in a dark wood on the edge of the aerodrome with a mess waitress—as some, the less fastidious, found. Or in a rigid denunciation of excess in any direction out of a motive largely governed, not by any concise belief, but by fear of consequences. In complete solitariness, or in a crowd.

Naturally, when it was all over, some of them—and he was one—looked for something different. They found it in music and poetry and in cities not destroyed—Paris and Athens and Rome and in Bruges, as he had done; and in French cooking and wine. They searched with fastidiousness. For they were not—as he had read men were after a former war—cynical, or easily converted to strange creeds, filled with righteous wrath against fathers who had begot them, wanting to become missionaries in a new world of their own desperate making. A new world had been established in the years they were busy obeying orders. Theirs but to do or die! And they disliked very much the slogan-infested society, for which it was alleged they had fought and won, where a sense of personal responsibility was in the process of being taken from man and emphasis laid on his material welfare, with often a disregard of his spiritual needs. So they began to yearn for what they had never known, for a Europe where frontiers were open, for an age of gracious living, even for the artificial splendour of courts and *salons* and an attendance of wit and fashion. From the company of uniformed, rough-voiced amazons, whose unfortunate clothes turned them into a travesty of womanhood, they reverenced the mature, the gracious, the kindly, the innocent, the wise. Old age, they said, had no terrors for them, and indeed some—but not himself—looked forward to its many compensations, promising themselves that they would attain it with dignity and be modest about their own achievements. The trouble was, Adrian knew, they were all in danger of becoming prematurely pompous. It was what he must watch out for in himself!

The tram in front started off with a screech over the crossing points and the car slid forward. In the afternoon sunlight, although the trees were turning yellow at the edges of the leaves, Bruges had never looked so mellow or so beautiful. He wanted it to be the same every day for Elizabeth. The thought of her so near to him made his senses tingle and his heart turn over. But there was another thought, which, whenever it cropped up, he had put away from him in a cowardly fashion. Had she properly understood

why he had stayed away so long? And could she ever understand, if he tried to tell her, the strange sensation that came
to him in Julie de Fermandois's house when Pierre was
there, that the whole of his past life had been leading to
that moment? And that Elizabeth, herself, through her
mother's friendship with Julie de Fermandois, was the
instrument of that destiny?

He had gone there rather reluctantly, putting it off for
a fortnight, because there was so much to discover every
day in Bruges, not only in the city itself but, he could think
now, about himself. He had not known until he arrived
there how much in need he was of solitude and quietness
and of time in which to think and rest from thinking, to
let that atmosphere of Christian civilization redolent of
the past, but as alive in the present as ever it was when
men were martyrs for their faith, seep into his consciousness.
He walked, and sat in churches and outside cafés, and
looked at paintings that filled him with ecstacy and excitement and peace. He liked all he saw in the city and in the
surrounding country; the thrift and the industry, and the
importance that was given to the pleasures of the table—
a lost art in his own country. And if there was also—which
he could not fail to perceive—the salutary acknowledgment
of the necessity for a preparation of an end to all those good
earthly pleasures eventually, he did not quarrel with that.
The method was not for him, because he had not been
brought up to it. There his conservatism was the prop
to his principles, but he did not altogether shelve the
question, as one to be considered when he was an older
man, because he had seen men die and had been close to
death more than once. Meanwhile life was never sweeter.
Rested and revived he knew he must pay a call on the
American woman, married to a Belgian, who was a friend
of Elizabeth's mother. He found her kind and sophisticated
and very talkative, surrounded that day by boxers and
Siamese cats, understandably proud of her achievements
in the garden surrounding that old Flemish farmhouse,
as well as its enchanting interior. Her husband joined them
at tea, wearing his farm clothes—the patched trousers and

wooden clogs of a peasant. And in contrast—for he had just returned from Brussels—there was her brother-in-law, correct and elegant in a dark suit. It was quite ten minutes before one realized. And then the shock came and went and came again, like the plunging of a knife into the breast, because of the laughter that ran through his voice, to be drawn away again as conversation, easy and animated, in that atmosphere of very civilized living, continued. But one did not know the rest of it. And then, how small and unimportant was one's own past contribution, how limited one's previous comprehension of the word sacrifice!

Bruges was behind them, and the car was speeding down a country road when Pierre said, "I am going to Brussels tomorrow and I shall see Michel, who is back from Italy. I am taking him a copy of the first act."

"But, suppose," Adrian said, "I don't do the missing scene. Never can do it?"

"Oh, I feel you'll do it all right—one day. And even if you don't, it could be left out, without damaging the rest of the story. It's a good enough story, as it is."

"But you've said," Adrian reminded him, "and we both agreed—it had to be written. Now I'm all twisted up about it! Wondering if Michel will—like what you show him, well enough to——"

"I have an idea he will," Pierre said. "You know the history of opera is remarkable for the rare occasions in which librettist and composer have been in equal value. There are the great classic collaborators, Mozart and de Ponte, Verdi and Boito, and Strauss and von Hofmansthal. The wit and apparent simplicity of de Ponte's words are matched, but not overshadowed by the same qualities in Mozart's music. I believe a librettist should prepare the synopsis, which although it is an occasion for music, is really a kind of blue-print for a stage performance. And that is what yours is. It has the feel of a stage play. An opera with only musical form is not complete opera, any composer left to make one without a good librettist is so handicapped he can never really overcome it."

"When I hear you talk like that," Adrian said. "I feel like an Olympian! When I was sweating over it I felt desperate sometimes."

"It is salutary to sweat," Pierre laughed. "It makes you mortal again."

"I owe it all to you. In fact it is just as much your composition as mine."

"Don't talk nonsense. Think of the pleasure I have got out of it, listening to it as you wrote it."

They came to a village where compact little brick houses and shops stood back from the street, and the shadows of the symmetrical rows of pollard elms fell across the smooth cobble-stones, so that they drove through bars of darkness and light. Under the trees a figure moved with an unhurried gait. There was a glimpse of a pale face below the wide brim of a black clerical hat that was raised in greeting, the folds of black skirts, the bright gleam of a silver crucifix.

"The *curé*," Adrian said, "on your left." And Pierre waved his hand.

The village was behind them, and in a field, vivid against the blueness of the sky a windmill stood with motionless brown sails.

"Stop at the gates," Pierre said to the chauffeur. "And than take Mr. Morbeigh to Ostend, and afterwards with the ladies back to Bruges."

The tall, iron gates of the château stood open, and when the car had stopped Adrian jumped down from it and gave Pierre his hand.

"When shall I see you?" he asked.

"Next week. I will telephone. I want you all to come to lunch as soon as I am back."

Pierre's left hand had thrust itself into the loop on the Alsatian's collar, and his right one clasped the stick. But that, Adrian knew, was because the chauffeur was watching, and the concierge's wife, who had come out of the lodge with a shopping basket on her arm, had made her presence known. Presently, when he was alone, he would let the dog go free. For a few moments Adrian stood by the car and watched him, a lonely figure walking up the avenue towards the house. He had been right. Less than half-way up Pierre had released the dog, who was bounding ahead of him. His independence could often make the heart stand still.

Adrian got back into the car, which could not, now, take him fast enough to Ostend and Elizabeth.

CHAPTER II

ENGLAND had disappeared and the thin green and grey
and yellow coastline of Flanders was growing clearer every
minute. Gradually skeletons of buildings grew out of the
coastline, and some of the passengers got up from their
chairs and pressed near the rail forward to stare. The sea
below the rail was a smooth silvery-blue, flecked with gold,
and in the wake of the ship was a frothy-cream train of
foam. A gull was perched on a mast-head.

Down the whole length of the deck passengers were
relaxed in rows of long wooden chairs, and having lunched
well, and gorged themselves on ration-free chocolate, the
majority had their eyes shut. Lady Fulmer was one of these.
Also, the Channel crossing was not a novelty to her. But if
Elizabeth wanted to get up and walk about she could,
although it would be very foolish to tire herself out because
there would be plenty of standing and waiting to be done
when they landed. Immediately on this advice Elizabeth
got up, and made her way to where passengers were standing
and pointing out the different landmarks and naming them
inaccurately. But there was very little to see, after all.
Watching that coastline was like watching a kettle boil,
and her impatience could not draw it nearer. When she
was tired of standing and seeing so little she went back to
her mother, who still had her eyes shut.

She looked at her mother's profile below the small hat
that was suitable for travelling, critically, as a stranger
might look at it for the first time. Even in repose, after a
too-heavy lunch, it was hard and uncompromising. The
gloved hands that had relaxed their hold on a magazine
were capable. Their caress was claw-like. Whatever they
touched they held on to. They had held on to a child, a
growing girl. But the hardness in the profile was misleading.
It hid the foolishness, the sentiment, the bouts of indecision
that were apt to follow on a rigid and uncompromising line
of action, the tendency to gush, and only showed the pride

and the snobbishness and a domineering nature. It was the
finely-cut, good profile of many Englishwomen. The whole
face, Elizabeth thought, matched it. The eyes were a shade
too small and the lips were now too thin, and the tip of
the straight nose had become a little sharp. It was a very
English face, Elizabeth decided, but it lacked kindness.
Anywhere her nationality would be unmistakable. The
clothes were almost a uniform. A tailored coat and skirt,
in grey or brown tweed, worn with a woollen jumper in
winter and a blouse in summer—and pearls. A hat that
was a covering for the head and missed being smart. But
sometimes in London there was worn a confection of veiling
and feathers, much too frivolous and young for the face
beneath it, with a fox fur and plain, mannish coat over a
flowered-print dress.

Lady Fulmer opened her eyes. The magazine slid off
her knee and Elizabeth picked it up.

"We're not there yet."

"No. Not nearly there."

"Excited, darling?"

"I suppose so." It was a child who spoke now—not the
woman in Elizabeth who had been observing her mother
with critical intolerance. A child who was uncertain of
herself, filled with anxiety lest this holiday should be spoiled
by her mother's interference.

"This hotel Adrian has chosen for us is much more
expensive than I hoped, so we shall have to be very careful
and not waste francs on unnecessary things. It is a pity
Julie could not have us. After all she did suggest we came
over to stay sometime."

"But she has her sons home, Mother, and their friends
for the holidays. I expect if we get broke she'll help us out."

"S-hush," Lady Fulmer mouthed.

"Oh, *all right*. But you said it yourself."

"What I may say at home, darling, is not what I shout
in a public place. Daddy warned us, you know."

"I *know*. His career. Always his career. It must be
an awful burden to carry about," Elizabeth sighed.

"I don't know where you pick up these ideas."

"Perhaps I don't pick them up anywhere. Perhaps they just come into my head."

Lady Fulmer opened her mouth to speak, but thought better of it, and shut it again. She would do nothing at the beginning of a happy holiday to make a daughter more 'difficult' than she already was. "How handsome and pretty your ring looks," she said soothingly. "It must have cost Adrian a lot of money. I am always afraid you will leave it in some hotel wash-basin."

"I never take it off," Elizabeth said. "Adrian didn't buy it. It was his mother's and his father gave it to him for me."

"You never told me that."

Elizabeth looked down at the ring sparkling in the sunshine. No; she had not told her mother that at the time, for reasons she could not, even now, clearly define. The ring was a symbol and yet it was not. In her heart, proud of it as she was, she had not wanted it when Adrian had put it on her finger. But it had come with her mother's embraces and her father's reserve concealed by his artificial bonhomie, following Adrian's serious, almost rehearsed, proposal of marriage. It had seemed, in her anxious mind, to sever her from rather than bind her to him. But before that simple conventional act, had not her mother's solicitude, her embarrassing benignity, her encouragement and her interference begun to banish the magic and the utter sweetness and bliss from it all? To keep their love apart from the circumstances of their lives—hers and his—had proved impossible. Those circumstances had brought about their meeting and proved in the end too powerful.

She stretched out her legs. They were long, but although shapely, like her arms and wrists they were heavy because she had been stuffed in her childhood and adolescence by endless glasses of milk and all the starch that had to make up a wartime diet. But her neck and shoulders were beautiful. They rose out of low, deep-cut evening dresses with a flamboyant perfection, as smooth as marble. Her light brown hair curled naturally round a very young and pretty face. She was tall, and in evening dress she looked superb and statuesque, when she remembered to curb her natural clumsiness and move with restraint quietly. As a child she had been delicate, and that delicacy of health had clung to her like a legend she could not discard. A serious attack of measles when she was seven had left her heart reputedly weak, so that all forms of strenuous exercise had been denied her, such as riding and swimming, although later on she had been allowed to play what was called gentle tennis, and to dance. It had kept her at home until her fifteenth year in her grandparents' house, and sheltered her. And, she often thought, it gave her mother an excuse not to follow her father to unpleasant, dull parts of England or abroad, where his profession sometimes sent him.

A week after Adrian left for Belgium Elizabeth's parents had taken her to live in London. Before that they had been occupying a country house under the auspices of the Office-of-Works, which was filled with reproduction Chippendale. Every room was like a sample room in a Tottenham Court Road furniture shop; and the men and women who lived in those rooms unconsciously seemed to acquire the appearance of dummies seen through plate glass. Each one seen against that background belonged to a set piece. The servants—there had to be servants in that official life, as there had to be a special food allowance for entertaining—were servile, adequate, and impersonal. A gracious hostess, her mother. A jovial host, her father. And who could not say his joviality was not part of an act, also? Herself, the debutante daughter. Adrian, her father's Personal Assistant. That was the picture. There it all was.

She first saw Adrian from an upstairs window, as he got out of his car and ran up the steps. She had been away and he had arrived to take up his duties during her absence. But she did not have any conversation with him until a few nights later, when she asked him, "Where do you go— what do you do in London when you go up?" It was a dinner-party, and her father was being his most genial self to two junior officers' wives. And they, ex-W.A.A.F., were wide-eyed at so much ceremony, and shy because they came from bungalows or rooms where there were dart

boards and pictures of aeroplanes and snapshots on the walls
—and sometimes, as a concession to culture, a framed print
of Van Gogh's sunflowers. And an evening meal was something snatched out of the larder and eaten anyhow. She
had gone returning calls with her mother, who couldn't
have disliked those afternoon excursions more because
she said it was as bad as slumming. They were shy, poor
women, because it mattered to their husbands' careers
how they behaved and impressed the old man and his
lady. The old man could be gracious to women, in his
pompous fashion, but although he made fighting speeches
in the war on recruiting drives, saying they were wonderful,
he insisted on having, when hostilities were over, a P.A.
of his own sex.

She knew Adrian's father lived in London.

"You mean, lately? I usually go up to the Proms."

In time she came to accompany him, to drive up to
London in the middle of the afternoon, to walk in the park
first and to eat a late supper in a restaurant afterwards. He
took her to his home and she met his father, who frightened
her a little because he was a judge celebrated for his caustic
wit and his severity, whose remarks, especially on juvenile
delinquency, were always quoted in the Press. And Adrian's
stepmother, young enough to be his father's daughter;
and his brother, older and married, following the career
of the father, who had the same tall, lean figure and fairness
of complexion and hair, which in the father's case was
grey and grizzled above lined, red-apple cheeks. Were they,
the brother and the father, in appearance older, and very
much older, editions of what Adrian would become? That
was hard to decide, because there was something elusive
and complex about Adrian, and he had not yet got their
sense of belonging to an established order in society, with
a definite place in it. His father's home was an enormous
flat, where Adrian had one room. There were weeds and
grass growing among rubble and broken stones where the
Morbeigh's former London house had been. He had been
away on his own since he was seventeen, so perhaps he did
not look on that flat as home, only somewhere to hang his

clothes and dump his books and gramophone records. Once, on a wet afternoon, they sat in his room, and while he played his classical records she looked at his books. She did not know then if he really loved her. That was in the days—soon to end—when they were alone together, getting to know each other better, before his future came to be discussed and argued over, his very soul, it seemed at times, pulled apart and dissected, when her father's *bonhomie* and advice failed before Adrian's firmness and his obstinacy. Only her mother was their ally. And how! When she knew about his published poems she thrilled and cooed, and became in a twinkling the blue-stocking daughter of a country squire, forced by a conventional marriage to lead a narrow, circumscribed life and told him to call her Olive. She began to talk of Auden and Eliot and Gertrude Stein—muddling her up with a novelist called Steen. These were all tokens of a mother's approval against the voiced misgivings of a father. But when the advantages of a service career failed to impress or appeal to a quietly determined young man, and all the offers of help were met by a look that would have stilled the voice of a more sensitive man than that Air Chief Marshal, there was no more to be said, or done, except wish them happiness and reluctantly consent to an engagement.

But it was extraordinary how a father's misgivings and doubts could sink more deeply into the consciousness of a daughter, than did a mother's overflowing blessings. If Adrian really loved her, would he not conform? Those thoughts came repeatedly when he had gone to Belgium, and having gone appeared to be staying indefinitely. But he had made up his mind the previous year, before he knew her, how he would fill in the time before going up to Oxford. He wanted a break—and he wanted to work. He wanted to achieve something—for her. Her mother approved of his going to Bruges because there was Julie de Fermandois living near to keep an eye on him. And, who knew, Julie might invite them all to stay with her later on? Elizabeth knew what was behind her mother's late-flowering friendship with Julie. Continental contacts were essential these times if there was a daughter who had only been to Switzerland and Paris. But no invitation was forthcoming, though there must have been hints in plenty for Julie to write and say she was very sorry, but perhaps next year.

Then Adrian stayed on. When she read his letters from the château her belief in him was as a bright light shining on all her days, guiding her in all her actions, making her more affectionate towards her mother and less critical, making her kinder, making her be as he thought she was. Should she have let her belief in him guide her to stay in England and not be brought across the Channel until he had finished the work he was on? Not listened to her mother? Not to have clutched at the suggestion—when Julie could not have them—about a nice little holiday over there? But when it was there, spread out on the table in shiny, bright travel folders and it was said how thrilled he would be, how could she resist? All that summer, when they had settled in the London house, in the intervals between official engagements her mother let drop her questions, let drop and let drop, like a Chinese torture. How was Adrian? Had he seen Julie again? What was it he was doing? "Something to do with medieval times, Mummy. The crusades." (*He's not trying to wriggle out of the net you cast. . . . But, if he loves me, when he comes back, surely he'll give up Oxford? That will be three years! How can I wait three years?*)

"And while we are over there," her mother said, "you must see Brussels. We can go on one of these coach trips from Bruges, quite cheaply." But because her mother did not want to pay for Adrian—and she didn't want to embarrass him and put him to the extra expense on top of his hotel bill—they would go on their own. So the preparations began. And now they were nearly there.

She saw the ship was turning and that passengers were getting up and putting their things together. The land was very close now. "I'd better go below," she said, "and tidy up."

The ladies' room was crowded with women struggling to see themselves over the wash-basins, where two little

girls were slowly and unconcernedly washing their hands.
Elizabeth pushed her way forward and stood behind them.
They were laughing and one of them was spelling out the
word, 'Chaud'. They were twins, plump and fair-haired,
dressed alike in gingham frocks and little woollen cardigans.
She had noticed them in the saloon at lunch, because they
and their mother—if she were their mother, dark and slim
where they were the opposite—were attracting quite a lot
of attention. Twins, of course, always did, though she
was thankful she wasn't one. When their mother took them
out all the stewards smiled and bowed, and it could not
be because she had over-tipped them. It was because she
was uncommonly beautiful, although no longer young.

Over the twins' heads Elizabeth bent her own and
began to do her face. She knew they were watching her,
and that they would have stayed had not their mother
arrived to pull them away. In the mirror Elizabeth's eyes
met her eyes—and they both smiled fleetingly. Yes, she
was really beautiful, Elizabeth decided, but she looked
pale and tired, as though she was in need of a holiday. But
a moment later she had forgotten her. Her hand was shaking
as she held the lipstick. Now the woman had taken the
children away she could see herself properly, and she could
think only of how she would look to Adrian after all that
time. Why had she ever harboured any doubts about the
wisdom of coming to him before he had finished his work?
For surely he had finished it by now?

All these women pressing round her, rattling the catch
of the toilets, fumbling in handbags, and the one with the
twins, what were they going to meet when they landed?
What were they going to find on their Belgian holiday?
Thump-thump-thumper-thump went the engines of the
ship. It was like the beating of her heart. She saw her mother,
and heard her say, "Oh, there you are, darling," in the voice
she always used in public. "Hold my things a minute, will
you?"

Presently they went up on deck and in the bright
sunlight Lady Fulmer glanced, not with entire approval,
at her daughter's face. "I don't like that coloured lipstick,"

she said. "It is too purple. Smooth it down, dear, just a bit."
They collected their hand luggage and joined the queue.
On one side were the private cabins, in which were expensive
pieces of luggage, rugs and white pillows, and dull, elderly
travellers. Sailors were busy with ropes. The wharf was
sliding nearer; the division between land and ship was
narrowing. People behind were pressing, pressing. A man
in front was carrying a bag of golf clubs, the end of which
lunged against Elizabeth's knees. Her temper began to
rise, the temper which, in childhood, had to be coaxed
out of her because of her heart.

They were holding landing tickets, passports, all the
paraphernalia of travel, besides the hand luggage. Would
the gangway never be put down and porters appear? Her
arms felt as though they were breaking. Why hadn't her
mother sent all the luggage registered through to Ostend?
Resentment rose in her heart against her mother, for her
coolness in this heat, for her efficiency and her general
management of everything that had ever happened. Then
the crowd began to move slowly; a man took the landing
tickets they had been balancing between their fingers.
Their feet were upon the gangway and their arms were
lighter, their hands emptier because porters in blue smocks
had torn the luggage away. Everything looked very bright
and clean, and smelt different. Stepping down the gangway
behind her mother Elizabeth looked quickly along the
wharf and then to the right of a shed where a fence enclosed
some waiting figures, and the one longed-for figure standing
apart from them. She saw Adrian, tall and very lean, hatless
in the sun, waving to her.

·   ·   ·   ·   ·   ·

The most anxious, most agonizing moments to two little
girls was when the great crane began to pick up the motor-
cars in its claw-like pincers. Suppose it dropped it! Suppose
for one awful moment one saw those claws open and the
car, their mother's car, the car that had belonged to their
father who had been killed before they were born, the most

beautiful and fastest car in the world, hit the quay with a sickening crash?

Sensitively aware of her children's fears Clare Ainslie held their hands. To be on foreign soil again after so many years brought formalities she had forgotten; and with the excited children beside her she submitted to the inspection of automobile papers, passports, and luggage, remembering that on previous occasions those things were always seen to by someone else. The children each had their own passport, which described them respectively as Jane and Matilda Ainslie; and she pretended not to know they had each presented for inspection the passport of the other. This joke would continue to be one of never-failing delight for many years.

"Remember," she said to herself, when the formalities of arrival were over, and the twins had climbed into the front seat beside her, "to keep to the right. Go slowly to start with."

She had first seen this country when she was thirteen. And was it anything more than a sentimental memory of an ice-cream, coloured pink and coffee, eaten at a café on the Grand' Place in Bruges that had brought her back with her children? She had gone to France and Switzerland and Italy and Austria with their father, and those countries would have held his ghost, as the quay and the customs shed had half an hour ago, when the babble of foreign tongues brought him back with momentary vividness. She must drive slowly, not because of the different rule of the road, but because it was the first glimpse of abroad for Jane and Tilly, and she wanted them to remember it, as she did. Why was it she particularly remembered one afternoon of that long-ago summer holiday at Knocke, when her father had spared a precious afternoon from his golf, while his wife was playing in a tennis tournament, to take his young daughters on a little sight-seeing tour of Bruges? But that afternoon, out of the whole holiday, stood out painted in shining colours, with the sun reflected on rose brick, on carved figures that adorned the façade of an old building; and music was in the bells. Sweet, vibrating music that had echoed in her dreams ever since. She wore a pink frock and her hair was in two plaits. She was tall for her age and leggy, and the pink frock was getting a little too tight for her. Her head was full of dreamy nonsense, so that her family often reproved her for not paying attention to what was said. While her sister, Joan, three years older, had been conscientiously reading aloud out of a guide book, and their father had been leaning back in his chair with his hat tilted over his eyes, herself had been listening to the bells, while she licked the ice-cream off a spoon with sensuous delight. No ice-cream, before or since, ever tasted quite so good as that one.

Tilly nudged her. "What is it?" Clare asked without looking at her.

"It does look a little like England—just here."

The child was perhaps right, for it was like parts of East Anglia, with the beet fields, the willow trees, the streams and the low, squat, red-roofed farmhouses and the windmills. But the Flemish houses all had bright green shutters; and there was a neatness about those small fields, a certain well-arranged orderliness. And now and again there was a single house, three stories high, which indicated the value of the land it was built on. Like a doll's house, with curtains draped so neatly they might have been painted on the glass. Peace had come to this land again, to the inhabitants of those little homes; and she wondered about the lives of all those who dwelt in Flanders, then and now. Being a tourist she would never enter into them. She thought of the armies that had marched through Flanders; and once again they had left no mark, for already the scars were healed, the holes filled and the houses rebuilt. Was a country happy that had no history? She did not think so. She saw a girl walking by the side of a stream leading three cows; and sheep with wooden cross bars round their necks were nibbling grass in an orchard where the apples were red and ripe. The cows were spotted— like china cows. Beside a little river, where some boys were fishing, stood another windmill. She passed the road to Jabbeke, and where the new *autostrade* began

at a little red-brick bridge cars swept past her, leaving
the Bruges road to roar along the new double track to
Ghent.

"But why," everyone said, "are you taking the children
to Bruges for a holiday? Wouldn't it be wiser to take them—
if you want to go abroad—to the sea? Bruges in late summer,
when the canals smell worse than Venice, can't be healthy."
They were the same voices which had said, "Why do you
insist on keeping the car when you can't afford to run it?
You would get a good price for it, if you sold it now."
She couldn't sell Jock's car, because it seemed like part of
him, the part she had shared—the happy part. Those same
voices had said, "Why do you go on living here—alone,
like this? How are you going to manage? Have you never
thought it would be better to take a job of some sort—you
are capable—which would bring you in more than this
sewing does, and take you out of yourself, and then you
could send the twins to a nice little nursery boarding school.
Children, believe me, Clare, are much happier away from
their parents along with others." A widow was at the mercy
of the world's advice.

The attack had not been renewed when she said she
would take the children to the sea every day from Bruges,
except to remind her that now she was to marry again she
ought not to go gallivanting off for three weeks because her
fiancé had gone to America on business. Since she had made
that sensible decision for her future everyone had been
pleased with her, and she was clucked over and kissed and
showered with goodwill. They all thought it was so suitable,
and nothing could have turned out better for poor Clare.
But she ought, they said, to stay at home and start getting
her trousseau together, and see about selling the car and
the cottage, and put her affairs in order, so there would be
nothing to worry Claude with. They were all very suspicious
about the state of her affairs. But it was because she was
going to be married again that she had brought the twins
on this holiday, for it might be the last one they would
spend together for many years. She wanted them to have
something to remember of the years they had spent alone

together that was different, something, perhaps, to treasure
when they came to share her with Claude Spencer-Perry.

Was this the Porte d'Ostende so soon? She brought the
car to a standstill behind a van filled with bottles of beer,
and on every side of her cyclists were waiting. A bridge
was being slowly raised to let a long boat go through, and
a policeman in a white helmet shouted to the driver of
another car who had nosed his way out of the waiting line.
The sun beat down and the wait seemed interminable. She
looked at the cyclists: young men in knickerbockers
and berets; little boys in very long plus-fours; and girls
with flowing hair and sun-tanned legs. Slowly the boat
passed; and slowly the bridge was lowered again; but the
line of traffic city-bound waited for the traffic leaving the
city to cross first.

Then they were over, and she raised her eyes for a brief
second, and a thrill of expectancy ran through her. Presently
they were in a narrow street lined with shops. One window
was filled with religious medals and statuettes and pictures
of saints and coloured reproductions of Memlinc and Van
Eyck. A *patisserie* displayed pyramids of chocolate bars
and trays of cellophane-wrapped toffees and glass bowls
filled with pink and white and lavender sugared almonds,
and mouth-watering cakes. A stocking shop. Oh, the nylons!
A big window full of flowers. Two nuns went by with
hands folded and eyes downcast. Some schoolgirls with
leather satchels. A Capuchin Father. A Benedictine. Some
black-clothed priests with pale, æsthetic faces, wearing
spectacles.

She stopped in the Grand' Place to ask the way and
as she did so the bells rang out from the Belfry. It was all
as she remembered, as she had known it would be. Another
day shining in soft colours on rose brick, on Gothic magnificence, on pointed gabled roofs, on grey cobble-stones. A
town of spires and towers, of churches and convents, ringed
by its waterways, shadowed by trees. But, how alive!
There was not one empty chair at the cafés on the pavement
opposite. But when she remembered that the town had
stood on the road from Cologne to Canterbury the centuries

narrowed, and the Place was filled with princes and peasants, soldiers and rioters, bishops and conquerors, pilgrims and queens. The children were silent. Perhaps there was suddenly so much to look at their eyes were dazzled—or they had been at the sight of that *patisserie*. They mustn't have bilious attacks!

They drove along an embankment, where under a tree an old man sat before an easel, and over another little bridge. Houses rose straight up out of the water, and weeping willows bent their feathery shadows over it. Two swans glided under the bridge. A little motor-boat disturbed them. She turned the car slowly into a square, where there was a fountain; and over an oak door, in Gothic lettering was the sign:

HOTEL DIERICK D'ALSACE

She was, at first, disappointed to find their rooms did not face the water but the square where she had left the car with its nose to the entrance. But it did not really matter. She would wake in the morning to the sound of bells and of footsteps hurrying over the cobble-stones and perhaps to the sound of the milk-cart. Were they still drawn by dogs in harness? While waiting for the luggage to be brought up she leaned out of the window, heard the bells again, and the clanging of a tram in the distance. She looked across the square at the row of lop-sided houses with their façades painted cream and yellow and pink, and at the uneven red-tiled roofs, then down at her car. There was another car beside it, which had been there when she arrived; a large black, chauffeur-driven limousine with a Belgian number-plate, which had brought the party on the floor below from Ostend, for two of them, a mother and daughter, had been on the boat. There was a young man with them now. But it could not be his car, because he was English.

The children had gone exploring, and she wondered where they had got to, and hoped they were not trespassing. There must be other rooms on that landing than the ones whose doors she had seen, perhaps approached by a secondary staircase from below, because the first-floor landing was more than twice the size and had twice the number of bedroom doors.

The children returned with the luggage and a fair-haired young chambermaid and a youth with the look of an idiot, a harmless, pathetic, friendly, happy fool, who grinned as he put the luggage down.

"I will unpack later for you, Madame," Marie Berlearts said, "if you will leave me your keys. But for the moment I must attend to guests below. Madame is satisfied with the appearance of the rooms? Ah! but how alike are the children!"

The children's demands for tea drew Clare into the busy streets away from the quiet backwater where the hotel stood, to look for a café where their appetites could be satisfied, and she took them to the one on the Grand' Place where she had eaten an ice-cream long ago. It was crowded, and they could only find seats at a table set on the edge of the roadway, where the awning did not reach. Watching her children's faces, pink and flushed, their eyes lighting first on one thing, then on another that was new and fascinating, the happiness in her heart swelled to overflowing, and with that happiness there was a sense of release from care, from tension and stress. She was used to the children being noticed everywhere—as twins always were—but she did not know that herself was the object of many glances also, that many, that afternoon, outside the café looked at her and looked again; or that a passing priest had momentarily caught a glimpse of a mother and two children seated at a café table in a crowd and had gone on his way thinking that her face might have been painted in an earlier century to grace an altar.

They sauntered slowly back to the hotel, stopping to look in every shop window and to read every Flemish sign. When they climbed the stairs to the second floor the children's feet began to drag a little. They were tired and the excitement had died down. They had all got up very early that morning to drive to Dover. But the dirt left in the high-water mark in the bath was a matter for pride and boasting, and they thought it sweet of the management to have a little baby's bath in there too. When Marie brought them cups of soup and asked which was which they sleepily played their favourite game on her. Clare heard their prayers, and when they had risen from their knees and scrambled into bed there was a gentle knock on the door; and when it was opened an elderly woman said, a little nervously, "I wondered if they would like a piece of chocolate?"

Miss King, unobserved in the little *salon* off the hall, had seen them arrive. She had seen them, through the open door, get out of the car and bring a breath of fresh air into a stuffy hotel with them. A veritable breath, she had thought, of moorland air, where there would be ponies and gorse and heather and legs scratched by brambles. She held out a chocolate box lid, her shyness dispelled by Clare's smile.

"Oh, it is kind of you," Clare said. "But, please, not all that. One little piece each, perhaps."

"My name," the visitor said, "is Muriel King."

"And mine—Clare Ainslie. Jane, and that one is Tilly." Loneliness! Clare thought, smiling into Miss King's spectacle-framed, guileless eyes. "Have you been here long?"

"Four days. And I am staying three weeks."

Were those three weeks, Clare wondered, stretching before Miss King, as a void to be filled in—somehow? A long-planned holiday abroad already losing all purpose, an unaccustomed freedom of hours hard to employ and enjoy? At the gathering dusk outside in the little square she offered with her silent thoughts, as she put the mosquito frames in place across the windows, a prayer for all lonely women, whose arms were empty. There was laughter behind her, from the twins' beds, in which Miss King was joining in; and after a few minutes Clare left them to go and have her bath, knowing that they would question Miss King without restraint, and having done so would, perhaps, allow her to enter into the intimacy of their own lives. It happened like that sometimes, but not always. To some advances they could be as close as oysters, and they were not always discriminating. Lying in the bath, relaxed in the hot water, she thought of some of the embarrassing occasions when they had not shown discrimination or been tactful, and laughed. She would have stayed in the bath much longer had not someone tried the door, perhaps even fallen asleep in it, because being able to relax at that hour was an unaccustomed pleasure, as was an evening in front of her with nothing to do.

The bedroom, now the luggage was unpacked, had a different appearance. It belonged to her, and her possessions seemed already at home. Yet, I have no home, she thought, any longer. The anchorage of the cottage was already being pulled up, since she would leave it for good when she married in November. The diamond and emerald ring that circled her finger above her wedding ring was a reminder. She was to marry Claude in London and fly to Paris for a honeymoon.

Her previous honeymoon had been spent in Cyprus, and she and Jock, after their wedding in Cairo, had sailed for Famagusta in a Greek ship from Alexandria. Three months later they had gone to England, and from then, until two years before his death, they had had no home to call their own. That one she had bought without consulting him, and on his death she had been left with debts and an overdraft, which his decorations for bravery did nothing to reduce. He had not, at first, wanted her to have children, but to wait awhile, so the years had gone by until it was near to being later than they knew. He had gone out that last time without knowing she had got her wish; and in those months when she had known there was no hope, while friends and his father and her mother and sister listened every night to the German broadcasts, which they said would announce his name among those of captured bomber crews, she had known he was dead and believed that she carried his son. Of that time, what could she remember now? A fire in a cottage sitting-room that smoked perpetually, and his dog who still looked wonderingly, who leapt up when a caller came wearing the same uniform, only to sink disconsolately on to the rug again and lie there shivering. The cat that curled indifferently at one end of the couch. A row of empty clothes on hangers in a cupboard. A row of shoes on a shelf. The rains and winds of spring. Fitful sunshine and more rain at midsummer. The melancholy chill of autumn. And it was decided officially, that Jock was dead. Her mother came, and they sat together knitting baby clothes. She was a widow, left to face the world's advice in all its abundance. And she hadn't been carrying Jock's son, after all.

Afterwards, when she left the hospital with two roaring bundles with old, red, puckered faces, the advice began all over again. She should not bury herself, they said. Bury herself? The word 'bury', meaning, in the dictionary, commit to earth or tomb or sea, consign to oblivion, brought a significance they were unaware of. To be consigned to oblivion had, at first, been her desire, but it was no longer because the physical needs of two babies were all-embracing round every particle of her energy. And the economic needs of the three of them were pressing problems also. She was aware of the passage of time by the manner in which those problems were solved, and by landmarks in the progress of her children's growth; their first faltering footsteps, the first intelligent sentences. The war was a sound of fury in the distance, a storm over the hill. The American army was in England. Italy had surrendered. British and American forces had landed in Normandy. The days and nights were noisy with the sound of aeroplanes. But those sounds were now impersonal. One by one the last of Jock's followers were killed, or became household names. Her brother-in-law was knighted for his distinguished military services.

When she took herself up to London she was a stranger in a foreign city, among men and women keyed-up to a pitch of excitement and hope she could not share, any more than she could involuntarily sway her body and move her feet to the dance music that was relayed at railway stations to ease the monotony of a queue waiting for a train, as they did. But sometimes she could feel the beating of the pulse of London and of England, feel the rhythm of its strange new sensuality, share with an A.T.S. girl in an underground passage the kisses of a sailor—and pass by.

The war ended, echoing an atomic explosion far away in Asia. In reality two wars ended, with speeches and flags and

C

prisoners returned. Over cottage doors were garlands o
welcome, a band at the railway station and tears an
embraces. Between those two wars' endings a lady of goo
works sent her handing political pamphlets, printed in blue
in at doors that would, in the ordinary way, have bee
opened wide to a gossip and a kind inquiry, but which wer
opened merely a slit and evasive looks and evasive answer
given to the intruder. Not that she was qualified to question
or to instruct; nor, strangely, did she greatly care. And thi
was wrong of her, the lady of good works said, and spok
of the heritage Jock and others had left by their dying fo
liberty, for England, and for the four freedoms—which, a
Clare could make out in her desultory reading of one daily
newspaper, were fast disappearing from more than hal
the world. But Clare did as she was told and attende
meetings and listened to speeches, and she became a membe
of the local Conservative Party and paid her subscription
She tried to evince interest in the resignation, after hi
defeat, of the elderly gentleman with the Ouida-esque white
moustache, who had sat so safely and so silently for so long
as a member for that constituency, and in the nomination
of his younger successor, Major Spencer-Perry. He was
soon to drop his military title, as he had only held wartime
rank.

Looking out of the window at the sky above the roofs
opposite, and then down at two peculiar looking white dogs
with long, curly tails rolling each other over in the gutter
by the lamp-post, she was ashamed of her first critica
thoughts about Claude. But she had been critical of him
because he wore success so easily, and there was nothing ir
his life she could discover to his discredit. Not that she
cared. It was only that so much success and correctness
must have a flaw somewhere? Surely, once in his life, if he
were human, he must have made a mistake and suffered
a humiliation? But those were her thoughts when she first
heard him speak in public, at the meeting to which the lady
of good works had taken her, and she watched his practised
gestures with tortoise-shell-rimmed glasses, heard the rise
and fall of that well-modulated voice, which she had unjustly

hought at the time had almost a too sincere, too honest
ing in it to be true. It was at that lady's house, the same
vening, that she met him, when he was being sustained with
ood and drink after he had expended so much eloquence
nd drive and had dealt with hecklers with such merciless,
unruffled repartee. His duty done by the committee members
ie made his way to her side, and asked if he might drive
ier home. She had no drink to offer him, but she made some
offee and he stayed and talked. He was very easy to talk
o. He knew Joan's husband, and had once served under
iim. He admired him, and she was glad because Joan's
iusband was the only member of the family who had
efrained from giving her advice. That was the first evening.
5he had never imagined there would be anything more.

He took to dropping in on her when he was in the
ieighbourhood. She liked him, really liked him, for the first
ime when he was tired and didn't talk much, but sat there.
Apart from his business, which took him all over Europe
ind sometimes to America, on what was called the Export
Drive, he was throwing his heart and soul into that now
rather hopeless constituency. And she wanted to say to
iim, "Is it worth it?" Perhaps her values were different.
Perhaps she hadn't any. He sat and watched her sewing,
at and stared at her, when he wasn't looking into the fire.
He said, "Poor sweet, you shouldn't be having to do that."
And she had gone on sewing, and pretended she hadn't
ieard.

Gradually she came to rely on seeing him, aware of her
oneliness, aware that when a woman lived entirely alone
vith her children she was only half-alive, and she was out of
ouch with the world. She might become in time as withered
.s a spinster who had never known love, never known male
ompanionship that was needed to balance most feminine
iatures, unless they were exceptional—and she was not.
)ver the next few years she saw more and more of him—
ometimes in London—and recently he had asked her to
narry him. She knew that was no hasty decision, but he
iad thought it over very carefully for quite a long time.

That was the outline, and as figures outlined only

she knew they lacked substance and reality. But there wa
substance enough in Claude, enough to insure him one day
a place in the nation's political history, as it had brough
him already fame in the war for a dangerous exploit, and
a reputation before that at Winchester and Balliol he wa
doing his best to fulfil. He was thirty-eight, two years he
senior. He was kind, and she had not, so far, seen him los
his temper. But perhaps that, like everything else abou
him—even his love-making—was under control. Sh
suspected he could be passionate, and she wondered if sh
would come up to his expectations. She made the discover
—through her sister Joan—that he had been for years th
lover of a married woman, and the affair had ended whe
he took up politics. She regarded that fact with indifference
felt no jealousy and no inquisitiveness about the woman'
identity.

Everyone was pleased. Her mother especially, becaus
now her widowed daughter's future was secure. From quarrel
ling with other elderly residents in a Hampshire Guest House
from asserting her right to the best chair by the fire—because
after all, hadn't the house once belonged to her cousins?—
and from continually talking about the past in India and
Egypt, she had been raised by both daughters to a new
status. As well as being the widow of one general and th
mother-in-law of another, she would be—God willing, nex
election—the mother-in-law of a Conservative member o
the House of Commons. Clare's only sister was delighted
because, like their mother, nothing succeeded better wit
her than success. Failure and sadness bored her, especiall
among those who would not take her advice.

"Do I love him?" Clare asked herself, and knew th
truth in the silent answer: "Yes, as much as I am capabl
of loving any man again." "But as much as any mar
rightly demands from his wife?" her conscience asked
and not for the first time. 'I can,' she thought, 'when th
time comes. I know how.'

'I am happy,' she thought. 'Happier than I deserve t
be.' The warmth of the cobble-stones on which the sun had
beat down all day, and the warmth of the walls that sur

ounded the square on all sides, save for two narrow
ntrances, and the stillness of the evening stole into her
wareness. But the stillness was broken; in the distance
. tram clanged down a street; and the bells rang again.
he bells of Bruges she had heard in her dreams for years,
hat played a melody of her youth. On the landing outside,
ootsteps were hurrying towards the stairs. They were
going down the stairs. A man's footsteps, but lightly,
wiftly, and he was singing as he went. The young man in
he room opposite, who had tried the bathroom door.
She would peep in at the children to see if they were asleep.
They really ought not to have eaten that chocolate after
hey had cleaned their teeth. But it would have hurt that
nice woman's feelings if they had been told to keep it until
morning.

There were voices below, and a smell of cooking. That
rich, unmistakable, aromatic smell of Continental cooking.
Hot butter. Meat sizzling over a flame. She was hungry.
And she would have a glass of wine at dinner.

CHAPTER III

COFFEE had been served, and they were waiting until the last drop had trickled through the perforated metal cover into the cups. To Lady Fulmer and Elizabeth this was a novelty. They were delighted with everything, Lady Fulmer said; with their rooms and the service, and especially the dinner they had just eaten. The excellent soup, that shrimps dish, the steaks cooked to their individual taste, the golden-yellow potatoes fried to a perfect crispness, the salad glistening with dressing, and the grapes, tender with bloom, for dessert. Not to mention the white rolls, the spotless napery and the extra-special attentions of Henri, the head waiter. It was always important to find out the waiter's name, because it made the service just that little bit more personal. If Adrian knew what she meant? Of course it was more expensive than they had bargained for, and she hoped it was not putting him to any inconvenience to be with them? And about their rooms—hers and Elizabeth's—they were charming, and such a nice view, but they could quite easily have shared one. In fact, could not this be arranged, and a saving made?

Because there came into Elizabeth's face an expression with which Lady Fulmer was too familiar she decided—if the holiday was to be a happy one for everyone—nothing more, for the present, could be safely said on that subject. So what, she asked, as she lifted the aluminium top off the coffee cup and she began to stir a lump of sugar and a generous spoonful of cream into it, had Adrian been doing with himself, apart from writing? Had he been bathing much? Playing any golf?

"I don't play golf," he said. "And I haven't bathed much because, when I was here, it was rather an effort getting there, and I always seemed to miss the tram."

Lady Fulmer smiled indulgently. "I thought we might all go and bathe tomorrow and take a picnic lunch. I expect the hotel will provide one, and make no extra charge?

62

After all, we pay for three meals a day, don't we? This time, Elizabeth and I shall see you don't miss the tram."

Elizabeth was silent and left it to Adrian to say it would be very nice at the sea tomorrow. It would be lovely by the sea, but not much fun for one who could not swim in it. If her mother was going to organize every minute of every day they might as well have stayed at home.

"I understand," Lady Fulmer said, a little reproachfully, "that you haven't seen much of my friend, Julie de Fermandois?"

"I am afraid I haven't," Adrian replied. "And I do feel awfully sorry about that, and I hope she understands. But I have been working quite hard, with the help of her brother-in-law, and the time just flew."

Lady Fulmer nodded, not entirely with approval. She wanted to ask him what he had been working on, because—like her friend, Julie—she felt that anything to do with the Crusades, which was all she had been able to drag out of Elizabeth, was too remote to be practical. But she was pleased he had made friends with Julie's brother-in-law, to the extent of being invited to stay with him, so she asked, "Is the château very beautiful?"

"It is very large," Adrian answered. "But I wouldn't call it beautiful, not if you compare it with those in the Loire country. For one thing, although its foundations go back centuries, it was only built—what you can see now—about a hundred and twenty years ago. You could call it Victorian Gothic, or Scottish baronial, either would fit, yet neither description would be accurate. But it suits the landscape and it suits, in a strange and paradoxical way, the owner. Possibly because I have not known him anywhere else, I feel it does."

"I suppose full of family portraits and all that?" Elizabeth asked.

"Oh, lots. Some good. Some bad. The room I know best, and love best of all, is the library."

"An interesting one?" Lady Fulmer wanted to know.

"Very," Adrian told her. "Classics in every language, rare editions, some priceless. And early Flemish and Latin

manuscripts, mostly out of monasteries. And a very earl¬
German bible that must be worth goodness knows what
Then Italian works. An ancestress was Italian in th
eighteenth century, and these came with her, with som
miniatures and a couple of Italian primitives on the wall
They were formerly altar panels, like the Flemish ones
Oh, and a lovely *Book of Hours*, a fourteenth-century
illuminated thing, priceless. To me that room spells Europe
Of the past. Europe that is eternal. Europe, too, that ha:
suffered so much and has always survived—like Pierr¬
himself. Also," he laughed, "it is the most comfortable roon
in the house, with wonderful arm-chairs."

Lady Fulmer nodded. Well, that all sounded, she thought
most interesting and quite satisfactory. And to think thi
opportunity for Adrian had all come about through he:
having met Julie that day! She would never have imagine¬
—even if she had given her a thought in all those years—
that noisy, rich, and vulgar Yankee, Julie, marrying int¬
the Continental Catholic nobility, which she had alway:
imagined was extremely conservative, and making a succes:
of it. The poor thing must have gone through it in the war
if you could believe all the stories. But that was over an¬
done with now, and it was irritating to see countries tha¬
had capitulated now so prosperous. The dinner, for instance
they had just eaten. And all those well-fed, rich-lookin¬
Belgians, who had just got up from their tables and gon¬
out! At one time in Belgium one only saw the English ir
these sort of places. Never before had one needed to bothe¬
about foreigners, or about forgotten school acquaintance:
who had married them. It was really an unenviable position
to be in, to be dependent on them, grateful for loans ir
their currency to be paid back, when they came to England,
in pound notes in an envelope.

"Adrian," Elizabeth said, "do you know, I feel rather
scared of meeting—Pierre, as you call him. Frightened o¬
putting my foot into it. Because you said one wouldn't
know at first. Saying isn't that a lovely tree, or a beautiful
sky. Or else not being able to say a word to him. Being
dumb."

Adrian laughed gently. "Darling, he won't let you be that. And you mustn't feel that way. If you do say anything about a tree, for instance, he will know which one you mean. And if you call his attention to the sky he will know the beauty of this big sky over Flanders has impressed you, and that will please him enormously."

Their table was in a window alcove, and he sat between Lady Fulmer and Elizabeth with his back to the room. He could see the lights behind him reflected in the window-glass and the waiters hurrying to and fro, lifting covers and unused cutlery from tables, and putting baskets of fruit back on the long serving-table in the middle of the room. He could see Elizabeth's profile against the glass, the curve of her throat and soft rounded breasts, the sweep of her hair curling on to her shoulders. He wanted to be alone with her, to walk with her round Bruges, to tell her all he had to tell her, to hold her in his arms.

"Did you have this table when you were here alone?" Lady Fulmer asked. "It is quite the best position in the room. It must be very nice in the day-time. Does much traffic pass along the canal?"

"Only the motor boats filled with tourists," he answered. "No. I sat over there." And he turned his head.

"Where she is sitting?" Elizabeth asked. "That dark-haired woman, alone? She was on the boat, with two little girls. Twins. Aren't they on your floor?"

"Yes," he said. "I heard her putting them to bed. And she kept me out of the bathroom."

"Don't you think she's attractive?" Elizabeth asked.

For a moment he hesitated. He was about to say he thought she was, but he remembered a couple of occasions, soon after they got engaged, when Elizabeth had drawn his attention to another woman in a restaurant, and on his saying he agreed she was lovely—agreeing with her question —she had appeared to be annoyed, as though in praising a stranger he was dishonouring her. "I haven't really taken her in."

"She's not young."

"No. I suppose not." But she had seemed young, he

c*

thought, when she came out of the bathroom, young and slender, moving swiftly past him, with her hair pinned up in plaits that made a little crown on top of her head, and her lips were like the lips of a statue, carved in stone, but fresh and smooth without paint, soft as a girl's were soft. There had been a curious sense of intimacy in that glimpse of her—which after all, was a common enough incident in any hotel—and it remained with him as he turned the taps on in the bath she had just used.

"Getting on for forty, I should say." Elizabeth smiled happily, and he met her smile with tenderness in his.

They got up then from the table, and as they went down the dining-room towards the little *salon* Clare Ainslie was walking in front of them. They saw her go to the window and stand for a few moments looking out at the lights reflected in the water below, before she turned round and picked up some magazines that were lying on the top of a squat little revolving book-stand. None of them was English, and nearly all of them were the kind issued by travel agencies and air lines, with shiny pages filled with advertisements and pictures of Alpine scenery and Provençal towns. But she selected one, and sat down to read it in an arm-chair, which had a Cluny lace antimacassar over the back.

Lady Fulmer continued to stand, with Adrian and Elizabeth uncertainly at her side. Having an audience she began to speak in the tone of voice that always made Elizabeth embarrassed to listen to. She was going to bed very soon, and she was sure they would like a little walk together, wouldn't they? And she had just remembered she had never asked Julie, when she telephoned before dinner, what time the car would come for them on Thursday. Had Adrian any change? The coins were found in his pocket, dull little metal ones, which were taken to the light and sorted.

Claire Ainslie looked up at them as they stood there counting the foreign money. One could not read or concentrate through some women's voices! Then she put down the magazine on seeing Miss King approaching shyly and

uncertainly. "They did so enjoy that little treat you gave
them."

Miss King smiled and hesitated. One never wanted to
intrude on people and bore them. But Clare stood up and
pulled another chair forward, and they both sat down and
began to talk. Sitting there, they watched the other party
of three move away. Lady Fulmer went into the office to
telephone, and the young couple, whom Clare guessed
were lovers, went through the door into the square with
their arms linked closely, into the magic and mystery of
Bruges at night.

* * * * *

At first it was the shops all brightly illuminated, and
many, in the main streets, still open, with which Elizabeth
was fascinated. She remembered how the shops in Lausanne
had delighted and excited her, and how she had spent all
the pocket-money that was supposed to last one term in
the first fortnight on stockings and sweets and cosmetics.
It was all part of being abroad, seeing shops filled with things
you could not buy at home, and cafés with tables on the
pavement.

She said to Adrian, "I want to see where you stayed
first." But he answered her evasively, saying it was a humble
little place and it would be noisy at that hour. He did not
want to take her there at night, into the bar, which was the
only public room, nor did he particularly want to take her
there in the day-time, and introduce her to Monsieur and
Madame and Denise their daughter. They were usually so
busy, and if they were not, they were sitting down to one
of their good, hearty meals, making the proper Flemish
business of eating a matter not to be hurried over, or
interrupted.

"But what is wrong with it?" she persisted.

"Nothing is wrong with it, darling. Only I don't think
it would amuse you. I've got so much to tell you, and I
can't in that place."

"But I just want to have a peep inside."

"All right. Just a peep then. But we shall have to have a drink. And I know places you would like better."

He guided her along a narrow street and over a bridge, and in the darkness under a tree he stopped and took her in his arms and kissed her as she had wanted to be kissed ever since her arrival, and as he had wanted to kiss her. The night air was warm and still, and not a leaf of the elms that shut out the sky and hid a moon three-quarters full stirred above them. The water below the bank was pierced by little rings of light that fell in a reflection from windows set in the walls that rose up from the opposite bank. Wrapped in his arms she felt the whole of that strange, brooding city was enclosing them, and a little of the mystery and awe of the great churches and the silence of the little squares and dark waterways stole into her consciousness. She felt the pressure of the centuries and of history, against which they, themselves, were insignificant. Then suddenly she was afraid, not of the darkness under the trees, and the weakening of her own defences, defying a code of behaviour she had set herself to maintain—as he had set one for himself too—but of something in the very air of that city which was alien to her. Whatever it was—and she could not name it—she felt it intrude into the ecstacy of their embrace, parting them and bearing Adrian in spirit away from her, leaving her on the outside, frightened and alone.

But the lights and the cheerfulness and the noise in the inn, a startling contrast to the quietness of the streets, restored her confidence, and she thought how odd it was to find such a place near a corner on which hung a statue of the Virgin Mary decked with tinsel jewellery and paper flowers in an illuminated glass case. They went into the bar, where Adrian was greeted by a woman behind the counter, and by what appeared to be the woman's husband, a red-faced man in an open shirt and no tie, and a young girl with bare legs and merry black eyes who was serving drinks. Along each wall were marble-topped tables and at the far end near the counter, there was a juke-box into which someone had recently put a coin, for a hot jazz tune suddenly burst out of it, and the music throbbed in that small, hot room with all the primeval beat of tom-toms, while up and down between the tables working-class couples bobbed and jerked.

"What will you drink?" Adrian asked her.

"Oh, anything. What you are having. Beer?"

They sat down at a recently-vacated table near the door, and the girl with the merry black eyes brought the drinks in two long glasses. Round the girl's neck, half-way to her high, prominent breasts, there hung a little gold cross on a fine gold chain.

"What was your room like?" Elizabeth asked.

"Clean and small and cosy." Adrian answered. "But it began to get a bit stuffy. It was just under the roof and got the sun all day. I had to move the bed under the window —to Madame's horror. I used to lie in bed in the mornings watching other people across the street getting up. Quite educational at times."

Elizabeth giggled. At the next table there was a joke being repeated, for two men and one woman were laughing until tears came. It had perhaps been a mistake to come there. The music had started up again. But she knew Adrian would not ask her to get up and dance—not there. Under the table their knees were touching, and on top of the table he put his hand on hers. All the way down, from their shoulders to their knees they were touching each other.

"It has been such a long time without you," he said.

"Have you only just realized that?"

"No. Though perhaps not so strongly as now—what I have been missing all this time, when I was working."

"You were luckier than I," she said. "I had only you to think about. But I shall always keep your letters. When I am an old woman and you are an old man and we are bored with each other, I shall take them out and read them."

He looked at her. "One or two of yours worried me. About the Chinese torture."

She turned her head away, knowing that her cheeks had reddened suddenly. What you wrote when you were desperate, as a kind of confession, you didn't want mentioned again. Not now. Her mother had brought her here, after all.

"You said your mother——"

She forced a smile. "Perhaps I exaggerated a bit. Perhaps very few girls get along with their mothers."

"You are sure? But it does worry me, still."

"Oh, it needn't."

"I cannot bear the thought of your being unhappy."

'Yet, you didn't come back!' she thought. He had finished his drink, and when he asked her if she would like another, she shook her head. "No, let's go. It is so stuffy in here."

They said good night to Madame and her husband and Denise and went outside. "That's better," Elizabeth said, and she took his arm.

Presently they came to the Place du Bourg, and as they were crossing it and walking towards a seat under some trees in a little avenue off it he said, "Just before dinner you asked me who Dierick d'Alsace was. It was he who brought the Holy Blood to Bruges, and it is kept in the church over there—behind us now, in the corner." They sat down; and he went on, "It is kept in a reliquary of the most dazzling precious stones, and they say the crystal vial is the same one he received it in from the Patriarch of Jerusalem in the twelfth century. Every Friday it is exposed for the veneration of the faithful. Many times in the history of Bruges it has been taken away and hidden for safety. It was taken away in the last war, and the one before. They say it was seen to liquify before 1914, but not before the last war."

"Do you honestly believe that?" she asked..

"Yes."

"Adrian," she cried. "You're not thinking of becoming an R.C. or anything, are you? I mean, since you've been here, soaking yourself in all this?"

He laughed. "Good heavens, no. And if I were, I wouldn't be ready for a long time. But you have to hand it to them."

"I think it is all a bit creepy. And——" She did not finish.

He laughed again, and kissed her. "It is the worst possible subject to argue over."

"Who started it?"

"My darling! I don't know."

He took a strand of her hair and curled it round his finger. He was filled with love and tenderness for her, and with delight that she was there with him. He knew, now, what he had been missing—without realizing it—all summer. Her head was resting on his shoulder. "Sleepy?" he asked her.

"No. Wide awake. But just thinking of us and the future."

"Awake enough to listen to the story of what I have been doing, with Pierre's help, the story of one of the Counts of Flanders and his wife, Marie of Champagne?" He bent his head close to hers. "It is for us. It is for you," he said. "I have written it for you," believing with all his heart that he had.

.   .   .   .   .   .

There had been no need to ask Adrian for change because the hotel telephone stood on the desk in the office, and Madame De Jonkheere obtained the number Lady Fulmer required and said it was of no consequence. Then she tactfully withdrew into the inner room to finish her own dinner. Rene had not yet returned, and as she sat down between her husband and her mother Madame De Jonkheere rehearsed in her mind what she would say to him when he did. It was no use discussing him with his father. No use at all.

"Where is Rene?" Monsieur De Jonkheere asked, when she sat down. And when she told him he laughed. Sometimes his thin nervous laugh irritated her. He spoilt Rene too. Because he had suffered so much for Rene's sake the boy was doubly precious and could do no wrong. "The new English guests," he ventured, "are all you expected? They will make no trouble, even if they do not spend lavishly outside the weekly arrangement?"

"They are well-connected," Madame De Jonkheere said. "Naturally."

"They are very English, so fresh, so lively, I can see."
As he spoke his eyes smiled as well as his thin lips parted
above his broken teeth, and Madame De Jonkheere's black
eyebrows rose towards the roots of her hair. "Those little
twins," he added. "Not the friends of Monsieur Morbeigh."
Then at the mention of that name, he ceased to smile, and
his thin fingers plucked at a roll of bread. He was trying
to remember, and the effort was too much for him. But he
said, before his wife's stern gaze in the direction of his
fingers pressing the bread into pellets, "He told me something.
Monsieur Morbeigh. It was important."

"To do with what?"

"I forget."

Madame De Jonkheere drew in her breath, frowned at
her old mother who was about to speak, but said gently,
"If it is important he will mention it again. Do not worry
yourself about it. Get on with your dinner." And she dismissed it instantly from her mind because the telephone
conversation in the office was being a prolonged one, and
that was a cause for annoyance.

"Julie?" Lady Fulmer said, after an interval in which
a servant had gone to find her. "It's Olive. . . . I hope I
haven't brought you away from dinner? . . . You were in
the garden? . . . Yes, it is a very hot night. . . . Oh, it is most
comfortable and an excellent dinner. Although"—Lady
Fulmer lowered her voice—"I think Adrian could have
found somewhere a little cheaper. . . . Yes, I expect they
are, but you know how it is with all the poor English these
days who are having to pay for the war on top of all their
other effort. What I really rang up about is Thursday.
You didn't say, or have I forgotten, what time you want
us to be ready? . . . Right, my dear, we'll be on the dot."
Lady Fulmer hesitated. She had not rung up Julie to ask
that, not entirely. She wanted to talk to her about Adrian,
and discover if Julie knew exactly what he had been working
on at her brother-in-law's château. She wanted to talk, as
one woman to another. And as one woman to another they
talked for over half an hour. Not of Adrian or of Elizabeth,
or of the engagement for all of that time. They merely talked.

And Madame De Jonkheere put her head round the side of the door once or twice and shrugged her shoulders and compressed her lips. It was bad for the hotel business for a guest to have the exclusive use of the telephone for all that time.

When the conversation came to an end Lady Fulmer was no wiser; nor, in truth, had she expected to be. She felt tired as she went upstairs; and the comfort and luxury of her bedroom, when she entered it again, filled her more with annoyance than pleasure. She could only blame Adrian, unless Elizabeth had had a hand in it, which she suspected on arrival and found they had a room each. It was really too early to go to bed, and should she, she wondered, sit down and write to Freddie? But she had nothing, except their safe arrival, to report to him. She wondered how he would get along in her absence, and if the Latvian couple a friend had got out of a D.P. Camp for her, would look after him all right. Freddie did not particularly care—any more than she did, in her heart—for foreigners. But who else could you get to work in a house these days? They ought to be grateful for employment, but they never were. Gratitude, she often felt, was rarely found in anyone—not even in one's own child. And it was ridiculous of Freddie—on one of the few occasions he had interfered in his daughter's upbringing—to say one was a fool to expect it. Still, he hadn't really interfered very much.

In acknowledging that fact to herself Lady Fulmer was being honest, for in the early years of Elizabeth's childhood her father's profession absorbed most of his energy and there was little time to devote to his only child. Also, he wasn't a domesticated man, and he was content to leave her upbringing largely to his wife. As a bachelor, he had sometimes observed the married life of his contemporaries with pity. When he married, if he ever did, he promised himself it would be different. And so it proved to be because he married well, and if not for money itself, where there was ample means to assure a smoothly-run household for which his wife footed most of the bills, and he was therefore able to devote his full attention to his career. He knew that such an enviable position was not shared by many, and it was all the more reason why he could not fail to succeed. In his magnanimity he gave full marks to fellows who could do their job while beset with domestic and financial difficulties, but he could never have seen himself doing it. He knew his own limitations and that knowledge was as useful as knowing his capabilities.

When he arrived to take command of a squadron in one of England's fairest and least-known counties he took stock of the neighbourhood and called on the owners of the big houses in order, he said, that good relations could be established between the station and the county, and prejudice overcome. He had recently returned from a tour of duty overseas, where weekly perusal of English papers devoted to country pursuits and the social round, and the conversation of cavalry officers—whom he professed to despise, but whose manner of speech he came to imitate —had given him a taste for a way of life he had never previously known. He developed an appetite for good living, and his favourite enjoyment at week-ends was to go to a good hotel and order dinner and a bottle of wine for himself. Over it he would brood and give rein to his private ambitious fancies. This did not deter him from entering on other occasions, into the pastimes of his fellow-officers, but he did so—knowing that he had to get on with them and make use of them and their talents—with reserve and restraint. Naturally he wasn't popular, but he earned excellent confidential reports, which were stowed away in the secret archives of the Air Ministry and were as good for his future as gold in a bank. He never put a foot wrong; and his marriage was the result of careful planning, because opportunity comes oftener to those who plan, than it does to those who don't.

The bride of his choice had grown up in country society that gathered together at Point-to-Points, Conservative Fêtes, hunt balls and in the hunting field, and it regarded the most junior service, which it still called the Flying Corps, with prejudice and dislike. In that society a man who knew anything about engineering or aviation was seldom a gentleman. But gradually towards the end of the decade that followed the slaughter of the 1914–1918 war, unmarried daughters began to turn their eyes on the nearest aerodrome as offering a possible means of escape from their spinsterdom. Although they were contemporaries of the Bright Young Things, not many of them had ever been inside a night club. And green hats were sturdy affairs, made to stand the wind and the rain. After a presentation at Court, and one or two unexciting dances in London, they returned to the country, only visiting London for the sales, the Horse Show and the Royal Academy. Sometimes they went abroad, strictly on the cheap, travelling second-class and sitting up all night, to Paris and Rome, and Switzerland for the winter sports. They never went to Cannes or Eden Roc. Their parents thought the Riviera unhealthy in summer. Although they travelled second-class on the Continent, and at home third-class, it was not because —on the whole—their families were poor. They did not worship money—for indeed they professed to despise the making of it—but they were careful of it, and although many indoor and outdoor servants were employed the household bills were kept to a minimum and economy was practised in the catering. Any foreigner sitting down in a dining-room, surrounded by Lelys and Romneys and Raeburns—singularly, after the early nineteenth century few portraits were commissioned—would have been appalled at the food. The women scorned the use of make-up, except for a little inexpert dabbing of a puff dipped in too white powder on a shiny nose. To make-up in the country stamped one as common, as having come from a town. It was 'shop-girl'. As were high heels and sheer stockings, except for evening.

Olive Gilbart was a pleasant, energetic and not unattractive looking young woman, who looked her best in tweeds and on a horse. In her voice and manner there was abundant inherited self-assurance; but as the years went by, with no permanent romantic attachment, only a profound student of human nature would have detected a tendency to smile too often and too readily when anyone of the opposite sex paid her attention in a public gathering. When she eventually married out of her class and family environment naturally the unanimous opinion in the county was that Squadron Leader—when they remembered not to call him Major—Fulmer had done very well for himself. He wasn't out of the top drawer, but only the most super-critical would detect it.

When Elizabeth was born Olive wished the baby had been a boy. Although she had never been on really romantic terms with anyone until Fulmer had gone punctiliously dropping cards on the county, she had always got on with men in a comradely fashion. She had two brothers, which, as she always said, made a difference. She had always been very happy in their society until they married. She liked their friends, and the sight and sound of all that masculinity about the house, when they came down to shoot or for the hunting. They looked on her as a good sort. But there the baby was, and as it was early May she christened her Jonquil, Elizabeth Jonquil, where it should have been, if not Christopher Robin, at least Christopher John or Julian Frederick. She took her maternity very seriously and read books on mother-craft and child-psychology. The first time she found her child out in a 'wopping fib' she flew for advice and comfort to her women friends. She had quite a number, although, as she always said, she got along better with men "A boy," she said, "would be so much simpler." Elizabeth baffled her, and at times infuriated her. Thwarted of her desires in any way, she sulked or flew into tempestuous rages; and it was all very well for Freddie to be lenient, he didn't have to put up with it. Then the child got measles, and she had to be indulged because of her heart. And it was such a disappointment that, as a result, she wouldn't grow up good at games.

In 1940 Olive had to make the hardest decision of her life. She had to decide whether to take her only child—who, suddenly, in that hour of danger, became unbelievably precious—to safety in America, or whether to remain in England. She decided to stay in England more out of a wholesale dislike of Americans, and the fear that Elizabeth might be contaminated by those children she had read about, who used cosmetics in their 'teens and had 'dates', than out of patriotism or courage. Freddie, anyway, was against their going. So she stayed, and she did her best to see that Elizabeth did not suffer from too many shortages. There were two jersey cows and there was all the butter and cream they needed, and pigs and poultry. Freddie was going from strength to strength, and as there was nothing to worry about on his account—he was too senior to fly, except as a passenger—she was left free, apart from W.V.S. work twice a week, to devote herself to her daughter. The 'teens were, according to the books, notoriously difficult years.

She confided in the headmistress and the housemistress of the school—her own old school—to which she sent Elizabeth later, which did not make the girl's path as smooth as it might have been. "She is apt to be sulky and highly-strung. And she does not, I am afraid, always speak the truth." It was only when Elizabeth was eighteen and had come out in the limited way that was only possible after the war, that it dawned on Lady Fulmer that she had perhaps talked too much of her daughter's shortcomings, because Elizabeth had made few friends of her own. She should not, perhaps, have told anyone of that terrible affair when Elizabeth was sixteen. It had been ghastly, because she had been well-brought up. She had been told the facts of life and had been given little books to read on the subject years ago. Not that there was anything of that sort, not for one moment. But with foreigners, especially Poles, one never knew. It was bad enough for Elizabeth to have been meeting the boy—he was only a boy, nineteen or twenty, and it was true his uncle had been an ambassador, even though he was only a private in a smelly, khaki battle-dress and black hob-nailed boots—down by the river. How could she! She had known by this—and a mother did know, after reading books that made things so much clearer and wrapped up nothing, as things used to be wrapped up—that Elizabeth would be happier if she married early and suitably. There was a charming, domesticated side to her, and it only needed Mr. Right to bring it to the forefront.

She remained moody and sulky, rude and casual in her manner, and easily turned to tears—until Adrian came into her life. And then, what a change! Right from the start, from that first dinner party. Certain little details were pointers. More interest in her appearance, more attention to matching accessories—although still inclined, if not watched, to pin an unnecessary flower on the shoulder and adorn a neat jacket with those common 'scatter-pins'. If Adrian did not entirely personify the son Lady Fulmer wished she had had, he soon qualified for a place in her affections, by his appearance and his good manners and his background; and she was willing from the first to accept him into the family circle and make him feel at home. She even, occasionally, was indiscreet enough to pass on to him a spicy piece of service gossip concerning a member of the Air Council that Freddie had told her in the privacy of the bedchamber. She did not, privately, blame Adrian for refusing a service career, when her husband talked disgruntedly of his throwing away chances, she only regretted his obstinacy because Elizabeth's happiness was at stake. She knew Adrian liked her, in her rôle of his chief's wife, for did she not understand his artistic temperament, even his diffidence when he feared he had so little to offer her child? He knew she was his friend and ally.

The dear things had been to a concert in London again. This had become a habit, and occasionally she had wondered where Adrian got the petrol from to be driving up and down so often. She hoped he wasn't patronizing the black market. Now the war was over it was morally different—you could really say it was only hurting the Socialists and no one else. But if Freddie found out there would be ructions. That night the dear things got back very late. Fortunately Freddie was away on a tour of inspection, and she had waited up for them. Normally Adrian would leave Elizabeth on the door-step and drive off back to the mess. But that night she intervened. It had gone on long enough, her having to deceive Freddie about what was going on. It was two o'clock in the morning, and the concert must have ended about ten, and it was only an hour-and-a-half's drive. She opened the front door when she heard the car, and said, "Well, my dears, have you enjoyed yourselves?"

She got them both into the drawing-room, and Elizabeth began to yawn. "You are tired, my pet, aren't you? So run along to bed." She kissed her fondly and squeezed her hand. "I want to check over the engagement-book with Adrian, and the lists for the sherry party."

Elizabeth stood there, with her hair untidy and her lipstick smudged, and she looked first at one and then the other. She looked longest at her mother, a long, long look of curiosity and strange innocence, like a dog, trusting, yet a little afraid.

"Have a drink, Adrian," Lady Fulmer suggested, when Elizabeth had gone upstairs. The drinks were on a side-table, whisky and soda and lime juice and beer. He had a glass of beer. She did not refer to the engagement-book again; she lit a cigarette and sat down on the arm of a chair. He stood on the hearth-rug, very tall and very young, in a dark suit. A little tired, perhaps, and rather pale. She asked him about the concert, and she nodded and smiled. She didn't ask him why he was so late. She waited for him to tell her. They had had supper in a restaurant in Jermyn Street, and then drove home. He was afraid they hadn't hurried. But he hadn't realized how late it was.

"That is all right," she said. "Quite all right," and smiled. "Only if they know in the mess how late back you are and who you've been out with——"

"You mean," he said quickly, "Elizabeth might be——?"

"Oh, I don't mind," she hastened to assure him. "I don't mind in the least. You are"—she hesitated—"fond of each other, I know." A pause. "Or is it more than that? Tell me, Adrian, and I shall understand and do my best to help you. Are you both serious? If you are not, then I fear——"

"Yes," he said very quietly. "Yes. I think we are. Although I haven't got anything to offer her."

She got up and kissed him. Nothing must stand in their

way. Nothing. She said love would find a way. It always did. So much she wanted them to be happy. So *much*. He mustn't worry, because everything was going to be all right. Of course, she had never anticipated she would lose Elizabeth so soon. So he must forgive her if she was a little tearful. She just stopped herself in time from saying she wasn't losing a daughter, she was gaining a son. She went upstairs and found Elizabeth in bed, awake. She bent over her, "Darling, Adrian has asked me if your father and I will consent to your engagement." And all Elizabeth could say was, "Oh, *Mother*!" before she started to cry. Nerves, of course.

Freddie had not been very accommodating when he was told. He'd had three days of tiring inspections and had evidently found much to criticize. And all that seemed to influence what he said. But she knew it would all come right in the end. It had got to come right, even though she knew Adrian's father—that sour old judge—thought it was a mistake. All the same the little ship of love was launched, but when it would come safely into harbour, Lady Fulmer did not know.

She had to bring Elizabeth over for this holiday. They had been separated for too long in such an early, and critical, stage of their engagement. Before he went up to Oxford and became engrossed in his studies, making new companions and, perhaps, finding other interests—not necessarily feminine or dangerous, but ones that might tend to sever him from Elizabeth—they must have two or three weeks together, and then all return to England the same day.

She finished a brief letter to her husband, in which she ended, conventionally, with her love. They had long since done with that word in its fullest meaning, if it had ever, in a spiritual meaning, existed between them. She was proud of his success, and he acknowledged the help she had been to him, so they lived together, except for occasional friction that blew up into rows, in a highly-satisfactory relationship. Through her family connections he had been admitted—before the war earned him fame and a title— to two of London's most exclusive men's clubs. It all helped. Nowadays he had to confer with Labour politicians, and his own background and upbringing were assets there, for he was clever enough to be himself when required.

She heard voices on the landing outside, low and laughing, followed by a silence. Then the door was opened.

"Well, darling, had a nice walk? Say good night, and go and get some beauty sleep."

Elizabeth walked to one of the french windows. "Lord," she said, "it's stuffy in here. Why have you got them shut?"

"Mosquitoes," Lady Fulmer said. "When the light is on they pour in. Oh, darling, must you—*always*——?"

Elizabeth had opened the window and stepped on to the little balcony. She stood with her back to the room looking at Bruges lit by a three-quarters-full moon, at all its pale and ghostly but beautiful sombreness. A few lights still showed here and there, a few danced in the inky blackness of the water below.

"Where did you go?" Lady Fulmer asked.

"To a pub. Then we sat outside near a square called the Bourg, I think. Adrian has written a libretto."

"A what?"

"A libretto. A play for an opera."

"Darling, you needn't explain."

"Isn't it wonderful?" Elizabeth turned into the room again, and the light shone on her smiling face. She felt quiet and calm and at peace again, and her happiness was of a quiet, not an excitable kind. She glowed in this new-found contentment, and was ready to share it, even with her mother.

CHAPTER IV

THE sun pouring into the room had awakened Clare Ainslie
early, and she had lain for a while listening to the sounds
she had expected she would hear, of a city stirring to life
in the rumbling of wheels and the tread of feet hurrying over
the cobble-stones, the barking of dogs and the ringing of
bells. Jane and Tilly burst in before she rose, and went to
the window and hung out of it. "Oh, come and look," they
cried. "The milkman has a big dog pulling his cart." She
got up and looked, feeling the warmth of the day on her
face and bare arms. Because it was going to be hot they
must go to the sea.

After breakfast, when she went to look at the car Rene
de Jonkheere was standing beside it. His mother had dealt
with him for his absence yesterday, and he was, for the
moment, feeling small and mean and of no consequence.
He was to take the cash to the bank and to return immediately. But as one of his chief interests in life was automobiles
he stopped to study Clare's. And as his other interest was
beautiful women he took his cigarette out of his mouth
and bade her a respectful good morning. When he wasn't
dreaming of one he was thinking of the other, and longed
to be rich to own both—a blonde and a Buick for choice.
Clare had seen him the previous night; when going up the
stairs to bed he had followed on her heels, and as she was
shutting her bedroom door he had glanced back at her over
his shoulder, as he opened another door on the landing that
led to his family's quarters.

"Good morning."

"These were good models, in that year, madame."

"They still are, I think. In spite of their age."

"In spite of their age," he agreed. "Have you seen,
madame, the latest Buick, the new Cadillac?" She was
like her car, he thought, of aristocratic English lines, beautiful, but no longer young. Younger models had the looks,
the flashiness, the speed. Nevertheless . . . nevertheless. . . .

The older models wore better, as you could see. He bowed to her, wrenched his shoulders back, extended his chest, and smiled at his thoughts. He no longer felt small and mean and of no consequence, and he walked away, humming softly to himself.

Half an hour later Clare and the children got into the car with their bathing-suits and towels, and she drove slowly out of the square towards a hump-backed bridge. As she was negotiating the awkward turn three pedestrians had to go in single file and keep close to the wall to allow the car to pass. They were fellow-guests from the hotel, and by the appearance of the bundles the young man was carrying they, also, were bound for the sea. She recognized the young lovers and the girl's mother, whose nationality, she thought, even back view was unmistakable, by the way the feet were put down in a determined way on the hot cobble-stones. The girl, bare-legged in white sandals and a simple cotton frock, with pretty silken hair worn loosely, was like any girl of any nationality going to the sea to bathe. But although the young man wore rope-soled sandals and one of those gaudy open-neck shirts, that had probably been bought at the Bon Marché, he couldn't be anything but what he was—English and probably an undergraduate. When she had driven over the bridge Clare stopped the car and waited. She leaned across the twins, who were beside her and opened the door on their side.

"If you are going to the sea," she said, "may I give you all a lift? That is, if you are going to Zoute, by any chance?"

There were coats in the back, and an empty biscuit tin and a thermos flask and a pair of her own shoes she had forgotten to pack, which had to be cleared away first. It was very kind of her, the girl's mother said. They all, in turn, said it was very kind. Now and again, when Bruges was behind them, murmurs of conversation in the back floated forward, but Clare did not pay much attention for she wanted to watch the road. Once, on a straight stretch, for the fun of it again, she let the car out; then remembering the comfort of her passengers behind she slowed down; and presently in what seemed a totally new and large

straggling town of villas she found herself driving up the
Avenue Lippens in Knocke. There was the old Grand Hotel
on the left at the top, the *digue* in front, and a bright sea
facing her in a blinding light. She turned to the right, and
the sea was in the hot air, salty and fresh. In Zoute, by the
little Place, she stopped.

"I see you have brought lunch with you," she said.
"And we are going back to Bruges for ours, so I can't offer
to drive you back." She smiled at them, and they thanked
her; and she drove on.

For a few moments Elizabeth and Adrian stared after
the car. "Lucky thing," Elizabeth sighed. "I wish we had
brought ours over, Mother." Then they crossed the road,
and Elizabeth led the way and jumped down on to the hot
sands. They hired two cabins and three camp-stools, and
staked their claim to a few feet of that crowded shore.

Lady Fulmer emerged from the cabin first, wearing a
plain, serviceable black swimming suit, and Elizabeth
followed in an abbreviated two-piece that fitted her figure
so finely it might have been painted on her young, ripe body.
At the water's edge Lady Fulmer adjusted her hair under a
workmanlike, plain red-rubber cap and fastened the snap
of the chin strap. Elizabeth put one foot into the sea and
laughed. But the laugh was uneasy and self-conscious,
because she couldn't swim. And everyone could swim—her
mother magnificently—who hadn't once had a weak heart.
She felt Adrian's hand suddenly clasped in hers, and felt
him leading her deeper and deeper, up to her knees and
over them, into that deliciously cool sea. At their side
Lady Fulmer was splashing forward with her arms thrust
out. "Don't take her too far, Adrian. We'll give her a
swimming lesson presently," were her last words before
she plunged, and set out with even, masterful over-arm
strokes, in the direction of Kent.

"Go on," Elizabeth urged. "Go on, Adrian. Race her."
He laughed. "I couldn't catch up with her."

He put an arm under her waist and another behind her
knees. "Let yourself go back. I've got you. Gently. That's
it. Now you are going to float."

She forgot what her mother had said, and obeyed him. The sea rocked and swayed behind her head and she could see the whole panorama of brilliant blue sky and yellow sands and grey buildings, hotels and shops and cafés, and cars moving along, and crowds and gay umbrellas. He was behind her, holding her, and she was being towed farther and farther away from the children paddling and the lazy, inexpert swimmers and boys and girls playing with rubber canoes. The sky had tiny white flecks of cloud, high, high up. The sun was in her eyes, on her face, warm glowing. That was the way she liked it, and she wanted it to go on for ever. Then he turned and towed her back to the shore, and she struggled to find her feet, and to find something solid to put them on, amidst laughter and splashings. She covered him with her splashes, all over his bare chest and face, and when she put her arms on his shoulders the bare flesh of their bodies touched, and if there had been no one near them she would have kissed the hollow at the bottom of his throat. But what she had felt he had felt too, for he brushed her shoulder with his lips, bit into it with his teeth— and in a flash had gone into the water again. Then her mother came back, and a swimming lesson began. "One-two-three. One-two-three. Don't open your fingers. Watch how I do it."

Elizabeth and Adrian lay on the sand afterwards between the two cabins, and Lady Fulmer sat on a camp stool under a sunshade, with a towel knotted round her waist like a sarong. If they were not going to use the camp-stools, she thought, it was a waste of francs to have hired them.

Lying relaxed at Elizabeth's side, Adrian's mind became slowly emptied of all thoughts that were not related to the surrounding scene. The sun beat down on his naked chest, and the smell and taste of the salt sea were in his nostrils and mouth. He was observing the colourfulness as though it were a painting; the sun-tanned women and girls and men and boys and children, their bright clothing, the gay umbrellas. He felt happy. And he didn't, for the time being, want to think of the libretto or of the heroic past of Flanders, which had been absorbing him until

yesterday. He couldn't, lying there, summon any of it to
his mind, even if he had the will. He could not recapture
the thrill of his first discoveries in Pierre's library, nor any
of the exaltation of spirit those discoveries had given him,
which, at the time, had seemed not only to equal but to
surpass the sensation of love. The love he had come to bear
for Elizabeth was sweet and different. It had touched him
gently with a wand, not pierced him with an arrow. It was
perhaps the discovery of her inner loneliness that had first
drawn him towards her, and then finding that her desire
for companionship and love matched his own mood at that
time. There was the thought that his own hunger had caused
her awakening, so it was in order that she should come to
mean to him the promise of physical fulfilment hallowed
by the sacrament of marriage, a sharer of his nights and
days. As it was written, or was ordained—it read—for a
remedy against sin. It was all very simple, looked at like
that. And as she lay beside him on the sand, he didn't
want to think of it any other way. He didn't want to remember that they had seemed to be on the edge of an argument
—over religion of all things!—in the Place du Bourg last
night. He lazily scooped up a handful of sand and let it
fall through his fingers.

Lady Fulmer looked down at them and lowered her
sunshade. "Shall we all have one more swim before lunch?"

Elizabeth did not stir. "I'm thirsty," she said. "Can't
we go and have something to drink at one of those cafés?"

"Having those odd drinks and things at cafés," Lady
Fulmer reminded her, "is where all the francs go."

"You said we could borrow from Julie if we get stuck."

Adrian got to his feet. "May I take you and Elizabeth
for a drink at a café across the road?"

"You two go," Lady Fulmer said. She had untied the
towel round her waist and was standing up putting the
rubber cap on again. "I hope," she began, "I do hope,
Adrian, that we are not running you into too much expense.
I said so last night. And you have been here a long time."

He laughed. "I think the bank can stand it."

"I think I know what you mean. Though I don't think

we should be discussing this quite so loudly in such a public place. Well, if your father and your—er—banker don't mind."

"They are going to meet," Adrian said. "In October. My banker is coming to London, a visit he has promised himself for some time." He looked out to sea; and the sea narrowed. The crowds were no longer there. 'Noon strikes on England, noon on Oxford town,' he thought. 'Noon of my dreams, O noon. . . .' He would like to have Pierre with him one day in Oxford. He would. . . . But what was the matter, why couldn't he see them there together? Perhaps Elizabeth was in the way, physically in the way. And if this went on, he'd give in.

When they were dressed Elizabeth and Adrian sauntered hand in hand across the road, dodging cars that drove past them, and found two seats on a café terrace. "Really," she said, "the way mother goes on!" She drank thirstily of the pale, cold beer in the tall glass, and then laughed. "I told her—I didn't think you'd mind—about the libretto. Though, of course, it isn't quite a certainty, is it? Until your friend has seen the composer?"

"No," he said, "it isn't a certainty. And as I told you there is one scene I haven't been able to do." He looked away from her, at the crowds on the sands, and at the sea. It was all as gaily coloured as a picture postcard, and it was all he wanted—with Elizabeth—at that moment. He didn't want to think about anything else. He wanted to enjoy the present—and not think. But her next words brought him back with a jolt.

"If the composer is agreeable, and you finish the scene you haven't yet done, and it gets produced and makes you famous—you will be able to chuck Oxford, won't you?"

"It won't make me famous," he answered slowly. "Who remembers the names of the men who wrote the words of any opera, outside real opera lovers? It will be the music that will count."

"Then why," she demanded, "have you done it?"

"Because I wanted to. Had to. And then Pierre said it

was made for music. That was an added inspiration for me, half-way through."

"But you'll get something out of it, surely?"

"I suppose so. But to tell the truth, I haven't thought about that very much."

"But you said you'd written it for us, for me."

"I have dedicated it to you. And because I love you, you must have been behind all my inspiration." He smiled at her. Their eyes were hidden from each other behind dark sun-glasses, but he watched her mouth, always expressive of her moods, pouting a little, like a child's, but seductive enough for him to want to kiss her.

"Adrian," she said seriously, "I believe you are very unpractical in some ways. And you haven't answered my question." She paused. "If it is a success, and you do make money out of it, would you then give up Oxford?"

"No."

She bit her lip, and her mouth set. She, now, turned her face from him and looked at the sea. He said gently, "Elizabeth?"

"What?"

"You accused me just now of being unpractical. It is because I am the opposite of that as far as you and I are concerned that I wouldn't be such a fool as to let this—if it were a success—go to my head. I want to give you the best that is in me—and I'm not qualified to do that yet. In the old-fashioned way of putting it—I want to give you what you've been used to having, and a bit more."

In the past he had thought she had understood. Hadn't she? It was like being back in that house again among the Tottenham Court Road antiques, in the drawing-room where there was a photograph of Lady Fulmer in Court feathers on the grand piano, and one of Elizabeth as a little girl by Marcus Adams; and Lady Fulmer was being understanding and asking him to call her Olive. God! He was being a heel, for she'd been very kind. But he was in the room called the library of the Air Chief, looking at old service groups and a framed snapshot of a Sopwith Pup in World War I, with 'Fearsome' Fulmer as a second-lieutenant posed beside it in field-boots and breeches. And the old man was being pontifical, fiddling with his top tunic-buttons, and staring at him with those piercing, almost hypnotic, cold blue eyes, which, with the short black moustache, gave him at first glance, the most uncanny resemblance to Hitler. Hell! he thought. Forget it!

He stretched his arms out across the table and touched her hands, felt the flutter of response in her fingers— and held her hands tightly. "I thought," he said, "you understood, and were with me. Are you, still? Or not?"

"Yes, Adrian," she said, "I do understand. And I am with you—really."

"It means waiting, darling."

"I know."

"It's not all that easy for me."

"I suppose not." She smiled, and there was the sunshine in her smile, and the carefreeness and happiness of the holiday crowd down on the sands, the blueness of the sea and the brightness over everything. The lovely day was theirs and they were young in it, and in love; and if the waiter, coming to take their order for more drinks, knew they were lovers they were happier still because of his knowledge of it.

Inside the café a radio was playing dance music, and under the table Elizabeth's feet began to move in time to it. She would love another drink before her mother joined them. "After lunch," she said, "mother will tell us not to bathe on a full stomach, so let us go and look at the shops. I saw a nice one on the corner when we got out of the car, with dresses and scarves in the window. It was a bit of luck getting that lift. I wonder who she is."

"I wonder."

"Those twins don't look at all like her, do they? She is attractive, don't you think? Or haven't you taken her in yet?"

"Yes," he said slowly, "she is—beautiful. Seeing her close to, this morning. There is tranquillity in her face and, well, a kind of stillness that makes you think instantly of——"

D

"Of what, Adrian?"

"Spiritual grace."

Elizabeth burst out laughing. "What funny ideas you do get. There wasn't much tranquillity or stillness about her when she let the car roar up to seventy in one place. I thought mother was going to pass out. She distrusts every woman driver, except herself."

Adrian laughed with her. "I expect it was just the feel of the glorious morning—that holiday feeling. Darling, what would you like to do tonight?"

"You mean, just you and I, together?"

"If your mother won't mind?"

"She won't. Why, I'd like to go dancing somewhere. Could we?"

"Yes," he said. "We can come back here. I'll hire a car and we can have dinner where there is a band, and then we might go to the Casino and try our luck."

"Do we dress up?"

"We can, if you like, though not many do."

"I'd like to. I have two new evening dresses you haven't seen. A white and a very special red. Which shall I wear tonight?"

"The white," he said. "I love you in white."

"And keep the red for another time?"

.   .   .   .   .   .

At the far end of the shore—as far as she could take the children to bathe on that well-regulated pleasure beach—Clare lay after her swim watching them making friends with a Belgian family. Before that they had drifted, fascinated, towards a bright, peroxide-haired woman with an enormous shaggy dog. The more outrageous the *poule*, Jock had always said, the bigger the dog. The woman had an artificial coating of orange tan on her legs, arms, and face, and the dog wore an expensive wide leather collar studded with brass. She lay under a red umbrella, and on one finger of the hand that clasped it there was a ring with a big red stone. On her feet were wedge-soled sandals, five inches thick. Everything about her was bright and outsize. Fascinated, the twins had stroked the dog and stared at her; and she had smiled at them and at Clare. Then Jane began to watch some children playing with a big blue ball, and within no time Tilly left off stroking the dog and they both had joined in the ball game.

Their voices rang out as merrily as birds' song. Clare was often afraid that they had the inherited sense of gravity borne by all children whom war had deprived of a father, and who had, in consequence, become too early in their young lives acquainted with the economic problems of their mother's existence. But it was leavened by a natural zest for enjoyment, by their innate love of the plain ridiculous, best expressed when their spirits were at the highest by an ability to stand on their heads and turn somersaults. Her own contemporaries—her sister and the few friends left whose way of life she could compete with in the straitened circumstances of her widowhood—at times criticized the twins' upbringing, saying they were too old for their years. They appeared to be shocked that both children could read two years ago, when they were six, and write a moderately steady and even hand. They called it being forced, although Clare thought other children's fashionable backwardness in those essentials meant that their natural development was being retarded and they were the victims of modern experiment, from which, in many cases, it would take them a long time to catch up.

Neither Knocke or Zoute proved that morning to be as she remembered. Before she took the road back to Bruges she drove to the end of the promenade and turned inland among houses that might have come straight out of Beverly Hills and been the homes of film stars and millionaires. The gardens were filled with exotic plants, and roses bloomed below stone terraces, and green lawns grew where there must only have been sand dunes at the end of the war. For nearly all those palaces looked as if they had been recently built; there was a newness and a brightness and a solidity that spoke of enterprise and prosperity unknown in post-war England. She looked for landmarks she remem-

bered—in vain. The pine woods where she had picnicked
as a child had disappeared, and a township of villas stood
on the site of it; and where the old golf course, her father
had played over, and the tennis courts had been, were
avenues and more villas, with new courts and a new
championship course made in a new place. It was absurd
to regret change, to imagine anything stood still.

The next day she took the children to Wenduine. They
climbed up the hot dunes, where sand clogged their feet at
every step, so that for one step forward they seemed to
be making two steps back, until they pulled themselves
up with handfuls of *oyats*, before they ran down on to a
golden, and less crowded shore. In the sea at Wenduine on
the second day Jane and Tilly gained confidence, and
each swam three strokes alone. The passage of time was still
being marked in her mind by steps in the progress of her
children's development. But for the first time since they
were born she was beginning slowly to be aware of pleasures
in which they had no part. And the thought came to her,
at the end of that week, that she was leading two lives,
for what she was discovering in her afternoon walks round
Bruges, when the children were resting after their morning
bathe at Wenduine, belonged to herself and could be shared
with no one living.

More and more in those walks and explorations she
began to feel that she was being drawn away from herself
and her ordinary life and responsibilities. And what was
stranger, and could not be explained—neither could it be
called 'that holiday feeling'—was the thought that the
life she had lived at home for many years was one alien
to her nature. She was finding a kind of enchantment
everywhere, that lulled her mind and brought a sense of
quietness and ease to her heart. At the Beguinage one afternoon she wondered what thoughts ran in the heads of those
old ladies, as their fingers plucked at lace bobbins. In that
ancient seclusion and security, had they done with the world,
and forgotten it? Were they as remote from it as the nuns
with downcast eyes?

The first time she passed the Chapel of the Holy Blood

she could not enter because she was bare-legged and without covering for her head. But the next afternoon, clothed as the rule of the church demanded, she climbed the dark stairs from the crypt and gazed in awe upon the reliquary, whose precious stones seemed to be afire. Afterwards, when she was staring at the strange pulpit, a carved terrestial globe of polished wood, she turned to face the young English lovers from the hotel. She smiled at them, as she held the ends of the thin blue scarf she had put over her head, and when she went down the stairs she heard the girl ask the young man a question, and because he did not seemingly answer immediately, repeat it sharply and demand if he were suddenly deaf. That incident disturbed her own tranquillity, offended by its irreverence in so holy a place, for the girl had also asked why he was staring. At herself, Clare knew was meant. But she put the incident from her mind when she collected the children from the hotel and took them for a ride in a motor-boat; and later, in the great kitchen of the Gruithouse she wondered why, when one pictured oneself living in another age, it was as the lady with a tambour of needlework in her hand, not as greasy Joan stirring the pot below stairs. And laughed at herself, because, after twenty-three years, her head was still full of dreamy nonsense. Now it was her children who rebuked her for not paying attention to what was said, who clamoured to be included in her thoughts; and who asked her on the Saturday afternoon, after they had been to Damme, and were having a picnic tea on the bank of a canal near a destroyed bridge, what she was reading, and to read aloud to them, where her finger was on the page.

So she read aloud: ". . . my lady Margaret was married on Sunday last past at a town called The Damme, three miles out of Bruges at five o'clock in the morning; and she was brought on the same day to Bruges to her dinner. . . ." But as she read, for their clearer understanding, she translated the almost Chaucerian English of John Paston into a twentieth-century idiom. " 'And as for the Duke's court, as of lords and ladies and gentlewomen, esquires and gentle-

men, I heard never of none'—I never saw anything like it—
'save King Arthur's court.' "

"Like King Arthur's court! Go on!" they begged.

The sun by the sea had sprinkled their faces afresh with
freckles, lightened their already flaxen hair to a whitish-
silver on top. But that must be enough for one day. So pack
up the picnic things, scatter the cake crumbs for Flemish
birds, and stretch out the arms and look straight up the still
canal water and see the spire of Notre Dame in Bruges
piercing the sky, and give thanks to God for this day and
all the days that have been this week since Tuesday. Give
thanks to God tomorrow.

In Notre Dame, where she took them for half an hour
the next morning she thought, with a gentle smile, how
horrified their grandmother would have been, with all her
prejudices against what she called spikiness and the exhibi-
tionism of High Church practices, to see them, after having
watched two Belgian schoolgirls dipping their fingers in
holy water and touching each other's hands with the sacred
drops, imitating those gestures with pink, serious faces. As
they knelt, and then sat down on chairs at the back of the
cathedral she wondered what impression the strange ritual
of that service was making on them. The details were not
easily followed, but she was sensitively and acutely aware
of the feeling of the continuity of Christianity through the
centuries, as she listened to the music and the singing that
soared up to the great roof as though borne on invisible
wings. She took the children away before they began to get
restive, and outside in the sunshine they met Miss King.

They knew all about Miss King now, all she had told
them. And there could be little else, with that bland innocence in her eyes, that ring of unaffected honesty in her
placid voice. Miss King had been a V.A.D. in World War I
with the Belgian Red Cross at La Panne. In the second war
she had worked in the censorship in Liverpool. She kept an
embroidery shop in a south-coast town, which Queen Mary
had once honoured with a visit, and at one time she had been
connected with the Royal School of Needlework. She liked
pottering about the lace shops, and said it was sad to find

here, as everywhere else, that fine craftsmanship might come to be a dying art because the younger generation in a machine age had not the patience.

Miss King was returning that Sunday morning from the Brangwyn Museum in the old Hôtel Arents, which she had found was only open on weekdays. Had Mrs. Ainslie, she wanted to know, been to any of the galleries yet? Clare had to confess she hadn't. She had been keeping the Flemish paintings as a delight in store, not wishing to crowd her days with too many pleasures all at once, and she wanted to see them only after she had absorbed more of the atmosphere of Flanders, read a little more of its history every night before she fell asleep.

The twins had taken off their hats. Could they, please, have ices? They all went to the café on the Grand' Place, and the ginger-haired waiter, who was beginning to know them, served them with ices for the children and beer in tall glasses for Clare and Miss King. Sunday church-goers strolled past. Elderly women in black carrying prayer-books and beads, wearing pious but satisfied expressions, going home to good soup and good beef—whatever was special on that day of the week. Children in Sunday clothes holding the hands of parents, prattling as they passed by. Cars swept past, many bearing foreign number plates. And into that holiday scene of crowded cafés, amid the clamour of the bells, the young lovers from the hotel appeared, accompanied by the girl's mother, and sat down two tables away. The twins smiled at the young man, and he smiled at them. Presently a voice Clare had come to know was heard saying, as a guide-book and a travel brochure were produced out of a capacious handbag and laid on the table, "It is for Elizabeth, for her education. But, if you think, Adrian——" And then the girl's voice rose petulantly, "It's no good telling Adrian again. It's too late to get on that excursion. You said it was yesterday."

"What isn't any use telling Adrian again?" Tilly asked. And Jane answered, "That you can go to Brussels and Waterloo in a bus. She's cross he can't."

"You shouldn't listen to what other people are talking

about," Clare said. "It has nothing to do with us. And I don't think you should call him Adrian, either."

"We don't know his other name," Tilly said. "And he said we might."

"When was this?"

Both children giggled and nudged each other. Then Jane nonchalantly lifted the metal ice-cream bowl to her mouth and began to lick the sides.

"Jane!"

Jane put it down and smiled serenely. "One night. After you'd gone down to dinner. You said we could leave the door open. So we—— So we just——"

"Just—what?"

"Said hello and he came and talked to us and sat on Tilly's bed and had a biscuit Miss King had left. Then his lovey-dovey-cat's-eyes came up to find him."

"Yes," Tilly went on. "Last night, too. You always keep him out of the bathroom, so while he was waiting he came again. He asked us about us, and you."

"And you told him, I suppose?" Clare's eyes were mock-serious. The twins had told Miss King the first night about their father and about Claude Spencer-Perry as well, so that yesterday morning, when they had all come to the Grand' Place to see the Saturday market, and met the lovers again strolling among the crowds by the stalls, Miss King had said, "How nice it would be if your fiancé could join you here." One could follow the train of her thoughts, for she was a romantic, and those young lovers had become almost her chief topic of conversation, and much enjoyed by the twins, who could not hear enough.

"No," Jane said, firmly. "No."

"We teased him," Tilly said. "We said we were Hot and Tot from Africa."

Miss King laughed. "You didn't tell me that."

"No," Tilly answered. "Of course not. You knew. Mummy told you who we were."

That night Clare wrote to Claude in America. She tried to tell him what she had been doing and to describe what she had seen. But as her pen moved across the page she found that all feeling was receding from her and what she wrote down. It was not as though she were writing to a stranger, but what she wanted to put could not be expressed, so that the descriptions she gave of their arrival and their outings to the coast, and of her personal explorations were strictly pedestrian. She described the hotel—that would interest him, for he collected addresses of promising hotels in a little note-book—and the food, because that would interest him, also.

She was writing in her room, because the little *salon* downstairs was crowded. She had left her door open to let some air circulate—it was an unusually hot September night—and the door of the young man's room opposite was open also, as were his balcony windows. And suddenly through his room, into hers, from somewhere outside, at the back across the water, there came the strains of Mozart's 'Requeim'. It came louder, with all its terrifying power, sounds which from the depths of grief and shuddering repentance explored the farthest horizons of human longing for immortality, ending in the last clear, serene chord of faith. With the ending of that last chord she rose to shut her door, to shut out the possibility of that requeim being repeated, and in doing so saw the occupant of the room opposite standing on his own threshold.

"Someone," he said, "is often playing that record across the water. It's an Italian recording."

"I haven't heard it before. I mean—not here." 'Nor am I,' she wondered if she should add, 'sufficiently musically educated to know what special recording that was of it.' But he was on his way downstairs, on his way out, she knew. And tonight there was a moon. Ah, youth! 'Be happy,' she wanted to say, to him. 'Those chords, those sounds, those voices were not speaking to you.'

She went back to the table and picked up her pen again.

She wrote: "I want to be a good wife to you and help you always and bring you happiness." But as she wrote those words she knew with a conviction she had not admitted before, that she would fail in that purpose and desire unless Claude would be content with less than she considered to

D*

be his due. That was the truth, and there was no way out of her dilemma. How she had arrived at that truth within herself she did not know, since she had looked out of that same window on the evening of her arrival, and answered a question she asked of herself bravely and confidently. She must try, then, to recapture that lost confidence in herself and her future as his wife. What she had found in those afternoon walks that could be shared with no one living, the feeling that she was being drawn away from herself and her ordinary life and responsibilities were all but transitory sensations. They could have no possible lasting influence on her future.

With this thought in her mind she arranged to spend the whole of the following day at Wenduine with the children; where she swam until she was tired, and ran up and down the sands with them in endless games, and swam again, knowing that she would sleep that night without dreams. But when Tuesday dawned in misty dullness, and they had been there exactly a week, for which payment must be made, she did not take them to the sea, but instead for a walk in the town, as far as a bank in the Grand' Place, to cash some travellers' cheques.

CHAPTER V

THE bells had just chimed the hour of half-past ten. Waiters were setting out chairs and tables in front of the cafés, which at that hour of the morning had few clients beyond three or four elderly men of no apparent occupation, who were sitting down reading their newspapers over cups of coffee. An artist sat on a camp-stool with his back to the Panier d'Or Hotel and Restaurant painting the Belfry, and women were hurrying along with baskets of groceries. Although the morning was dull and misty, there was a promise in the sky above the roof-tops that the sun would presently break through. The air was fresher than it had been on preceding days, with an unmistakable breath of the sea in it.

Suddenly aware of an unforetold, unexpected interest among passers-by and casual loiterers, the waiters paused before laying clean cloths on the tables, before setting the cane chairs in position, and the elderly gentlemen sipping coffee put down their newspapers. The artist looked up from his palette. Some boys who had made an appearance from a side street stopped and laughed, and the drivers of the cars that were coming round the corner past the bank braked gently and swerved to the left. Then laughter as gentle as the breeze that was freshening the morning and stirring the leaves of the trees blowing the sea mist away broke from everyone's lips. What good sense! What perfect accommodation! On the cobble-stones opposite the cafés there was a thin layer of sand, which had probably fallen from a passing cart. It lay there a bright and conspicuous island in the grey *pavé*; and a tabby cat was walking deliberately towards it.

Pierre de Fermandois, who was crossing the Grand' Place towards his waiting car, felt he was at home again in the air which that morning hung so much fresher over Bruges than it had over Brussels during the last few days. He was always happy to be back, and he was proud when intimate friends in the capital teased him for being a provincial. Life in Brussels—even as he remembered it before the war— was becoming hurried and losing, he felt, its former special distinction, becoming cosmopolitan. While here, in what he liked to call his home town, civilization had not lost touch with rusticity and simplicity. Here the best of both town and country blended in harmony, which not even the tourists could spoil. Summoned back a day or two earlier than he had intended returning, by Julie, who was giving an afternoon party—partly in honour Jean had said on the telephone, of her English friends, and partly because the weather, if it didn't break, called for one last outdoor festivity—he was thinking how happy he was to breathe again the good air that on cooler days always had a smell of the sea in it. And to be able to walk in familiar surroundings, and not be dependent—or in an attempted independence be confused by noise, even with the dog's guidance, he was also thinking when he became aware that something was attracting universal interest, and of a pause in the morning's activities, and of a diversion of traffic that was not in his aid.

In front of him a child's voice in English called the attention of a companion to what it had seen. "Do look," the child cried. "Do look! How sweet! And all the cars are being so careful not to disturb it!" And he heard the soft murmur of feminine laughter falling gently into his ears, mingling with the full-throated, robust merriment of more than one child. So there were three of them, he judged, and intent on observing whatever it was that was causing such amusement they were unaware of his approach. He felt the decisive tug of the dog guiding him to one side. But he stopped, when he was immediately behind them, and said, "Will you please tell me, madame, what the incident is?"

Puzzled and surprised at hearing the voice of a stranger ask that question Clare turned quickly round; and instantly she understood. "It is a little tabby cat," she said, "who naturally thought some sand opposite the cafés on the cobble-stones had been placed there for its special benefit."

The laughter had died from her voice, which had dropped so gently and musically into his ears, but it returned before the humour that lit up his whole face and creased the corners of his hidden eyes, and came to mingle with his laughter.

Still laughing, he thanked her, as Jane's hand, which had begun to stroke his dog's head, touched his hand, and on his other side Tilly laced her small fingers in his.

"It has finished," Tilly announced. "And it is going back now to the café where it lives."

"You are a visitor, here in Bruges, madame?" he asked Clare. "For the first time?"

"Oh, no. It is not my first visit, although it is my children's. I came here when I was very young, and I always wanted to come back."

When he had been a boy the English had thronged Bruges. Church of England clergy and their wives, and colonels, and spinsters who painted in water colours. They stayed at the Flandre or the Commerce—some of them all the year round—and made up a little colony, and played whist in the evenings among the potted palms and the plush furniture. Most of them had come to the autumn of their days. Those were the years that followed the discovery of the Brugeois of the antiquity in their midst, which they had begun to exploit and advertise, when little boys with heads in the clouds devoured tales of troubadours and crusaders, Flemish counts and Burgundian dukes, and knights of the Golden Fleece. The years when he was young, when the officers of the Third Lancers were to be seen riding to the races in blue, gold-laced dolmans and shakos, and the Benedictine Fathers never missed the sight of the Saintonge hounds. The years when landowners met their farmers at the Cornet d'Or for their feudal transactions, and would look up from their business for a brief second when strangely-dressed English tourists invaded their sanctuary, to continue again, having brushed aside that interruption as they would have a fly. After the first war very few of those elderly English people came back, and a different class began to come over; tourists by the thousand on cheap excursions, young men and women seeing Bruges and Ghent and Brussels and the battlefields before rushing on farther into Europe. When the last war ended the English began to come over again, and they came as prisoners released from behind bars, mostly to eat and to drink and the women to buy stockings; and they to the very old, conservative Brugeois were a new race entirely. Not many of them—one heard from complaining shopkeepers and from gossip that drifted out into the country—lived up to the ideal that every Belgian patriot, were he a Fleming or a Walloon, noble, shopkeeper or peasant, had cherished in his heart during the war years about his coming liberators, and had found personified in every British and Canadian soldier who had fought his way from the coast. An Anglophile in every fibre of his being Pierre knew that this was all part of the inevitable post-war *malaise* and distrust which the English writer, Kipling, had described—of the generation that had come to maturity in France after 1870—when he had called it that "defeatism and costive ill-will that crawls like a snapping cur on the heels of war."

The children's hands were still holding his, and Clare touched their arms to withdraw them. The four of them and the dog were making now another island, round which the traffic had to pass, and she knew that a chauffeur standing by a black limousine—which she remembered having seen before—was waiting for the blind man; waiting, and watching his master with a smile of amusement at the interruption in his passage towards the car. And dodging the traffic, coming towards them from across the street, hurrying, smiling also, as all the world, all Bruges, seemed to be smiling that morning, was the young man from the hotel, who lived on her floor, who had come from Ostend on the day of her arrival in that same black limousine with his fiancée and her mother. She would have drawn the children away and said good-bye, had not further words detained her.

"So you liked Bruges so much, as a child, you wanted to come back?"

It was not exactly a question, although it ended on a

note of interrogation, as though the speaker wished for a confirmation of her statement because it had given him pleasure.

"I hope it has proved to be as you remembered it. That it hasn't shrunk in beauty or size, as places do that one has often remembered and treasured a picture of."

"It is all as I remembered it," she said. "It hasn't shrunk. I spent one afternoon here, when I was thirteen. That was all. But I wanted to bring my children here and——" But she did not finish.

"Here's Adrian," Tilly announced.

"So you know Adrian," Pierre asked, before Adrian cried, "Pierre! When did you get back?"

"Of course we know Adrian," Jane said.

"Then, Adrian," Pierre said, smiling, "will you please introduce me to your friends?"

Adrian looked at Clare and hesitated, then down at the twins, and laughed. "They say they are Hot and Tot from Africa, but I know their names are Jane and Tilly." That was all he knew. Her name, her surname, was part of the gentle mystery he felt surrounded her. And he hadn't cared to penetrate it, even to probe and ask. Yet he had asked. He had asked her children more than he should have, and they had known—with the instinct of children—that he was attempting to trespass into her privacy. He looked at Clare again.

"It is Ainslie," she said.

"Mrs. Ainslie, this is the Count de Fermandois. And Pierre, these are the Hot and Tot twins from Darkest Africa. Jane and Tilly. Or the other way round. I never know which is which, and they never tell."

They all shook hands, and they were all laughing at the moment the sun burst through the clouds and shone down on them; on Adrian's fair hair and eyes that were lit with pleasure and laughter, and on the children's even fairer hair and sunburned freckled faces wreathed in smiles, and on the dark glasses that hid the eyes of one who could not see any of them. Nor, Clare thought, the smooth, dark brick façade of the Belfry made a richer colour, and the whole

scene suddenly vivid, bathed in a golden light that emphasized the velvet shadows on the grey *pavé*. Only the artist
sitting by the Panier d'Or, who had been painting the
Grand' Place and the Belfry in the silvery-grey muted
colours of a cloudy September morning, put down his
palette in annoyance.

She had been at once aware of an intimacy between
the young Englishman and the Count de Fermandois, into
which she felt she was intruding; and she was prepared to
leave them to go their ways together. But, after she had
said good-bye, the count put a hand on his young friend's
arm and said to him, "I shall see you and Elizabeth at Julie's
this afternoon. No, don't come with me. James is waiting
with the car over there." So they stood still, and watched
him walking with his dog towards the car.

Clare never quite knew how it came about that she and
the young man and the children began walking along
together, and in the direction they took. But after a while
there was not enough room on a narrow footpath for them
to walk abreast, so the twins walked in front; and when they
had an ancient, high brick wall on their right, and the
cathedral of Notre Dame rose skywards on their left across
a narrow street down which the cream trams rattled and
screeched, and the twins asked where they were all going
she was able to tell them they were going to the Hôpital de
Saint Jean to see the Memlincs. Under the gatehouse two
hospital nuns came out in spotless starched white from head
to foot, with downcast eyes and folded hands. And white,
Clare noticed, were their faces, as white as the face of Marie
Stuart in the celebrated portrait of her in a white linen
coif when she was the Dauphin's widow.

"Is the Count de Fermandois's blindness due to a
war injury?" she had asked, when they had seen him drive
away. "Is he—totally blind?"

"Yes," Adrian had said. "Yes, he is now."

A car was being reversed, and he had put an arm out
and drawn Tilly out of the way.

"Yes," he had said, when they had crossed over to the
other side of the Grand' Place. "It was a war injury, though

not in battle. When Belgium was invaded the Germans took his house, and he and his wife and son went to live in a villa near Ghent. Two years later his son escaped through France and Spain and got to England. But right from the beginning, you can imagine the kind of work the count got mixed up in. In fact he was one of the leaders of the *armée blanche*. But he wasn't caught in the end for that particular work, that's the bitter irony, only for something he did that wasn't in his own routine at all. You know they all had their special tasks. And I never have got out of him what his was. Perhaps in this uneasy peace none of them tell."

"I can understand that," Clare said quietly. And to the children, "Go on in front. There isn't room here. Not to let anyone pass." She looked at Adrian. "Please go on."

The street was crowded, and they were walking slowly under the awnings that shopkeepers had unrolled over the windows. What street they were in, where they were going she did not know.

"He went into Ghent one day," she heard her escort say, "to get his hair cut, and an acquaintance he met in the street asked him if he could hide an American airman who'd baled out near his home in the country, and this man knew the Germans were combing the neighbourhood. Of course he took the airman and passed him on to those who were looking after allied airmen and escaped prisoners. But he was caught—through carelessness, he insists. There was some trace of that airman, the butt of an American cigarette. Something like that, in the villa. He was imprisoned and tried and—— Well, you know, you've read of the methods used, and it wasn't only that, it was slow starvation as well. But that isn't all that happened to him. His wife was taken and sent as a slave worker to a factory in Germany. She was delicate, and she died under it a month before the Americans broke into that town."

Clare had been walking without knowing where she was walking, and she looked up at the bright sky above the roof tops so that the young man at her side should not see the tears that had sprung to her eyes. In that story a hundred memories had been loosened. It was as though she had been pulled apart, and she was now defenceless. The screen she had placed round herself had been hurled down. But she could not conceal her tears. She was aware that the children were looking at her, wonderingly, sadly, with too-serious eyes. They, too, had heard, and they were sad and puzzled, because it was all beyond their understanding—man's inhumanity to man, some knowledge of which she had tried, perhaps foolishly in the world they had to live in, to protect them from. She saw that the young man's eyes were upon hers, and turned from his look to wipe away her tears. He was not so very young, she decided, after all. His experience in some ways had perhaps outrun hers. And why did she feel he was no longer a stranger, whose surname she had not even learned?

She said, when she could trust herself to speak again, "Please tell me your name." And when he had done so she called him Mr. Morbeigh in her next remark, which was an ordinary and trivial one. They all stood still at a street crossing to let a tram pass, and she looked at him then, critically, although she knew his face well enough, having seen it in the hotel every day, and had collided with him more than once on the landing and met him on the stairs. But she knew it better when they had crossed the street. She knew the colour of his eyes and the way his hair grew back from a scholarly brow, and the changing expression the lips could form in the whole face. The lower lip was full and a little sensual. But it was his eyes that held her interest because they were older than the rest of his face, which was lean and young and not yet lined. It was a thoughtful face, and although his body, as he walked beside her, looked young and lean and fit, because maturity or a sedentary life had not yet softened or coarsened it, she had the impression that he was not very strong physically.

They talked together, Mrs. Ainslie and Mr. Morbeigh, as any chance acquaintances in a foreign city might talk, whose paths appeared to be going in the same direction, of what she had seen so far in Bruges. And because she had not seen any of the pictures, and they were not far, he said,

from the Hôpital de Saint Jean, he would like to show them
to her. Had he put it like that, or merely said he would
like to see them all again?

As soon as they entered the small room where the
Memlincs were exhibited they saw Miss King, and immediately the twins' greeting of her, when they saw her sitting
down facing the triptych of the Mystical Marriage of Saint
Catharine, drew Clare's attention away from the painting.
But there was room for all of them to sit down, and it was
a little like being in church, so silent did they all become
before the central panel of the Virgin on her rich throne,
with the Child on her knee leaning forward to place the
ring on Saint Catharine's finger. They were all silent, rapt
in contemplation until Jane's eyes moved to the left-hand
panel, and she drew in her breath and let it out again.
"Oh, Mummy!" she cried. "Blood!" Both children were
staring, fascinated with horror at the scene of the execution
of John the Baptist, and at his headless body prone upon
the ground with hands thrust forward, and at the small,
round column of neck from which blood was pouring into a
little pool on the ground. Tilly's face grew pale and
puckered, and as Jane hid her face against Miss King's arm,
Miss King jumped up and put her hand over the child's eyes.
"Shall I take them out, Mrs. Ainslie?" she asked. "No,
don't you come. You stay and enjoy them."

They had all risen, and behind them the caretaker was
standing with a magnifying glass in his hand. Another
party of tourists had just left, and he was ready to attend
to them. "Yes, please," Clare said. "Will you, Miss King?
Perhaps an ice-cream would——" She did not finish,
because at her side Adrian said quickly, "But not for a
minute. Come here, Jane—and Tilly. I want to show you
something." And he took them by the hand and showed
them the little panel of the Virgin with the apple. He took
the magnifying glass from the caretaker, and made them
look through it at the waves in the Virgin's hair, at the
pearls in her bandeau, at the jewels embroidered into the
top of her robe, at the bright pink apple, and at the curling,
sprouting tendrils on the Child's head. He lifted them up

in turn so that they could see better. Then he made them
look at the worn velvet on the sleeve of Martin van Nieu-
wenhove. "You would think," Tilly said, "he would have
bought a new tunic to be painted in." And then in the
centre of the room he showed them Saint Ursula and her
attendants setting out from Boulogne.

They had forgotten John the Baptist, and being very
careful not to look in his direction again they went
happily out into the sunshine with Miss King to eat an
ice-cream.

Clare was standing with her back to the big triptych.
"Thank you," she said. "You did just what was needed."
She sat down again, with Adrian beside her; and they
began to discuss the strict and rigid training of an artist
apprentice under the patronage of Phillip l'Asseure, in the
fifteenth-century renaissance in Flanders of intellectual
activity in music and poetry and painting. She knew that
after the discovery of the sea route to Asia, which ruined
the trade of Venice and Genoa, and the Hanseatic League
lost its power, Philip's realm became the chief mart of
Europe. Erasmus said that in all Christendom there was
no town equal to Ghent in size, wealth and power, and
Bruges, Philip's capital, was equally spendid. All the cities
had their Guilds of Painters, and the ones in Flanders were
the most interesting and most despotic organizations of
their kind ever existing. And painting to the medieval
mind was a trade—nothing else. "How strange," she came
to say, "that out of such tyranny, from tyrants like Philip
and his successor Charles came the encouragement and
endowment of such great art, of painters like Memlinc and
the Van Eycks and David and Roger Van der Weyden."

"And the first tyrant," Adrian said, "the richest prince
in Europe, came to pass the last days of his life in a little
workshop, dyeing old fragments of cloth, and fitting together
pieces of broken glass and sharpening needles."

A silence fell, as they sat alone together, watched by
the custodian in the background; and Clare thought again
that it was a little like being in church. Then she rose and
looked once more at the Virgin with the apple; and they

went outside. Crossing the courtyard, he said to her, "There is plenty of time—unless you would like an ice or a drink?—to cross the street and go over the little bridge and through the garden of the old Hôtel Arents, and for you to see some of the pictures in the Musée Communal."

"Plenty of time for me," she answered. "Yes. But surely I am keeping you from your fiancée?"

"She had an appointment with a hairdresser," he said. "And then she was going shopping."

They walked round the side of Notre Dame and crossed the little bridge into the garden, and went through a gateway down a short path. The garden was green and quiet and overhung with trees, with walls surrounding it; and in contrast the entrance hall of the Musée Communal seemed bare and gaunt and dingy. An attendant tore off two tickets from a roll, and they went into a corridor hung with sage-green canvas, empty and silent. "This," she heard her escort say, "is what I have really brought you to see," and she felt the touch of his hand under her elbow. "This, first of all, before you look at anything else."

She lifted her eyes to the picture that hung before her, and a tremor ran through her as she beheld for the first time Jan Van Eyck's altar-piece from Saint Donatian's. She looked in wonderment at the scene in the apse of an old Byzantine church, glowing with colour; at the columns of shining porphyry; at the pavement of encaustic amber tiles, and at the pale green, unearthly light pouring through the arched windows set with little panes of bottle glass. And then at the Virgin with the Child on her knee, seated on a sculptured throne beneath a canopy; at her outer garments of red silk, her blue kirtle, and the rich carpet spread before her. The face of the Child was so old, so wise! And in the Virgin's hand the bright green plumage of a bird. A sigh broke from Clare's lips, and words, which to the ears of her companion were as a bow being played on a secret string in his heart, "Ah! *The parrot!*"

Her eyes strayed from the Virgin to the figure of Saint Donatian, his face too stern, she thought, for a saint, with the pastoral cross and the traditional wheel with five lighted

tapers. Then it was with the figure of the kneeling prelate
she was fascinated; the donor, George Van Der Pale, a
thick-necked, asthmatic, obese old Flemish canon, with
his horn-rimmed spectacles and prayer book, and a squirrel
stole over his left arm. She smiled at his wrinkled, worldly
old face; and then looked at the youth standing behind him
in polished mail, who was politely raising his helmet. He
was a very joyous, tolerant young saint! But once again,
Adrian knew, it was the figure of the Virgin on which her
eyes were resting—the centre of that great painting filled
with the feeling of divine peace. "Give me beautiful models,"
Adrian could imagine Jan Van Eyck saying, "and I will
paint you beautiful pictures. But give me ill-favoured ones
and the pictures will still be remarkable, for I shall not
flatter them. I will neither make a fat man thin, nor a coarse
woman refined. I will portray every blemish and every
wrinkle. But their surroundings shall be magnificent. I
will set them in the midst of courts and temples and
array them in costly garments. I will shower them with
jewels. Thus, for centuries to come, I will compel men
to kneel and recognize and worship the splendour of
truth."

He wanted to show Mrs. Ainslie the Memlinc of Saint
Christopher, show her the colour of his bare feet seen through
the water; but she said in almost a whisper, so low was
her voice, "Today, no more! Not after this!"

She was not ready to meet the bustle in the streets, the
clamour of trams. Did he, she wondered, understand? In
the peace of the little green garden overhung with trees,
she said to him, "Do you mind if I sit down for a few
minutes? No, it is not that I am tired through standing."
It wasn't, she thought, sightseer's feet—turnstile feet,
Jock used to call it—that she was suffering from, but too
much emotion, too much loosening of forgotten feelings,
perhaps too much wonder at too much beauty in one who
had been starved of that for so long. "Thank you," she
said, "for giving me this." And as he sat down beside her,
he said, "I would like to thank you for having shown me a
little of what it meant to you."

"I don't quite know," she said slowly. "I can't describe what it has all meant. There are no words for it. But, tell me—do you paint?"

He shook his head, and she wondered what he really did, what his profession was. But, of course he was so young—though not as young as she had first thought. Then he told her he was going up to Oxford, and that he had only recently come out of the Air Force.

"Were you glad or sorry?" she asked. "I suppose that is obvious—else you might still be in it?"

"It all seems like another life," he said, "now. Like something that happened to someone else. But I suppose I ought not to say I was extremely glad to get out, because my last job, P.A. to Elizabeth's father, was the means of our meeting."

Clare looked at him, "Fulmer," she said. "Of course! Not 'Fearsome' Fulmer, it wouldn't be?"

"How do you know?" Adrian asked. "How do you come to know his nickname?"

"I had a husband," she answered, "once, who was in the Air Force." There was a pause. "I am a widow."

The sunlight through the leaves made a pattern on the grass. They might have been far away, she thought, from the town and the traffic, there in that little enclosed garden. An old man was snoozing on a bench near. There were always old men, and sometimes old women too, in every city, snoozing on benches, nodding their remaining days away. Slowly for them was time passing, as the movement of a clock running down. The leaves of the trees were yellow at the edges; a few had already fallen.

"It is funny," she went on. "I never connected the name at all. Of course, I never met him—Fulmer, I mean. He was just a name—a nickname. I have been out of touch with things, with that life, I didn't even know he'd got a K. Jock, my husband, was killed early in 1942, and after that I dropped out of everything completely."

"Did you say," Adrian asked her, "that your husband was Jock Ainslie?"

"Yes. Why? You didn't know him?" The young man

at her side couldn't have known Jock, he wasn't old enough.
When Jock was killed, he'd have been at school.

"No. I never knew him. But I remember how awful
it was—reading that he was missing. You won't smile,
when I tell you he was my hero?"

Quickly she answered, with her cheeks suddenly aflame,
"Why, is it something to be ashamed of—now?"

"No."

"But you—have grown out of hero worship?" she said
gently. "I know."

"I don't think you do," he ventured to say. "I only said
that to you, in shyness, feeling you had heard so many say
that, as well as having an idea you knew how far short I
fell of the ideal he set."

"How old were you, then," she asked, "when he was
killed?" And when he told her she nodded, thinking he
could not have been more than nineteen at the outside,
when—to use his own words—he fell short of the ideal
Jock set. "There were many," she said, "who came after
Jock, who not only equalled his record, but one or two
surpassed it. Why did he have that special place in your
worship of valour?"

"Because he stood alone," Adrian said, "didn't he?
Their list of honours may have equalled his, but the record
of sacrifice couldn't be equalled. When he had reached the
rank he had—and at his age, for he was older, wasn't he,
by that time?—he could have sat back. A lot did. And he
had done so much already."

"Don't," she whispered. "You are saying something I
never have said—out loud."

"Please forgive me, Mrs. Ainslie. I wouldn't for the
world have——"

His youthful confusion touched her, and she smiled.

"And I wouldn't, willingly, have embarrassed you.
Anyway, it is all over—that life—for both of us, isn't
it?" And that, besides the morning and what they had
seen together and talked about, was something they now
shared.

"Are Jane and Tilly like him to look at?" he asked.

"No," she said. "Not a bit. Jock had my colouring. They look exactly like a portrait of my grandfather, whom I never actually knew. My parents brought me and my sister home from India to live for a while in his house after he died. The portrait was one of those presentation ones, and it had hung in the Academy. He was in a pink coat and holding a hunting-horn, and his face was round and rosy and fat, and he had very fair hair. He was a little man, with rather a tummy. He must have looked like Jorrocks, sideways on a horse. I must have gazed and gazed at that painting—it was in the dining-room—at meal-times, to be able to reproduce him later on in my children." She laughed. "I hope they fine down. No, they don't look in the least like Jock. Not even their blue eyes are his blue eyes."

She stood up. "How long have we sat here? Talking like this and forgetting everyone?" She hoped he would not look at his watch, and he didn't. He rose and smiled at her under the trees, and it was so quiet in that garden, it might have been midnight, not long after midday, perhaps long past the hour of lunch in the hotel.

Outside in the street, she asked him, "Is the Count de Fermandois a very old friend of yours?" And Adrian told her how he had come to meet him. "You haven't," he reminded her, "told me how you came to make his acquaintance this morning?" And when she had described the incident she joined in his laughter.

"It was just like him—to want to know, and to ask someone."

"I am so glad he did. That brief conversation, before you appeared, and then what you told me, I shan't forget very easily. But what is this work, you mentioned, that you have been doing in his house?"

"Oh, just attempting to write about some medieval characters who lived here, in Bruges."

"What period? The one we were discussing?"

"No. Earlier. The twelfth century. About one of the Counts of Flanders—and his wife—who both followed the Crusade."

"I have often wondered," Clare said, "about those

women who did that. And I am very ignorant. Did this one share all his adventures right to the end?"

"No. She died, waiting for him in Syria."

"Oh!" A little, half-whispered cry of dismay broke from her lips. "But what kept him from her?"

"It is a long story, Mrs. Ainslie. What keeps men from——?"

They had reached the square, and almost the entrance to the hotel, when she said, "You have already written it? Then you know."

"I believe," Adrian said, "that you could tell me what I don't know. For suddenly she lives—his wife."

"What don't you know—about her?"

"It can't be asked," he said, with a smile. "And it can't be answered now."

"That sounds very involved. Very mysterious."

"No, Mrs. Ainslie. It is all relative—really."

They were very late, and heads were turned when they entered the dining-room. She did not watch him go up to the table in the window, where Lady Fulmer and Elizabeth sat drinking coffee, to make his apologies. She sat down opposite Jane and Tilly and asked them what they had had to eat. She did not hear the conversation at the other table.

. . . . . .

When Julie Fermandois gave a party she brought all her qualities of generalship into play, and these allied with an American flair for hospitality made an occasion her guests enjoyed and remembered long afterwards. "We'll have a party," she had said to Jean on Sunday, when he had returned from Mass with the boys. "A party for Olive and Elizabeth, a proper party. On Tuesday. Tomorrow is too short a notice. We'll ask everybody. And find out where Pierre is staying in Brussels, will you, and tell him he's got to come back for it?"

She gathered her sons and their friends round her, while she telephoned to friends in Brussels and in the country and those who were still to be found in their villas along

the coast, and made them write down the acceptances.
There were very few refusals. And the two English boys
found her extremely entertaining, vastly different from
what they had expected their Belgian friends' mother
would be.

Belgian society, almost the last stronghold in Europe
of strict Catholicism and conservatism, had been a little
disturbed when a member of the Fermandois family—noted
in the past for conventional marriages—married a young
woman of Anglo-American parentage, and a non-Catholic.
True, there was mixed blood in the ancestry of Pierre and
Jean, but except for an Italian, most of the foreigners had
been French, sophisticated ladies, whose portraits hung
beside those of their more sober-countenanced husbands
in the château. Like them, Julie had brought wealth with
her, but the Fermandois family was not in visible need of
more when Jean was pursuing Julie from Europe to America
after he had seen her ski-ing down the slopes above St.
Moritz. Pierre's marriage had followed the expected convention, uniting two ancient and distinguished families, but
no one in their immediate circle doubted that he and the
beautiful, delicate Ghislaine were not passionately in love.
At her Requeim Mass in Saint Gudule after the war, those
who mourned her remembered the splendour of her nuptials,
and her death for many was a symbol of their country's
sacrifice. They knew Pierre would never marry again. But
a year or two later they were beginning to say that if he
did he would naturally pick a wife as he had picked one
before, and if not for beauty and youth this time, it would
be suitably a woman in his own circle. Not like Jean.
Nobody had anything against Julie—especially when they
remembered the war—but she had been brought up to
different standards and she was indiscreet and had once
mocked and flouted their conventions. When it was known
she was looking for a residence in the *Flandre*—a farmhouse,
she insisted—it was thought to be a whim, and a sign of
improvement in her health; and things were certainly
getting back to normal if Julie could concoct one of her
wild-cat schemes. There had been so many! If one hadn't

a château in the country, or a villa at the seaside, then one rented a villa for the children's summer holidays. Only peasants lived in farmhouses, no matter what Julie said was done in England and Connecticut. And nobody could live in the *Flandre* in winter. You did not buy a Flemish farmhouse in the middle of beet fields and rip its inside out and add wings and several bathrooms and central heat and make a permanent home unless you were Julie— and mad.

But gradually it became clear that it was no whim, when it was known that Jean was buying cattle; and then it was remembered that, after all, he had often boasted of being a Fleming. Although, had not Pierre called it, in the beginning, Julie's '*Petit Trianon*'? Or was that the name he gave to the model dairy, where it was said her own cows were milked to Beethoven? Or to the thatched roof chalet she had built beside the swimming-pool, with changing-rooms and showers, when it was described to him? And was it true, the question was being asked in dressmakers' show-rooms, at receptions, at cocktail parties, wherever Julie's friends met in the previous winter season, that she was importing a pack of English foxhounds? But they were fond of her, dear, brave, extravagant, tactless, interfering Julie, a friend in need, if ever there was one. And the conventions she had flouted long ago were, since the war, not so rigid. Yes, the war had tamed her. And you never knew whom she was going to have at one of her parties, from abroad.

For an hour that afternoon the *concierge* had been standing outside his lodge at the gate directing the drivers of cars where to park. Tables and chairs and gay umbrellas had been placed on the brick *patio* below the pool and on the parched lawn. There was the exercise of swimming and diving and the fun of water polo, and there was talk and there was tea, one of Julie's famous teas, with American angel cake. And it was surprising how much talk there could be among her guests who all knew each other inti-mately, and saw each other frequently. It was not surprising how much they ate, when tea was served, of the angel cake and chocolate cake and little rolls of fine white bread stuffed with delicacies, because good food was a serious matter, meant to be enjoyed and not hurried over.

Her tireless generalship kept her guests busy and on the move—before and after tea—breaking in on little groups that were tending to keep together too long, bearing one guest away, bringing up another. She did not, however, separate Pierre and Elizabeth too soon, because he clearly did not want that. Elizabeth was being much admired, Julie was delighted to observe, by everyone, for her English freshness of complexion, her good figure, her pretty hair, her bright eyes. Her figure was just right for the fashion, for that dirndl skirt, and the simple little blouse top cut low showing her lovely throat and shoulders. The boys, Gaston and Lucien, and their friends, Gerald and Richard, were quite bowled over. Of course they were at an age when a grown-up girl had more appeal than their mid-'teens contemporaries. And in spite of her engagement and an occasional air of maturity and thoughtfulness, she was in some ways a bit of an overgrown schoolgirl, subjected to sudden attacks of shyness and gaucherie in the presence of older men and women. As she had been, Julie had noticed, in the beginning with Pierre. But she had that freshness and dewiness of youth, that one could sigh over, because it was so transient! How pretty she had looked, sitting on the edge of the pool, as she looked up to watch Adrian make a swallow dive off the high board!

But how serious and grave, at first, with Pierre, until he melted her shyness and made her smile and laugh. Was the poor child shy with him because of his affliction? That showed, of course, what sympathy she had, and how immature and inexperienced not to be able to conceal it; not to know how very much he was embarrassed by that kind of reaction. But she had seemed grave, and serious too, in her manner towards Adrian this afternoon—not as she had been last Thursday when they all came to lunch, and certainly not as she had been when she and Adrian had come out on their own, on hired bicycles, on Saturday afternoon and stayed on for dinner and played Canasta

with the boys afterwards. On Thursday it had occurred to
Julie that Olive talked too much, and dominated her too
much, and did not give the girl a chance to be natural.
As she moved among her guests that afternoon Julie felt
she knew what was wrong, why there were signs of restraint
between the lovers. She would speak to Olive about it—but
not yet. Olive must meet everyone. Was there anyone to
whom she had not said, "I want you to meet Lady Fulmer,
who is the wife of a famous Air Chief Marshal? We were
at school together. Yes, isn't the daughter pretty? Yes,
her fiancé was in the R.A.F. too. . . . Yes, he has been
staying with Pierre." Eyes were turned upon the young,
fair-haired Englishman. Eyes smiled on young lovers.
Whose wouldn't?

Having risen from the side of an old friend of the
Fermandois family—an elderly lady, not over-fond of Julie
in the past, but who had softened towards her as the years
had proved her to be a more devoted wife and mother
than had been expected, and who always felt herself in
duty bound to attend any function to which Jean's wife
invited her, if it was only to see who was there—Julie saw
Pierre walking alone towards the house. She caught up
with him.

"Pierre, you are not going so soon?"

"Of course not! I am enjoying your party far too much.
I am giving a luncheon party on Thursday for your English
friends. I hope you will all be free to come to it."

"You are sweet. Olive was thrilled to meet you, and
she's dying to see inside the château. Adrian has talked so
much about it. Just us, I suppose?"

"No," he said. "I am hoping to have fourteen altogether.
You and Jean and Gaston and Lucien and their two friends.
Aunt Matilde is coming tomorrow for a day or two."

"But that is only—eleven."

Pierre laughed. "So it is. But I am hoping to make it
fourteen. Eleven is an awkward number, and it mustn't be
thirteen, must it? If Adrian is disengaged presently, will
you ask him to come to me? I have some news for him."

Julie went back across the lawn. Tea was over, and

there must be a suitable interval before her guests could be offered cocktails. The pool was empty, and no one appeared to want to risk indigestion and swim again. She saw Adrian sitting on the grass with Elizabeth and the boys, and she gave him Pierre's message. Adrian jumped up and smiled. And Julie knew that his legs could not take him fast enough into the house to discover what that news was. Elizabeth watched him go, and then her attention was drawn away from his retreating figure by something one of the boys said to her. And Julie walked on.

Under an orange umbrella Lady Fulmer's face broke into a smile, and she held out her hand and squeezed Julie's as Julie dropped into the chair Jean had just vacated. "I think it is time," Julie called out to Jean, as he was walking away, "to see to the cocktails. I'll start moving everyone indoors in about twenty minutes."

"Well, now," Julie said to her friend, Lady Fulmer, "now we can really talk."

"Such a lovely party," Lady Fulmer exclaimed. "It is so good for Elizabeth to see something of this sort abroad. And that charming brother-in-law of yours has asked us all to lunch." She smiled, first at Julie, and then in general at the other guests, and on the whole scene. "You know, dear," she went on, "looking at you all here, it is impossible to imagine you ever had a war. If it wasn't for your brother-in-law. And, even he——" She stopped, and seemed to be trying to choose words that would not sound too unsympathetic. "I mean, he looks so well, so happy."

"He doesn't always," Julie said. But today, she was thinking, he did. "And you should have seen us all at the end of it."

"I saw you very soon after," Lady Fulmer reminded her. "And to think of it, if I hadn't, Elizabeth and Adrian and I wouldn't be here." She laughed. "I often think Fate has a very strange way of working itself out." Then, quietly, "Tell me, my dear, quite frankly, you like Adrian, don't you?"

Julie smiled. "Very much—what little I've seen of him. But I think if I were in your position I'd be very happy."

That was true. The more she had seen of him the more
she had liked him, and being at heart a romantic she had
found his tenderness and his air of protection towards
Elizabeth very touching to see, both on Thursday when
they all came to lunch, and again on Saturday, when he
and Elizabeth came out alone. And she wished there was
not the impression of an unnatural restraint between them
today, which she had gained very strongly and could not
dismiss from her mind. "When," she asked, "are they
getting married?"

At this point in the conversation both women instinctively edged their chairs closer together. The gush that
had previously been overflowing in Lady Fulmer's apprecia-
tive remarks was stemmed, and a suggestion of apprehension
and doubt crept into her voice. "Oh, Julie, that's it! When?
Adrian's prospects—his immediate prospects aren't exactly
encouraging. Not from our point of view."

"It is not good for them," Julie said firmly, "to have to
wait too long. Not when they are so much in love."

"I know. But what can one do?"

"What was the idea, to start with," Julie asked, "when
they got engaged?"

Lady Fulmer sighed. "I suppose Freddie and I were
content to let things drift for a while. And I know Freddie
and Elizabeth hoped Adrian would fall into line, so to speak,
and if he wanted to marry her he'd take a job. But no, it
must be Oxford."

"My brother-in-law," Julie said, "is of the opinion that
Adrian is right over that. You know he has seen a great
deal of him this summer, and I believe he thinks very highly
of him, and of his talents."

Lady Fulmer nodded. That was all right, as far as
it went, she thought. But how far did it go? England was
where Adrian's home was, where he had to live and work.
Counts might be counts in Belgium, with land and châteaux
and a place in society, as clearly this one had—poor fellow!—
but they didn't cut much ice in England. Not from a practical
point of view. It was all very nice on a holiday. Very nice
indeed. "Do you know anything about this thing Adrian

has been working on all summer?" she asked. "This libretto?"

"Not much," Julie answered. "I didn't know it was a libretto. Pierre was rather vague and non-committal about the whole thing. What is it?"

"I don't know," Lady Fulmer had to confess. "He has only told Elizabeth, and she has told me. But apparently your brother-in-law, when he was in Brussels, was going to see a composer about it. Someone called de Castelberg."

"Michel!"

"Do you know him, then?"

"I've met him. Jean thinks he is tremendous, with a great future before him. Jean, you know, although he is a farmer now, is the musical one of the family, and studied to be a concert pianist—only he wasn't just that little bit good enough. Michel was with Pierre in the *armée blanche*."

"Does that," Lady Fulmer asked realistically, "apart from your husband's opinion, make him a better composer?"

Julie laughed. "No, it wouldn't. But it would give him a chance—as it has given him one already."

"I don't quite see——"

"With Pierre, I mean. He has helped him considerably since those days, to get known."

"You mean, helped him in a practical way? One always hears musicians have to struggle to get known." Lady Fulmer hoped she was not showing too much surprise. "But is he really so good?"

"If he hadn't been," Julie told her, "Pierre would not have bothered. He's not all that a philanthropist. Belgians are a very practical race. Oh, Olive, if this is true about Adrian having written a libretto for Michel, it is simply wonderful. Isn't he over the moon about it? Pierre had something to tell Adrian, just now. This must be it. Oh, isn't it exciting?"

Lady Fulmer made herself smile. It might be exciting, she felt, if it were something she knew more about, something she could feel certain about. And she wanted to pin the

E

whole thing down to something practical that she could understand. "Will he make anything out of it?" she asked.

Julie was thoughtful. "I don't honestly know. It will depend on many things, I suppose. It may be months, a year or more—I don't know how fast composers work—before the whole thing is complete. And then it has got to be produced."

"So it won't make all that difference," Lady Fulmer said, "to the future?"

"Not the immediate financial future, Olive. It can't."

"So we are back where we were."

"Yes and no. Don't you feel there is a different outlook now?"

"Frankly," Lady Fulmer answered, "no."

"Oh, Olive!" Julie felt she would like to shake her. Couldn't Olive see? There were those two lovers eating their hearts out, and beginning to get on each other's nerves, probably, because there was nothing so wearing to true love as uncertainty. Really, Olive was very obtuse, very unimaginative. "Can't you risk it, darling," Julie said quietly, "and let them marry soon?"

"How can they?" Lady Fulmer turned a far from happy face on her friend. "She can't live in rooms in Oxford with him, though I know it is done now. But he doesn't want her to."

"No," Julie agreed. "That wouldn't be a good idea. I can't think how married undergraduates ever do any work surrounded by nylons and nappies."

Lady Fulmer shuddered.

"But what is there to stop them getting married and Elizabeth living with you in term time? How big is your house in London?"

"It is a big house, Julie," Lady Fulmer admitted. All her defences were now down in face of Julie's persistence. And perhaps, after all, Julie was right. There was a difference now, in the outlook. Though what Freddie would say to it all, she couldn't imagine. Since he had reluctantly consented to the engagement he seemed to be having more to say in a great many other things. This holiday in Belgium, for instance. He had advised against it. Said if Adrian was a writer, a poet, as they all seemed to believe seriously, and he was at work on something, they'd both be wise not to interfere with him. "It is quite a big house," Lady Fulmer repeated. "And I have often thought we could let the whole of the top floor. People do, you know, these days. And people are glad of anywhere. Of course, I'd have to be careful and insist on references."

Julie burst out laughing. "You are a goose, Olive. Just kidding yourself, aren't you? You know perfectly well what is in your mind now. It's all there! Why didn't you think of this before, your top floor? Or have you?"

"I don't know." Lady Fulmer didn't know. She had been content—up to a point—to let things drift. Things had been drifting until she took a hand in them again. "Except," she went on, "we only moved there after Adrian had come over here. I don't know what Freddie would say."

"Why don't you put it to him?"

"When we get back," Lady Fulmer said, "I will."

"No," Julie said firmly. "No, I wouldn't wait, if I were you. I'd tell him now, as soon as possible." Deliberately she avoided use of the word 'consult'. "Write," she said, "write to him tonight. Or better still, stay for dinner and telephone him this evening from here."

"That is most kind of you." Lady Fulmer thought of the saving of francs, if she did telephone Freddie from Julie's. She would have to make the gesture, of course, with a fold of franc notes in her hand.

"In my bedroom," Julie said, "where you can have a long, intimate chat."

Those words decided Lady Fulmer, not to telephone her husband. Long intimate chats on the telephone were what he most disliked, and he would probably ring off before she had finished. And if it were a long conversation she would have to make more than a gesture of paying for the call; and Julie might accept it.

"I think it would be better," she said, "thank you, all the same, if I wrote to him tonight, instead. I can explain it all much better in a letter. But I won't tell the young things, because it wouldn't do, would it, to raise their hopes? Not just yet."

"No," Julie agreed. "Not until you have very definite news that will make them happy."

.   .   .   .   .   .

"You simply must," young Gaston de Fermandois said to Elizabeth, "come to the *kermesse* in my uncle's village next week. You and Adrian mustn't miss it."

"But I am going to Brussels with my mother," she said.

"Get out of it! Can't you get out of it?" she was being urged by the boys on every side, as they sat on the grass, and she saw Pierre and Adrian walking towards the little rose garden. It was quite a pretty garden, she thought, or it would be if everything was not so dried up by the drought. Of course you couldn't compare it with an English garden; the grass was too yellow and the flat fields where the black and white cows were grazing utterly uninteresting. There were too few trees and not very tall ones, except the poplars that stood in a line beyond the barn as though they had been painted against the sky.

She had never mingled before with Continental society of that kind, where all the women looked so well-fed and well-groomed, with shining hair and polished finger-nails and good make-up, and had such fabulous but discreet jewellery. Now and again, when there was a fresh arrival, a man would bow low and kiss a woman's hand, but it would be an elderly woman or one of some extra distinction. They were gay, but there was a certain decorum in their gaiety. She wondered if they would loosen up after the cocktails they were evidently all to go indoors for presently. It was rather like one big family, for they all seemed to know each other so well. And you knew they were only being polite when you were introduced; and you'd never know them intimately. But Pierre was different. It was different with him. You couldn't be shy with him, after all. He was *friendly*. And he'd even got her mother laughing, and he seemed to make her more natural in her manner, because she stopped talking in that silly way almost at once. Perhaps, Elizabeth thought, her mother was a little out of her element with all those foreigners. Or was it because the awful gaff she had made at lunch was still rankling? All the time, Elizabeth knew, she, herself, had been thinking of it. When she had been sitting talking to Pierre de Fermandois she had been thinking of it, and nothing else. Nothing else.

It would perhaps have been wiser if she and her mother had not stayed to watch Adrian eat his lunch, when they had finished theirs, and question him and listen to him. You couldn't, not for one single minute, put those feelings down to jealousy. That was too ridiculous, although she had been a little cross with him for being so late, and then to come breezing in with the mother of those twins. When he said what they had been doing, it was all right. Then he said—and she wanted to remember it word by word, so she could get it right, and know where it had all gone wrong suddenly—"Did you know her husband was in the Air Force, and that he was Jock Ainslie?" To her mother, Elizabeth remembered he had said that. Then to both of them. "She is the widow of Jock Ainslie."

"And who," her mother had asked, "was Jock Ainslie?"

"Ought we to know?" Elizabeth had asked. And Adrian had not answered.

"There were so many of them," her mother had said. "Was he a regular, or just in for the war? Your father would probably know. We must remember to ask him when we get home."

"Yes, there were so many of them," Adrian had said. And you could not tell why, in that moment, the room felt cold. Perhaps the waiter had switched the fan on. " 'Their shoulders held the sky suspended . . . they took their wages and are dead.' "

"When was he killed?" Elizabeth had asked. And when Adrian had told them, her mother had said, "As long ago as that?" As though time lessened the importance of a man's death and made it insignificant. "I suppose," she had gone on, "being who we are, I ought to say something to her, oughtn't I? Say I didn't realize, or something?"

It was seldom that Elizabeth had seen her mother so unexpectedly flustered. Then an idea must have crossed her mother's mind, because she frowned a little before she flashed a brief smile at Adrian. "As, of course, she must have known at once who I was, and felt too shy to introduce herself."

"She hadn't," Adrian said, "the foggiest notion. The name meant nothing to her."

Elizabeth saw her mother flush suddenly, an ugly scarlet flush that went down into her neck.

"She has lived a very quiet life ever since," Adrian said, "with her children."

And then her mother appeared to be trying to smooth things over when she went on to say Mrs. Ainslie couldn't have been left very badly off, as so many women were, who had to be helped by the Benevolent Fund. She sat on a committee connected with that charity, and Adrian had no idea the number of sad, deserving cases that came up for review. They had only to look at that Bentley and the children's hand-made smocks and that magnificent emerald and diamond ring Mrs. Ainslie wore, even down to the sea, and the fact that she could afford to stay at the Dierick d'Alsace, to know. To know—what? Elizabeth had felt Adrian was wondering. And after that, she had known that whatever else was said at the table, or perhaps even for the rest of the day—she and her mother on one side, and Adrian on the other, would not be speaking the same language.

Her mother had risen from the table and said, "Come, darling, and get ready for Julie's party. You won't forget, Adrian, will you, that the car is coming for us at a quarter past three? And we ought not to keep the chauffeur waiting." Elizabeth knew she ought to have got up then, and gone with her mother. She ought not to have remained sitting there with Adrian, sitting there and finding nothing to say except, "It must have been a bore for you having to show those pictures all over again to someone, after having shown them all to me."

She had got up then and left him; and when she passed Mrs. Ainslie's table she smiled at her to show there was no ill-feeling. She had gone upstairs and wondered what had got into them all, what the shadow was that had just appeared to spoil the day. But it had been spoilt. Why couldn't it have all been like the evening they spent at Knocke, always? They had a wonderful dinner and champagne and then they danced. When they went to the Casino he gave her all the chips, because it was her first time and she would be lucky. She grew excited and happy and the chips piled up in front of them, for she couldn't go wrong, she couldn't lose; and a crowd gathered behind them to watch. All the world knew they were engaged, and that she was bringing him luck. She had never seen Adrian look like that before, not even when he was drunk on the music and colour and movement of *Sleeping Princess*. He grew paler and his hair was untidy, as they went on and on, putting on their stakes, gathering up the winnings. They left with his pockets bulging with notes, laughing and laughing, and went to a café that was still open for hot coffee and something to eat. He had oysters and she had a plate of shrimps. They walked on the shore afterwards, where it was cool and fresh, and there was a moon shining on the sea, and he said if they could only go on walking there for ever, to the end of the world with the sound of the sea in their ears. And he fell asleep in the car taking them back to Bruges, with his head on her shoulder.

And then there was Saturday, when they came back from Julie's through sleeping villages, where the only sound was the movement of the bicycle tyres over the *pavé*. They stopped by a bridge for a rest and a cigarette. There was one of those little wayside shrines close by, all lit up; and there was a stillness and a warmth over the whole land, of which they were the possessors, because there was no one there but themselves.

How happy they had been! And perhaps it was only her imagination they were not so happy now, that something had come between them. She looked at the sunburned face of the schoolboy beside her, and at his laughing companions. "I wish I could go to the *kermesse*," she said. "But perhaps when I get back from Brussels Adrian will take me."

She saw Jean de Fermandois walking towards them, and the boys all got to their feet. Jean smiled down at her and took her hand. "I have been sent," he said, "to bring you all indoors."

She looked back once or twice as they walked towards the house, but there was no sign of Adrian and Pierre.

.   .   .   .   .   .

When Pierre and Adrian had crossed the lawn they walked down the little path between the rose beds and came to a fountain where water gushed through the mouth of a stone dolphin into a round pool, which Julie had filled with carp. They sat down on the edge of it, and the gush of water was a pleasing sound.

"Any carp left?" Pierre asked.

"I don't see any at the moment?" Adrian answered, as he peered down into the water. He could see the reflection of the sky and his own face blurred in little ripples, and the shadow of Pierre's back. "Did you have a good time when you were away? And do all you wanted to do?"

"Yes," Pierre said. "That is what I wanted to see you about. I saw Michel, and I have left the copy of the first scene with him. I told you he has made a speciality of medieval church music, so that, as you would say, is right up his street. He'd like to have the rest."

"You mean," Adrian cried, "that he'll do it? He wants to do it?"

"Yes. I mean all that."

"I feel dizzy, Pierre. I can't believe it is true." Adrian put one hand in the water, and let the water run through fingers that were trembling. "But is he really willing to— waste time on it, just on the chance?" And when Pierre nodded, he went on, "You must have influenced him? Did you?"

Pierre did not answer. He lifted his head as a flock of starlings passed over across the sky. When they had gone and the silence was only disturbed by the gushing of water into the pool, Adrian said, "Pierre, you haven't offered to

subsidize him over this, have you? This is going to take time
—time he might spend on something else."

"You do speak the most abominable Civil Service English
at times," Pierre said. "Subsidize!" He reached out for
Adrian's hand and gripped it. "Listen. Michel was thrilled
with that first scene—genuinely thrilled, and excited over
the idea of the rest. You once said I must be filthily rich.
I am more vain than anything, and vanity is perhaps one
of the few sins left to me to enjoy. I've often thought I would
have liked to have been a medieval patron of the arts,
subsidize—what a word, it is catching. I must look it up.
I mean I must get Prendergast to look it up for me—a
painter. Only I wouldn't enjoy that because I couldn't
see the results. Music I can hear and take pleasure in,
more now than ever before. So let me have this pleasure.
This vanity. What's the matter?"

"I think," Adrian said slowly, "if I were a woman I
suppose I'd weep now. I've never wished I were one
before. It must be a relief to them. Oh, God! What can
I say?"

"You have said it all. So let Michel have the rest. But
what about the scene in Syria?"

"It can't be left out," Adrian said. "It's a sort of—
hinge for the rest. No, I can't just leave it with the news
of her death reaching him. I've asked you often enough—
what were her motives? And you've never given me a
straight answer yet. Oh, I know what it ought to be to a good
Catholic. But can't you tell me as a man of the world, as
well?"

"What can I tell you?" Pierre said, after a pause.

"I have no experience to go on. And you have."

"You mean of women and love—and marriage? Those
things might not necessarily teach you to interpret Marie of
Champagne's motive for following the way of the Cross."

"Nor would living in a monastery. A monk would only
give one interpretation. But I, personally, don't feel it
would altogether be the right one. Yet, I am not sure.
He for God—only he wasn't altogether—and she for God
in him? She left her child."

E*

"As some women in England left theirs to join the Forces."

"Oh, Pierre! There's no comparison."

Pierre laughed. "It's an idea, though. And you wanted a new idea." Then seriously, "But remember, women can deceive themselves, even good women. At the end, I think, she would see the truth, what it had been, and what it was. As a Catholic, I know, right at the end, it would be God."

"But before that, Pierre?"

"Perhaps Him all the time. It is for you to find the answer. Find also—whether her love, if it were human love —blinded her to her husband's vanity." He drew a cigarette case from his pocket, and Adrian struck a match for him. The matches were in a little flat book, and the heads of the first two broke off.

"That's one thing you can't make in Belgium," Adrian said. "Decent matches." The tension was eased, but the excitement within him had lifted his spirit on wings. "Oh, Pierre, I can't describe what I am feeling. And I really do envy women their natural outlet. I saw tears come into a woman's eyes twice today. The second time was when she saw the Van Eyck Virgin in the Musée Communal."

"And the first?" Pierre asked.

Adrian did not answer.

"We ought to be getting back," Pierre said. "I am keeping you from Elizabeth. I have wished this afternoon I could see her." But he had seen her clearly in his mind— half child, half woman. A shy child to start with; shy because of his age as much as his affliction, he wanted to think. With an overwhelming, domineering mother—Julie's friend! But it was the woman, not the child, in Elizabeth, who asked him if Adrian's work would bring him fame. He pressed the half-smoked cigarette against the stone edge of the pool, and although Adrian had stood up expecting him to do the same, he did not move. "Could you describe to me," Pierre said, "the Englishwoman I met in such an unconventional way in the Grand' Place this morning? What is her name-again?"

"Ainslie," Adrian said.

"How is it spelt?"

Adrian told him.

"Continue," Pierre said. "You haven't described her yet." And he waited.

"She has dark hair," Adrian said.

"Go on."

"She's not easy to describe."

"Why? Is she uncommonly plain and ordinary?"

Adrian laughed, and turned the question. "Was that your impression, this morning? You have sometimes said you can tell by voices, and you are acquiring an extra sense. Was that your impression?"

"Not that she was plain—or ordinary." Then as Adrian was still silent he said, "I shouldn't have asked you such an impossible question to answer. At your age, were I in love, there would only be one face I could describe. Naturally, you haven't noticed if she is beautiful or plain, fat or thin."

"She is lovely, Pierre." Adrian spoke slowly. Then an inner surge of excitement ran through his words. "It grows on you. It is a beauty of a very rare and special kind. Perhaps it isn't everyone's idea, but it is mine, that what is in her face is spiritual grace. I don't altogether mean it in a religious—or what would be your interpretation of those words. But her spirit is graceful, as a body's movement is described as that." His voice had risen, as though with the pressure of inner excitement and ecstacy, up into the evening air, to the accompaniment of the sweep of birds' wings across the sky, and the sound of the water gushing into the pool. "Her eyes made me think of those lines of Stevenson's to his wife, for when they were filled with tears they were literally 'all gold and bramble dew'." There was a pause. "Her husband—— Have I told you she is a widow?"

"No. Go on."

"Her husband was my hero. He was killed quite early on, missing over Germany. It is so extraordinary, I suppose I must have read at the time that he had a wife, but I'd forgotten. If I had wanted to think of a wife for him—and mind you, I know nothing about Jock Ainslie beyond his war record—and that was terrific—she is just what I would have imagined she would be like. And if you hadn't stopped and asked them what everyone was so amused about, I don't suppose I'd ever have found out. Or do we give the cat the credit?"

Pierre laughed gently; and he stood up. "Why did she weep the first time?" he asked.

"I don't really know, Pierre. Honestly. Nothing."

"She must be a very emotional woman if she weeps about nothing so easily, and in the company of a comparative stranger."

"She's not," Adrian cried. "She's not emotional. That picture, well, I felt like crying the first time I saw it. It is so wonderful."

"You haven't given me an answer," Pierre reminded him. "You haven't told me why tears came into her eyes the first time." There was a silence. "Why did they?"

"All right, Pierre," Adrian said. "If you must know. It was—— Well, you had just driven away, and she asked me if it were a war injury. And I told her. I told her all of it." He stared into Pierre's face, which did not change in expression. The eyes were hidden, but the mouth betrayed nothing of his thoughts.

"Give me your arm," Pierre said. "I have been encouraging you to neglect Elizabeth."

*   *   *   *   *

It was very quiet in the Château Fermandois that evening after dinner; and it seemed more so after the noise there had been in Julie's drawing-room, when Pierre had entered it with Adrian. Sometimes he found crowds confusing, and that had been one of the worst occasions: so he had broken away and said good-bye to Elizabeth, who had been making conversation with him by the piano, in a strangely brittle and artificial voice. He had felt the unseen vibrations of her stress and unease, heard her shrill, forced gaiety after one or two of Julie's cocktails; and he had known that her head had been turned provocatively away from

Adrian when they had reached her side at the end of their passage through that room, and he had asked her forgiveness for his neglect. On Pierre's own intervention she had remembered her manners, and she had sounded like a child forced to say how-do-you-do, against its will, at a party, and he had known that there was more amiss between those two lovers than Adrian's desertion of her for half an hour. There was something the girl was harbouring, an inner grudge, a resentment, which had brought a lessening of her confidence, that not even a couple of cocktails had restored. Ah! Youth! he had thought. Youth that alone could magnify so much from so little, either out of an unintentional slight, or attention!

"We can tell her, can't we, Pierre?" Adrian had said, amid the chatter and the noise. "We can tell her about Michel?" But he had left Adrian to tell her that news, and had made his way alone through the lane that was always made for his solitary progress, which isolated him, as royalty was isolated. But the passage was long because of interruptions, because of social duties to this woman, that man, with handshakes and bows. And their pity followed him. It was for ever on his heels, like a shadow he would rid himself of.

But when he was driving home, having dismissed Adrian and Elizabeth from his thoughts, he remembered, not for the first time that day, the sweet naturalness of an Englishwoman's voice and the touch of her children's fingers lacing themselves in his, and how she had answered his question with no hesitation, as swiftly and as spontaneously as he had asked it. Not even that instant's pause, to which he was used among strangers, and magnified to an intolerable length. But, later, when she knew. . . . (*But you should not, my sweet stranger, unless your tears were shed for the world.*)

When he had finished dinner he went out on to the terrace. The night was warm and close. On his heels hovered the bulky figure of his servant, Prendergast, whose Yorkshire voice came carrying through the darkness towards him, heavy, ponderous, deliberate, and distinct. "Your stick, milord. Would your lordship like me to read *The Times* or *Le Soir* in a little while?"

Prendergast was seventy-two, and although he had lived in Belgium for more than half a century his French and his English were equally overlaid by a north of England accent. He was more easily understood when he spoke Flemish. He had been groom to Pierre's father, and before that with an English trainer of a prince's stables near Boitsfort. But he had put on weight in his twenties after he married a Belgian wife, and his riding days ended as a result. When Pierre's father sold his horses and carriages and bought motor-cars a year or two before the first war, Prendergast, who refused to learn to drive one, came to work indoors. No one ever knew how that happened, but knowing how Yorkshire tenacity had been infused into little boys' riding lessons Pierre had never had any doubt that Prendergast had found himself work he wanted to do in the house, and nothing could shift him. He was steward, butler, valet; and in his painstaking handwriting, with the aid of a dictionary, he was sometimes a secretary. He had become a Catholic on his marriage; and in the old days, before her death and the loss of both his sons in the first war, when he made his confession in his loud voice in the village church, it was said he could be heard in ships at sea. That was perhaps why, in common with many other rustics, he went to Bruges on the eve of a great festival, to confess to a Capuchin or a Carmelite, instead of to the parish priest already too familiar with his shortcomings. He had the simplicity and sometimes the duplicity of a peasant. He looked like one, and perhaps that was why he had settled down into the Flanders plain as though he had been born there, for in that country the men and horses are broad-chested, and the fruit and vegetables grow to outsize. He looked like any peasant, in his younger days, who drove his cattle into Bruges over the level crossings, across the Place de La Gare, holding up trams, cars, and taxis, to dispute the fact that the clergy owned Bruges. He looked like a peasant in his Sunday best: dark suit, white collar, and cloth cap, holding his two little boys—in button boots—

by the hand, with his wife beside him carrying a missal and her rosary. But that was long ago, although it was how Pierre often saw him in his mind, in those faraway days when horses and carriages rolled over the cobble-stones and turned in at the château gates, sweeping into the court-yard, when visitors arrived to stay, or parents returned from Brussels or Paris.

When one lived alone in a darkened world, one found oneself dwelling more and more in a remote, and now almost legendary, past; not in the years between when Prendergast stayed on and became part of the life indoors until, after a second war, he was one's mainstay, the shoulder on which one's hand rested for guidance. But to hear him reading aloud was a painful ordeal to endure!

"Not tonight, thank you," Pierre said. "But I want to write a letter, so leave paper near the typewriter and an envelope. Tomorrow morning I want it delivered early at the Hotel Dierick d'Alsace. Have the car sent in with it, and to wait for an answer. I wish to see Marcelle after breakfast, because I am giving a luncheon party on Thursday, for fourteen. There will be children, besides my nephews and their friends, so there must be cakes and ice-cream, as well as fruit."

He could feel Prendergast smiling.

"Very good, milord. It is a long time since we 'ad a party of that size. What about oysters, to start with?" And he went on, as the subject was one near to his heart, only to be interrupted by Pierre, who said, "But it must not be too heavy a lunch, if this weather lasts. Besides, most of the guests will be ladies." There was a pause. "Do you think we have been too much alone here, since we came back?" His cigar smoke was almost motionless in the still air between them, but Prendergast coughed.

"Well, yes and no, milord."

"Be precise!"

"It's a big 'ouse for——" And he stopped.

"For just one man, do you mean?"

"No. And yes. It's different when Mr. de Castelberg is 'ere. And Mr. Morbeigh. Something goin' on all the time, then."

"I know," Pierre said. "It is too big, too empty. Too full of ghosts, perhaps. Tell me, do you ever see any ghosts?"

"No, milord. I can't say I've seen any."

And he wouldn't, Pierre thought, when he was alone again, and Prendergast had gone indoors, admit it even if he had. Blind men were spared that. They walked into an empty room, but for them it was not empty, nor eerie with the rustle of ghostly skirts, cold with the fleeting trail of a phantom. It was warm with the memory of life and laughter. When he and Robert had walked through the rooms on their return he had known there were tears in Robert's eyes, for what had been done to them, although fortunately there had not been time in the hasty retreat for all the treasures to be removed that bore the official seals on works of art to be taken from conquered countries to swell a maniac's collection of loot. And what had been taken the Allies had found and restored. But it was the desolation, more than the actual desecration of some of those rooms.

He lifted his head in the darkness on the terrace, as though he could see the crenellated tall outer walls pierced by rows of windows rising to the sloping roof and pointed towers. He could see the house in his mind from all sides; from the entrance on the north, rising out of elms and rhododendrons with a formality and austerity that gave no hint of the life there had once been within those walls. From the east and the stables, where a weather-vane creaked in wintry weather; and from the south and west, where swans glided across the small lake and there was the stream gurgling among the willows, where he and Jean had fished as boys. He supposed the lawns were parched after the drought, and he wondered if the box hedges were as neat as they had been in his mother's time and in Ghislaine's; and in what sort of condition the numerous summer-houses were in, which were dotted about the grounds like pepper-pots, where ladies before the first war used to sit and gossip over their needlework.

The windows of Ghislaine's bedroom on the first floor in the centre of the south wall that grew up from the terrace were shuttered; and this was not because he had ordered it. The room had been stripped of its furniture before his return. In that room Robert had broken down. The women of common soldiers or collaborators had perhaps taken the clothes that had been léft there in 1940. How often in those bitterly cold winters in the villa near Ghent had Ghislaine thought of that warm dress, or that fur cape! She had brought so little with her when they were evicted. But the thieves had left one pair of ball slippers, pink satin ones, Robert had said, on his knees by the wall cupboard in her dressing-room. And it was then, in that moment, Pierre had thought, 'He must not stay here and brood among ghosts. He must get away, out into the world, for a few years.' And Robert had wanted to go, which was healthy and normal. When some of the contents of Ghislaine's room had been found and returned he had had them put elsewhere, saying that before they were put back in place, the room must be redecorated; and he had not yet given the order. Perhaps he would never give it, and it would remain as it was until one day Robert's wife would take possession.

He went indoors. These warm nights made him restless. He had been content in his isolation—until the last few months, because when a man came back from the dead it took some time to get adjusted to the world again. He had often thought how incomplete was the story of Lazarus, for it was not told whether his family and friends shunned him in fear ever afterwards, or whether they treated him normally, as before. Lately, when he was alone, he had become more and more aware of his isolation becoming a prison of his own making; and when Prendergast was reading to him, murdering English or murdering French, he had inwardly groaned with uncharitable impatience. He had begun to feel ill and irritable, and when the village priest dined at his table to wish the good man had a bath oftener. Even with his friends he sometimes felt irritable, for they would talk of politics, and each one had a cure for every crisis. Politics, the curse of Europe! If it were an English fault to over-simplify them, it was the fault of Europeans to make them too confused and intricate. He had two Polish exiles living on the estate, and he often strolled down to their cottage to talk to them, because he knew

their country and could speak a little of their language.
Was not the betrayal of Poland by the Allies one of the roots
of Europe's present sickness? An example of the weakness
in that tendency of Anglo-Saxons to over-simplify a political
issue? Sometimes he heard those exiles' voices raised in
song, old Polish songs, sung in unison and with a nostalgic
fervour; and hearing them he was ashamed of his own
discontent and irritability. If another army had liberated
Belgium, where would he, as well as every good Catholic
and sturdy Flemish farmer, be now? Then sometimes,
sleepless in an endless night, he would try to summon
Ghislaine, summon the feel of her hands across his eyes
giving him the miracle of light that was eternal. When
Masses were sung for her he craved for himself the peace
that was hers. He had craved it with a hunger that could
not be appeased. But he wondered, when he had made his
way to his desk in the little room where the business of
the estate was conducted, and felt with his hands for the
keys on the typewriter, in what form the peace he had
desired had really been, whether it were altogether peace
of the soul for the soul's sake; and why the sound of such
sweet naturalness in an Englishwoman's voice, and the
touch of her children's fingers lacing themselves in his,
had brought a glow of warmth into the chill of his heart.

He slept soundly that night; and in the morning he
rose early and went outside into the promise of another hot
day. He lifted up his face towards the sun and felt it warm
on his cheek, as he smelt the dried grass mingling with the
sweetness of ripening apples in the orchard. He tore a leaf
from a branch and pressed it between his fingers, inhaling
the scent from it. He picked an apple, and walked back to the
house eating it. The Alsation had come lolloping after him, but
he did not need him. Every step he knew, and every path.

Prendergast was in the dining-room. "The answer to
your letter has come, milord. Shall I read it?"

"Please do," Pierre said, as he sat down.

"The lady accepts, milord, for 'erself and 'er children.
But she says, that 'as she 'as 'er own motor she will not
trouble your lordship to send yours for them."

CHAPTER VI

WHEN Clare looked at herself in the mirror after that most unexpected invitation had come from the blind Belgian she had met in the Grand' Place the previous day, she said to herself, without vanity, "It must be the steaks." And the sea bathing, she thought, as well as the freedom from care. For it was not the same face that had gazed sadly at her in the last years, with ugly shadows under the eyes, thin and drawn. The invitation lay on the dressing-table; and she had read it so often and looked at his signature—in the bold Continental lettering of his own hand—she knew it by heart. And the morning was half over, with no decision made how the rest of the day should be spent. She had washed the twins' best muslin frocks and she had asked Marie if she could borrow her iron again. And it appeared Marie knew where they were all to lunch the following day, for, as Marie confessed, had she not seen the car drawn up outside and had she not borne in person the letter upstairs? She held up the children's dresses. "Such fine work, madame! Worthy of the best work in Belgium." Such handwork, she added, cost vast sums of money to buy.

There had been a subtle pleasure in that morning's inactivity, save for the washing of the children's dresses, a pleasure emphasized by an even sharper awareness of her surroundings—the view of the square framed by the window of the lop-sided houses opposite, and the little fountain that did not play. How often had she watched the passers-by! And heard, now, those bells! And the figures that moved against that background had assumed definite personalities. Henri, the head waiter, with a mole at the side of his nose; little Marie, forever on her feet, running to and fro; the happy idiot Jules, forever going up and down the stairs with luggage. That tight-laced, lacquer-haired business woman, Madame De Jonkheere, presenting the first week's bill, with a curtain over her shrewd dark eyes, until the bill was paid with big crackling notes without any item being questioned, when they softened with a

smile that creased her thin, carmined lips. And Rene, he
too fat son, with his insolent eyes that stared too much an
too long after the girl, Elizabeth Fulmer, and at Clare hersel:
who would sometimes rub down the bonnet of the Bentley
not because he enjoyed work but because he enjoyed wastin
time that might be put to a more useful purpose for hi
mother. In the early morning she had seen from her window
the father of the fat Rene setting out for the fish market,
thin, grey-haired, bent figure, with haunted eyes. He
like Miss King, sometimes gave the twins a piece of chocolate
and once or twice they had gone with him before breakfas
to do the marketing. And in the background of the D'
Jonkheeres' lives was Madame's mother, a shadowy wraitl
with white hair and a complexion the colour of lard. She
went to church very early, and flitted silently across the
square in dingy, voluminous black.

Visitors came and went; American, English, Belgian, and
French. Only the Fulmers and Mr. Morbeigh and Miss King
and herself and the children remained, so they all acquired
a permanency with the De Jonkheeres and the servant:
after the first week. But they were divided, not because o
their ages, but because their pleasures were different. Nov
and again they spoke to each other, in the *salon*, in the hall—
usually about the weather. And there was, of course, the
sense of intimacy that had arisen between herself and the
children and Adrian Morbeigh—as well as with Miss King—
which was inevitable when living on the same floor and
sharing the same bathroom, although she had not known his
surname until yesterday morning. Now there was a stronger
tie between them—because Jock had been his hero. That
discovery, and the conversation they had had in the garder
near the Musée Communal she had remembered for the
rest of the day, so she had been reproved by the twins once
or twice for not listening to what they were telling her
She had taken them to Wenduine in the afternoon, and
because Miss King did not bathe and did not like sitting ir
the sun on a hot shore, they did not invite her to go with
them. And she had felt, for once, she did not want to talk
to her, or to anyone. She wanted to think about Jock again,

nd about the Count de Fermandois, because of what
Adrian Morbeigh had told her. She wanted to watch the
children—the children of the visitors to that coast, not
only her own—playing on the sands that had once been a
tangle of barbed wire, who did not know what men had
endured that they might play there freely.

"Such fine work," Marie repeated. But Clare turned
from her to greet the twins who had returned from a walk
with Miss King. Still excited over the invitation they asked
Clare what she was going to wear, and which hat.

"You can't," Jane said firmly, "wear your old hat."

Clare had intended to take them to Brussels one day,
and this day, which had begun in that way, might be turned
to that purpose, with a visit to a milliner's thrown in.

There was only time, as they did not leave until after
lunch, to buy a hat and have tea at a *patisserie*, and to stare
in a few shop windows as they sauntered along. Because
it was the beginning of the winter season, it was found
possible to buy at a reduced price a straw hat, which in the
spring would have cost a fabulous sum. It was a very simple
hat, but it possessed that simplicity that only the continent
of Europe can combine with delicate craftsmanship and
design. Then Clare remembered, when she sat holding the
hand-mirror and turned her head slightly to one side, watched
by the saleswoman and the twins and Miss King, that the
Count de Fermandois would not see her hat; and when she
came to pay for it with precious franc notes her fingers
fumbled with them and she could not read the figures.

Afterwards, as she sauntered along carrying the hat
in a white cardboard box she caught a glimpse of a forgotten
social order, when a massive door was opened to admit a
caller, who stepped out of a car into a stone house with iron
grilles and balconies. There were white blinds at windows,
edged with Cluny lace, and placed prominently, as there
were in many shops and private houses in Bruges, a picture
of an absent king. There was a smell of Continental tobacco,
as well as perfume, and the sparkle in the sunshine of jewels
in a woman's brooch; a drift, again, of perfume, as she passed
them under the chestnut trees. They halted before the

window of a children's dress shop, and stared at hand-made
layettes and smocks and dresses trimmed with the finest
lace. "But not," Tilly said, "any better than you do."
Jane plucked at Clare's sleeve, and pointed. "That one,"
she said, "the one with the red ribbons and the little bows.
You could copy that." But she smiled, because now her
mother was going to marry Mr. Perry, she need not sit sewing
hour after hour for a London shop, so they might go on
living where they were and have what they wanted, and
say boo to Auntie Joan and Grannie, who had other ideas
for them all.

In the *patisserie*, where they were having tea, Miss
King said to Clare, "You haven't much appetite, my dear.
Aren't you going to eat a cake?"

Clare shook her head. On all their excursions she had
paid for herself and the twins, as Miss King did for herself,
sharing the tips. "I'm not hungry," she said, and she put
her hand on the lid of the hat box. She was ravenous, and
she could hardly watch the twins and Miss King eating
slices of chocolate cake. If she had been alone she would
have done without even a cup of tea. What appalling piece
of folly had she indulged in that afternoon, when her host
would not see her hat, and there would probably be no one
else there? But if she did without the luxury of a glass of
wine at dinner every night, then the francs saved would
add up to the price of the hat—or very nearly.

"The Fermandois family," Miss King said, "is very
well-known round Bruges. When I was a young girl it was
quite a sight to see their carriages drive into the town."

Clare wondered, not for the first time, what Miss King
had looked like when she was young. She was old, but
because she was kind and uncomplicated in character,
simple and good, she was ageless; and she tried to trace in
her features the lines they had had in youth. She tried to
picture those kind eyes, a little weak and faded in colour,
alive with merriment and hope; the prim little mouth pink
as a rosebud, the soft, straggly hair not grey but fair, and
the figure that was now shapeless in a flowered rayon dress
lithe and slim with the fashionable waist of those years.

or perhaps round and plump like a little partridge, with dimples in her elbows.

"I remember," Miss King went on, "it's funny the way names and events come back. At La Panne. There was a Fermandois lady, very formidable, nursing in the queen's hospital. Are you really not going to eat a cake, dear?"

Clare shook her head, and avoided looking at the trays of cakes and pastries on the counter. She had been, in more ways than one—some she could name and some she couldn't—tugged away from herself and her responsibilities on this holiday. She had not been listening to what Miss King had said about the Fermandois family. She had returned to herself and her responsibilities. She was remembering a child's frock with cherry-coloured ribbons and bows. "Tell me, again," she said to Miss King, "how you started your shop? Did you just open one or buy a business?"

"I bought it," Miss King said, "when the war was over. Women are taking to fine needlework again, although most of the trade is in dull things, like knitting wools and patterns."

"Do you remember what you said the other night— about having children's things?"

"Yes. There would be a big demand for them. There isn't a decent shop for hand-made frocks in the whole town. And it is a rich town. If you came in with me, there would be much more for you than what those Bond Street places pay you." Then Miss King laughed. "But, my dear, it's an absurd idea for you to be thinking about, under the circumstances."

"Are there schools in your town?"

Miss King laughed again. "It is full of girls' schools."

Clare could see them; gaunt buildings set round playing fields. She knew the twins were listening, and apprehensive. (*My darlings, it may happen. It may very easily happen.*) After all, they'd got to be educated—somewhere. She stood up. "I'm going"—she said—"to eat a cake after all." It was unwise, she told herself, to drive when one was hungry; and she had never had such an appetite for years as she had here in Belgium.

It was all the fresh air, she thought, and the sea bathing,

and the steaks, and the freedom from care. It was all in
that incredible sense of contentment and peace, and that
unusual feeling of excitement and anticipation. It was
seeing the children happy; as they were, she thought again,
on the journey back through Ghent to Bruges, when that
happy day was dying in a red and golden sky, leaving the
promise of another on the morrow.

And when, the next day, she was driving them again in
the country over ancient roads, over level crossings where
signs called attention to danger in Flemish and French,
it seemed that each hour, and every minute of each hour
had been gathering speed to meet the moment when she
would drive through the gates of the Château Fermandois,
and up to its front, which rose out of elms and rhododendrons very much as she had imagined it would, with a
tower and crenellated walls and sharply-sloping roofs.

In silence the children got out of the car at the bottom
of the steps and looked up at the house. They had sat very
carefully in the car so as not to crush their muslin frocks,
and they wore new hair ribbons, tied in Alice-in-Wonderland
bands. They involuntarily straightened their backs with a
dignity new to them, as the massive oak door was flung wide,
and an old butler, with pendulous red cheeks and a large
stomach, welcomed them indoors and led the way through
a dark-panelled hall through an anteroom to a long *salon*
which looked out on to a terrace.

Clare had given her name, and it was boomed out across
the long room to the Count de Fermandois, who was standing
with his back to the brilliant light, which was streaming
in through the long windows, talking to a group of people
near him. He advanced towards her; and when he took her
hand the shyness that had engulfed her at the sound of
her own name fled instantly. It was to his aunt he presented
her first, a very old lady with white hair strained off a
pale, wrinkled face into the confines of a fashionable black
hat. Only the hat distinguished her as a Continental of her
age and upbringing, for her black silk dress dotted with
tiny white spots, and her plain black shoes and absence of
jewellery, save for a single string of pearls, might have

graced the elderly chatelaine of any English country house. Hearing her addressed as 'Aunt Matilde', it was Tilly who broke the ice by saying, "My name is Matilda, but I think Matilde is prettier," which brought the flicker of a smile to that aged face. "Then we shall have to call you Matilde," Clare heard the old lady saying, as her hand was taken in turn by her host's brother and his sister-in-law and four schoolboys, two of whom were English. Clare knew that under the almost flattering scrutiny of Julie de Fermandois's candid gaze that everything about herself from her shoes to her hat—especially the hat—had been passed and won approval from a worldly but kind woman. With Jean de Fermandois she felt immediately at ease. There was humour in his eyes, and good nature in his whole round, rosy face.

It was a very formal room, designed and used, she imagined, for only formal occasions, but nothing was out of harmony, looked on as a whole. There was a lot of gilt; in ornaments—in a French clock and Empire furniture; many formal chairs and stiff-backed little couches; little tables holding precious china; two crystal chandeliers; and an Aubusson carpet on the parquet floor. Perhaps too many pictures on the green walls. But there was one modern painting of a girl in a white dress, in the style that was fashionable in the mid-twenties, whose beauty gazed down from the wall with a poignancy that could momentarily still a heart's beat, in that gathering of men and women and young people, in the room which had once been hers.

"So you are staying at the Dierick d'Alsace," Julie de Fermandois said to Clare. "Then I expect you know my friends"—as those friends of hers were announced by the butler—"Lady Fulmer, Miss Fulmer and Mr. Morbeigh."

Presently Clare found herself walking through the ante-room, through the hall filled with tall Flemish cupboards and hung with portraits, with her host walking between her and Lady Fulmer; and when they reached the dining-room in that order they sat down, with Lady Fulmer on his right and Clare on his left. His aunt sat at the far end of the long table, facing him; and she had the children round her; the boys and the twins; and in the middle were his

brother and sister-in-law facing each other on opposite
sides. Jean de Fermandois sat between Lady Fulmer and
Elizabeth, and on Clare's left was Adrian. White-capped,
white-aproned women servants waited on them. The old
English butler with the north country voice directed them
and handed the wine. The table was loaded with silver,
with a heavy éperne in the centre and flanked with many
little silver vases holding top-heavy flowers. The table was
covered with a white-embroidered linen cloth, criss-crossed
with wide lace insertions. Now and again from the other
end of the table came the gentle ripple of children's laughter.
"*Oui*, Madame. *Non*, Madame," there came occasionally
from the English schoolboys, pausing in their fun with the
twins to answer the old lady, who sat presiding over them
like a benign deity who had not altogether forgotten a
childhood of nearly seventy years ago, although it had not
been permitted such unrestraint at the table with its elders,
nor very often to sit down with them.

And with what effortless grace had the host been keeping
the balance of conversation between the two women guests
on either side of him, Clare thought, as she turned her
neglected attention on the younger man on her left. How
easy it was seeing the Count de Fermandois at his own table,
in his own house, to forget, temporarily, his affliction and loss,
and to think only of how brimful his life must have been
once not only of happiness but wisely-contrived pleasures.

"It is through you," Clare said to Adrian, "that I am here."

"Or the cat."

"Or the cat."

"I shall always worship them, I think," he said, "from
now on. Like the Egyptians did. Strange, inscrutable
creatures—like destiny."

"I have always loved them. And Jock did too. They
used to follow him in the street and sometimes would jump
on to his shoulder. And haven't you always hated the type
of Englishman who thought it was correct to like dogs and
hate cats?"

"That," Adrian said, "must have a very primitive origin.
Something to do with witches, I fancy, and the fear of the

gnorant and cruel for what they don't understand. How long
re you staying in Bruges?"

"Until a week on Tuesday. Twelve more days, to be exact.
have started to count the days that are left. And you?"

"I am supposed to be leaving that day, too. So we shall
ll be going back, probably, on the same boat?"

And that, Clare thought, was where this slender acquain-
anceship would end. On the quay at Dover they would
ll return to their separate English lives. Claude, of course,
night be there to meet her. Across the table Lady Fulmer
vas describing to the best of her ability, in a voice that was
aised a fraction above her ordinary one, to a foreigner—
vho could not possibly really understand—the rigours of
ife in England under a Socialist Government. And Elizabeth,
vho always felt uncomfortable when her mother raised her
voice, tried not to listen, and not to watch Pierre de Ferman-
tois's controlled expression, his lips, which, she thought,
night in an unguarded moment crease with amusement,
vere he not so practised a host, so clearly experienced in
he society of feminine bores; and she talked rapidly and
vithout stopping to Jean about Switzerland. Now and again
he glanced at Adrian. He was talking seriously now to
Mrs. Ainslie. But she could not hear what they were saying.
What with her mother and those children!

"I only had that one visit to Gstaad," she said, "where
he slopes are fairly easy for a beginner."

Julie leaned across the table. "Next time, Elizabeth,
you should go to——" A former expert on skis was naturally
nterested. "We are all going next January. You and Adrian
hould join us." And there was a smile, a little understanding
smile, full of the kindness and generosity of her heart,
a Santa Claus smile that promised fulfilment of hope to
a child who was not yet certain.

"I owe you so much," Clare had said to Adrian, "for
all you showed me the other morning." From there she had
drawn him to speak of his work, for she had thought of that
subject often since he had told her about it. "Oh, it will
come to you," she came to say, "the scene you can't do,"
before they all rose from the table.

When they were all on the terrace Lady Fulmer spoke t
Clare of the interest they had in common; and Clare answere
her appropriately. The twins appeared to have take
possession of the four schoolboys, and to have acquired i
the process of sitting down with them at a grown-u
luncheon party—where they must have eaten far mo
than was good for them—a maturity beyond their year
But the boys had stooped down to them, shedding th
cloak of sophistication they had worn a little self-consciousl
when they had surrounded Elizabeth in the *salon*, and wer
alternately teasing them and treating them as equals i
age. In the company of those new-found friends they ha
forgotten their admiration of Adrian—or they had abdicate
from an uncertain position in his affections, and from hi
attentions, in the presence of their rival, whom the
referred to among themselves as his lovey-dovey-cat's-eyes
and with a bound they went over the stone balustrade wit
the boys, and went racing across the lawns.

"My daughter's fiancé told me," Lady Fulmer said t
Clare. "My husband must have known your husband, o
course. Where are you living these days?"

"In the country," Clare answered. She put her hand
on the stone balustrade, and felt it hot beneath them.

"What jolly children your twins are! So completel
natural, aren't they?"

Her duty done by Clare Lady Fulmer turned away t
give her attention to the old lady; and for a short time th
guests stood about idly on the terrace. The children ha
disappeared but their voices could be heard in the distanc
when Clare walked down the steps and across the lawns i
their wake. Only the young lovers stayed behind, for th
girl was to be shown the library.

It was a very formal garden to match the house. There
were many little paths intersecting the broad lawns and
little summer-houses here and there, and flower beds ir
the shape of stars and crescent moons. Clare walked besid
Julie de Fermandois, aware of, and amused by an undis-
guised but friendly curiosity. In front of them the elderly
aunt was walking with Jean de Fermandois, and holding a

lack and white silk parasol. But gradually the distance
etween them and Clare and Julie grew wider, as Julie's
ace slackened, and her curiosity was diverted from Clare
) the conversation that was taking place behind them,
etween Lady Fulmer and the host. It was impossible not
) hear, and not to know—by the time they all reached the
ake—that an anxious mother had questioned and been
ssured of the literary ability of her future son-in-law.

Jean de Fermandois's red face was perspiring. It was
)o hot, he was thinking, for luncheon parties. And from a
armer's point of view, a waste of a day. As he stood there,
is mind went back to other days of more stately hospitality,
hen little boys did not mingle with guests, but peeped
t them from afar, and were only occasionally summoned
ito the presence. How different from today! He remembered,
lso, a time that was not so long ago, when he and Julie
ame to stay with Pierre and Ghislaine. He thought of
hislaine with the dull, numb ache in his heart, which even
ow, after all this time, came to those who remembered
er; as he looked with pleasure and appreciation at the
nusually beautiful face of the Englishwoman at his side.
t was the first time, to his knowledge, that Pierre had
ivited a woman guest, on her own, to his house since his
eturn. Julie had been ferreting! But she had other interests
t the present time, so perhaps they would be enough to
eep her mind occupied. He saw his aunt—who felt the heat
nd never had been known to take a walk in it—make a
iovement to return to the house; and Lady Fulmer and
ulie followed her. Julie's hairdresser had overdone the blue
inse for this light—it looked purple. He'd have to tell her. It
vas funny how little things, unimportant things, you'd say,
ould prick the heart. There was nothing unnatural in a woman
rowing grey—not in the ordinary course of events. But they
adn't been ordinary. So when he remembered the old
hestnut-brown curly luxuriance he could forgive any
erreting even if it concerned a woman guest of Pierre's.

For a moment or two Jean still stood there looking down
n the lake and the swans. To have followed the women,
xcept the beautiful one, since Pierre hadn't moved, might

have looked a little contrived. How well Pierre looke
today!

"Same old swans," Jean remarked. And Pierre, on th
other side of Clare, laughed.

"Descendents. My brother," Pierre told Clare, "has neve
cared for them since an incident in his youth."

In the distance the children could be heard shoutin
and laughing.

"They are in the orchard," Pierre said to Clare. "Do yo
want to see what they are doing?"

"Not to spoil their enjoyment," she answered, "althoug
it is time I was taking them away." She wondered how tha
scene would look in winter, and if the lake ever froze. I
it did, she thought it would look like a Ruysdaal paintin,
when the trees were bare, and the ice reflected the col
colours of the sky.

"That would spoil their enjoyment," he said, "as we
as mine."

"But I think," she suggested, "I should see what the
are up to. If you wouldn't mind?"

They left Jean, who strolled off alone towards the house
and went together to find the children in the orchard, not t
summon them—Pierre insisted—or to interfere. She ben
down and picked up a dropped hair ribbon, and took a
apple from one of the boys. Sheep were nibbling the gras
and came to cluster round the trunk of a tree to snatch i
their mouths the apples that were shaken down, as betwee
the laden branches the twins' laughing faces looked down o
her; and one of the Belgian boys swung himself up like
monkey to join them. Laughing back at them Clare stumble
in high heels over a mound in the tufty grass, and in steady
ing herself had for support a blind man's hand instinctivel
thrust out and closed upon her left one, and on the sharpnes
of the big ring on her third finger.

"They really should come away, now," she said.

"But they sound so happy," he insisted. "And it isn'
often I have guests. May we leave them, Mrs. Ainslie, for
little while?"

"Perhaps for about ten minutes."

When they came to the path that bordered the lake the
rest of the party could be seen in the distance on the terrace.
But she was not taken to join them. "It hardly seems worth
while," Pierre said, "walking all that way to the house, if
we are to come back again so soon," as they were passing
one of the summer-houses. So they went inside, and after
he had dusted the seat for her they sat down.

．　　．　　．　　．　　．　　．

"So it was here!" Elizabeth said, on the threshold of the
library, an immense room, with Venetian blinds down over
the long windows, shielding the treasures from the blazing
sun. She looked round at the walls lined with books, and at
a great globe in a polished-mahogany stand, at an enormous
desk and tables on which rested volumes too large to be
fitted into any of the shelves. When her eyes had become
accustomed to the shaded light after the brilliance outside
on the terrace she saw everything that Adrian had described,
and in a glass-topped box table, when Adrian had rolled
back the velvet cover, the *Book of Hours*, the German Bible,
the manuscripts and some miniatures in jewelled frames.
In a space between bookshelves on one wall there hung an
ivory crucifix. You couldn't, she thought, anywhere in
Belgium get away from religion. It was everywhere. In all
those little shrines in the country, and in women's faces
as they went into churches in Bruges to dip their fingers
in holy water stoops and say their prayers on any day of
the week. It was in the little gold cross worn round the neck
of that sexy-looking girl, Denise, in the pub, and in the
silver one worn by Marie in the hotel.

She walked slowly down the room with Adrian at her
side, and came back to stand before the large fire-place,
where, in winter, she thought, huge logs would burn. She
looked up at the high stone chimney-piece, and at the fan
vaulting of the ceiling picked out with gold and blue and
pink where there were roses alternating with a coat of arms.
She put her hands in Adrian's, and he kissed her lightly
and led her to a window seat at the far end.

"You do love me, don't you?" she asked.

"Yes, Elizabeth," he answered gravely.

"As much as you ever did?"

"As much as I ever did."

"Then," she began, and stopped before the new and uncompromising seriousness of his face. "Then, to please me, can't you definitely give up this plan of yours about Oxford?"

He did not answer. And she felt afraid in the sudden silence of that big room. She loved him, she went on, and must she wait indefinitely for him, while he became engrossed in study, in a life she could not share? And, anyway, wasn't he too old for it? Would he be amused by the society of boys not much older than Gaston and Lucien? Wouldn't it be like going back to school? What was he smiling about? she demanded.

H e laughed, "Oh, darling, what a long speech on a hot day! I thought we had all this out before and you were on my side. Though God knows you've been bringing it up enough lately I suppose I ought to have known you weren't. But in the beginning you backed me up. I don't want to be selfish. I want you to be happy."

"But I want you to be happy making me happy—else I wouldn't be."

She got up and walked towards the globe and began to turn it slowly. "This must be a very old one. Look at all the strange names on it." She went back to where he was still sitting on the window seat, and the slatted bars of light from the drawn Venetian blinds fell across her face and the new discontent and unhappiness in it. "Oh, Adrian, don't let's quarrel!"

"I don't want us to quarrel, Elizabeth."

"No. But lately, somehow, things seem to have been going wrong. Why have I been thinking that?"

"Is it anything I have done?" he asked.

"No, nothing. Nothing really. Except ever since the other morning——"

"Which morning?"

"Two days ago. Tuesday. When you took that widow to see the Memlincs and mother and I had never heard of her husband. And you were cross—and rather impertinent to mother about that."

"Darling, you are saying the most ridiculous things."

"But you were cross," she persisted.

"No. Only I forgot something—that you are so very oung. A girl."

"But you are only a few years older. Is it dull, then, nd uninteresting because I am so young and have led what ou once said was a sheltered life?"

He smiled. "I wouldn't have you any different."

"But my mother isn't young. So there was no excuse, vas there, for what she said? Adrian, you don't know what ıy life has been like always. How frightened I used to be f her, so I told lies and deceived her, when I was small. t is better now. It has been better since I met you and we ell in love. We did fall in love, didn't we?"

He pulled her down beside him and stroked her hair. What else could it have been?"

"I don't know. But lately you are different. You have hanged. Not only towards me, but in yourself. Haven't you?"

He did not answer. He could not answer. But in the end e said to her, "While you are away next week I promise ɔ think over what you want me to do."

"You will, seriously?"

"I promise."

He looked away from her at the table where he had one most of his reading and nearly all his work that ımmer. It was as though she had asked him—and he had romised—to deny his faith. In a way she had, for she had sked him to deny the faith he had in himself. Had she lways wanted that? Where was the girl whose moods had reviously matched his own, who had invited those tender ıve scenes and companionship between them with innocence nd warmth? But remembering her rebuke for his moodiness, hich she had called 'crossness' the day he had taken Mrs. inslie to see the Memlincs, what right had he, whose xperience had only touched the fringe of the war's grim ɔtal of human endurance, to judge anyone's ignorance of, r disinterest in, one of its heroes? Pierre had said that when was all over—he had been speaking of his own country, nd it must have been the same in others—there was at

F

first a sharp division that could, in some cases, never b•
bridged between those who had suffered and those who ha(
not. Among many who had there was the tendency, in thei
egoism and pride, to think they were of the elect, and amon₉
those who had escaped privation—often through no faul
of their own—there were many who were embarrassed an(
who felt themselves cut off from the brotherhood of th•
rest, and gradually came to avoid them. All of which wa
wrong on both sides. The best thing they could all do wa
to forget, and to forgive, not only their enemies—if Go(
would give them that grace!—but the transgressors and th•
ones of weak will, the ones who had been afraid, the one
who had played for safety. How could a girl, who had bee╻
a child in those years—or a woman, for that matter, con
cerned only with the upbringing of that child—know wha
the example of supreme courage and sacrifice of a ma╻
like Jock Ainslie could mean to those who followed him
and know, or understand the faith that cast out fear?

"I wish I could believe in your promises," Elizabeth said

He jumped up and went and stood by the empt\
fire-place and looked down into it. He put his hands agains
the stone carving of the chimney-piece and laid his hea(
against them.

"You've been beastly, ever since lunch on Tuesday.'
Her voice seemed to come to him from a great distance
"Yes, you have. And I've got a headache."

"I'm sorry," he said, without looking round.

"We sound as though we were married almost. Jus
like my loving parents. Were yours the same?"

"No," he answered abruptly.

"It was all that wine at lunch. The old butler kep
filling my glass. Do foreigners always eat and drink s•
much? Fancy his asking Mrs. Ainslie and those twins.
thought you said he hardly ever had anyone here. Does h
make a habit of picking up strangers in the Grand' Place?'
She laughed. But her laughter died because there was n
response from Adrian by the fire-place. "I didn't," sh
said, "mean it in that way." But she did not know wha
she had meant. It was true, she had a headache, and ╻

burning sensation behind her eyes, and a desire to cry. "Adrian," she said quietly. "Come here."

He lifted his head and dropped his hands to his side. He turned round and walked slowly back to her. He knew, with a deep conviction, that he would not now fulfil the plan he had long ago made for himself; but he could not bring himself to speak the words that would bring her happiness and banish the misery in her eyes, which had first looked at him in her parents' home with such child-like uncertainty and appealing trust. It seemed, as he walked towards her, from the fire-place to the window seat, that he had said good-bye to a number of things; and as he stood before her he knew that everything was ready to fall one way or the other, in that moment of concealment. There was a queer, blind pause, when everything, their whole future, was in the balance. He could have reached out for her hand and said the words for which she was waiting; as he could have, equally—had he not put aside, partly in fear, the cold uncompromising knowledge of the truth that had come to him in the last few moments—broken then and there the image she had been cherishing of their future.

But voices broke upon their fatal silence, and they were no longer alone. She got to her feet and answered Pierre's question, "Well, dear Elizabeth, and has he shown you everything?" with a false, self-conscious little laugh. How could anyone like him look so happy, so pleased with the world? He had taken off his dark glasses, and there were little wrinkles of laughter round his eyes. He was old, she thought, and you wouldn't call him handsome. A face a bit like a Red Indian—side face. Only of course, paler, olive skinned, that was what it was called. His teeth were square and strong and there was a division between the two front ones, that was supposed to be lucky. But he hadn't been lucky.

"Oh, yes, he's shown me everything." She saw Adrian advance to the side of Mrs. Ainslie, and then walk slowly down the room with her, pausing beside the table that held the treasures in the glass case under the velvet cover. She saw him rolling the cover back, and their heads bending

over it, close together. She saw Mrs. Ainslie raise her head
as the cover was replaced, and Adrian look at her.

Elizabeth could not think of anything else to say. She
couldn't remember what Adrian had shown her in that
room. They had begun to quarrel almost at once; to argue,
except for those long silences. But Pierre de Fermandois
was still smiling; and was it because he thought that lovers
would not have wasted all that time looking at books? Yes,
that was what he clearly thought.

"You must come again soon, my dear. Next week we
have the *kermesse.*"

She saw her mother and Julie and the old lady coming
to surround them, and the little girls and the boys filling
the door on to the terrace. And her mother and Julie had
begun mouthing and whispering together. Then they broke
apart, to talk to Pierre, the centre, really, of that gathering,
the host and owner of all this old-fashioned magnificence.
It was time, time they were all going, now Adrian and Mrs.
Ainslie had stopped looking at the treasures, the books,
and were coming back from the other end of the room.

"Ready, darling?" Lady Fulmer said to her daughter.

.   .   .   .   .   .

The twins were eating grapes to finish off their supper,
and while they ate them—first a black and then a green,
not knowing which really tasted the best—and spat out the
seeds and sucked skins on to a plate, they discussed the day.
The grapes were a present which had been put in the back
of the car, in a basket lined with cotton wool and leaves,
and they had only discovered it just when they were driving
off.

"You wouldn't," Tilly said, "ever be frightened of him."

Jane nodded and pushed her plate away. She was full,
and she couldn't eat any more.

"Who do you like best?" Tilly asked, "Count or Adrian?"

"Adrian. No—Count. Who do you?"

Their thoughts were identical, as they lay in the twin
beds, too full of grapes to eat any more. One of them would
often say what the other was about to say. But sometimes

they fought, with tooth and nail and a good deal of expert footwork, although if either of them were attacked by an outsider they were immediately allies in a masterly, and not always bloodless, defence. Adrian or Count? They didn't really know. They were abroad and they could ask, now, for things in French, and they had been to lunch in a château, which meant castle.

Marie came to take their plates away, and when she spoke to them they squealed with laughter and tried to imitate what she had said. Then they got up and cleaned their teeth in the wash-basin, not very thoroughly. Sometimes they only wet the brush under the tap and put it back in the mug. They knew that was deceitful, and they wouldn't do that tonight, any more than they would have played their special game on *him*—who had asked them to his château—"Guess who I am, Tilly or Jane. Jane or Tilly?"

"Hurry up," they heard their mother say in the doorway. So they hurried. They rinsed their mouths and turned the tap off, and went to kneel by the side of their beds. Tonight, they added, of their own accord, another name in their blessings.

"What did you talk about," Tilly asked, when they were in bed. "You and Count all that time? When you were in the summer-house?"

"We saw you."

"You forgot us."

"What did you talk about?"

"Many things," Clare said.

"About us? And the war? And—daddy?"

"A little."

"Did you tell him about Mr. Spencer-Perry?"

"No. And now it is time you both tucked down."

"When will he ask us to the *kermesse*?"

"Will he take us there?"

"What else did you talk about?"

"Mr. De Yonk-Yonk knows him."

"Mr. De Yonk-Yonk said he is *si brave*. Very brave. When we went to the fish market with him this morning he said——" Jane laughed. "Mr. De Yonk-Yonk is so funny.

He forgets things. He forgets things often. He forgot this morning what Mrs. De Yonk-Yonk told him to get."

"That will do," Clare said. "Monsieur De Jonkheere was hurt in the war. If I let you go to the market with him again you must not laugh when he forgets what he should buy."

"We didn't."

"We only laugh about him to you. Kiss me."

Clare bent over their beds in turn, and felt their arms close tightly round her neck.

"She is tired," Jane said, when Clare had gone.

"She is happy," Tilly murmured. "I know when she is happy. I have another tooth loose."

"She has shut the door. It is your turn to open it."

Tilly got out of bed and opened the door ajar, and then raced back into bed again. They could see across the landing the doors of Miss King's and Adrian's rooms closed upon their curiosity. But they had not long to wait. Miss King came first, as she always did. And tonight they wanted to tell her about the party and what they had had to eat. It would have continued without end, the recital of the events of that day, had not Miss King said it was nearly dinner-time. "Shall I shut the door?" she asked.

She said that every night, and they always gave the same answer. And they always waited, although sometimes they fell asleep watching Adrian's door, and they never knew whether he had been to see them or not. This time they were rewarded. They saw his door open, and they called out to him, and he came to them and sat down on Jane's bed.

"Tell us," Tilly said, "about when you were a little boy."

"You are much too sleepy," Adrian said. But Jane's hand was holding on to his. A pink, plump, but long-fingered little hand had Jock Ainslie's child, Funny, serious little pair! Full of curiosity. And was it a good world, he wondered, that they were discovering, peep by peep? Was it the world Jock would have wanted for them? Perhaps he hadn't known? And did he know now? In that mysterious universe, about which conjecture got one nowhere, did he watch them? Flesh of his flesh—and hers.

"Don't go," the child said, holding tighter on to his hand. And he smiled at her, thinking that he didn't want to go. It was curiously comforting, her hand on his, curiously satisfying, temporarily entering a little world where his own problems did not exist, where there were two pairs of sandals, recently whitened, drying on top of a suit-case in the corner, and a tin of Blanco beside them, two buckets, two spades, some picture-books and a plate of Pierre's grapes on the table. With her other hand Jane broke one off the bunch. "Open," she said.

"Bandits approaching," Tilly announced.

The door opened, and Clare stood there. "Oh," she said. "Oh!"

But she wasn't really cross, Jane and Tilly decided, although Adrian had gone very pink in the face, when he had got up off the bed, and said he had only come in to say good night and he hoped she didn't mind. She was smiling and he was smiling, and of course he was because she had that nice dress on she only wore when she went to London to meet Mr. Perry, which made her look prettier than anyone else's mother in the whole wide world. But she was firm, though, most decidedly firm about taking Adrian away, and putting out the light and shutting the door.

They could hear her laughing outside.

.   .   .   .   .   .

Pierre could hear the click-click of knitting needles, and in his mind he could see the ivory, wrinkled hands that held them, and below them a little woollen garment would be taking shape for the charity of Saint Vincent de Paul. His aunt had never in her life sat without work in her hands, either at home or when visiting relatives. His own generation had quailed before her piety and her opinions, and he did not think she had mellowed. But her courage and her staunchness he could not despise. Put in a glass case with a few other survivals of a bygone age, she would serve as a model for an out-moded way of life. She had always worn black—like Queen Victoria mourning a husband dead for over forty years. It was profitless to remind her the world had changed. In a personal way, she had done with the world, having long ago renounced its pleasures. But she enjoyed sitting in judgment on it, especially on its follies and mistakes and disasters. Before a silence had fallen between them the conversation had been solely on family affairs, mostly about relatives he seldom met, except on the occasion of a wedding or a funeral.

He was glad of the silence. Family affairs were, of course, part of his background, the roots from which he had sprung. Mention of them reminded him of his boyhood, when subjected to long hours of study under severe tutors, a boy's impressionable mind was striving after personal discoveries. So a man in middle age, in the warmth of a September day, searched, but not with confidence, this time, towards what was hidden and out of reach. He unclasped his hands and lifted them from his crossed knees, and touched the tip of each finger with his thumbs; and he relived an interlude of the day that had passed, remembering the sound of one voice only and the soft and gentle laughter that fell from those hidden lips in the orchard. To rely on another's description of the essence of beauty was not enough! He could smell again the dried grass of the lawns, the mustiness of the summer-house, and feel a renewal of the glow that reached him from so gracious a spirit, in the fleeting touch of hand on hand, the brush of a soft sleeve against his wrist.

"Pierre."

"Yes, Aunt Matilde?"

The knitting needles had ceased to click.

"You should, I think, go about more in society."

He smiled at such unusual advice from one who had shunned its pleasures for so long. And when she expected an answer from him he reminded her, unnecessarily, that he was handicapped. Then it was her turn to remind him, sternly, that many other men had been—and were—who had not his advantages. She spoke reprovingly, as though he were ten years old; and he was ashamed, for she still possessed that power over him—the only one left of his parents' generation to wield it. Then with surprising anima-

tion in so old a voice, she spoke of the luncheon party.
"It was very enjoyable, Pierre. And those English children
—I refer to the little girls—quite nicely brought up. The
mother, I thought, had distinction. It was kind of you to
invite them, and Julie's friends too, for I am sure it gave
them all great pleasure. I hear social life in England now is
practically at a standstill."

She spoke of London, as she remembered it on a visit
made fifty years ago, and then returned to the subject of
the luncheon party, as the old are apt to dart from and
return to a subject. She thought Prendergast still performed
his duties quite well. But he was getting very old, and perhaps
it would be wise to pension him and engage a younger man.
But it would perhaps be even wiser if Pierre were to engage
for himself a secretary, someone who could accompany
him abroad? He agreed it was a good idea, and one which
he had, at one time, contemplated. He agreed, again, that
the situation was one which would require the most careful
selection. But he did not think he would pension Prendergast
just yet. He was unprepared for her next remark.

"You would do better," she said, "to marry again.
Robert shows no inclination yet? And even if he should,
you still have your life."

He shook his head. "That side of life is over. For me,"
he added. And he wondered why the words sounded flat
and devoid of meaning, as though they were not his own
words. It was not true. He had known the last two days
that it was not true.

The room suddenly felt stifling. As a concession to her
dislike of even the smallest current of air circulating in
any apartment in which she sat after nightfall, in winter or
summer, the french windows had been closed. He got up
then, and without asking her permission, he opened one.
It was not only the airlessness. Nerves! he thought, as he
stepped forward on to the terrace and put his trembling
hands on the stone balustrade for support. He stood there
putting the returned remembrance of one particular year
of his life away from him. He knew she had risen and
followed him, and that she was fumbling with a shawl. He

felt for the ends of it, took it from her, and wrapped it round her thin shoulders.

"Please forgive me."

Calm and sure of himself again he half expected to hear a rebuke from her lips. But she said, very gently, almost timidly, "It is no better, then?"

How did she know? he wondered. Jean knew, although it had rarely been spoken of. He had kept it all to himself and his doctor—who had to know, and who said, "In time it will go. You have great resources and self-discipline. The body is cured." To his priest and confessor he took the rest . . . all the confusion and the sin of spiritual pride.

"It has been better," he assured her, "until just now. It is not too cool for you, out here?"

"No, Pierre. It is quite warm, thank you. I know, you know—how this returns sometimes. Do you think I don't know all that was done to you?" She touched his arm. "That is one reason why she must not be too young."

Puzzled, he asked, "Who mustn't be too young?"

"Your wife."

"My wife!" Involuntarily he raised his head in the direction of the shuttered windows of Ghislaine's room above.

"We were talking about this, were we not, indoors? I was about to say——" And she faltered.

"If you have forgotten, it does not matter. You will perhaps think of it in the morning."

"I have not forgotten, Pierre. I was about to say this: There are girls who would think it an honour, whose mothers might instil into them the advantages." Then as he laughed she said sternly, "This is not a matter for joking. We can be frank about such things, you and I. At your age, it need not be an affair of sentiment, of the heart."

The light from the room behind them shone on his face. He was still laughing, when she began to speak and to rebuke him for his levity. But he was laughing no longer when he spoke, and she listened in silence. He was glad, he said, she had reminded him of his age, although she exaggerated the attractions that any girl—any woman, perhaps

—would find living in the country with a middle-aged, afflicted and often irritable man, a man, prone as she had seen, to sudden attacks of frightening claustrophobia. But if he ever did bring himself to propose marriage to a woman again, it would be for one reason only—because he loved her.

"But you wouldn't be foolish?" she ventured, when they had returned indoors.

"To do—what?"

She did not answer. She picked up her knitting from the chair and stowed it away in her work-bag. It was in his mind, she thought, already. Otherwise he would not have spoken as he did. And she was both pleased and agitated.

She put her frail old white hands on his sleeves. "I shall pray for you, Pierre. I shall pray she is a good woman." Then never in her life had she made so easily a concession, or arrived at a compromise. "I shall be pleased whoever it is. I shall pray that if you already care for her that she will come to care for you, equally."

He took her hands and pressed them, and kissed her ivory cheek. "I was teasing you. Nothing is farther from my mind. I have other things to occupy me, about which I shall tell you tomorrow. That young Englishman you met today has written a libretto on Baldwin of Constantinople, for de Castelberg. He wrote it here, this summer."

As they crossed the hall towards the stairs, she said, "The one who is engaged to that girl? It is of her and her mother's making, I think, more than his."

"What gave you that idea?"

"He does not give her the attention with his eyes that he should, and they were not at ease with each other when they left. He has a look in those eyes."

"What kind of a look?" Pierre asked.

"One that is not of this world. I have seen it before. He is not a Catholic?"

Pierre shook his head.

"Then I do not know what it means."

They had reached the top of the stairs when she spoke again. "He has known that nice Mrs. Ainslie a very long time? Knew her in England, perhaps?"

"I believe not," Pierre had to say. "But her husband was one of England's Air Force heroes, whose memory young men still revere."

"I understand," she said. "Now that would account for it."

. . . . . .

The night was hot, and Clare was sleepless in it. Once she had risen and gone into the twins' room to find their coverings had been kicked on to the floor. She had replaced them and returned to her own room, but still sleep would not come. One light in the square still shone, and a stray dog worried a bone filched from a refuse bin noisily in the gutter. A distant clock chimed the hours. A mosquito came and went and came again with its own particular note. A tom-cat sent forth his lusty howl of desire on a roof near.

When she got back to the hotel after the luncheon party there was a letter from Claude. He wrote that America was suffering a heat-wave, and by all accounts—he did not appear to have received her letter—it was the same in Europe, so he hoped she was not overdoing it, and that she was spending as much time as possible at the sea. She would have been much wiser to have made her head-quarters by the sea, if she had not been so set on Bruges, which, as he could remember, was not a very lively or very healthy place for a summer holiday. What was the attraction there? (She could picture his indulgence.) Places seen in childhood seldom came up to expectations. But as everything concerning the conference was going swimmingly and according to plan, he would be back sooner than he thought. So he might fly over to Belgium and join her for the last few days of her holiday.

When he came would he share her delight in everything, or would his indulgence merely enable him to make the pretence? Would he find her changed after so short a separation? She knew there was a change in herself, and she could not altogether account for it. It was an inner change, and one which might not be detected by him. With that change had come a quickening of her senses, a feeling of pure and innocent delight, a strange, submerged excitement, and withal a sense of peace. It had been a gradual process leading to a scene where parched lawns were yellow under a golden sun, and a house stood mellow and formal and solid in the distance, when she sat with one who, like herself, had known sorrow and irreparable loss—and *more*. But she had known his life had value again, because of the triumph of the spirit. They forgot the time—and she her children, who came in the end to look for her.

In the library they had disturbed the lovers. The afternoon was over, but the magic of it had not quite receded when Adrian Morbeigh walked the length of that great room at her side, drawing her attention to this treasure, pointing out the rarity of that. (He should not have let himself be enticed by the twins to go and talk to them. And he ought not to look into one's eyes with those serious ones of his, either.) But was he not responsible for the loosening of all feelings, that had been locked away in a frozen heart? He had, after all, only come to please and spoil Jock Ainslie's children, as many another like him might have come had Jock lived. How many of them had come to the cottage to snatch an hour of quietness out of the tumult of their days and the endurance of their nights? When the strain of endurance was temporarily eased they were as children allowed up long after their accustomed hour of sleep, heavy-eyed. Men who were children. Children who were men, who carried the burden of men prematurely.

Going down the stairs with Adrian Morbeigh she had told him, as severely as she could, not to do that again; and when he had promised he would not, unless she gave him permission, he had looked at her, as he had looked at her at the luncheon table and in the library, as though there was a secret in her life he would discover. As though he were questioning what kind of a woman was she, whom Jock Ainslie had married? And she had wanted to say, "Do not probe too deeply. Do not search for the truth in me."

She turned her face from the light that shone up into her room from the square, and prayed for sleep that would

not come. She thought of Claude—and was afraid. She
knew she had grown far from him in that short time, and
that she had always been far from him, in her inner self.
She tried to picture his arrival, the scene of their meeting,
and failed. She knew he would come, but the circumstances
of their reunion she could not see.

She was back in the library of the château, in the hall,
where there had been the politeness of leave-taking, in
which the children, in torn and crumpled frocks, played
their little parts quite creditably, a little overawed, perhaps,
at having so many hands to shake. The old lady bowing
stiffly, as though stays were tight round that thin body.
Grins from the four schoolboys, and hands sticky with fruit
and gritty with tree-bark. A friendly smile in the inquisitive
brown eyes of the American sister-in-law. Another smile in
her husband's blue eyes that held no inquisitiveness to
establish one's identity, one's background, or the reason
for one's presence there. Nods from the Fulmers, which
said, "We shall see you again. We see you every day.". . . A
moment in which there was the thought of offering them a
lift back to Bruges, but dismissed because one wanted to
be alone, to drive back slowly, to take a round-about route
through villages, past shrines. . . . To stop the car by one
and get out and . . . Her host's hand in hers. "Will you
come again, Mrs. Ainslie? We have our annual *kermesse*
next week, which Jane and Tilly might enjoy. . . ." A basket
of grapes in the car. "He has asked us to come again,
Mummy. What did you talk about when you were alone
with him?"

Before the little shrine and the little flower and tinsel and
jewel-decked figures, with the children at one's side. . . .
The sun in her eyes . . . warmth in her heart. . . . "Mummy,
what's *kermesse*?"

Just before dawn she fell asleep, and in her dreams the
children asked that question incessantly.

CHAPTER VII

BECAUSE Lady Fulmer had begun to regret the expense of taking Elizabeth to Ghent and Brussels she was determined, on the morning of their departure, to practise the strictest economy throughout the trip, and would not, therefore, hire a taxi to take them to the Grand' Place. So Adrian, with the reluctant assistance of Rene De Jonkheere, who had been screamed at by his mother to do this task, carried the two suit-cases. It was again very hot, and although it was early the streets were full, and it was dusty, and the canals had a strong and peculiar smell of their own, that had not been noticed so acutely before.

The long, grey motor-coach was waiting, and they were almost the last to board it, but there was just time for some last minute advice and solicitude from Lady Fulmer. "It is going to be very hot, Adrian, so don't stew in your stuffy room all the time. You have been looking a little tired and washed out lately."

They both kissed him in turn. "Good-bye, my darling," he said to Elizabeth. "I'll be waiting here for you on Thursday." He watched them climb on board, and before the coach turned the corner he saw Elizabeth was looking back out of the window, and he blew a kiss and waved to her.

"It is going to be very hot on that journey," Rene commented. "It is not the most comfortable means of travel."

For a short distance while walking back to the hotel Adrian had Rene's company. He had come to dislike the fat youth, and thought him insolent and probably vicious in a cheap way, but he did not, as Elizabeth had come to do, snub him unnecessarily because he always remembered what had happened to Rene when he was only a boy. Eventually he succeeded in parting from him when he stopped to buy cigarettes and *Le Soir*.

When he was crossing the Place du Bourg he wondered if he went into the Chapel of the Holy Blood and knelt down, if he would receive guidance to a solution of his problem. But he would feel self-conscious if there was anyone watching him, and a trespasser. In Notre Dame or Saint Sauveur it was different, there were always people kneeling there and coming in and going out, and his inexperienced gestures would pass unnoticed. But he felt too lazy to walk so far. The sun was hot on the cobble-stones, which were burning through his rope-soled shoes. He strolled on, and came to the little bridge near the hotel, where he stopped and leaned against the parapet and opened *Le Soir*. But he couldn't concentrate, so he folded it up, and drew a recent letter from his father out of his pocket. Never much of a correspondent with either of his sons he had, this time, chosen to write at some considerable length to his younger one. Reading it again, Adrian could picture the background against which it was written, as well as the circumstances that had contributed to its composition. He could see the rain and mist sweeping past the windows of the lodge in Inverness-shire, and his father, with an unwelcome cold in the head, putting in a morning's forced inactivity to good and—hitherto that summer—neglected use. And he could see Stella, his stepmother, in rubber boots and mackintosh going out with a rod, leaving him by the fire, being wise not to fuss over an old man's temporary indisposition.

In the letter his father did not criticize the manner in which his younger son had spent the summer, but the whole emphasis lay upon the future, with the parental hope that his son would not allow himself to be turned from his original purpose. He wanted to know what would be owing to the Count de Fermandois, when he came to London in October. There followed a gentle homily on extravagance, and another reference to Oxford and the future. He was very pleased to hear of the libretto, and it would be a wonderful thing if it came off. He hoped Elizabeth was well and enjoying Bruges.

Adrian smiled and put the letter back in his pocket. His father's most particular grace lay in the fact that his scholarship had never lost touch with life, nor had his

knowledge of the frailty of humanity learned in courts of
law dimmed his capacity for enjoyment. And that to a
sensitive and very young observer, who had been privileged
on more than one occasion to sit through a celebrated and
sordid case, was remarkable. He had sometimes wished he
knew his father better. Not that he could discuss with him
what was in his mind now. The answer—if he wanted one,
was in that letter—not to be turned from his purpose. But
that wasn't all, although it was the root of the trouble.

It might have turned out better if they had stayed at
Zoute, because there wasn't enough to do in Bruges for a
woman of Lady Fulmer's physical energy for games. But
even at Zoute, he reflected, there would have been, perhaps
even more nagging little economies practised daily. But he
could have taken Elizabeth dancing every night, and she
would have loved that. That first evening—although not
the luck at the Casino—would have been repeated. He
was trying, now, to pin down the difference that was
widening into a gulf between them to something tangible.
But even from Zoute they would have gone to lunch at
the château that day. They had gone there since then,
and to Julie's again, and he had been left alone with Elizabeth
at the château to wander where they pleased. But being
left alone together found them unusually reserved. They did
not speak of the future, and that left their conversation
rather limited. He had given her the libretto and both she
and her mother had read it. But while they were discussing
it in front of him, he had the queer idea that they were
discussing something someone else had written. Perhaps
someone else had, whom neither of them knew.

He stared down at the water. He had looked forward to
these days alone, in which to come to some decision, and
now he couldn't think what he was going to do with himself.
He might telephone Pierre and invite himself out there—
but that would be evading it all.

It was Tilly who saw Adrian first and nudged Jane.
They were in a souvenir shop near the bridge buying picture
postcards, and taking an endless time in choosing what
they wanted out of the revolving stands and on the trays

on the counter. It was a fascinating shop, full of pretty painted images and medals and gaily-coloured pictures and lace-edged handkerchiefs. They were well-known there because they frequently wandered in, to look oftener than to buy, as they had already become known at the Fish Market when they accompanied Monsieur De Jonkheere early in the morning, and at a grocer's and a confectioner's, where the proprietor sold them *dragées* and always added an extra few. Everyone in the neighbourhood was beginning to know them, although few could distinguish between them, and that was always a matter for joking.

On seeing Adrian alone, they made a hurried choice—two highly-coloured cards—and paid for them, and rushed towards the bridge. "Hello," they both said. They had seen him leave the hotel with his lovey-dovey-cat's-eyes and Lady Full-of-Side and fat Rene carrying the luggage, and they knew he was only going to the Grand' Place where the buses waited.

"We are going to the sea," Jane said. "What are you doing today?" He would be lonely now, poor Adrian!

"We are taking Miss King to Knocke," Tilly went on, before he could answer. "She is going to say good-bye to cousins. Mummy said it would be so hot for her in the tram."

"Come with us," Jane said. "There will be plenty to eat. There always is plenty when we take lunch with us. Salami and rolls and butter and soup in our thermos and chicken and salad and pears and cheese and——"

"Come with us," Tilly pleaded.

Two cyclists passed over the bridge, ringing their bells, followed by a car, and as it slowed down he drew the children closer to the parapet until it had passed. He had already seen their mother walking along the bank on the worn grass under the trees, seen the pattern the leaves made on her light-coloured dress as she moved. When the car had passed and she came up to them there was a moment of shyness, of embarrassment, as the children cried, "He's coming too. He's coming with us. He *wants* to come." Her eyes asked of him silently, with amusement in their depths,

'But do you—honestly?" as her lips moved to say, "Please
do. It is going to be hot again, and if you'd like to, we'd
love it," drawing him into their completeness and making
him part of their plans for that day. There was suddenly
no other way of spending that empty and purposeless and
very hot day, except with them, in driving to the sea and
having a picnic lunch there. So when they turned and
walked back towards the square, where they saw a black
limousine drawn up outside the hotel next to Clare's car,
and they saw Pierre standing there talking to Monsieur
De Jonkheere, the arrangements for the day were made,
and Adrian had no wish to change them. If Pierre had come
to ask him to lunch or anything, he would explain why he
could not go.

"Here they come," Monsieur De Jonkheere said. "Madame
Ainslie and the twins, with Monsieur Morbeigh." He was
holding his loaded shopping basket, and his haunted eyes
were smiling. He had seen the big car turn into the square
and stop outside the hotel; and he had said, with diffidence,
"Good day, monsieur le comte."

"Who is it?"

"De Jonkheere, monsieur."

"Jean-Christophe De Jonkheere?"

"The same, monsieur."

Their hands clasped. "And how are you, these days?"
Pierre asked. They spoke of business, which was good, and
of the general prosperity and of the inflation, which was
not so severe as last year; of the present, not of the past.
Until Monsieur De Jonkheere said, "Here they come."

"They are," he said, as they came nearer, and the twins
broke away from Clare and Adrian and ran towards Pierre,
"the little friends of all the world." But, Monsieur Morbeigh.
. . . What was it he wanted to ask him? What was it Monsieur
Morbeigh had said, about his room? But he could not ask
him now, in this moment, for he was intruding. And there
were the fish and the meat to deliver to the kitchen.

It was not Adrian whom Pierre had come to see, but
Clare, and as the twins smiled up at him Adrian knew he
had come to fulfil a promise which they must have been

remembering for days. Tomorrow they were to go to the
kermesse; and if their mother were to find it too hot for such
a tiring, noisy entertainment, would she allow them to go
with his old servant, who loved a *kermesse* and would take
the greatest care of them?

"What about you, Adrian?" Pierre said. "Will you go
with them? Or stay in the garden with Mrs. Ainslie and me,
listening to the fun in the distance?"

"May I see when tomorrow comes? If it is as hot as
this I think the garden will win."

"Then I shall expect you all about three o'clock."
And as Pierre stepped into his car, he added, to Adrian,
"When does Elizabeth return?"

"The day after tomorrow," Adrian told him.

All the way to Knocke, when he was sitting in the
back of the car with the twins, and Miss King was in front
with Clare, he tried to answer the children's questions as
to what a *kermesse* would be like out of his memories of
English fairs when he had been their age. And he thought
perhaps he would go with them tomorrow, however hot it
was, and ride on a hobby horse, and try his luck and have
his fortune told. That might be as good a way as any other
of getting his problem solved.

The scene was the same; the golden sands; the colourful
crowds; the gay umbrellas; a riot of colour set below the
grey-white embankment. And the first glorious plunge into
the sea was the same; the taste of salt spray; the sun in
eyes; the sky a canopy of pearly-blue. Because it was the
kind of day when quotations from great minds dropped into
lesser ones, he remembered that Gertrude Stein had said
that 'everything is the same and everything is different',
which was, he thought, today at Zoute compared with
every other day he had spent there.

Today the shore—although there were still many
holiday-makers—was less crowded than it had been on
other days. They were able to lay the rubber mattress and
rugs and cushions down without trespassing on the preserve
of another party; and to lie, after lunch, and relax, without
running the risk of being trodden on. While the twins were

resting, to let their digestions settle before bathing again, he made up a story for them, and gave to the characters a travesty of Flemish names. Clare lay near him, in a loose cotton coat, cut like a Chinese coat, that reached to her knees, covered with a pattern of blue flowers, and the short, wide sleeves fell away from her arms that were crossed behind her head. Her eyes were hidden behind sun-glasses, but he could watch—when he thought she was not noticing —the line of her lips. Those lips, he thought again—as he had the first evening—that were as the lips of a statue carved in stone, but soft, as a girl's were soft. Not even that merciless sun could mar her beauty, disclose flaws in it. She could not be unaware of the beauty of her own face, but she was, he knew, indifferent towards it, and at times, careless of it; almost as though she was weary of it.

Clare's eyes were upon the sea, as she lay listening to the adventures—that appeared endless, under the twins' insistence for more—of characters with the funny Flemish names. They had come—as she had done on that first morning— as far as they could up that well-regulated bathing beach, and today, as before, there was the same *poule*, with the same dog, in the very same place. This time it was not the twins on whom her eyes had rested, but on a young man, on his young, thin body, before she also looked out to sea. It had been a glance of appraisal, with no thought of gain in it. Sensuality oozed from her, all over the shingle, the warm pebbles.

"Do you belong to a large family?" Clare asked, when the story had come to an end, and the twins had run off and joined in a game of Bumble-Puppy with some other English children. That was how the conversation began, lightly on her part, answered equally lightly on his. Now and then she glanced at the game of Bumble-Puppy still in progress, and wondered if it were possible that the twins had grown and put on weight in that short time in Belgium because their swim-suits seemed made for smaller little girls. The tide was going out; the ribbon of sand between shingle and sea was widening. There was the movement of the swell, the slow lift of water, the curling ripples that fell in foam and dribbled in shallow streams over the wet sand and receded. She watched it over a breakwater, the same movement, relentless but even. She would remember it, she thought, whenever in the future she thought about this particular afternoon and what she and Adrian Morbeigh had talked of together. Their respective childhoods, to start with; and personal discoveries. But what did he seek now? she wondered. He was a solitary, she thought, by nature, and not because he had lost a mother so early. But not an introvert, although there might always be some part of him that was his own, hidden and secret—even when he came to marry. Had she caught a glimpse of that hidden secret self on Sunday, when light from a window in Notre Dame fell across the pillar against which he was standing, and gave to his whole face the elongated austerity and compassion of a medieval saint, heightened the cheekbones, narrowed the eyes and set the mouth gravely? The eyes were looking far beyond the high altar, but religion she had felt—the religion of churches and dogma was not then in his mind. From the safe distance of her own years and experience she could smile tenderly upon his youthful dreams, his aspirations, and his enthusiasms; and wonder, for a moment, if she were jealous of the girl to whom he had given his love, for such love would never come her way again with all its hope and sweetness. But she could share one enthusiasm—as she had shared a part of it in the Musée Communal—and say, "Yes, when I drive through this country I feel warm and contented. I like its air of well-being, the feeling of calm after storm. The industry and the good husbandry."

"Did you tell Pierre that, last week?"

"The Count de Fermandois? Oh, yes, I did."

"He must have loved hearing that. He dotes on this scene. And he can tell—though, of course, he wouldn't to you—the most outrageously Rabelasian stories of some of the peasantry in days not very far from these."

They both laughed. And then neither of them knew why they reverted to seriousness again. But there had been a reference as Adrian turned over to let the sun warm his back, to a certain mystical love of the soil; and she had wondered if the Church made for that feeling of unity among the Flemish people. In asking him if he thought they were wise to accept the teaching she knew how he would answer. His generation were not iconoclasts. Plunged in their youth into scenes of destruction—often, as in his case, impotent instruments of it on towns and cities—they turned for comfort to tradition, as a rock to lean against, in a world beset with confusion and doubt.

"I think they are," Adrian said. "Man needs a certain discipline, for freedom is a much ill-used, much misunderstood word. Men need it more in peace than in war. War gives them a form of discipline for material reasons. In a war, a man who has no belief of any kind—Pierre de Fermandois has said this—can die as bravely as one who has a belief in an after life and in God. Men will die bravely for all kinds of things, because they love a fight, because their blood is up—and calmly because they are doing their duty, acting according to their training. But in peace—if a man is to survive as an individual, he needs more." He turned his head and looked at her and smiled. "Those aren't really my words, although I believe them. They are his."

"I should have liked to have listened to some of the things you discussed together."

"And I should have liked to have had you there. I don't think I have ever felt for anyone what I have come to feel for him."

"I can understand that," she said gently. "It would be easy to——" And stopped.

"There are not many people one can talk to," Adrian said, after a pause, in which she did not finish her broken sentence.

"That is terribly true. I have talked to no one for a very long time—of the things we have been talking about."

"Nor I," Adrian said, "ever before, except with Pierre, until today with you. Somehow I find it easier——"

She waited; and then asked, "To do—what?"

"Talk to people who have lived and have known———"

"Sorrow?"

"Forgive me, yes. Does that sound morbid?"

"Why, no! At least you are not afraid. A great many people are, you know."

"That is what Pierre says. You and he are—I was going to say alike. But that is not what I mean. Being with you is like being with him, in many ways." After a moment or two, Adrian said, "You must have been gloriously happy —as well."

She had taken off her sun-glasses to wipe them; and her eyes clouded as she looked out to sea. She could tell him the truth—the whole and bitter truth. But there were squeals of laughter as Jane poured a handful of sand down Adrian's back, and Tilly caught hold of his hands, and he struggled to his feet.

Because it was so warm they stayed in the sea for a long while, swimming, and playing with an abandoned rubber canoe that no one claimed. They kept close to the shore because of the children and the tide that was pulling out. When they were dressed and everything had been put into the car they went and had tea at a *patisserie*. The sun by then had swung far into the west, and they sat watching the crowds going home and the sea growing darker, as they drank very hot and weak tea out of cups that had daisies painted on them. And when Clare said, "It is much later than I thought, Miss King will be wondering where we are," he knew it was not the ending of that day, but the beginning.

The car was parked by the kerb, and when they reached it Clare said to him, "Would you like to drive?"

"Will you really trust me?"

"I want to trust you," she said, as she got in beside him. "It will be nearly dark when we get to Bruges, and I am not very good at dusk driving when there are many headlights." She wanted to trust him. She wanted to sit beside the driving-seat and see another pair of hands on the wheel.

In the avenue where Miss King's cousins lived children

with buckets and spades, and boys and girls with tennis racquets were sauntering home under the trees, their feet rustling the dry leaves that had fallen. An elderly man and woman came down the path with Miss King and stood by the gate; and with kisses and hugs Miss King took leave of them. At first the children sang, but the words died on their sleepy lips, as their heads rested against Miss King's arms, and the only sound was the even hum of the engine as the car sped through the twilight and the deepening dusk. And then Adrian spoke.

"There are some lines of Verhaeren's about this country, Pierre told me one day. Only my French isn't very good."

"Can you translate them?"

"Country of toil-worn pride and searing rage
When your life is thwarted or hands laid
On your destiny.
Country of heavy fists and fierce brows,
Country whose force of will is patient, dark and deep."

In the silence that again fell between them they wished for nothing more from that hour than the hour itself could give them.

But when the children were having their baths that evening Clare went into Miss King's room. On the dressing-table were gifts she had bought to take back to friends; a lace-edged handkerchief; a lace collar and two pairs of nylons; some sweets in cellophane packets. And beside them was a list she had already written out for the customs at Dover. Marie had turned down the covers of the bed, and laid across it was a pair of pink cotton pyjamas sprigged with forget-me-nots. Miss King was wearing a dressing-gown, an old-fashioned silk kimono, which by its freshness, Clare thought, she must keep to wear only on holidays.

"Miss King," Clare said; and she faltered because the request she had come to make was one she had never dreamed she would ask, although it was one which Miss King had once suggested, if the occasion rose. "Miss King, if you are not going out—and you did kindly offer, otherwise I wouldn't have dreamed of asking you. But Mr. Morbeigh has asked me to have dinner with him at the Panier d'Or."

.   .   .   .   .   .

The landlord had been through both wars, and from his bedroom window above the restaurant he had looked down on two triumphal scenes of liberation, on 18 October, 1918, and 12 September, 1944. When Adrian had dined there once with Pierre he had listened to them exchanging reminiscences. "I felt," he told Clare, "that I was listening to a saga of ancient times, impossibly remote from these, and that he and Pierre had taken their place in a pageant with the Burgundian dukes, De Conninck and the lords of the Gruithouse."

From a discreet distance the waiter was watching them; their appreciation of the dinner, their smiles, and what was growing, he felt, into a very intimate conversation. He had approved of the good taste the gentleman had shown, in ordering—with the lady's consent—after the cold *consommé*, a dish of lobster so eminently suitable for a warm evening; lightly poached—as he had explained to the lady, with artistry and pride—in *estragon* and water, and served with melted butter and chopped *estragon*. And naturally to follow, *poulet au gran*? With a *salade romaine*? And for wine? A *Liebfraumilch*? They knew each other very well, he thought, but they knew each other even better when dinner was half way through. But as their intimacy grew so did they become more serious. Ah! But she had such distinction! And her eyes were beautiful enough to break your heart, break anyone's heart—as they were clearly breaking the heart of the young gentleman. Because a young man did not look into such eyes on any woman as he was doing and not love her. It was obvious to an observer what was growing between those two; and they must be aware of it.

They were aware of it. But it was the setting, Clare thought; the pageant of history; the food; the wine; and the

memory of that drive back from Zoute in the deepening
dusk. It was Adrian saying that the landlord and Pierre
had taken their place with the Burgundian dukes, De
Conninck. . . . And one could picture those waves of invasions;
the dead of Ypres; hear the rumble of liberating armour
and Canadian and Scots' and Irish and English voices,
hear the allied thunder in the skies.

"Did you ever come this way?" she asked Adrian.

That had begun it; but they had gone far from his own
experience—measured in time six months—in the casual
telling of which, under her questioning, he had involuntarily used an expression of speech that made her smile in
remembrance of other days. Far from it when she came to
say, "He was dedicated. Right from the beginning he was
dedicated. I did not understand at the time, and only now
am I able to, a little."

She went on: "There was that quality in him we have
been discussing—absolute truth. But he sought it in individuals and their actions, which were related to his own ideal,
rather in the inanimate things we have talked about—
although they, to us, have the spirit of absolute truth behind
their creation. But Jock had one steadfast purpose, and
there was little room for anything else. But don't think—
please never think he was a dull companion, especially
when he was, on rare occasions, resting from his purpose."
She smiled then, and memories that were happy ones lit
up her eyes. "To have watched the growth of a hero is
something not given to everyone. I should have been
proud—to serve."

"But weren't you?" he ventured.

She did not answer. Instead, after a little silence, she
said, "This afternoon you said I must have been gloriously
happy. I have often wondered if a different kind of woman
would have been." And she looked down at his hand which
he had laid upon hers on the table and felt the warmth
of the pressure of it flowing through her as he spoke her
name for the first time: "Clare, if this hurts!"

"No," she said. "It doesn't any more. I can look back
now on the growth of a hero I watched in those years, as

I can at the same time look back on my own growth from
a girl into a woman, as though it were someone else."

She could trace, she told him, the progress of Jock's
development as one who was detached from it. She had
gone with him, after a prolonged honeymoon abroad, to a
part of England that was remote—but beautiful. They
lived amidst cornfields and downland—and later on surrounded by low, beech-covered hills. When the wheat waved
like a golden sea they rode up a Roman road, and if she saw
the sun glinting on the ghostly helmets of legionaries, a
younger warrior's eyes would search the skies for weather
signs, for clouds that would gather and dim the stars at
nightfall and lose him hours that were precious because
they were few, and he was gathering them unto himself,
for his squadron's training, for the purpose of that special
dedication.

"But he had more," she said, "than a singleness of
purpose. He had the gift and personality that could communi-
cate his faith to those he led. No one honours more fervently
than I all those who were heedless of the growing danger
to our country in those years and who came to share it
equally as bravely, and to die. But the few of Jock's kind,
who worked for his ideal, theirs was the duty in those years
of indifference to prepare the way. That was his very source
of life, besides which any personal feelings—love for instance
—sank into insignificance."

Yes, she could see the wheat fields, the downlands, the
beech-covered hills, and the hideous little colonies that
had been built there. The rawness of that rash of red brick
buildings; the feeble grass that tried to sprout between
white coping stones; the spindly little trees that still bore
the horticulturist's labels; rose bushes stampeded by the
wind into grotesque shapes, but flowering bravely. The
gaunt, grey hangars, divided from that rash of red brick
by a road. The road became a kind of symbol, a dividing
line, between Jock's world, a man's world, and the one she
inhabited, which was rather like a Planned Socialist State,
where the ones at the top had certain privileges denied the
rest—such as more book shelves, larger rooms. She preferred,

when it was possible, to live away from the colony. She preferred the loneliness of rooms in some isolated farmhouse, or a primitive cottage, to a house provided by the government, and neighbours with whom she had often little in common. "All these trivialities," she said, "must sound unimportant. But they are part of the picture, and increased my discontent. The real background of Jock's development, beyond that road, is what you know more about than I. It is the weather, always the weather! But I learned to watch skies too, for clouds and treacherous mists. And I, from the other side, have known the terror of fog and—noise. I, also, have heard and seen what you have, and not known who it was. . . ."

She turned then to the individuals of Jock's world, the men with whom he worked. At the time, being young and intolerant, she was unjust towards them, critical of the professional good fellows, the clowning heroes of a guest-night dinner; the lazy; the mean; the coarse and insensitive; the ambitious and the career-conscious, pompously senior, many for whom the service was a means of livelihood and no more, and of limited duration. But there were some with a selfless devotion and the eyes of visionaries, strict but tolerant, looking into the future with a confidence, that at the time seemed out of proportion to the material at hand. And there were the younger ones, of her own age. On their shoulders the fate of the world was destined to rest. Perhaps never in history had there been the need, in those years of preparation, of men possessed of quiet certainties, to lead and to inspire. "The women," she said, with a laugh. She hadn't said anything about the women, had she? "With one or two I made friends—real friends. But I rarely see them now. They have been lucky and I haven't, and it embarrasses them, but it seems to embarrass their husbands more. They are nice men, able, and I like them. But all they can do is ply me with drinks and avoid mentioning Jock. Or if they do, they do it nervously in case I may get emotional. Oh, dear, but misfortune can be a very lonely and bitter thing, Adrian. One is never taught that when one is young. But the women on the whole. It wasn't

always easy. I wasn't a snob—but where men with men can
find a bond of interest in their work, it's not so simple with
women who have different upbringings, different tastes.
And then the danger wasn't shared by all. The *sense* of it.
And when it was, that made a barrier too. It was perhaps
the barrier of—fear, which many of us carried in our minds
and never spoke of."

"Please go on," he begged.

"You mean about the trivial side of it?"

"All of it."

"Oh, well—and this will make you laugh. There was the
calling system, peculiar to Jock's service, devised I feel by
some suburban mind that had been feeding on tales of
Indian nabobs. When you arrived in one of those colonies,
although everyone else called on you, you had to call on
the top lady. I mean call, ring the bell with cards, even if
she lived a few yards away and you had a bird's-eye view
of her underwear on the line on Monday morning. It was
like saying, 'I have come to report'. Then she would return
your call. It struck me as idiotic. Perhaps it is all changed
now. Jock was very patient with my impatience. His mind
was on bigger things, and he would tease me gently."

Clare was poised, Adrian saw, between laughter and
tears; but the laughter triumphed, and it was the girl of
those years he saw before him, radiant, high spirited, brimful
of gaiety. "Then the senior, very senior ones," she said.
"Oh dear! I can't think my mother's experience of general's
wives—or even she, when she became one, tiresome as she can
be in some ways—ever approached such regal behaviour."
Then she stopped. She shouldn't, she paused to think, be
telling him those things, under the circumstances. They
both laughed, and their eyes met. They had gone too far
by then in their growing intimacy for those circumstances
to be remembered.

"But those things—they make me laugh now," she said,
"were only a little part of it. We used to go abroad always
for long leave, and then it was different, he was different.
But when we returned and he changed into uniform to
cross that road he changed too. You have the picture now.

the background. All the cheap and frustrating trivialities.
I left out the humour. The fun. I was young too then, as
they were, Jock's boys. Out of the grief I can still hear
their laughter, see them in our house after dinner. . . ."
There was a break in her voice. But she had gained control,
when she said softly, "In the heaven of their rest I would
have laughing angels to keep them company."

One by one the other diners left. There was now only
one table beside their own that was occupied. The Grand'
Place, seen through the windows, was empty. She shook
her head as the waiter came with liqueurs, with brandy.

"A *fine*, Clare?"

"I never do."

"A benedictine or——?"

She shook her head. "I'd like some more coffee and to
watch you with your *fine*."

She watched his hands curling round the big glass,
as he said, "And all this time, it was coming nearer?"

"Yes. All this time. From quite early on I began to
live with the expectation of his death. But not morbidly.
Just something I came to accept. And when one lives with
that expectation one does not deny much to a man, or let
him deny himself. This is what I could not say at luncheon
that day at the château."

Adrian looked down into the glass his hands were still
holding, as he had looked down at a pear lying on a blue and
gold dessert plate, with pity and rage choking him, remembering a reference to her children's smocks. She had been
asking him on that occasion to tell her more about his
work on the libretto, and when he had, again, confessed,
his inability to complete one elusive scene she had said
she knew nothing about creative work, as she only worked
with her hands; and pressed for a more definite description
of what she did she had told him. At first he had misunderstood, until she had answered his question: "No, not only
for Jane and Tilly."

"Not many people," Clare said, "understood that. Then,
not very many people lived our kind of life. I know there
were some who did live our life who did make sacrifices—

women who let their husbands deny themselves many little
pleasures so that they, the women, should have security
in case of an accident. I couldn't. Yes, it was all coming
nearer. Sometimes I went away by myself, to London, or
to stay with my sister. My parents came home from their
last tour abroad. My father died. But even that, even they
had become by that time something quite apart, and outside my life with Jock. Sometimes in my absence Jock would
have had a couple of youngsters, new to the trade, sent to
him. One might be from Cranwell, and one might be in
just for a few years. Or oftener they would both be in
for a few years, and they were going to be very dashing,
joyous years, with few responsibilities, and it was Jock's
job to stiffen their backs with pride and courage, to take
an interest in what they did when they were not on duty—
which I fear everyone didn't do. They were his children
and he was an elder brother to them, on and off duty.
Our house was their home, especially if they came from afar.
Then it came. The war came to us all."

But at first, she said, it had not seemed very different.
She had to move out of her house in the colony, but she
found a cottage and bought it. Fortunately it was within
reach of three stations he was on, right up to the end, so he
could come home to sleep. No, it wasn't very different. She
could hear them go out, and count them coming back—
as she had always done. But now he would come, and before
he slept he would give her names and addresses of women
she must find, or failing to find, write to.

"Women?" she said. "They were girls. Some of them just
out of the schoolroom. And I would find them in hotel
bedrooms, where there was still the impress of a man's
body in an unmade bed. What comfort could I bring, I,
who had lived with this for so long, I, whose world was still
whole? I would go back to find Jock sleeping like one dead.
Only the dead do not talk in their sleep. I have sat by him,
wanting to share what he knew. I watched him age. Then
he was promoted, and again promoted. I thought we were
safe, that he was safe. He had led the way and there were
others, thousands to follow on."

She looked at Adrian. "I suppose you were one of them. And I would have accepted their sacrifice and yours, but he wouldn't, he didn't. He used to bring some of them to the cottage, to rest, to sleep, to relax. Boys from the Dominions, many of them. I noticed their skins, how tired and grey they looked, and that colour that people with cancer get, as though strain and fatigue had drained their blood away. Once two brass hats came, full of clichés and *bonhomie*, and there was something queer about their eyes as though there was a curtain over them. I thought if they could see through that curtain into Jock's reality they would be very frightened. They were very brilliant, clever men concerned with higher strategy, not with personalities, except how those personalities could carry out that higher strategy, not concerned with flesh and blood. Perhaps they dared not be. The whole thing was growing, had grown into a colossal concern, like some machine. Anything to do with flesh and blood—the human side—was given to—Oh, my God!—psychiatrists! What could such men know of our lives? Our inner lives? Or see that road as a symbol cutting Jock's life and mine in two before we came to the war? And really, you know, I often wished Jock were like them. You said, didn't you, that he needn't have gone on? That day in the garden near the Musée Communal?"

"I said it, Clare. But I know he had to. You don't think he could have lived differently?"

She did not answer. And Adrian went on: "You spoke of frightened men. Men who, if they could have seen into his reality, would have been very frightened, full of the fears of death he conquered. You can tell me of those things and still think he could have lived and died differently? Yet you stayed by him, followed him."

"I loved him," she said. "I would have gone to the ends of the earth after him, if he wanted me, and even if I wasn't sure whether he did. I did not understand his love for those he led. Yes, he loved them, and in helping them to overcome the fears he conquered, he found a greater glory. He need not, Adrian, have taken part in that last tremendous raid. He fought authority to lead it. It was all very secret,

G

but I felt something was brewing. But I never asked him, never questioned his right to—do what he wanted to do.'

"I would have given my soul to have known him," Adrian came to say. "To have served under him. You must know what it meant to others, who knew what he had to lose?"

"To lose?"

"By dying, by risking his life with them. You, Clare. Those men he brought to your house, to rest, you said, to sleep, to relax, men who were far from their homes."

"They were boys."

"But living as men. And with men's desires too. When they saw you they knew what he had to lose. We are filled with fear, all of us at those times. Many men are as little children in the dark. And when in the blinding search-lights——" He stopped. He could not add to her agony or remembrance. Neither could they speak of these things any longer, in that place.

The waiter was at his elbow; and the restaurant was empty. He and she were again as two ordinary diners in that famous restaurant, speaking of their enjoyment of the dinner to a smiling waiter, and leaving the man bowing his thanks in the doorway.

They walked across the Grand' Place and down empty silent streets, where the churches and convents rose up like a citadel hidden from them. They came to the little bridge where the twins had found him earlier in the day, and they stood for a few moments leaning against the parapet. They could see the stars reflected in the water. Neither of them spoke. And she knew when he was no longer looking at the water, but she dared not raise her head. After a few moments she walked away ahead of him, but soon he was at her side, and presently they came into the square, where a light shone above the hotel entrance.

Rene De Jonkheere was standing in the hall. "Good night, madame," he said. "Good night, monsieur." They said good night to him in turn, and his eyes followed them up the stairs.

Clare went straight to Miss King's room, and found her

in bed, nodding over a book. "Not a sound from them," Miss King said. "Did you have a nice dinner?" Clare stood by the bed and she began to describe the dinner, dish by dish, and even the wine, she thought, glass by glass. Then she bent her head and kissed Miss King. "Thank you for keeping watch."

"You are trembling, dear," Miss King said. "You haven't caught a chill, have you?"

"I don't think so." Clare said good night and went away. Adrian's door was open and he was waiting there. She walked towards him and held out her hand, "It has been——" She began, and could not finish what she had meant to say.

"Just come and look at this," he said, and she obeyed. He led her across his room to the balcony. "Be careful," he warned. "You mustn't lean on the rail. It's bust. Shut your eyes and open them slowly, for slowly Bruges with all its holiness and greatness will come out of the darkness to you, out of the night." He switched off the light in the lamp on the table behind her, and when she opened her eyes it was as he had described. Out of the darkness, like a miracle in the starlight, assisted by artificial lighting from distant windows, distant street lamps, Bruges rose out of the dark water, a city of towers and spires, of mystery and awe.

She stood beside him very quiet and still and composed. As still, he thought, as a statue, with those lips that might have been carved from stone. Would they quicken with life, with response, if his own were laid upon them? They did. And it seemed to her that her heart opened and he entered into it; then it closed again, like the petals of a flower at sunset, gently encircling him. And it was as though he were kissing more than her lips, but deep down into her tormented memories, healing them. "This is wrong," she told herself. "This shouldn't be. But. . . ."

"Put the light on," she commanded him, when she was sure of her voice again. "I have something else to tell you. The truth."

He stepped behind her and touched the switch of the

table lamp. She turned, and the light fell across her face, which was pale and filled with compassion and gentleness, like the face of a woman, he thought, in a painting, before which worshippers had knelt, before which he could kneel now, and into her hands, and upon her mercy offer himself.

She spoke in a quiet, emotionless voice. "I said I recognized Jock's greatness. I gave you a picture of your hero, didn't I? But what I didn't tell you—was this. At the time I attributed other motives to him. I thought he sought self-glory. That being the leader of those boys, being their commander, fed his vanity, made him feel big and important. Going after danger, being brave, was directed not so much from a sense of duty, but because he sought that eminence, that personal eminence, that power of leadership because it exalted him. I thought him selfish towards me. And in many ways he was."

"Yes," Adrian said. "That is true, as the rest is true. Most men's motives are mixed. Didn't you know that?"

She looked at him, wondering at the wisdom he had beyond his years; and she sat down in the chair he had pulled forward. "I wanted you," she said, "to think of me differently. You have been creating something about me, haven't you, in your mind? He was your hero, and to say what I did——"

He knelt at her side. "It hasn't, Clare, made him any less so. Men admire men for certain qualities at certain times. He fulfilled his destiny, his mission. If I did not love you, if you had not become 'what my heart awaking whispered the world was', I would perhaps ignore your sacrifice, your contribution." He looked at her eyes, bright with sudden tears, and felt his own lids stinging, and a thickness in his throat.

Her hand was resting on his head when she spoke again. "What sent you to me," she said, "to help rid me of my bitterness and regrets? I wanted him to belong to me in this world and the next. I now know that no human being should demand that of another. We can, if we love, only serve on this earth. I loved him too possessively. And I know now how slender are the ties of that earthly, possessive love, in comparison to what he must always have known in his heart. Because whatever the motives were, he must have reckoned with that ultimate destiny very early on. My love belonged only to this life. It has taken me years to know that truth. Perhaps I did not know it fully until now. Perhaps you have shown it to me. You have freed me of all my perplexities."

He raised his head and looked at her. "But is love never to be reckoned with in your life again? The love you bore for one man, can it never be given to another?"

"It will be different, Adrian, for I am not the same person. It was my first, immature love and passion that Jock had. And I cannot be a girl again."

"I do not ask that——" he said.

She stared at him through drying tears and rose from her chair. On the balcony she would have forgotten his warning had he not put his hands in hers and drawn her back. He turned her round so that she faced the light again; and momentarily blinded by her beauty, and because he could not trust himself to speak he bent his head and kissed her hands. He felt her trembling, felt her release one hand and place it across his lips to seal them against the words that came from his heart, his very soul. But he lifted her hand away and put his lips on her lips again. Then in a pause that held as tremulous and expectant a pause as in music he looked at her, and read in her eyes a plea for the restoration of their separate identities. When she would go from him, he did not restrain her, for into her hands— as upon her mercy—he had surrendered himself.

She had gone from him; so swiftly and silently he had not heard the opening and the shutting of his door. On the balcony he stood looking at what he had brought her there to see. But he was seeing beyond it, and tracing in her story, in her love and sacrifice a resemblance to that of a woman who had lived seven centuries ago, there in that same place.

CHAPTER VIII

"PIERRE," Adrian said. "I have finished it."

They were sitting under a tree near the lake. In the distance, down in the village, there was the noise of the hurdy-gurdies, the grinding music of the merry-go-rounds and all the clamour of the *kermesse* to which Jane and Tilly had gone with Prendergast. But in the grounds of the château it was quiet and still and warm and oppressive. Not a leaf or a blade of grass stirred, and the little lake shimmered under the sun with scarcely a ripple. But although it was as warm and as close as a midsummer day there was a mellowness in the sunshine that foretold the waning warmth of a dying season. Autumn was in the drooping dahlias, the withered roses, in the bravery of the bronze chrysanthemums, and in the curling yellow edges of the leaves of the great trees that spread their shadows over the parched lawns.

"The scene in Syria?" Pierre asked. He leaned forward and took the manuscript which Adrian held out to him; and for a few moments he did not speak. Clare watched him turning the pages over, counting them, almost, she thought, as though he were able to read them, and in reading judge the merit of that scene. Then his request surprised her. "Will you read it to us, Mrs. Ainslie?" And when she consented, he said, "Thank you. A feminine voice will be a softer medium for Marie. Do you know the story? Have you already read—this?"

"Yes. And the rest too. Adrian gave it to me this morning."

She had been sitting at her table breakfasting very late when Adrian came down. The children had gone upstairs and she was alone. She had been looking across the room, and through the window near where he usually sat she could see the water and the houses on the opposite bank, and the sunlight on the mellow brick, as she drank her coffee. She watched a swan glide past. The pure whiteness of its plumage was like a ship of snow on the water. She heard the bells ring out, and then his voice at her side speaking to her. "If you could come out with me," he said, "there is something I want to show you." When they were outside she knew where he was taking her, to the little garden near the Musée Communal, and when they reached it they sat down on the same bench as before. Because it was early there was no one else there. Only now and again a woman passed through from the street and went towards the little bridge and Notre-Dame. Women going to pray. "Because it was here," Adrian said. "Here, that first morning. Will you read this, Clare?"

He watched her as she read. And when she came to the end she lifted her eyes from the page and looked not at him but beyond—far beyond that little garden through the mists of time. "Yes," she said. "Marie has been waiting and asks why he had to burn with that zeal. She has news that other men have won victories and been content. She has seen the sun go down on that road and on the hills, to rise again to renew her faith that he will come. When hope is dying, oh, how she sees him again as a seeker after self-glory, not all for God! . . . Then she is stricken and she cries to her women and to her chaplain. . . . At first she does not want the reassurance of life everlasting, which promises that in heaven there is no marriage or giving in marriage . . . only Baldwin, whom she has followed. . . . But as life recedes from her so do all earthly desires. . . . The chaplain returns to anoint her . . . she rises from her couch to go to the light, and in a blinding flash of revelation she knows that reconciliation with God fulfils all. . . . She knows the truth. . . . We rail and weep when we are earthbound, forgetting we make every final journey alone . . . as each discovery we make we cannot really share, except with God, through our inner selves, our consciences. . . ."

She gave the pages back to Adrian and looked at him as a woman might look at a son she had borne, whose achievement was beyond her understanding, although it had sprung from the love she bore him and its seed had lain within her. She looked at him, and knew they loved each other perilously.

She took the manuscript from Pierre, and as she did so she thought, "He knows. The Count de Fermandois knows. But how have we betrayed ourselves?" Then she bent her head and began to read aloud, conscious that Adrian's eyes were again upon her, watching her and the movement of her lips. Then she forgot him, as she had temporarily forgotten him in the little garden of the Hôtel Arents; she forgot both her listeners and became oblivious of her surroundings. She was a woman of seven centuries ago waiting as she, herself, and countless thousands had waited in the war. The noise of the *kermesse* was as a sound in another world. It was incessant, loud, throbbing, filled with the lusty laughter of the crowds surging round the gaily painted stalls, the swings, the circling hobby-horses, the side shows, the freaks; but neither of the men who sat listening to her reading aloud were now aware of it. One of them felt he was being borne on wings, so light in spirit was he, and a cigarette lay balanced, unsmoked, between his fingers. All the tension and the uncertainty of the preceding days had gone out of him, and he was filled with a sense of wonder and amazement that what she was reading had been his own accomplishment and creation. There was a lull in the music of the *kermesse*. The end was approaching. Clare had the last page in her hands. Her voice was low but distinct. What a sense of timing she had! She was bringing movement into it, the slow, stumbling steps of Marie, the halting words. Some of her own words! . . . And that last, desperate but triumphal cry. Oh, speak, Pierre, say something! He had grown pale, Adrian noticed.

To Pierre the reading was a revelation, the proclamation of a truth half guessed at before, when they had arrived with her children on Christian-name terms, intimate with each other, where they had not been yesterday. Of this he was thinking; for what, in the main, was revealed in that scene, which she had read so movingly, the interpretation Adrian had at last arrived at, unaided—except by a woman who had suffered similarly?—was too poignant, too near to him to dwell for long on now.

"Well," Adrian said, "will it do?"

"It will do." Pierre answered slowly, trying to put words together, the words of praise that were due, that would not betray his own inner confusion. "I congratulate you." He turned to Clare. "Thank you, Mrs. Ainslie. You read very beautifully, very movingly." She had read those words, he thought, as though they were her own—and perhaps they were.

"Now it is done," Clare said. "How do you both feel?"

"It is for Adrian to say. How do you, my son?"

"But I know," Clare persisted, "Adrian has told me that you have collaborated to a great extent in all of it, except this scene."

"He exaggerates. A fault, I think of poets. One would be wise, Mrs. Ainslie, not to believe all poets say."

A woman servant came walking across the parched lawns to tell them that tea was served on the terrace; and they rose from their chairs and followed her. Pierre put his arm in Adrian's. "It is very good, my son. And I do sincerely congratulate you."

"Why," Adrian asked, "is there so much of your son all of a sudden?"

Pierre laughed. "You are the age of my son. But young as you are, you have succeeded where I failed. I was, of course too old, too unimaginative. He has made this woman, Marie, live. Hasn't he, Mrs. Ainslie?"

"Yes, indeed he has."

"Did you ever imagine what she looked like, Adrian, when you were writing that scene?" And when Adrian did not answer, Pierre went on, "If she were dark or fair. And if, for instance, she had eyes like the eyes of Stevenson's wife. 'All gold and bramble dew', you once quoted to me. In Julie's garden, do you remember? That is another trait these poets all have, Mrs. Ainslie. For every occasion they have a line that meets it."

The tea-table was set at one end of the terrace in the shade of tall elms that grew on that side of the house.

"When Jane and Tilly come," Pierre said, as they sat down, "we will have fresh tea made. Or do they drink milk?"

G*

"They usually drink milk. But they are quite used to tea."

Pierre asked her if she would pour out for them, and Adrian rose to help her. As their hands touched over the handle of the large silver tea-pot her eyes asked of him silently, "Do not attend to me too much. We are shutting him out of our intimacy. And I will not be a conspirator in this guilt before him." But she knew he knew. For what else was behind his teasing of Adrian, and that gentle mockery? Before such teasing she felt young and foolish. Before his wisdom and knowledge—inexperienced. Not what she was, a woman of her age, with children and many responsibilities, old enough—in all conscience!—to know better than to believe this was anything but make-believe and a dream. But she knew his mockery hid something else— some memory that in him had stirred when that scene was read.

The children came on to the terrace from the house, and broke up the conversation that had become polite and a little forced. They were flushed and exhausted, untidy and happy. Prendergast shuffled in their wake. He held a bowler hat in his hand and his red, perspiring face smiled broadly. "A proper pair of cautions, they are, madame."

Clare laughed, "I hope they were good. Thank you very much for taking them."

"Mrs. Ainslie," Pierre said to him, "has said they would prefer milk. And shouldn't there be ice-cream as well?"

"This is all going to be very difficult for me," Clare said, "when we are home again."

While they were busy eating, the children told of the wonders of the *kermesse*. "We went on the swings and the horses. . . . Prendergast too. . . . He rode on a horse and everyone cheered him. . . . He went up and down and round and round and waved his hat at everyone. . . . He blew kisses too, to a lady. . . . We saw Gaston and Lucien, count. . . . But not Gerald and Richard. . . . They have gone home to England. . . . There was a lady with a beard. . . ."

"It happens every year, then, at this time?" Clare asked Pierre.

"Yes," he told her. "It is part of our lives. Or it was—in our younger lives."

"Better than now?" Clare wondered. And she watched the expression change in his whole face as he began to describe to her the dream-like and fantastic *kermesse* of his boyhood, with all its astonishing richness of colour, and how it was even more exciting and wonderful after sunset, seen from an upper window, when the white flares of the acetylene lamps of those days lit the darkness. There was a man who offered for two *sous* as many raw mussels as anyone could eat without coughing. And for one *sou* there was the spectacle of a man pulling up handfuls of his skin and pinning it with safety-pins. A woman with no arms who opened a bottle of champagne with her toes and drank your health.

"I can never," Clare said, "enjoy seeing nature's cruel freaks."

"Small boys are insensitive, Mrs. Ainslie. I agree it isn't far from bear-baiting."

"Was there anything specially Flemish in those days that there isn't now?" Adrian wanted to know.

"I haven't been," Pierre answered, "since I took Robert before the war. But when I was a boy there was the Berard family. Berard and his wife and about six children, who gave four times a day a dramatic version of the Passion of Our Lord. So renowned was he, there was a song about him. '*Et le voilà, et le voilà, Ber-ard. Le plus comique de la Belgique, Ber-ard*'. Why he was called comic, I don't know, for his performance as Caiphas in the Passion was one of the most harrowing scenes you can imagine."

"You've never told me any of this before," Adrian said. "But what did your church say to it?"

"Oh, the priesthood was authorized to assist—naturally." And he added, "No, none of us would miss our *kermesse*. It is always a tragedy if it rains in that week. And much as the country needs rain, I hope it won't come tomorrow when everyone from here will be going—except Prendergast and myself."

He had been thinking of tomorrow evening—but not of the *kermesse*, although he had been speaking of it—and of actors playing parts distasteful to them, in a confusion of falsity and concealment, on the return of Elizabeth. Had he been filled with an uncontrollable envy that a young man, having touched some inner spring in the woman, whose child's head lay resting against his own arm, that opened her closed heart and her secrets, had loved her and been in turn loved by her? Not yet, perhaps, in the fullest meaning. Not yet. Was it envy and cynicism that caused him to think, "Adrian may never exceed this? This is his moment. He may never attain these heights again—never write with such passion and understanding?" But he was ashamed, that before her, he had, in his own confusion of mind, taken refuge in mockery; in cynicism teased a boy scornfully. Thinking of tomorrow evening and of a gracious spirit torn by perplexities, placed in a position that might cause her mental anguish and a false sense of shame he said to her, "Mrs. Ainslie, I think you should not leave Belgium without seeing a *kermesse*. Will you give me the pleasure of dining with me tomorrow night, and let me take you to it?"

In the little silence that had fallen before he spoke to her, Clare had known it was time she was taking the children away. They were tired. Jane was sitting quietly beside Adrian, with her hand in his; and Tilly's head was resting against Pierre's arm, her hair falling back over his sleeve. But they were not too tired to answer for her, "Oh, you must! You must go to the *kermesse*, Mummy. Mustn't she? And Adrian, too."

Pierre laughed. "I can't include you this time, Adrian. Elizabeth, I expect, will be too tired after her sightseeing in Brussels. And you will have so much to tell her, won't you, about completing the work in her absence." Then he turned to Clare and waited for her answer; and she gave it in a low but natural voice, looked at his hidden eyes and knew why he had given her that invitation. But it would depend, she told him, whether Miss King—another guest in the hotel, she explained—would keep an eye on Jane and Tilly. "If she is agreeable," Pierre said, "I will send my car for you." And when Clare protested, reminding him that she had her own car, he said, "The roads will be full of late revellers when you return to Bruges, and they are sometimes in the mood and the condition to be indifferent to traffic. I should feel happier if you were being driven by someone who has experience of them."

Clare thanked him again, and caught the eyes of both children; and presently she took them upstairs, with the woman servant who had announced tea showing them the way. And Pierre with his arm in Adrian's, went into the library, where he asked Adrian to ring the bell.

"We must drink to this," he said. "It should be drunk in the best of my cellar, and you will find what comes will be too sweet for your taste and mine. So I fear, will Mrs. Ainslie. But I am having Jean and Julie and their boys to dinner—they always come on the last night of the holidays— and it is for their younger palates. There is not time to have anything else brought up and served properly."

When the order had been given to Prendergast and they were alone again, Pierre said, "Michel telephoned last night. He will be here on Tuesday. It is a pity he can't get here before, because you are leaving that day, aren't you?"

"I was," Adrian said. "But, of course, I shan't—now."

"But when does Oxford term start?"

"October."

"That is soon," Pierre reminded him.

Adrian sat down on an arm of a chair. "I suppose it is. But I seem to have lost all sense of time, and season."

Prendergast entered with champagne and glasses on a tray. "Shall I draw the curtains, milord?"

"Thank you. No, leave them." Pierre walked towards one of the long windows. "Is it a good sunset tonight, Adrian?"

"Yes. The whole sky is scarlet above the trees and the park. I have an idea Mrs. Ainslie is watching it from an upstairs window while the twins are turning on every tap in one of your ornate bathrooms."

Pierre laughed. "I like those children." There had not

been, he was thinking, little girls in that house for over sixty years. Then he said, "But before they come down, I want to say this to you. I am very proud of you. That is why I called you my son."

"It seemed," Adrian said, "to shut me out. Put me in my place. I thought you were angry with me, for some reason. I'd never known you quite like that before. I thought, in spite of all you said, that you were disappointed—disapproved of my interpretation. And you haven't said if I can come back here on Tuesday—to meet Michel and all that."

"But of course you may," Pierre said gently. But in what mood, he wondered, would he come? On Tuesday *she* was to leave Belgium! What havoc would have been caused by then? Why was it impossible to think of Tuesday, as though it were an ordinary day of the week, made special only by the meeting in that house of a poet and a composer? What other and dire significance seemed to hang over it? He put his arm in Adrian's. "I was not disappointed. And I want to thank you for all you have brought me—this summer."

"There is a horrible sound of—finality in that, Pierre."

"Each phase of one's life has, when it is ended. And another has begun. Is the sky still red?"

"It is darkening," Adrian told him. "But there is a new and incredible colour, like plumes, of pure jade. And the lights are up on the fairground. I shall always remember this day."

"As I shall," Pierre said. "Now put the lights on in here. Not too many. The softer wall lights for us to drink to Baldwin."

And as the lights in the sconces on the walls suddenly cast their soft illumination into the room, Clare entered with the children. Smiling she raised the glass that was put into her hand and looked from Adrian to Pierre and back to Adrian. She had watched—as Adrian knew she had—the sunset from an upper window, seen the lights go up in a glow of white brilliance above the fairground. But she had turned from the window to stand before a *prie-Dieu*, and to drop on to her knees wondering if any woman had ever knelt there before in prayer, and been so inarticulate. The children were laughing in the adjoining bathroom. Perhaps it was their voices, intruding. . . . "My darlings," she said to them, under their insistence, "you can taste this, if you like. It will make you sneeze, so best to pretend." When they were big girls, would she one day take them to hear the opera, *Baldwin of Constantinople*? On that far distant day, would she remember this one? And see in her mind these two men standing side by side in this room?

They had drained their glasses. It was time to go. Her hand was in her host's. "I will telephone you, Count, as soon as I have asked Miss King."

She watched her children spontaneously reach up and kiss him; saw Adrian thrust his arm in his as they walked across the hall. They parted in laughter, on a note of merriment.

But when they had gone; when the sound of the car going down the drive grew fainter and fainter, the house seemed empty, haunted and desolate as Pierre turned back into it from the porch.

．　　　．　　　．　　　．　　　．．　　　．

That night, at the dinner-table, where Jean and Julie and their two sons were assembled, and where he played his part as the head of a family, Pierre felt strangely apart and remote from their interests. It was a charming, but antiquated custom, he felt, that made it seem necessary that an uncle should be consulted on the future of nephews when their respective careers had already been planned by the young men concerned and agreed upon by their parents. But to Julie, although he appeared tired, he had seemed to receive them with a good deal of his former gaiety, alternately teasing and complimenting, and at times talking with all his former brilliance. It was not, however, long before she perceived that much of that gaiety was forced, and he had something on his mind he was concealing from them; and she felt a little worried as her eyes rested on the dinner-table itself, and later on the flowers in the *salon*. One could not say the house was uncared for, but the spirit had gone out of it. And with old Prendergast almost in sole charge of what was done and what went on, the table, for instance, with all that old-fashioned silver, now looked as it must have looked fifty years ago. It was slowly, she thought, growing into a museum. Whatever must visitors think?

"Pierre," she said, when dinner was over. "I hear you had visitors this afternoon."

Jean had sat down at the piano. He had the thick, stubby fingers of a farmer and a pianist. He liked the piano in the *salon* of the château better than his own, because he had learned to play on it, and he always felt, when he touched that instrument, a return of his youthful hopes and confidence.

"Gaston and Lucien saw those little twins at the *kermesse* with Prendergast. I think their mother is so attractive. I'd like to have her over one day. How long is she staying?"

Jean went on playing softly, but keeping an ear turned to catch Julie's words. Sometimes she blundered. Sometimes her inquisitiveness led where she should not intrude. Though what was in his mind, what, strangely, had dropped into it on the day of the luncheon party, down by the lake, might be utterly wide of the mark. Might be. Might not? Although he and Pierre had followed different paths in life—married, for instance, very different women—there was a bond of youthful closeness, the growing up together, the deep roots they shared. And on that foundation instinct could speak clearer than words of a change.

"Oh, well," Julie said, "there isn't really time, is there?"

Jean felt happier and went on playing.

"Because," Julie went on, "Olive and Elizabeth will be back tomorrow, and they haven't much longer here, either. How was Adrian?"

"He seemed very well, Julie," Pierre answered. "Why?"

"Well, as I knew from the boys who heard it from those children that he was here this afternoon too, I just wondered." Julie laughed. "I can't keep it any longer, darling, though I promised Olive. I telephoned her at the Metropole just before we left. She said she'd let me know the moment she had any news, but I guessed she wouldn't want to waste money on a call, so I called her."

"And what was the news?"

"She's got Sir Frederick to give in. She heard this afternoon. Elizabeth and Adrian can get married as soon as ever they like. And they can have the top floor of Olive's house. This will mean they'll be quite independent and it won't interfere with Adrian at Oxford. Isn't it lovely? I really believe if I hadn't put this into Olive's mind it would never have come off. You can't tell me that long and indefinite engagements are good for anybody."

"No, Julie," Pierre said slowly. "They are not good for anybody." He lifted his head towards the piano. "Jean," he called out. "Stop playing Chopin—it is too sad. Play something else."

"Shall I make it 'The Wedding March'?" Jean said, laughing.

Julie laughed also. "It is really," she said, "all due to me."

.   .   .   .   .   .

They had finished dinner when Adrian said, "Shall we go out for a little while?"

"Yes," Clare agreed. "If Miss King isn't. Let us do that."

"Shall we ask her to have a drink with us first?"

"That would please her. She likes *crème de menthe*."

They sat with Miss King in a corner of the *salon* for half an hour, and when she said she would not be going out Clare went to get her coat.

"I wonder," Adrian said, when they were outside, "if a change in the weather is coming, and if this is the last of these wonderful nights." They walked slowly, and in silence after that, along the dimly lit streets and came to the Grand' Place. There they sat down outside a café and drank coffee; and in their eyes every detail of the scene surrounding them was sharpened. As her hand moved to

lift the aluminium top off the blue and white cup it was
momentarily dipped in the light that shone through the
open door of the café; and the smooth surface of the table
that divided them became in his mind a bridge between
his expectation and the eventual fulfilment of the heaven of
physical touch. To talk lightly and inconsequently of the
commonplace was merely a measure of their intimacy,
their increasing sense of ease in each other's company, to
know—with breathless expectancy on his part, that could
be controlled outwardly under a cover of gaiety that
matched hers—that they had reached in their relationship
a point of no return.

For her to analyse her feelings towards him did not
dispel the sense of a dream she was now living; it enhanced
that sense and gave it a symbolic significance. In opening
her heart to him she was embracing all the gladness and
the brightness and the courage as well as the fear and the
suffering that had been the portion of his generation in
the war. That he had taken from her what he had, all her
perplexities, all her sorrow and bitterness, all her loneliness,
and when she had gone from him last night used that know-
lege to that purpose, filled her with wonder and tenderness,
with pride and joy. There, she told herself, her own feelings
must rest, as well as his, imagining that the present sense
of gaiety and gladness would all-prevail, believing that
what he had already achieved through her brought delight
sufficient to put into insignificance any other desire.

A horse-drawn cab was waiting at the kerb, and the
driver, who had been watching them, spoke to them, when
they had risen from the table, in anticipation of a fare. He
was not disappointed. The spirit of gaiety was still present
when Adrian said, "Shall we go back in it? I have often
thought motor-cars are an anachronism here, especially
at night." And in that spirit she answered him, laughingly
assenting, as she gave him her hand and put her foot on
the step.

Their heads were covered by the hood, and now and
then a street lamp shone on the façade of an old house,
drenched the foliage of the trees in a translucent green.

The movement of the carriage over the cobble-stones rocked them gently in their isolation. They were lovers whose personalities were temporarily lost in time; and the words with which she answered his pleading belonged not to herself. He had declared it was the woman she was now whom he loved, but it was the girl she had once been who met his ardour with tenderness and surprise, with shyness that melted in wonder and ecstacy. The spell was broken when there were lights and a familiar thoroughfare that led into the little square, and there were words exchanged over the chink of coins and the crackle of notes passing from hand to hand, with the sound of the horse's hooves going clop-clop and the turning of the wheels and the creaking of harness as the carriage rumbled away. But it would return to them. It was destined so.

But when day came, with a scarlet sky that touched the towers and spires and bathed the little square with the flush of a rose, the phantom of her regained youth mocked her before it fled. And when a young voice would have restored it by his pleading, and in pleading would have screened the advent of day from her eyes, she knew, even before she bade him leave her, what her purpose that day must be. She knew, when she was alone, that she must act upon that decision and not once dwell on the reason for it. She would go to Ostend and arrange to return to England tomorrow.

CHAPTER IX

THE country looked exactly the same as it had looked on the painted canvas of the Rotunda, except it was autumn and the trees were darker and the harvest was in. It had not changed in a hundred and forty years. But at the end of two and a half days of extensive sight-seeing in Ghent and Brussels there was little the eye or mind could assimilate in that historic scene, and Elizabeth felt she had been wrung dry. But for her mother, who seemed determined to get every franc's worth out of the excursion she would have gone back to the bus and sat in it until the rest of the party descended from the Lion Monument.

Waterloo had been left to the last. They were to return to the Metropole Hotel for lunch and in the afternoon return to Bruges. They would be given half an hour on their own before the bus left, so, the guide explained, they could do a little shopping. He said this with no conviction that anyone had anything to spend, although all his friends, the lace touts, would be assembled outside. It was all part of the routine.

It was hot in the sun on the top of the Lion Monument, and the guide having come to the end of his recitation had gone down again, followed by the rest of the party anxious, evidently, to indulge in another orgy of picture postcard buying. Lady Fulmer did not move. She took a cigarette from the case in her large handbag, which contained their passports and a guide book, and she began to smoke in a manner which often indicated that she was giving some subject deep thought.

"There is nothing wrong," she said, "is there between you and Adrian?" She was not an over-imaginative woman, but at the same time she told herself she was not exactly blind, and there had been occasions during the last week when both Adrian and Elizabeth showed a strange reluctance to be left alone together.

"Why do you ask me that?" Elizabeth wanted to know.

"But is there? I hope there isn't. It has struck me once or twice that you and he seemed rather silent. You know long engagements can be very trying to men, when they are very much in love. And he hadn't seen you for some time, and then seeing you every day."

Elizabeth turned her suddenly reddened face away. She knew. It was all in those horrible little books. In the last instalments. The first had been filled with the love-life of flowers and plants. There ought to be a law against them, and against mothers who—— She said, "There is nothing wrong."

"Good, darling. Because I know the future has seemed very vague and unsatisfactory, hasn't it?"

Elizabeth did not answer. She was very close to tears. She looked down on the field of Waterloo; and at first she did not understand what her mother was telling her. And when understanding at last came—after she had asked her mother to repeat what she had said—she could not believe it. The field of Waterloo was hidden in a blur of tears. "Oh, why," she cried, "why didn't you think of this before?"

"Before—what?" Lady Fulmer asked sharply. "I had to wait until your father wrote, and I gave him the address of the Metropole, because I didn't expect an immediate reply from him. Then there is something up between you two?"

There had been, Elizabeth thought. There had been. But this—this would mend it. "No," she said. "No, there isn't."

"I am glad, darling. Because I can see now it was silly of daddy to try and turn Adrian against his plans."

"But you backed him," Elizabeth cried. "Having presented it all to daddy as a *fait accompli*—you lost your nerve. And it was all daddy this, daddy that. If only you'd left it alone! Left it all alone!" 'And if only I,' she thought piteously, 'had left it alone!'

"I have often wondered," Lady Fulmer said, "what I have done to deserve such an ungrateful and rude daughter. You were always difficult. There are times—and this is one of them—when I don't envy the man you marry, and I don't envy Adrian."

Below in the road the driver of the grey bus was hooting the horn. Lady Fulmer stood up. "Pull yourself together child. We shall be left behind if we don't hurry."

Elizabeth got to her feet. "I am sorry," she said in a low voice. "Perhaps I am ungrateful. I won't be." She could see the bus down below on the road, the bus that would take her back to Bruges. 'It is not too late,' she thought. And she smiled through her tears. She was ashamed of her churlishness, her ill-temper and her frequent displays of boredom on that excursion. Her mother had filled her heart with hope again.

*   *   *   *   *   *

Adrian put his signature to the letter he had been writing to his father and put it in an envelope. He had told him that he had not been turned from his purpose, and although he was remaining in Belgium for another three or four days, in order to meet de Castelberg, he would be home the following week-end. But the whole time he had been writing that letter he had wondered why Clare had not told him of her plans for that day. She had had breakfast before he was down, and when he went out into the square her car was not there. He had thought, at first, that she had gone to buy petrol, and for a long time he hung about and then went for a walk along the canal bank, where he thought he might see the car returning. Back in the hotel Miss King told him she had seen them going off very early with bathing suits and towels, but she did not know where they had gone.

It was midday when he finished the letter; and he went downstairs. Although he wasn't hungry he thought he might as well have lunch early. The dining-room was empty and when the red baize door swung open there was the smell of meat cooking in the kitchen, and it brought a return of his appetite. Rene passed through, and seeing him alone went over to talk to him. He was beginning to loathe Rene, and it was with difficulty he made himself polite to him when Rene inquired at what hour were Lady Fulmer and Elizabeth expected to arrive in the Grand' Place, and should a taxi be ordered to meet them. "Or are you, monsieur," Rene asked, "going to meet them to carry the luggage?" Adrian then found he could not remember what time the bus was due. About six, or six-thirty, he thought.

Rene stood by the table looking out of the window. He wore a pink shirt and a hand-painted tie of bright emerald-green silk on which were a number of bright yellow fox's heads. "It is hot again," he said. "Very hot. But it will be very pleasant for Madame Ainslie in Ostend."

"Where?" Adrian asked; and he could have killed himself for asking, and for answering fat Rene with his knowing, leering eyes.

"Ostend," Rene said. "When I inquired of them outside early this morning if they were going to Wenduine or Knocke one of the little girls told me no, they were this time going to Ostend. It is far to go to bathe. But perhaps Madame felt she needed a change."

Adrian said nothing, and after a moment or two Rene strolled away. The dining-room was beginning to fill up. "You are not hungry, monsieur?" the waiter said, eyeing Adrian's almost untouched plate.

"No. Not very. It is so hot." Adrian got up then and went upstairs and found his bathing trunks and a towel. On his way down he overtook Miss King. "Going to bathe?" she said. "It ought to be very nice in the sea."

When he was waiting for the Knocke-Zoute tram to come up from the station and the sun was beating down on his bare head, he suddenly felt dizzy. The street was very dusty and filled with the glare of the sunlight. But the tram came along and he boarded it, and because it was crowded he had to stand most of the way. He clasped the back of a seat where two women were talking in Flemish without pause, and every time the driver rang the bell and the tram jerked over crossing-points the jolting seemed to jar through his whole body in the heat. But just before the outskirts of Zoute were reached he was able to sit down, and by the time he got off the bus at the bottom of the Avenue Elisabeth he felt better. And he knew he would be all right the moment he got in the cool sea. Purposely he had not thought of Clare for the last hour—or of her going off for the day without telling him—because what had been between them was too beautiful, and almost too sacred an experience to be remembered anywhere but in complete solitude. He would think about her when he was in the sea.

He wanted to swim a long way, far from any other swimmer. But because the guards in the boat shouted at him he had to turn round towards the shore again, and then he thought he would swim a mile parallel with the shore, to where the last house was. If he got tired he could turn in to the shore, and walk back to the cabin. But although he was not tired, he did, now and then, turn over on his back and float. And it was while he was floating, looking up at the sky, he felt happy again, happy and exalted and free. Into her hands and upon her mercy he had surrendered himself; open, he had known, if her heart were to be sealed against his pleading, her body rigid and unresponsive to his desire, to the banishment of her dismissal. And now, as another man had gained confidence and strength and courage from her, he had done so, and would for ever afterwards be firmer in every resolve he made because of her.

He would now swim to the last villa, keeping close to the shore. Let the guards in the boat follow and shout, if they had nothing better to do, no straying children to watch, no occupants of capsized rubber canoes to rescue. But the last villa was farther away than he thought. Leave it, he thought once, leave it for another day. Then he knew he was tired, and he was farther away from the shore than he had thought. But he knew enough not to panic, and there was no need to fear anything because the men in the boat would see him if. . . . Not that he wanted the disgrace of being picked up and being lectured to. The tide was pulling out fast, and he was struggling against it. But, don't panic! He could feel the unseen pull of the sea against him, but he kept on. . . . And he couldn't any longer . . . keep on. If he turned over and floated he would lose distance, with the tide going . . . out. He had almost lost the power of thinking when he put a foot down and felt the shore. He went under and came up again and swam three more strokes, which as he made them, seemed to be tearing his swollen heart out of his chest.

Afterwards, when he was lying on the sand, he could not account for it. He felt cold and the press of his body against the warm shingle at first brought no warmth to his limbs. His fingers stretched out were numb. When he had come out of the water he had collapsed in the shallow hollows of wet sand from which the sea had receded. A man spoke to him, asking if he were all right, and he had tried to laugh, with what seemed to be his last breath. All he could see was darkness, then as light came so did the coldness of the wet sand send him to stagger forward to where it was dry and warm. There he lay, and wondered what ailed him, and cursed himself for being a fool.

He lay with his eyes closed and very slowly his breathing became more even, and there was a tingling sensation in his skin where the sun had dried the salt water, and he could hear, as though it were very far away, the conversation in French of two women lying a few yards away from him. Feeling came back into his hands, and he opened his eyes and looked at them. Was that what would come one day? A slow paralysis in the limbs? The shortness of breath? The mind incapable of coherent thought? He shuddered.

He made himself rise then, and he trudged slowly along the sands, and presently he saw a towel lying unclaimed, which was his own. He found the cabin and got dressed. He lit a cigarette, but it had no taste, so he threw it away and climbed the steps of the embankment and crossed the road. When he came to the first café he sat down and ordered a *fine*. It warmed him and it steadied him, and made him feel better. He wouldn't think about it any more, or remember the trick memory had played when the blackness, when he came out of the water, dissolved in a blinding light that showed him the face of the wireless operator; or how the feel and the play of the sea had been the force of the search-lights that held one in a Mephistophilian power, and one engine was hit and they were losing height, and the crew were stolid but watchful. And it was on him! Don't panic!

It was dusk when he arrived back in Bruges; and he

knew he had not had the courage at any time during that day to think over what it was his duty to think over, and every time he had remembered it he had thrust it from his mind. But it came back to his mind as he entered the hotel and he saw suit-cases in the hall and heard their voices talking in the office—and he remembered he should have met the bus. For a moment, it was like the day they arrived, when they had gone in there to register, and he had helped Marie and Jules carry the luggage upstairs. This time Marie was not there—or Jules—so he carried the suit-cases alone; and came down again because Lady Fulmer wanted a cup of tea brought to the *salon*.

He had been kissed by both of them, and they wanted to tell him about their trip. They had bought picture postcards and they spread them out on the little table. And really, Lady Fulmer said, it was a wonderful way for Elizabeth to have seen everything, and they couldn't have done it so cheaply on their own, although the other people on the trip had been rather dreadful—Americans with cameras round their necks, and some English Midlanders, by their horrible accents. She had a slight headache, and there was thunder in the air. Didn't he feel it? She swallowed an aspirin with the first cup of tea. There was a cloying sweetness in her manner towards him, which embarrassed him, and he tried to avoid her eyes. Elizabeth was sitting opposite him, drinking tea and smiling; and he did not think he had ever seen her look prettier. They both wanted to know what he had been doing with himself. And it was like that first evening all over again.

"Well, what have you been doing?" Elizabeth asked, for the second time.

He tried to tell her. He told her he had spent the first day at Zoute, and with whom he had spent it; and it was as though he were telling her of another man's day, not his own. "And yesterday," he said, "I went out to Pierre's in the afternoon. I worked in my room all morning."

"On the libretto? Not on the missing scene?"

"Yes. It is finished—now."

"That's wonderful! Really and truly finished?" Her eyes

ere shining, like two lamps, he thought, that had been
ghted inside. And sooner or later he would have to quench
hat light of happiness in her eyes.

Lady Fulmer congratulated him. A clock on the wall
truck seven and the waiter had switched all the lights on
1 the dining-room. Adrian beckoned him. "Yes," Lady
ulmer said. "That would be nice, before we go up and
ath. We must drink to you and to Elizabeth. To your
appiness." And she smiled. "What a wonderful holiday
his has turned out to be, hasn't it, Elizabeth? Hasn't it,
ny darling?"

He ordered a whisky and soda for Lady Fulmer, a
ocktail for Elizabeth and a *fine* for himself. He saw Lady
ulmer raise her eyebrows at that, and look at him search-
ngly. Then she said, while they were waiting for the drinks,
"The hotel seems very empty."

"Yes. Everyone seems to be pulling out now. Miss King
oes tomorrow."

"How did you get out to the château yesterday?"
Elizabeth asked.

He told her, and added. "The twins went to the
ermesse."

"Didn't you go?"

The questions were coming fast. And he wondered how
much longer he could remain sitting there answering them
vith half-truths.

"He is very kind," Lady Fulmer commented. "He is
very kind to strangers—evidently." She laughed. "But she
s a very pretty woman."

"He doesn't know that, Mummy," Elizabeth said.

Lady Fulmer laughed again, very good humouredly.
"Oh, I expect there are ways of finding out. Perhaps Adrian
as told him."

The drinks came, and Lady Fulmer raised her glass.
She looked first at Elizabeth and then at Adrian. "This is
a double toast," she said. "A very important and happy one."

Adrian was sitting facing the door, and as Lady Fulmer
spoke the street door opened and Clare came through it
vith Jane and Tilly. She went straight upstairs, and only

the children paused to see him and to wave. But he had
heard. He had heard all that followed. And he looked a
Elizabeth, at her smiling eyes. He heard his own voic
answering, but he did not know what he was saying. H
made himself smile. He swallowed the cognac and it seemed
to set his mouth on fire.

Lady Fulmer was laughing. Then she was serious again
"You are not drinking brandy, Adrian, for any reason
All this Belgian food is far too rich. I swear by ordinary
bicarb. of soda."

They all went upstairs together and Elizabeth put her
hand in his and gave it a little squeeze. "We'll meet you
downstairs," she said, "in about three-quarters of an
hour."

He left them, and went on up the next flight, and on
that floor there was silence. The bathroom door was open
and there was warm steamy air coming out of it. The other
doors were shut, and he knocked gently on Clare's. "Come
in," her voice said; and he entered.

.   .   .   .   .   .

She was seated in front of the dressing-table and she
was already dressed to go out to dinner at the château.
And as he stood before her he said, "I don't think I have
ever pitied Pierre before—that he can't see you, as I see
you now." He had never before noticed her clothes, because
they were simple and unobtrusive, and insignificant, he
thought, compared with her beauty. Her clothes were a
frame for her—not as clothes were for many women, something that called for attention. For a moment he felt shy
before her, conscious of his own attire, not very clean
flannels, a creased jacket, and sand in his shoes. Was this
she, whom he had loved and possessed? This beautiful
but strange woman? But when he looked at her eyes he
wanted to kneel before her and tell her all over again, and
to be with her in solitude and silence. The words he had
spoken to her had not come easily; and he felt a wave of
giddiness sweep over him. "Do you mind," he asked her,
"if I sit down?"

She sprang to her feet and pulled her chair forward. When he was seated she put a hand on his forehead. Concern and fear were in her voice, "Is there anything—wrong? You have grown so pale."

"I'm all right," he managed to say. "I swam a bit too far this afternoon."

She went over to the wash-basin and filled a glass with water. She held it while he drank. "That's better," he said. "Thank you." Then, "What did you do today? Why did you go to Ostend and not tell me?"

"I thought," she began, and faltered. "Dearest, I thought I was acting for the best. Oh, we just went, and it was very hot and thundery and headachy." There was nothing more she could tell him about that fruitless day, when she had been unable to secure accommodation for the car on any boat leaving before next Tuesday, the day of her reservation. She must therefore remain here, since it was unlikely that Madame De Jonkheere would relieve her of the obligation to pay for the rooms for the next five days, and she had not the francs to go elsewhere. When Adrian had stripped the years of her maturity away from her, and she had slipped back to her girlhood for his young love, she had not only forgotten her responsibilities, but thrust his from her mind also. In that spell of enchantment she had not thought of their being caught and imprisoned in an intrigue that would tarnish the essence of those brief hours.

"I know why you went," he said.

She took the glass back to the wash-basin and returned to his side. She looked at him, thoughtfully, and said gently, "You are not well. Have you ever had anything like this before? What made you swim so far?"

"Because I wanted to feel happy and exalted, to think of you right away from people. Perhaps it is a touch of the sun. I felt queer waiting for the bus. But I am all right now. Honestly, I am all right now." He felt her arms enclose him as he laid his head against her breast. "And you went away from me all day. But now you are back, and I am with you again."

He was with her, he thought, as he would always be

with her, in the spirit. But he knew, even as he felt her lip
rest against his forehead, that he had created her in the
spirit and he had not reached her in the possession of he
body, and that the ecstacy of the union of the flesh wa
but an illusion of possession. In the spirit she would remai
with him, through eternity. That was the life everlasting
"But all day," he said again, "you went away from me."

'I had to go,' Clare thought. 'As I should go from hir
now and never return. As I should send him from me, bac
to his responsibilities, which we have never spoken of b
name.'

There was a knock on the door, and she released hir
and went to open it. Marie stood there and announced tha
the car had come. "I am ready," Clare said. "Please tell th
chauffeur I will be down in a few minutes." She shut th
door again, and went back to Adrian. He was still sittin
down, and she bent her head and kissed him. "Good-bye,'
she whispered.

"But you are only going from me to Pierre—to th
kermesse. I wonder what made him suddenly want to go
because crowds so often confuse him, though I know h
wanted you to see it."

"The *kermesse* was perhaps an excuse for kindness."

"Kindness?" he repeated. "Yes. But—can it be——
Yes, I do see now. Do you mind, if he has—guessed?"

She shook her head. "No. Because all that has happened
has been a kind of dream, and he is part of it too."

"Am I—then?"

"Yes—and no. But apart. As I have been—with you.'

"Apart, yes," he said. "As heaven is apart—and fa
from this earth, this world?"

"But we live in this world, Adrian."

'Which I could renounce,' he thought. 'All of it.' He fel
dizzy again, but he did not tell her that. He felt alone anc
remote and afraid; and he reached for her hand, for th
very feel of her flesh, for comfort. "Come and see me," he
said, "when you get back and tell me all about it. I shal
be waiting for you."

He saw her hesitate, and her eyes looked away from hin

at their surroundings, as though, he felt, she was looking at them for the last time, and would not see that room again with those same eyes, those same thoughts.

"I will come," she said, "but to talk of what we have never talked about—the world we both have to live in, to return to, but separately." Was he, she wondered, on the way to accepting the finality of their intimacy, their love? She prayed he was. For what was the nature of his intuition that had read her thoughts as she had given that room a last glance? Did he know she would not be the same woman, the woman he had loved, when she entered it again, after having made her real farewell with him? Or was this, now, their real and final farewell of the spirit as well as the body? Henceforward she must pray for strength, for mental strength, to live through the remaining days in Bruges—to put from her this dream.

She could not—neither could he—speak again, now, in that place. Neither did they, when he had put his lips to her hand, touch each other again. In silence they went from that room; and he stood and watched her going down the stairs.

.   .   .   .   .   .

Pierre de Fermandois had said to his servant, "Tell me when you hear the car bringing Mrs. Ainslie," and it seemed a long wait in the silent house until Prendergast announced the car was approaching. He went into the hall, and he could feel the drift of air from outside, and heard the crunch of the tyres on the gravel. He heard her voice, her footsteps; and then her hand was in his and she was apologizing for having kept the car waiting. The voice was animated, he thought, as though she were pleased to be there; but in her footsteps, as they walked towards the dining-room, there was an impression of tiredness she could not conceal. When they sat down at a small table placed near a pair of open french windows, and he asked her what she had done that day—as any host might ask a dinner guest in politeness—and she told him she had been to Ostend, he was not surprised.

In the background Prendergast hovered. Noiselessly he went from them, and noiselessly he appeared again The corners of the room were in darkness; the chandeliers unlit, but the little strip lights shone above the portraits and out of the darkness of the walls the men and women in the dress of another age were a silent audience of that dinner for two. The air was warm, and heavy with the threat of thunder; so still, the flames of the candles on the table burned into two straight plumes. In the distance the lights of the *kermesse* made a white glow in the darkness of the sky, and the throbbing music continued without pause. Hovering in the background Prendergast listened to the murmur of their voices; and heard, more than once, the sound of gentle laughter; and his eyes softened. Once he heard the sound of his own name; and knew that an account of his adventures in the war with Madame Jean was being repeated. His lordship, under her insistence, was telling her many stories, of Belgium, of Flanders, of the countryside, of his own boyhood, of the family, of Master Robert. Of the war, but not of his own war. Some day he might tell her that? But she wasn't eating anything much. A pity! Just pretending to eat. Had the English lost the habit of enjoying good food?

He removed the champagne glasses, placed coffee before them; went from them and returned with liqueurs. "What time do you want the car, milord?"

"Not just yet. I will tell you." And when Prendergast had gone, Pierre said to Clare, "The day in Ostend has tired you, hasn't it? I feel you would rather not go to the *kermesse*?"

She at once felt dismay that her tiredness had been so apparent. "Did you," she asked, "want to go very much?"

"Only if it would have given you pleasure."

"This," she said, "all this, is giving me pleasure enough. Just talking to you."

And when they had risen from the table she placed her arm in his, as she had before, when he had taken her into dinner with more of an old-fashioned courtesy in that gesture, than in reliance upon her guidance in his own familiar house.

They went into the *salon*, which, that evening, seemed
as deserted and as lifeless as a room in a house whose owners
had long since left and bequeathed it as a monument to a
forgotten age. And she wondered if he had read her thoughts,
when he asked what the flowers looked like. "They are
dead—most of them," she told him. And at her side he
said, "I thought so. I can smell them. So we will not stay
in here."

But her eyes had strayed from the dying clumps of
white and yellow and bronze chrysanthemums in the many
urns and vases to the walls, and came to rest on one portrait,
on the face of a girl who was dressed in the fashion of the
nineteen-twenties. It was a face that Watteau or Fragonard
might have painted, for apart from the delicacy of the
colouring, the fragility of the hands and wrists, the slender-
ness of the limbs, there was a certain roguishness of expression, a happy, very feminine look in the brown eyes, seduction
in the soft lips and in the careless grace of the curling tendrils
of golden hair. She must have been tiny, Clare thought,
five feet one or two, and gay and happy and loved her
whole life through.

"You are looking at Ghislaine?"

"Yes. How lovely she must have been. Adrian—told
me."

His name had not been spoken before; and Clare spoke it
now as though there was no significance attached to it,
surprised that she could speak thus, as though he were
merely a mutual acquaintance.

"I know," Pierre said. "He told me he had." And he
remembered the occasion, in Julie's garden. Should he,
he wondered, have known then? Foreseen this, then?
But he went on: "I suppose that fashion looks quaint, if
not absurd now. Just before the war Robert was always
complaining about it, and Ghislaine wanted to have the
dress painted again and made to cover her legs. But I
wanted it left alone." There was a pause; and then he
said, "Come, let us leave this mausoleum of dead flowers,
which was not expecting anyone this evening. You have
asked me so much, about Flanders, the family—everything

H

that interests me, shall I now be an old-fashioned host and
bring out the family albums? Or would that bore you?"

She laughed. "It would not bore me."

In the library he opened a deep drawer in a cabinet
and took from it a number of albums, which he placed on
table. "I don't know," he said, "what order they are in
But you will find them all dated."

She sat on the floor with the albums all round her
and he sat on the arm of a chair behind her. The long
windows were open, and the sound of the *kermesse* seemed
louder than ever in that close, heavy air. It was as though
the whole earth outside, the whole of Flanders was moving
to the rhythm of that music, moving with laughter and
high spirits and shouts. But the library held the quietness
of a sanctuary. She began with a wedding book, and smiled
at the fashions of that day, and looked long at the faces of
the bride and groom, whose formal clothes could not detract
from the aura of happiness in their whole bearing. And
as she went on, turning over pages that depicted other
happy scenes—in which a little boy made an early appearance—not only in Belgium but in other countries, he said
"They only show you the times when she was well." A little
later Clare paused before a picture of a palace that might
have been—but clearly was not—a slightly smaller Ver-
sailles or Schönbrunn, hesitated over the pronunciation
and spelt it out loud. "That," Pierre said, "was in Poland
The summer of 1937." And they fell to talking of Poland
as she held the album in her lap, dispassionately but sadly
She remembered then, as Pierre said, "I should like you to
meet my two exiles. They are touchy about accepting hospitality in the house, and it gives them pleasure if I take my
friends to them, gives them the honour they prize so dearly
and an illusion of a return of their lost independence,"
how Claude had explained to her why it had been necessary
to betray England's first ally, and had gently rebuked her
for calling it a betrayal.

She picked up the last album, and when Pierre asked
her which one it was, she told him, "Yugoslavia, 1939."
And she listened while he described the last holiday abroad

he and Ghislaine had. "She had been ill again that winter
and when spring came she wanted to go somewhere we hadn't
been before. So we went off in the car. It was May. The
country was unbelievably beautiful, and the inhabitants,
Serbs or Croats, with a sturdy individualism all their own."
He went on to speak more of the Serbs and Croats, to take
his thoughts, she knew, away from more poignant memories
of that last holiday. And to help him to keep to the subject
of the country and the races that inhabited it, she said,
"My fiancé was there in the war. He was dropped by para-
chute to help Tito. A few British officers were, you know."

They both stood up. She with her arms full of albums.
He took them from her and put them back on the table.
"Thank you," she said, "for letting me see those. For
letting me——" and could not finish before the sudden
sternness in his face. 'What have I done?' she thought.
'What have I said?' And knew what she had said. She went
past him and stood in the open doorway. No stars were
visible now. There was only the glow of the lights of the
kermesse; and the air was so heavy it seemed that the sky
itself was descending on to that scorched earth, pressing
down and down, as the music of the *kermesse* throbbed
and throbbed. He was at her side, speaking coldly, but
wishing her happiness. "Marriage," he said, "is very much
a matter of temperament. You were happy before, so you
will be happy again."

Her sudden quietness, and her inner stress were apparent
to him; and it was as though the beating of her heart lay
under his hand's touch. "Is he a professional soldier?"
he asked.

"No. He is hoping to be a Member of Parliament after
the next election."

"Interesting," Pierre said. "I think you will find it
so, won't you? Provided, of course, you are quite sure of
your feelings."

She did not answer. She stepped forward on to the
terrace and leaned her arms on the stone balustrade. She
knew he had followed her, and that his hands had come to
rest beside her own. "What makes you think I am not sure?"

she asked. "He is brave. He had already fought in the deser
before that adventure. Why do you laugh at me?"

"But you would never choose," Pierre said, "to link
yourself with any man who did not conform to certain
standards. Though they are not everything. You make
me think of an Englishman I once knew, who was his younger
sister's guardian, and when a suitor presented himself
considered, first of all, whether he would be any good in a
fight, whether he would like him at his side in a tight corner."
As he spoke there was a flash of lightning to the left of the
glow from the *kermesse,* and a distant rumble of thunder
"May I ask you something?"

"Please do," she answered in a low voice.

"Why did you go to Ostend today?"

"To try and arrange to go home tomorrow."

"Because your fiancé is waiting for you, and you have
been away too long?"

"No," she cried. "You know that is not why. You have
known all along. Because you have guessed, haven't you?
How was it betrayed to you? In the reading of that scene?"

"Partly then," Pierre said. "For he could not have
completed that scene—unaided. Were you successful—
today?"

"No. It is the car. I would go tomorrow, but I can't
very well leave the car here."

"If I can help you in any way," he said, "in this—
predicament, will you let me? Where would you like to
stay for the remaining few days?"

"In Ostend. Because if I were on the spot I might get
someone's cancellation for the car. But I can't accept that
from you. For when could I pay you back?"

"I shall be in London next month."

"That makes it easier for me," she said quietly. "And
you have made all this seem——" She stopped, and searched
for words. "All this—my predicament, and your saving me
from it, with a dignity I don't merit." She stopped again.
"I don't seem to be able to talk properly, or say what I
mean."

Was her distress, he was wondering, indicative of how

deep was this experience? What had happened was not an uncommon occurrence on a holiday abroad. Often it was a tonic necessary for jaded nerves, forgotten impulses; and in the ordinary course there would be a return to matrimonial duties, or commitments, fortified by secret memories. But that behaviour, he knew, was not for her. She would not, now, he felt, marry her politician. And what of her future relations with Adrian, when his engagement was broken—as it would be? When she returned home she would be possessed of a sense of guilt, and she would torture herself, putting herself in the position of the girl who had been betrayed. Standing beside her, listening to the storm which was coming nearer, he knew she was already torturing herself. "Don't take it to heart," he wanted to say to her. "It would have happened without your intervention." Then pity took hold of him, thinking of all of them, in that triangle. It was flowing out to him from the woman at his side. How long could such hopeless love endure? It would not endure long if there came a sense of loss of dignity and pride, when the complications of the intrigue—even if she fled from Bruges—became too involved. It would be impossible in England to conceal their relationship. One of them would begin to tire of it; tire of the subterfuges, the explanations—and perhaps, in his case, the insinuations of his university companions, their mockery. Or she would terminate it, having first abandoned the security of her future, in ruthless disregard of her own feelings, in Adrian's interests.

There was another volley of thunder and a deafening crash above the roof of the château, and a splatter of rain fell. "Here it comes," Pierre said. "The rain the country needs. The rain to ruin the *kermesse*, as I feared." He took her hands and drew her back indoors, and he closed the long windows against the sudden downpour. Prendergast came into the room and shut the other windows. He moved slowly, and spoke of the storm and of the ruined *kermesse*.

When Prendergast had gone Clare said, "But it is over. It will be all over, when I see him when I get back. I shall not harm his—future. When I have told him——" She did

not finish. There was another burst of thunder over the
house that seemed to shake everything in the room, and
she felt a sense of impending doom as unnamed fears rose
and engulfed her. "Please," she cried, "please, I must go.
I mustn't stay here any longer." And as Pierre put a finger
on the bell by the fire-place, she said, "No, Jane and Tilly
are never frightened of thunderstorms. But I must go all
the same."

Prendergast came in answer to the ring, and the order
for the car was given. They went into the hall and waited.
The thunder continued, and the rain was lashing against
the windows. "Would the day after tomorrow suit you,"
Pierre asked her, "to move to Ostend. I must make the
arrangements for you. And you have to pack, as well."

She was only half listening to him, as though what he
was saying concerned someone else. Would the car never
come to take her back? If she had come in her own car
she would by now have been speeding along the road back
to Bruges. "But there is tomorrow," she heard him say,
"when you are not busy packing. Will you bring Jane and
Tilly to lunch here, and stay for the afternoon?"

She heard the sound of the car, as she put her hand in
his. But what words could she summon to express her
gratitude? What had she said, that had brought a smile that
lit up his whole face with compassion and tenderness,
except, "In your pity, pray for us?" Her fears had gone;
fled before his understanding and his strength, his wisdom
and his knowledge of the frailty of human behaviour. The
door was opened, and a gust of rain blew inwards as they
walked towards it; and her fears returned, the unnamable
fears that had engulfed her in the library, and she seemed
to be walking away from safety, from sanctuary towards
them. But whose was the greater reluctance that she should
face those fears, and alone?

"Until tomorrow," Pierre said, as he raised her hand
to his lips.

CHAPTER X

DINNER that evening in the Hotel Dierick d'Alsace might have been—except for the number of empty tables—any other evening when Lady Fulmer and Elizabeth and Adrian sat down together. But this time they were to drink champagne, to celebrate the coming marriage.

"Early in the new year," Lady Fulmer said, half-way through dinner, "and then you might join Julie and her boys at the *end* of the honeymoon, in Switzerland." She had already begun to plan the wedding itself, and the reception in the house. "So fortunate," she said, "those first-floor rooms have folding doors." 'I am not here,' Adrian kept thinking. 'It is someone else who is answering these questions, making these comments.' Someone else who was becoming acquainted with the geography of the Fulmers' house in London, and especially of the top floor; someone else who was agreeing that he ought to have at least a 'cubby-hole' of his own, to work in. He had no appetite, and he remembered that he had had little to eat all day. Once Elizabeth noticed what he had left untouched on his plate, and he told her he had eaten too many cakes at tea. The night was so warm and close he felt he could hardly breathe, but when Elizabeth complained, and asked the waiter to switch the fan on, he immediately felt cold.

He remembered that they did not know that he was not returning to England with them on Tuesday, and he wondered—when Lady Fulmer said, "We have only got a few days left, how shall we spend them?"—if this would be as good a moment as any to make that announcement. They would understand, when they knew de Castelberg was coming. But he could not bring himself to tell them even that, because he was walking in his mind across the Place du Bourg, going under the groined archway that pierced the Maison de l'Ancien Greffe, down the little street called Blind Ezel Straat for the first time. And standing outside the house on the bank of the Roya, where it

was said Malvenda hid the Holy Blood. . . . On the littl
bridge near the hotel two days ago, with Jane and Tilly
and Clare was walking along the bank under the elms. H
was on the balcony, showing her Bruges rising out of th
darkness, with all its mystery and awe. . . . And Elizabet
was saying. . . . She had never looked prettier. It hurt t
look at her and remember.

"What shall we do tomorrow, Adrian?"

"The *kermesse*," he found himself saying. "Didn't yo
want to go to the *kermesse*?"

Lady Fulmer fanned herself with a handkerchief. How
close it was tonight, she exclaimed. There must be thunde
in the air. "If you want to go out, you two, hadn't yo
better take mackintoshes?" But what they all really ough
to have, she went on, was an early night. She confessed t
a return of her headache and she told the waiter that sh
would not have coffee in case it kept her awake. "And you
my precious," she said to her daughter, "ought to go t
bed early." Adrian, too, ought to do the same. He didn'
look too well.

"Don't," Lady Fulmer said to Adrian, when they ha
eventually risen from the table and gone into the *salon*
"keep Elizabeth up too late. I know this is a night of al
nights! Are you going out?"

Neither of them answered at once. They looked at each
other, and both were waiting. Then to his surprise and
relief Elizabeth said, "I am going up too, Mummy. I am
very tired." She smiled at him, and he looked into her eyes,
which were happy and candid and innocent, and his heart
was stricken. They wished each other good night, formally,
with no endearments. He kissed her, and there was nothing
else to say. Not then. Not tonight. She went up the stairs
with her mother, and while he was still standing there,
watching them, Miss King came down the stairs and went
into the office. She was dressed in her travelling clothes, a
tweed coat and skirt and a dark jersey, and she was carrying
a large handbag. He could see her paying the bill and talking
in her good French to Madame De Jonkheere. When she
came out of the office, stuffing the receipted bill and change

into her bag, he asked her to have a drink with him. He wanted a drink and he didn't want it alone, and there was something about Miss King that was homely and restful and uncomplicated and kind, and he felt he could do with all those qualities in abundance at that moment. He remembered she liked *crème de menthe*.

Miss King sat down and took off her jacket. "It is hot!" she said, and she took a cigarette from his case. "I am on watch," she went on. "But they were so tired when they got back from Ostend, they just dropped off. Did your fiancé enjoy Brussels?" Miss King could look kindly on Elizabeth because she was young and pretty and engaged to Adrian, and it did her old parched heart good to see them together, but not even her innate good nature could find anything particularly endearing in the girl's mother.

While they were sitting there, Miss King sipping a *crème de menthe*, and Adrian a *fine*, the telephone rang in the office; and they heard Madame De Jonkheere speaking. "Allo. . . .'Allo," she was saying. "*Oui. . . . Oui . . . j'ecoute. . . . C'est l'Hotel Dierick d'Alsace. . . . Attendez, s'il vous plait, monsieur. . . . Un moment.*" Madame De Jonkheere popped her head round the office door. "It is for Madame Ainslie," she announced. "A telephone call from London. Madame is not yet returned?"

"No," Adrian answered. "Not yet."

The dark head popped back again, and they could hear her speaking to the unknown voice in London and repeating the letters of the caller's name. "I speak English, monsieur. . . . Yes. P . . . E . . . R. Double R . . . Y. Perr-y? . . . Yes, monsieur, I will tell Madame. . . . Tomorrow? At what time? . . . Yes, monsieur. *Bon soir, monsieur. Merci.* Thank you."

Miss King put down her empty glass and smiled. Dear Mrs. Ainslie, she thought, how happy that would make her, when she received that message on her return from the château and the *kermesse*! Tomorrow her own holiday was over. Such a happy one it had been, through the kindness she had received. And through this last little kindness of a young man asking an old maid to have a drink with him. She stood up and held out her hand. "I will say good-bye, Mr. Morbeigh, in case I don't see you in the morning. Thank you for that nice drink. It was kind of you. I hope Madame De Jonkheere won't forget to give Mrs. Ainslie that message."

"I shouldn't think she'll forget," Adrian said. "They are very good about messages here." A most peculiar thing had happened to Miss King's face. It was wobbling. 'God,' he thought, 'I'm drunk. But I can't be.' He blinked at Miss King and saw her a little clearer. He shook hands with her, and watched her go towards the stairs. She had said, "God bless you!" Someone came in from outside and passed him, and then he knew he must have some fresh air. It was supposed to be fatal—if he were drunk—but he knew he must have it. He went and stood by the open door and leaned against it.

"Going out, monsieur?" a voice asked. It was Rene, smoking a Belgian cigarette, and the smell of it seemed over-powering. "It is going to rain," Rene said. "This is not a gay city at night. Not like some. But it will be a storm—when it comes."

'Let it come!' Adrian thought. 'Let it come soon and end this unbearable closeness. Let it clear the air and my head, so I can think.' But he turned away from Rene in his natty suit, and the smell of that strong tobacco, and without speaking went back indoors and up the stairs, to his room.

The bedroom was stifling; the sun had beaten into it all day, and when Marie had come up to turn down the bed-covers she had shut the windows. When he had opened them he took off his jacket and undid his tie. Then he unlaced his shoes and kicked them off. They were a new pair, bought in London before he left, and he had only worn them a few times. On a hot night they were not as comfort-able as they might be. He meant to put them away in the cupboard, but the effort was suddenly too great, and he dropped them on the floor. Then he sat down at the table and picked up the manuscript, and when he read the dedication he smiled. But he wouldn't change it. It would be a little offering, a little—— He searched for a word, and dismissed 'compensation' as being crude and cruel. 'I am a little drunk,' he thought. 'I feel awfully queer.'

He got up and went to the wash-basin and turned on the cold tap, and ran the water until it was really cold. He bent over and let the water run over his head. The coldness of it was a shock, but it was making him feel better, making his head clearer. He went on rubbing it with his hands and letting the water run through his fingers in spurts and splashes. He did not hear the first gentle taps on the door that Elizabeth made, only her last impatient, insistent ones; and he looked up and called out, "Come in. But, who is it?"

She stood in the doorway, and she felt suddenly afraid. The gesture she had wanted to make of tiptoeing quietly up behind him had been arrested when he turned round, and he had left her bereft of the excuse that had been on her tongue, and bereft, also, of her confidence. But when she saw his wet head, and water running down from his hair on to his face, she laughed. She watched him reach for a towel and dry his head and turn the tap off.

"I'm sorry," he said. "But I wasn't expecting you. I thought you'd gone to bed." He stared at her. She was wearing a scarlet evening dress he did not remember having seen her in before, and he wondered why she was dressed so, unless she wanted him to take her dancing at Knocke.

Under his thoughtful gaze she was silent. But she stepped forward and pirouetted round. "How do you like it? It was the red dress we said keep for another time." She smiled and her cheeks were flushed through having run up the stairs and with twirling herself round so that the voluminous skirt of the red taffeta dress swirled out like a dancer's. But her colour ebbed away under his silence. "How do you like it?" she repeated.

"It is a lovely dress," he said gently. "It suits you. But you must go, now you have shown it to me."

"But why? This night, of all nights? Aren't you going to kiss me—properly?" She lifted up her face and waited. He kissed her lightly, and then taking her hands released their hold of him. "What's the matter?" she demanded "Are you ill? Or what is it?"

She had seen how pale he was, and how strained he looked, and how tired were his eyes. But she did not know that the sight of her dressed in that scarlet evening dress, like a child come for approval, for praise, turned his heart to ice for what he must, sooner or later, confess to her. For it was the childish aspect of her that was apparent, and to deny her would be to abuse and hurt a child. If he struck her across the face the crime would be less culpable. She was a child, with the body of a woman, and all her artifice was pitiable. He could regard her cruelly and tenderly in turn, hating and despising himself.

"It is nothing, Elizabeth. But won't you please go? Actually I'm not feeling very well. I swam too far this afternoon. And if you want the truth, I've drunk too much." He had, but he knew he was sober again.

"I'm sorry," she said. "Perhaps I had better go, and let you go to bed." But she sat down on the bed and looked at him. The air was heavy with their silence, and heavy also with the thunderstorm that was near. A peal of it suddenly deafened them. "I want," she said, when the rumble of thunder was spent and lightning flashed in the sky, "first of all to say I am sorry for the way I went on."

"You have nothing to reproach yourself with," he said.

"Because I am selfish? And have been brought up to be?"

It was the appeal of a girl from the heart, which she had made in the beginning, when her mood, striving for expression, for release from the bondage of the artificiality with which her mother surrounded her, had matched his own mood at that time. They had found release in simple pleasures shared, in the exchange of confidences and stolen embraces, and his heart had been touched in gentle pity for her loneliness. And he had loved her, with the love of a boy for a girl, for sweet companionship's sake, to the accompaniment of a popular, sentimental song.

"I am the selfish one," he said. "And I want—I shall ask you to forgive me."

There was another crash of thunder, and rain had begun to fall. He went to the windows and closed them against the sudden torrent. After the heat the rain had a sweet refreshing sound, as though it were washing the world clean. Out in the country it would be falling on the parched earth and on the dead summer flowers, on the fading leaves, on the grass that had grown over the grief of the war, drenching the dust of the roads, leaving that unforgettable smell. It would be ruining the *kermesse*, scattering the crowds for shelter beneath dripping canvas, and the music would grind to a finish. The hard earth would be sodden with trampling feet pressing the litter into the mud, and all the tawdriness and cheap finery and the glitter of the fair would be smirched. The rain was beating into the water below the balcony, sweeping into gutters, running over the cobble-stones, pouring off the roofs. Already the room was cooler, and he felt cold.

"What have I got to forgive you over?" she asked. The rain was the accompaniment to her voice, followed by another crash of thunder. "Why don't you answer me?" she cried. And when he had turned from the window, "Why are you looking at me like that? What is the matter with me? Why have you been so peculiar ever since mother and I got back? As though, half the time, you were not listening, when she told you we could——" She got up and went nearer to him. "Adrian, what is it? It can't be——" Her eyes were dark and troubled and her lips trembled. "You don't love me, want me any more?"

"Oh, my dear! Oh, Elizabeth, go to bed and leave me. We can't discuss this now, and here." He began, in his agony to think of trivial things, and to speak them. The storm would have wakened her mother and she might go into Elizabeth's room and find it empty. She might, at any moment, come up and find her. And the thought of Lady Fulmer's entrance into that scene, with all her penetration, as well as her understanding of lovers' difficulties, made him shake in fear. He searched in his mind for words to speak that would not hurt her, but before he found them she cried again, "Don't you love me any more?"

Involuntarily his lips forced a smile. "I do. I still do—in that way." He picked up the manuscript on the table. "Look. I wrote this for you. And it is still for you."

"In—what way?" she asked. "*That* way? What is that way?" She buried her face against his shoulder, and he held her and stroked her hair, as he might hold and hush a child in its distress, of which he was not the direct cause. "You are tired of me?" she asked.

"Not tired of you," he said wearily.

"Then, what is it? What has come between us?"

"Nothing," he answered. "Nothing new."

"Then something always was?"

"Yes, Elizabeth." And he heard himself speaking, as though it were another man, words that were conventional, and was puzzled that clichés should fall so easily from his lips, such as: his own unsuitability for marriage with her; that she would one day love a better man than he; that she must forget and forgive him. " 'Language'," he thought, " 'thou art too narrow and too weak to ease us now!' "

"I see," she said. "I see," and lifted her face. For a moment he saw a light in her eyes that transfigured her face, as though she had experienced a silent and secret victory, and had found the truth in herself and in him. But it was her piteousness and her defencelessness, as well as the challenge expressed in the putting on of the seductive scarlet dress that wrung his heart, when she said, with a curious smile twisting her lips, what he would never, in an extremity, have confessed to anyone—perhaps not even to himself, "You were caught, weren't you? By mother?" She was still smiling because she felt she knew him better than she had ever done, knew his charm and his weakness. Especially his weakness in a situation that might call for ruthlessness. But she knew, even as he still held her, even as she knew him better than she had ever done, the uncompromising and terrible truth. She had known it—or feared it—the first night in Bruges, that some power stronger than their love for each other had begun to draw him apart from her.

But when he had thrust her from him she knew that her

whole world, her whole existence, her future, were falling
into pieces round her. Hysteria rose in her, and anger and
scorn. She longed to humiliate him, and she knew she
could not because he was immune in some strange way.
But he was weak, she knew, weak as water.

"Will you do something for me?" she asked. "One last
thing?"

"Tell me," he said gently.

"Will you, just for a few days, until we leave, pretend
it is as it was before? Pretend in front of mother?" Such
pretence, she wildly thought, might help to re-establish
their relationship. And it would give her time to make her
own mind up, time to regain her pride. Then, only then,
might she release him with dignity.

For a moment or two he hesitated. He could hear the
rain, the blessed rain, he thought, that was washing the
earth clean. The summer was over. Summer was dead. And
he could not see another one, nor the miracle of spring. He
felt strange and remote again, and alone; as when he had
reached out for Clare's hand, for the touch of her flesh for
comfort. And there was another hand, Elizabeth's, thrust
out to touch his now, and he was denying her. For it was
but an illusion of comfort—and she was asking him to
create an illusion that would be a double betrayal.

"No," he said, "I can't. No, Elizabeth."

He walked to the door, to open it; to ask her, finally, to
forgive him, and to go. If she would not go, then he would
leave her there. The moment his back was turned she made
for the long windows, which he had pulled together to shut
out the rain; and the sudden rush of cold air into the room
made him look round. "What are you doing?" he cried.
Then he saw what she was doing, and he rushed towards
her. She had a knee on the balustrade, and whether in that
moment she was contemplating an idle threat, or an act of
despair and madness he had not time to consider. But her
weight was upon the balustrade when she lifted her other
foot from the ground; and as he cried, "You know it's
unsafe, for God's sake!" the bars broke and she fell with a
scream.

Her scream was in his ears as he jumped; and it guided him in the filthy, brackish water in the darkness to find her. He fought with her first struggles of panic and fear, and kept hold of her. Was she hurt? Then he swore at her in anger and fear, and it needed the whole of his strength to support her because she was heavier than he had ever imagined a helpless body would be in water that seemed to have the weight and the substance of treacle round his legs. Her dress was holding water. If he could only rip it from her! But she had ceased to struggle, and for a moment he recalled the first day at Zoute when he had towed her far from the shore, as he was towing her now in darkness. There were no lights to show him where they were, only far, far up, and distant. His breathing was becoming laboured and he tried to call out for help, but his voice came weak and thin out of his throat. Some driftwood caught at his legs; and as the rain beat down he wanted to drink it, and the taste of it was fresh and cold on his lips. But the force of it filled his eyes and blinded him.

Elizabeth began to moan and cry, and her fears were transmitted to him because his strength was ebbing. The rain was running out of his eyes with his own tears because of his increasing weakness. He felt her slipping. . . . She went from his grasp and they both fell and went under. But as he came up he heard her gasping and sobbing, and she caught at his hands. And he heard her not only gasping and spitting out the water she had swallowed but a strange, harsh laugh. "You—can—stand!" She began then to laugh, and she went on laughing in hysteria, as they stood in water that lapped over their waists. They were near a wall, slimy to their touch, of a height too great to climb. Without speaking they kept close to it, and kept their hands on it as they moved along, slowly, their feet slipping now and then; and he tried to remember where they were, how the wall ran on that side of the water, where there would be a break in it. He touched her naked shoulders, wondering if the slime was mud or blood. There was a sudden pain at the back of his head, and in his chest. Then she stumbled and cried out in pain. "Steps," she managed to tell him. "Steps."

He pushed her from behind, and she scrambled up them on her hands and knees. He tried to follow her, but he fell on the second step and lay there, half in, half out of the water. Up above him he heard her vomiting, and then her crying, like a lost child, between gasps. Sobbing, she called out to him, "Adrian, oh, Adrian!" He tried to answer her and could not, for every breath he now took was laboured and painful; and the pain of breathing increased. She called out to him again. "Go," he managed to say. "Go. For God's sake, leave me, and go."

There was silence. The edge of the step he was lying on was greasy with slime, and he began to shake with ague and felt the cold creeping through his limbs. He knew then, with clarity, between each laboured and painful gasp for breath, that he could not rise and climb the steps and follow her; and that there was no way back from the journey on which he had, unknowingly, set out. He could have answered her differently! Now he could cry aloud but no one would come. Or would they? Would the hand of a stranger touch him and lead him back—to what? Release me, he thought, God, release me from this pain! He opened his eyes, and he thought he saw a light, far above him. He shut his eyes, and the light played on his closed lids, as the light of searchlights, and he was giddy with the terror of them, falling like a bird that was winged.

The light was fading, bringing the peace he had known when his work was finished when Clare. . . . But who was she? He felt himself slipping deeper into the darkness. This was the way and he would not struggle.

When the water took him under again he did not know.

.   .   .   .   .   .

"Faster, faster!" Clare wanted to say to the chauffeur, when he was driving her with the care born of experience. Down in the village they came on to the crowds fleeing from the *kermesse* for the shelter of their homes. They were scurrying along under the trees with coats over their heads; girls with their finery ruined, squelching along in once-white shoes, carrying tattered, tawdry tokens of the fair.

Cyclists wobbled, with heads bent against the torrent. All
the bicycles in Belgium seemed to be on the road that
night. After a time she closed her eyes, and felt the movement
of the car increase in speed, and with it came an easing of
her tension.

But she opened the door of the car, when they reached
the hotel, without waiting for the chauffeur, thanked him,
and hurried inside. One small light was burning in the little
entrance hall, and the office and the *salon* were in darkness.
As she went up the stairs she noticed a trail of mud on the
red carpet, which ended on the first floor. She rushed up
the next flight and went into the twins' room. The window
curtains were billowing in the wet draught, and as she was
placing across Jane's bed the eiderdown that had been
rolled up at the foot of it, the child stirred and woke up.

"Mummy?"

"Yes, darling?"

"We heard it. The big storm. Miss King came. Did
you have a lovely dinner with Count, and ice-cream? Did
you go on the swings?"

In the next bed Tilly moved her head in the light that
shone into the room from the square. "What did you do?"

"I will tell you tomorrow," Clare said. "And tomorrow
we are to spend the day at the château. Now go to sleep
again." She kissed them in turn, and felt the warmth and
sweetness of their young bodies restoring her to calmness.
She was reluctant to leave them. In her tiredness she wanted
to lie down beside one of them and fall asleep—and not
dream—with that warmth and sweetness lulling her. But
she went from them and shut the door.

On the landing a strip of light showed beneath the
door of Adrian's room, but not from Miss King's. Therefore
she was asleep, Clare thought, and it would be unkind to
wake her to assure her that one had returned and all was
well. Outside Adrian's door Clare hesitated, possessed
suddenly of a strange reluctance to keep her promise to
him. But the light perhaps signified that he was waiting
for her, and if she hesitated too long she would not fulfil
the purpose of that visit—to tell him what she must tell

him, that would end, as possibly nothing else could, what had been between them. Even if she no longer believed in the security of her own future, her engagement was still a fact.

Immediately she opened the door the draught from the windows open on to the balcony blew papers off the table, and rain was sweeping in. When she had closed the door her first impulse was to prevent damage to his manuscript, and when she had picked up the scattered sheets she closed the balcony windows. The rain blew in her face as she did so, and the curtains, which she drew across them were wet. Then she sat down in the chair to wait for him, and tears came into her eyes for the words she must speak when he came. She had not realized how tired she was, and she leaned her head against the side of the bed. Not only was she tired after the day spent in Ostend, but tired emotionally, and beyond coherent thought.

She opened her eyes with a start. The room was cold and still empty, and she knew she had dozed off in sleep. For how long she did not know. And where was he? Where had he gone? It was still raining, and perhaps if he had gone out before the storm came he was sheltering somewhere. Or he was with——? And that was where he should be.

On the landing, as she was shutting the door, a voice spoke to her. "Good night, madame." "Good night, Rene," she had to bring herself to answer. In her own room, in the light above the dressing-table her own beauty mocked her, and she seemed to see reflected the face of a slowly ageing woman. There was a folded note propped up against a powder bowl, and she picked it up and read what was written on it. "Madame, M. Perry telephone you from London. Tomorrow he will telephone you again." She continued to stare at the note in her hand, as all feeling ebbed away from her. Cold and numb, alternately shivering and feverish, she began to undress.

CHAPTER XI

When Marie Berlearts took the trays of coffee and rolls upstairs the following morning her eyes were red with weeping. And to every guest she told of her sorrow, of the death of her grandfather in the village of Donk. She had to tell everyone in order to explain why she would be absent for the next few days.

Before the news came the morning had begun badly, with the breaking of a cup and saucer, and her attention had been drawn to a trail of wet mud on the stair-carpet; and a guest on the first floor rang to complain of the state of the public bathroom, with mud and dirt in the bath, and hairs in the wash-basin. That was a mystery, since the key was kept in a private place, Marie thought no one knew about, on a shelf in the cupboard where the brooms were stored. Then her sister had telephoned, and Madame De Jonkheere had strict orders that the staff were not to have use of the telephone, not even in emergencies. But, for once, she had allowed that rule to be broken, although she was far from gracious when it was known that Marie must leave on the first train for Donk, to be with her mother to assist in the funeral arrangements, and could not return until after the funeral on Monday. Tomorrow was Saturday, and Madame well knew it was too soon, and that the burial could not take place on Sunday.

She told everyone in turn. Downstairs, first, to Miss King, and received sympathy, "Poor little Marie!" and the expected tip. Then on the landing, to Mrs. Ainslie. "Oh, but Marie!" in Madame's good French, "I am so sorry," and a hand searched in a purse. "I am leaving, Marie, sooner than I expected. I am leaving tomorrow. . . . The twins will want to say good-bye to you."

The Lady Fulmer said she was sorry. But she was not leaving until Tuesday, so there was no need to remember the tip. And Monsieur Morbeigh would not be leaving either. He was not yet down and he had not rung. He never liked to be disturbed early. The last tray of all was for Mademoiselle Fulmer. She was sleeping very heavily, Marie thought, as she put down the tray beside the bed. Nothing of her showed, except the top of her head. Marie wished her good morning, and still weeping she began once more to tell of her sorrow.

Elizabeth opened her eyes, but she did not move. She listened to Marie without speaking, until she made herself ask, "What is the name of your village?" And she repeated it, "Donk," wondering why it struck her as funny, how it was that anything could strike her that way. When Marie had gone she rolled the bedclothes down and looked at the cuts and bruises. There was a lump at the side of her head, which was very sore. It had been bleeding last night when she had washed her head and had a bath in the public bathroom. How fortunate it was that she had once seen Marie hide that bathroom key! She ached from head to foot, and when she remembered everything tears began to flow, choking her, down her cheeks into the cup of coffee she held in two hands that were shaking. She felt sick too. Too sick to eat anything. She never wanted to see him again. She did not know what had made her do that, except she had wanted to frighten him, and make him feel sorry. She felt sick. She was going to be sick. . . .

She wondered, after she had been into the public toilet across the landing, and had got back into bed again, if the filthy water she had swallowed had given her typhoid. If it had, then he would be sorry. If she died, he would be. But she didn't want to die. She wanted to go home, home to London and try to forget. But what had she, now she had lost him? She drew her knees up for warmth because she had begun to shiver, and she whimpered now and again, as a child would, with her face turned into the pillows and her knuckles pressed against her cheek.

When Lady Fulmer opened the door a little later Elizabeth was lying on her back with her eyes closed, but not sleeping. The tears had dried, but not the marks of tears on the swollen cheeks, the reddened lids. Wasn't she up yet? Lady Fulmer called from the door. It was raining, so she must put on something warm. It was so easy to catch cold when the temperature had dropped. She noticed, first, the untouched rolls and pats of butter on the tray.

"Not well, darling?"

"Oh, go away, Mother! I'm all right."

"Well, have a nice long morning in bed. Adrian and I can amuse ourselves. Shall I ask Marie to fill a hot-water bottle?"

"Marie has gone to a funeral. Didn't she tell you?"

"Yes. I quite forgot. It is no good ringing. I'll fill it under the hot tap for you." Lady Fulmer advanced towards the bed. "Darling! Elizabeth! What is the matter? What is it?"

"Oh, go away! Leave me alone."

Lady Fulmer sat down on the bed, and Elizabeth turned her head away.

"Something, I can see, is very seriously the matter. What is it? Is it anything to do with—Adrian?" And when Elizabeth did not answer, "But when? What opportunity have you had since last night?"

"Stop it!" Elizabeth cried. "I can't bear it. It's all off. Will that tell you what you want to know? I want to go home. Please take me home, today!"

"We can't go today," Lady Fulmer said, with all the practical reasons why they could not, coming into her mind. "There isn't time to go to the bank, and pack." Besides, she wanted to see Adrian, to get at the bottom of this. She could not think—hysterical and upset as Elizabeth sounded —that it could be anything more serious than a lovers' tiff, which could easily be patched up. Knowing that she would get no more information from Elizabeth she left her, and climbed the stairs to the next floor to see Adrian, and hear what he had to say.

*　　*　　*　　*　　*　　*

Pierre was talking in the room he called his office to one of his farmers when the telephone rang shortly after eleven o'clock. They had been deep in country matters, the beet crop and the weather, followed, as always, with a little gossip—this time concerning a scandalous story of alleged witchcraft said to be practised by a certain widow. The village priest at lunch the previous Sunday, over his second glass of wine, had opened out on that subject, but not so thoroughly, or quite so humourously as the farmer who lived close to those fantastic occurrences. From the earlier occasion, when the priest had gone, Pierre had received English guests for the afternoon, Adrian and Elizabeth and Lady Fulmer, and he had found it strange, in the first moments of their arrival, to adjust himself to their world. So now, when an English voice spoke to him on the telephone, and appeared by its tone and by the substance of what it was imparting, to be disturbed and agitated he did not immediately react as he felt he should. He motioned with his hand for the farmer to remain; and it was perhaps that burly, stolid Flemish presence which accounted for his own inability to share in the alarm.

"No, Lady Fulmer," Pierre said. "He is not here. . . . No, not since the day before yesterday, Wednesday. . . . I am afraid I have no idea at all. . . . Yes, I can understand that. . . . Of course, I will telephone you immediately, if he comes."

He replaced the receiver, and turned his head in the direction of the farmer, and they continued the conversation where it had been left off. But not for long. The telephone rang again. This time it was Julie, on the same matter. It was a longer conversation; and he nodded in the direction of the farmer, and the farmer went. The door closed, and as Julie was talking, agitatedly, he heard the man's heavy footsteps going away down the stone passage. And with those footsteps went everything that was Flemish and stolid and unruffled and simple, as Julie said, "Olive thinks there has been a quarrel—but she doesn't know when." The room began to feel cold. "I'll let you know," he said eventually, "if I hear anything. I have already promised Lady Fulmer."

He rang for Prendergast, and when he came he said to him, "The house is cold. Have fires lighted everywhere. In the schoolroom too. If it is raining this afternoon the little girls might like to amuse themselves in there."

The rain, for which the farmers had been praying, was still coming down as he waited for Clare and the children beside a wood fire in the library. When she came he wondered what lay behind her quietness. Her children did all the talking, laughing and chattering on each side of him, telling him—and so saving him from questioning her—that they had been to Ostend again, this time to take their friend Miss King to the boat. At any other time Clare would have frowned in reproval at them, curbed their boisterousness by a glance of reminder that this was not their home; restrained them at the luncheon table from eating a second *gâteau* in the sweet course that followed a simpler meal than the previous one, with no meat, for this was Friday in a Catholic country. But they saved her, and, she thought, Pierre de Fermandois also, from the necessity of having to choose words that would not betray there was anything unusual afoot.

After lunch he took them up to the schoolroom, which had been his and Jean's and later Robert's. Cupboards still held the toys, and the shelves the books of two generations. There were pictures of King Albert and Queen Elisabeth and King Leopold and Queen Astrid on the walls. It was a boy's room, and the treasures were what boys everywhere liked to collect; shells from the seashore, flags and pennants tacked up, and a chief's spear from the Congo. On a narrow, high table stood a china figure of Our Lady. When Jane and Tilly were inside the big cupboard pulling out engines and horses and a whole farmyard of animals, Pierre drew two chairs up to the fire. He knew she would not leave her children that day to talk with him alone. But when the whirring noise of a mechanical motor-car was at its height, he said to her quietly, "You still want to go to Ostend to-morrow?" And she answered, "More than ever, now. I have given notice at the Dierick d'Alsace."

"I have made arrangements for you," he said, "also with a bank."

"There is no one who would have done this for me," she told him in a low voice. "No one, strangely, I could have accepted this help from."

Once, when Prendergast came and took Pierre away to speak on the telephone, she got up from the fire and went to the window and looked out of it. The rain had stopped, and she thought perhaps she ought to leave now, for he had devoted enough time that day to ease her predicament, and there must be many other demands on his attention. But when he returned to her, and the sun had burst through the clouds and was shining on the wet cobble-stones of the stable-yard below, he said, "If you have on a stout pair of shoes, will you come for a walk and meet the Poles? They will probably insist we stay for tea."

In the little whitewashed cottage where the exiles lived, she forgot, for the first time that day, her own problems. In the simplicity of those surroundings, in the faces of both men—neither of them young—there was a reminder of stoical endurance in their tragedy. She knew their history, for Pierre had told it to her as they walked there; and because it was not uncommon did not lessen the tragedy or diminish the courage of their gaiety. They spread butter on fresh bread—warm from the oven—and topped it with honey. And once or twice Pierre heard her laugh. It was a laugh so gentle, so innocent, he was puzzled.

On the way back to the château sudden rain sent the children running towards the house, and while Pierre and Clare were sheltering under some elms he wondered if he should tell her then. He had said, "Someone will come with an umbrella for you presently. I hope you are not getting too wet, meanwhile?" In release from pretence in front of the children she looked at the grey and sodden scene surrounding them, believing that was her farewell to it, remembering how it had appeared on her first visit there. When, in future years, she remembered this holiday she would think of this scene, drenched in autumnal rain, as being its ending. For her children, alone, she must henceforth live and work. There were schools—good ones—in the town where Miss King had her embroidery shop. On the quay at Ostend she had drawn her aside and told her of her decision.

"How much," Pierre asked her, "did you love him?"

"Adrian? With something that no longer belongs to

me," she answered quietly. "Perhaps it was my lost youth. But he took from me all that had been hidden for years. There was a certain quality in him that brought me to speak of it. I can't describe what that was. What was between us was something quite apart. He knows that now. He may have known it all the time. If there was a betrayal of Elizabeth in what we did, there was no sense of betrayal in our thoughts. It all had a magic and a rare kind of beauty. He created something about me—wrote of that creation. That too, although there was the foundation in what I told him, was his creation. I wonder if you understand? Or do you despise me?"

"Do you think, then, I am beyond understanding, Clare? That I have forgotten such magic and rare kind of beauty can exist? And it is over, now?"

"Yes."

A woman servant came hurrying towards them with a mackintosh over her head, bringing an umbrella. There had been a telephone call; and she repeated the number he was to ring. When they reached the house he asked Clare if she would excuse him, and she went into the library where the children were warming their feet before the fire. In the hearth their sandals were drying. She picked them up and felt the soles. She was saying, "Put them on again. You can take them off in the car," when Pierre returned. When she had finished speaking to the children, he said to her quietly, in French, "I have something to tell you, which I would prefer to tell you alone—in another room." And quietly she answered, "I will come." She made an excuse to the children, and went with him into the hall. There she stood still. "What is it?" she asked, and waited.

"I did not tell you before," he said. "But Lady Fulmer and then my sister-in-law telephoned to ask if Adrian was here. His room wasn't slept in last night. Did you see him when you got back?"

"No," she answered. "No. He wasn't there. I waited, and then when he didn't come—I went away. What are you trying to tell me?"

He caught hold of her hands. "I don't know. None of

us know. All day I have been trying to think it was nothing to worry about, and that he would turn up here, or he had gone back to England. But he hasn't. His money and passport are still in his room and they tell me——"

"What else?"

"His balcony rail is broken. The police, Clare, have been informed."

.   .   .   .   .   .

It was man's egoism to think that his own personal suffering and survival had left him immune, to be untouched henceforth by any calamity. But as the evening wore on, and Pierre sat waiting for the telephone to ring again, and hope—slender enough on the evidence—could not be revived, he knew how thin was the shell of invulnerability he had supposedly built round himself. When midnight came, and Prendergast suggested that no good would come through waiting up, he dismissed him and sat for an hour in a chilly room.

He did not sleep; and he was up again soon after dawn, disturbing a household not used to his appearance so early. He knew they all knew; and that when the telephone rang at about eight o'clock, they had paused in their work, and a hush fell upon every room. It was Julie who told him, sobbing, "He's been found, Pierre."

CHAPTER XII

Monsieur De Jonkheere was trembling, and his pale face puckered into lines of anguish as he tried to speak in front of his wife and English guests and the police, but no words came, none which could acquit him of his negligence, his crime. It was not his wife. She had said, "Sit down. Calm yourself. It is too late." For what? For excuses? It was the sight of uniformed authority again, and helmets—although these were not that grey-green colour of infamy and terror, of men come to question and question. Even though one knew who these men were, knew they were fathers of families, attended Mass, the uniforms hid their identity, their humanity. They would keep him standing with his hands high above his head, hour after hour. No. No. These had told him to sit down. But they did not understand what he had done. He forgot. He was always forgetting. Young Monsieur Morbeigh had told him about the rail, laughed and said. . . . In that voice of his that laughed so easily at a joke with the little twins. . . .

There was not room for everyone to sit down in the De Jonkheere's room behind the office, and Rene preferred to stand with his back to the wall, where there hung a Flemish calendar and a crucifix. His fingers reached in his jacket pocket for a cigarette. But better not. Bad manners. And this was a serious occasion, an upsetting one for his mother. His grandmother had been taken, weeping, to her bedroom. Poor father! Poor old man! Mother was hating this. It was bad for business.

But it was an interesting affair, all the same. And he would give much to know what was behind it. Was it an accident? Or find the woman? The English were not as unemotional as they were cracked up to be. That poor girl was crying her eyes out. And the other one, the one who had come out of his room so late that night, Madame Ainslie. Her eyes were painful to stare at for long. A man could drown himself in those eyes, when she smiled. And he'd seen her smile, often. Now they were the eyes of the Mother of Sorrows, tortured, haunted. "Cry," he wanted to say to her. "Let the tears come you dare not shed. You'll feel better for it. You went to the Panier d'Or with him, and he sat at your table the next night, and you went out for a little while. I saw you! I saw you come back. And what were you doing in his room when you came back from the Château Fermandois that night? The police have accepted your statement. I had to tell them what I had seen. They have accepted your statement that he had asked you to tell him about the *kermesse*, and that you closed the windows. But I do not know whether they believe that you did not notice the broken rail. You look so much older, so ill, with your beauty gone, your sparkle vanished, they are quite ready to believe that middle-aged women often go into the rooms of young men late at night for innocent reasons. There is nothing in that. They never saw you and he together, as I did.

"They must take it all down, slowly, word by word. You speak good French, madame, the French of Paris and an expensive education, which signifies you were well brought up. You will have to tell it all over again at the inquest on Monday, so be careful. But I wonder if the police think it is odd that you gave notice to leave this hotel yesterday, four days before you had planned to leave?"

The telephone rang in the office.

"Answer it, Rene," Madame De Jonkheere commanded her son.

"It is for Madame Ainslie," he returned to say. He looked at Clare. "From London. A Monsieur Perry—again. He could not get through last night."

"Tell him I am not available."

"You are excused, madame," the police officer said at the head of the table.

"Thank you," she answered. "But it is not important." She lifted her head and looked at Rene. "I am not available." she repeated. Rene shrugged his shoulders, went to

give her message, and returned. "Monsieur will telephone
again this evening." But she might not have heard him.
Her turn was over. It was now the girl's.

Lady Fulmer put her arms round Elizabeth. "Darling,
try and pull yourself together. You must answer questions,
I'm afraid."

Clare stared at the leather brief-case open on the table
in front of the officer, and at his hand, sunburned and large
holding a very thick fountain pen poised above an outsize
note-book. A sergeant sat beside him. Their helmets were
lying on top of a pile of sheets at the side of an old-fashioned
treadle sewing-machine. Someone had to interpret, and
Madame De Jonkheere would.

"I last saw him," Elizabeth said, "that evening. Thursday."

"Where, mademoiselle?"

"You are asked to say where, please, mademoiselle."

"Darling, darling, you must answer. You know where.
I was there."

"Yes. Yes."

"The exact place, mademoiselle."

"Downstairs. In—— Downstairs—the *salon*."

"At what time, mademoiselle?"

"He wants you to state the hour, mademoiselle."

"I—I I can't remember. Mother—what time?" She began
to sob afresh.

"My daughter cannot answer any more questions,"
Lady Fulmer cried. "Can you not see for yourselves?" She
began in French, and in her distress, faltered. She, also,
was crying now, as Madame De Jonkheere was also.

The police officer stood up and closed the note-book
and gathered his papers together. That, he informed the
company, would do for the present. They would be told
when to present themselves at the inquest, in the Cabinet
de Juge d'Instruction at the Palais de Justice, later. By
order of the Procureur du Roi seals had been placed on the
door of the room of the deceased. And he must inform
everyone present that they must not leave Bruges until
after the inquest. He was sorry. He bowed his head, in

the direction of the weeping girl, of her mother, and of everyone in turn.

.   .   .   .   .   .

Everyone stood, as the police went out, and Clare waited until Lady Fulmer and Elizabeth had gone through the door. As she walked towards the stairs she saw who was with them in the hall, who had been waiting for them. Pierre de Fermandois and his brother and sister-in-law. She passed by their sorrow unnoticed.

It was still raining. Mercifully, it was still raining. If one could think of any mercy this day! But she had set the children a painting task, promising a reward, and had demanded from them a promise that they would not leave their room until she returned. She knew, as she climbed the stairs with dragging footsteps—as a woman might whose body was wracked with pain—that she was in no condition to return to them yet.

"It isn't true," she said again, "it isn't true!" Everything in her room was unchanged. All her things were there, because she hadn't packed to go to Ostend. When she returned from the château she knew she wasn't going there. But in that long night of darkness and terror, hope had not died entirely. There was the strange hallucination that he was beside her, his youth calling her own youth back from the years. And into his understanding, and his wisdom beyond his years, she was pouring all her confusion, her bitterness, her perplexities; and he was taking her loneliness from her, banishing it.

She started, afraid of every sound. "Who is it?" she asked of the closed door.

"Rene, madame. Will madame see a visitor here? Monsieur le Comte."

"Open the door, please."

The door was opened. There was a glimpse of Rene's face, knowing and inquisitive, behind Pierre's. The door was shut, and her hands were a guide in the strangeness of her room, her body a shield from the sharp edges of unfamiliar furniture. There was nothing either of them could say in those first moments. The pressure of his own grief, and his grief for her, was rendering him incapable of speech. In cynicism he had mocked a boy in love, half-mocked the woman torn by her perplexities the night before last; and she had responded by stiff concealments. He felt a spasm of her secret, untold agony shake her from head to foot; and he put up a hand to her face, a finger across her tightly-closed lids, and felt them dry. And he was instantly incredulous, that in such a moment, there was in that very action transmitted to him from the tips of his fingers, that were as an instrument of sight, a vision of her face, which he knew he would never lose.

"Is there no one," he asked, "who could be with you? No one you can send for?"

"No one."

"You must not stay here. I want you to bring the children to the château until——"

"I have been forbidden to leave Bruges."

"That is a formality," he said, "that is easily overcome. Lady Fulmer and Elizabeth are going to my brother's."

"I cannot," Clare answered, "accept any privilege for myself. I must stay here. I cannot explain why. But I must. But I should like Jane and Tilly to go. If you could take them back with you, we can go and tell them. I mean that they are to stay with you until after——" Her voice broke. "Don't let me give way. I don't want them to see—— What have I done? What have I done to Elizabeth?"

His hand rested on her bowed head. "He did not love her, Clare. In some way she failed, poor child, to live up to his original conception of her. Had she fulfilled it, would he have loved you?"

"That is only conjecture. We shall never know. We shall never know any of it."

Having wished, for Clare's sake, to avoid any discussion that would increase her pain, under her sudden direct questioning he could only share her bewilderment. The purpose of the inquest would be to discover how he came to be in the water, so far from the hotel. If it were true, what Adrian had told her, of his swim at Zoute, was it possible that in a renewed fit of faintness he had fallen? Had possessed enough strength to swim a little way, and then collapsed? He knew she was unaware of, or if she were aware, she was indifferent to the position her action of going to his room had placed her in, being ignorant of the thoroughness of any inquest. Her thoughts were solely on others bereft through this tragedy; a father in Scotland; a girl she had helped, she said, to betray. "And you, because you loved him too!"

"Please take Jane and Tilly away," she begged of him. "But leave me, leave me to face this—alone."

"What," he asked, "are you going to tell them?"

"The truth. That there has been an accident. And if you really think they won't be in the way, I will tell them before they go. If you can face—what happens? I must pack a little case for them."

"While you are doing that," Pierre said, "I will take them to a café." And by the door, which she had opened, he stopped. He would respect her desire to be alone, and not intrude. But she would want to know how they were, wouldn't she? He wondered if he might come and tell her, after dinner?

Together they went into the twins' room, and he heard her tell them that he had come to see them. The children got up from the table where they had been painting—and not painting for a great deal of the time—and shook hands with him. They knew they were not going to stay in Ostend after all, but they did not know why their mother had changed her mind again. When she came into the room they were happy again, but in the heart of each child there was confusion and doubt about the permanence of that happiness. They were aware of unexplainable happenings that morning in the hotel; and they had seen policemen on the landing. But now there was a little reassurance that all was right with their world again, because if it were not, Count would not have come to take them to have ces?

I

They went down the stairs, and in the doorway they said to their mother, "But aren't you coming?"

"No, darlings. This is your treat. Your very own."

They linked their arms in Pierre's, and they were very careful to guide him round the puddles. The sun had come out suddenly, and there was a rainbow. Should they tell him? Everyone they met made way for them. They halted at street corners and the traffic, the trams and vans and lorries and cars and cyclists gave them the right of way. They walked round the Grand' Place to the sound of bells, on the edge of the clamour and bustle of the Saturday market, and everyone, again, made way for them. The drivers of cars sweeping round the square saw them, braked, and waved them on. It was like being with royalty, Tilly thought. Although it wasn't raining any more, it was too damp to sit outside the café, and the waiter showed them to a table inside near a window. When the ices were brought they did not immediately pick up the spoons and wafers, they waited until the last drop of coffee had dripped through the percolator into Pierre's cup. And it was Tilly who said quietly, "It is ready," and lifted the aluminium top. "You will have cream and sugar?" But it was Jane's honour to give him those. They looked out of the window at all the stalls of the market, and laughed and told him what they saw. They made the ice-creams last as long as they could.

When they walked back to the hotel they held Pierre's arms tighter, and the pressure of their hands told him more than any words could have done of the confusion in their hearts, of the doubt they had begun to have since early that morning that the security and happiness of their world were everlasting. They took him the longer way back, in silent conspiracy, to spin out the minutes of his company and comfort. And how, they wondered, did their mother know they would come back that way over the little bridge? Why was she waiting for them on the bridge, to walk on the other side of Jane, back with them to the hotel? Why did she say to Count, when they reached his car, "We shall be back again in a few minutes?" and leave him, and take them, not into the hotel, but back to the bridge? Her face was white and her eyes very big and dark. What was it? Was it anything to do with the police? There were a lot of leaves in the water, as they leaned on the bridge and peered over it. A lot of leaves had fallen in the rain.

There were some things you knew you had known, although you couldn't believe it when it was—Someone. Like Hugo, for instance, who had been their father's dog. He never came back. But She, who had always been there, and who would always be there—Mother—had been the reassurance that Heaven was not an empty or lonely place, nor was it only the home of God and angels with bright wings.

Count was waiting for them. "Who do you like best, Count or—or——?" they had played. Count wanted them. He wanted Jane and Tilly. His son was a long way away, too far away. . . . They clung to Clare. But when would she come? they demanded. How soon?

"As soon as ever I can. Trust me?"

They nodded and choked. They clung to her as she took them back to the car. They clung to her as she kissed them before they entered it. It had grown beyond their understanding. But, "Trust me," she had said. "Get in, darlings," she said now.

Count took her hand and held it and then he kissed it quickly, but they did not hear what he was saying. When he got into the car they slid themselves apart into the corners to make room for him to sit in the middle. Mummy waved once—twice. She had begun to cry. The car started. It went out of the square along by the water.

"It is very kind of you," Jane said, "to invite us to stay with you." Then she bit her lips, and choked.

"Very kind," Tilly repeated. But she couldn't go on. The houses were all blurred and wobbling like the water and the trees. It was raining again, when she looked up at the sky through the car window. She couldn't see it any more. She couldn't see.

Pierre put his arms round them as each one hid her face

against him, and their sobbing beat into the silent anguish of his own heart.

.   .   .   .   .   .

"I suppose we shall hear," Lady Fulmer said, for the fourth time that evening, "how soon the judge can get here."

There was so little left to say, so little anyone could say that had not been said before. Tears had dried. One talked of something else. But one always came back to it, Julie thought. The day had passed. A day, Julie knew, she would never forget, although it had been a day not devoted entirely to sorrow, but to the frustration of trying to get in touch with Sir Frederick as well as the judge. Sir Frederick had been found, eventually, in the country, where he was having a golfing week-end. He was due to arrive at noon tomorrow. And during a part of that terrible day a thought had returned which was puzzling, and still had to be solved.

They were in the *salon*, Jean and Julie and Lady Fulmer, after dinner when Julie thought of it again. It was too early to go to bed, although they all needed rest; and Julie could hear the rain outside again, pouring down on to the earth that had been parched for it for so long. But one of them should, she felt go up to Elizabeth; and Olive really ought to have allowed a doctor to come and give her a sleeping draught—aspirins were not strong enough. Again Julie was going over everything in her mind, right from the very beginning. "Did they," she asked suddenly, "have a quarrel?"

"Not that I know of," Lady Fulmer said quickly.

"But you said on the telephone yesterday morning——"

"I said, dear," Lady Fulmer answered, "that I wondered if there had been, when I found he wasn't in his room. But of course there wasn't. Elizabeth came up to bed with me, and we left him downstairs. We had such a gay little dinner, to celebrate. Perhaps he had—er—a little too much. The waiter served him with another brandy, it appears "

Julie was again thoughtful. And after a little silence she said, "You know, Olive, I feel sorry for that Mrs. Ainslie, because she's in the silly sort of position that might be misinterpreted. No, and I don't mean there is anything. But at inquests they ask all sorts of questions—and she's all on her own here."

"We can't help it, if she is," Lady Fulmer said. "I believe Adrian had quite a 'thing' about her husband." And as she sat beside Julie on a wide couch she put Mrs. Ainslie from her mind, for she had quite enough, she told herself, on her mind already. Her distress was made visible by the twisting of a ring round and round on her finger, and that constant motion was observed by Julie who, sympathetically thrust her arm in her friend's. They sat there for another half hour, talking of other things but always coming back to the same thing, until Lady Fulmer spoke the words she had been wanting to speak, and had dreaded that preliminary, to what, again, must be faced: "Now, I think, darling, if you don't mind, I will say good night and go and peep at my poor child."

In her agitation, earlier that day, she had taken a course which was, since she knew she was a truthful woman, one who had been brought up to certain standards, distasteful to her. She knew she had panicked. She knew she had been struck with horror, when, in making Elizabeth get up and get dressed to go downstairs, she had seen her legs covered with scars and bruises. She told herself, afterwards, that she would not have said what she did say to Elizabeth if they had been at home, or anywhere except in a foreign country, if they had not been who they were. All day she had been telling herself that exposure of the truth would not bring Adrian back. And the whole of the truth she did not know—why, to use Elizabeth's expression, they had been fooling on the balcony. She had been filled with genuine distress that the child had done as he told her—and left him.

Elizabeth had been expecting her. Lying in bed she had heard footsteps—her mother's and Julie's—coming up the bare polished stairs, then muffled along the carpeted corridor, their whisperings outside the door. "Not asleep?" she heard her mother say.

"How can I sleep?"

She turned her face and her body beneath the bed-clothes away from the repetition of what had been said to her earlier. She had been thinking, before her mother came, that she might one day write to Mrs. Ainslie and ask her about those two days, as a girl, who had lost a lover in a far country, might ask those who had been close to him in his last hours. But that would not tell her where she had failed. What her mother said now, was of no consequence. She must try and believe it was of no consequence, that it could not bring him back, undo what she had done in her hysteria, when she had only meant to threaten him. But as her mother was talking, touching her—and in distress trying to comfort her—she began to shake in another spasm of terrible sobbing. "How can I sleep?" she had asked, thinking she would never sleep again.

But when her sobbing had ceased, in the silence in which her mother sat watching her, sleep claimed her on an instant, and she did not know when her mother rose and switched off the light.

CHAPTER XIII

THERE were faces that would be for ever stamped on the mind; against a background of dark walls they were as figures on a medieval canvas. They were Flemish, with the steadiness of character that respected property and convention, had courage and bore physical evidence of good living. The lines at the corners of the eyes denoted humour. But there was little opportunity for a display of that quality today. The air was sombre and heavy with grief. With due solemnity the evidence was heard.

There had been, first, the medical evidence; and while it was being given Clare had been aware of the presence in the court of an English judge, who was there not in the customary role of one dispensing justice, nor as an interested spectator of foreign procedure, but as a father who had lost a son. Yet the law-giving aspect of his appearance was one which instantly came to mind, because a wig and scarlet robe would well become him. And from deep cuffs of black, purple-shot taffetas, those white hands of the law-giver would protrude, like the sensitive hands of an actor whose gestures were controlled. The face was set; the eyes beneath heavy brows thoughtful and searching, as each witness was called. After the doctor and police, Madame De Jonkheere. Then Lady Fulmer, who left the side of a weeping girl, round whose bowed shoulders a father had an arm. To be followed by the weeping girl, whose presence caused those stern Flemish faces to soften, their hearts a desire to spare her the ordeal of saying any more than she had said previously to the police.

When Clare was called she raised her eyes unflinchingly. "I do not ask of Thee," she prayed silently, "for any concealment for my sake, only for hers." She was ready for the questioning. "I do not ask," she prayed again, "that the secret of our relationship shall not be discovered, only that it shall not be believed by others who loved him." She was ready to be asked if she had known Mr. Morbeigh, and when she last saw him. And to answer. To speak the truth. To go back over her knowledge of him. Did they sound innocent pleasures? A day by the sea with her children. A dinner at the Panier d'Or. . . .

Friday evening. To tell what she knew of that evening. His going to her room. Her going, on her return, to his. And to describe the appearance of his room. To be asked to repeat when she last saw him. To be asked to repeat if his room was empty. To be asked why she gave notice to leave the hotel the following morning. To be asked what state of mind he appeared in, when she last saw him. To tell again of his having felt faint, and what he told her about his swim at Zoute. To be asked, again, what she did in his room when she was waiting for him. To be asked if she thought there was any reason why he should take his own life.

Then to hear, as though it were on a distant stage, an announcement that the court would rise and meet again at the hour of three.

That was all, when she was outside in the street, she could remember of the questioning, which would be resumed after lunch. But she could recall with fear the repetition of certain ones, the probing insistence on a more detailed answer to them. The sun was shining again, and the trees glistened with moisture sparkling among the leaves. Some more sycamore leaves had fallen. The water had risen; and its stagnant mire had been washed away. She would enter Notre Dame and sit there—and pray. Or should she go first to the little garden of the Hôtel Arents? She walked slowly, unaware of the crowds on the pavement, hearing the sound of bicycle bells and trams, the hooting of motor-horns as though they were in another world. But the beauty of that autumn day, after the rain, slowly opened itself before her eyes, and she observed buildings that had given her joy to behold, a joy she had shared with Adrian. How long had it taken for the grass to grow over the grief of the war out in the country? How long would it be before the beauty of creative endeavour in painting or poetry, the faith that such as Pierre held in God, shone into the darkness of the grief in her own heart?

She paused at a street crossing, and felt a hand on her shoulder, heard a voice speak her name. Who, in this city, would call her Clare with such authority? She knew who it was. But when she had turned round she could not yet answer. In a crowded street, on an even more crowded foot-path, with trams clanging, bicycle bells tinkling, and women and children pushing past, to have Claude's hand in hers and an arm round her shoulder was to be transported instantly into his solid world, which was no longer hers. It was a very orderly, sane world, and not to be despised. It did not lack courage, but it sometimes lacked imagination. To face Claude was to face his reality, which was far removed from the subject of the prayers she would have again whispered on her knees in a church which was not her own.

"How did you get here?" she asked.

He would tell her, he said, over lunch. He was hungry. And where could they lunch, and have a really good meal?

"Anywhere," she answered. "Anywhere is good. But we are too far from the Dierick d'Alsace."

He had put an arm in hers. He looked tired, and there was a hint of irritable impatience in his voice when he asked, "Then where else is good, that isn't too far? Where can we get a taxi?"

"I don't know, except at the station. There's the Duc de Burgoyne. The Sablon. And a place on the Grand' Place. The Panier d'Or." She was about to say, "Let us go to the first of those," when he interrupted, "I've heard of the Panier d'Or." There was no end to a road that was winding uphill, nor was a burden lighter, although he still had his arm in hers.

"I couldn't," he said, "get an answer out of you, so I hopped a plane this morning. Where were you every time I telephoned?" She did not reply, and as they were crossing the Grand' Place she said, "I shan't be able to have much time with you. But I will explain about an appointment I have to keep."

They entered the Panier d'Or, and the same waiter

1*

showed them to a table. She knew he had recognized her.
She watched him hand Claude the menu, and saw Claude
take his horn-rimmed glasses from a dark crocodile case;
and she shut her eyes quickly because her thoughts were
making the whole room dissolve into a mist. She was aware
that Claude was speaking to her, and that she had confessed
she was not hungry.

"Something up?" he asked. "I've guessed that. But
hadn't you better try?"

She nodded. She would try. It would be selfish not to,
and spoil his lunch for which he was hungry. "A little steak,
then. Nothing else. But you go on. Start with whatever you
want. I'll wait." He was already spreading butter on a roll
and biting into it. He would start with an omelet, but he
had had plenty of steaks in America, so what did the waiter
recommend? He was studying the wine list. And he knew
what he was doing when he chose the Chambertin 1934.
When she had drunk a little of it she would be able to talk
to him. She could, meanwhile, only listen to him, and hear
of his concern when he could not reach her on the telephone. She could nod her head when he spoke of the
success of the conference, and try not to look too blankly
at him when he suggested they might go to Brussels
tomorrow.

"But, I am going back tomorrow," she said. "Didn't you
know that?"

"Yes, I knew that, darling. But I have an excuse to
go to Brussels, so I thought we might drive there and spend a
couple of days. How are Jane and Tilly? And where are
they, at this moment?"

"They are very well," she told him. They have been
spending the week-end in the country. A kind friend took
them in. The hotel—suddenly—wasn't a very happy place
for them."

"You mean this inquest on young Morbeigh? The old
judge, and I think another son, were on the plane. And
they were met at Ostend airport by a blind man with a
car."

He was eating an omelet with enjoyment, and he paused,

to tell her how dull and tasteless he thought American food was, how omelets there were fluffy, tea-shop concoctions. "When I got to your hotel," he went on, "they told me you were at the inquest, so I went along there and hung about outside. I don't know how I missed you coming out. Quite a miracle finding you, wasn't it?" He smiled. He was feeling better now he had eaten something, and in the mood and the humour to regard her with tenderness and understanding for all her vagaries. But now he was regarding her critically, and he was shocked to see how ill and pale she looked. "I read about it," he went on. "Sort of silly thing that often happens, after a fellow's come through a war. I suppose he was old enough? But how do you come to be in it? I mean, why did you have to attend the inquest?"

"Everyone has," she said slowly, "who knew him in the hotel, who saw him that last day."

"Any clues?"

The waiter had returned, and he was uncovering the dishes, holding out for her inspection a succulent steak nestling in a bed of watercress. "A little piece," she said, "out of the middle." She picked up a knife and fork, and put them down again. She raised the glass of wine to her lips.

"I can see it has upset you," Claude said. "So I won't ask you any more. But I'll come along with you and hold your hand. Then I tell you what we'll do, we'll go and pick up the twins, and start off for Brussels this evening. How's the car been behaving?"

They talked of the car, and again of America. He was enjoying his lunch, and was in his usual good humour, wearing his success with an easy grace, a man who had little experience of humiliation in his well-ordered life. She made herself eat two mouthfuls of steak before she gained courage, before his good humour and his kindness, to say, "I cannot come with you to Brussels. I don't know, now you are here, how to begin to tell you——"

"What have you got to tell me?"

"Finish what you are eating," she said. "Then I will. And then I shall have to go."

"Is it about this inquest? But why are you mixed up in it? I can see you are—more than is usual."

"I went to his room, late, the night it had happened. He had been my lover," she said. "I didn't want to hurt you."

He pushed his plate away and then looked at her long and steadily. At length he said, "Has all this come out today?" And as he looked at her he saw an expression come into her eyes that he had not seen that day, dull and clouded and filled with sadness as they had been up to then. It was an expression of playful mockery, ill-suited, he felt, to the occasion. She had hurt him. She had hurt him damnably. "Has it?" he repeated.

When he had heard her answer he picked up his wine glass and drained it. "The thing is," he said, "you'd been a widow too long. Let's leave it at that. I understand. I'm damned sorry for you, Clare. It wouldn't have mattered. Just a flash in the pan. It couldn't have been anything but a bit of Belgian holiday foolishness at your age—and his—could it? And wasn't he engaged to some Air Chief's daughter? I know very well you'd never get up to tricks after we were married. You are not that sort."

She had hurt him. She had hurt his pride because he knew if he had behaved differently with her she would have repulsed him, even though she had been a widow too long. She was loving enough and affectionate—but that was all there was, and sometimes he had wondered whether she never looked at herself in the glass and knew her own beauty, so careless she was of it. He'd been going to deck that beauty, give her jewels and take her to good French dressmakers.

"But this publicity, Clare," he said slowly, "puts a different complexion on the whole thing. It is bound to be in the papers, if what you say is true." Then passion and feeling came into his voice, showing her a side of him that he had kept hidden from her previously. She had suspected that he would be passionate in his demands, and now she knew that he would lose his temper with servants, with anyone who could not safely answer back. "Why, in God's name did you ever come here?"

"If character is destiny," she answered quietly, "that will explain why."

"Only fools——"

"I am one, perhaps. But I do ask you to try and forgive me. I wouldn't have hurt you, willingly."

"I could have overlooked it," he said. "As I said. But there may be a General Election in November, or at the latest February, and it's going to need all I've got to win, now the boundary has been changed too. It's Cæsar's wife, Clare, I'm afraid. All those Baptists, erstwhile Liberals, down there in the town. You know what I mean?"

"Of course I see what you mean." She rose, and as he was about to do the same she put a hand on his arm. "Don't move. I must go now. You have planned your life always, and it has always gone as you planned it. You once said only fools did not plan. And I am one of them, so I would never have fitted in to your life. You have been good and kind and generous to me. I've let you down, and I am sorry."

But he ignored her hand, rose, and went to the street door with her. "Your ring," she said, and began to fumble with it.

"Send it back, if you must," he told her, "when you get home. The Customs would only soak me for it, and it would need a lot of explaining away. Clare, I can't pretend this hasn't shaken me. I forgot to tell you I bumped into Joan on Friday. She was coming out of the Empress Club. This will shake her, too."

Clare looked across the Grand' Place, remembering how she had sat at the café just a few yards away with Joan on that afternoon long ago. Claude and Joan would understand each other. They spoke the same language; the language of the planners, the successful. They would have a word for it. Clare had been a widow too long. And they would leave it at that.

"Good-bye," she said, and touched his hand quickly. "There is nothing more—except, be happy."

For a few moments he stood in the doorway of the

Panier d'Or watching her walking away. A Belgian holiday,
he thought. Oh, hell! Why did she ever want a Belgian
holiday?

.   .   .   .   .   .

Marie Berlearts, straight from the funeral of her grandfather in the village of Donk, dressed from head to toe
in black, with a little silver cross swinging against her plump
little bosom, got out of the train at Bruges station and
hurried through the barrier and out into the street. She
leapt on to a tram and leapt off it again at the recognized
stop, and ran the rest of the way to the hotel. She went in
by a side entrance and into the kitchen. It was the lunch
hour, and nobody looked up from the business in hand to
greet her. She could smell the soup, and her mouth watered
because she was hungry. The door into the dining-room
kept swinging open and swinging to again. When it was
open she could see who was in the dining-room. There was a
big party at a big table in the centre. Lady Fulmer and
Mademoiselle and le Comte de Fermandois and le vicomte
and la vicomtesse and three men, one very old, one not so
old and one younger who looked very like Monsieur Morbeigh.
Only he wasn't. Of course no Mademoiselle King, and no
Madame Ainslie and the little twins. They had left. Some
strangers. A party of tourists. Henri and his assistant
were very busy.

Henri, carrying a tray of oysters, asked Marie to move
out of the way. She obeyed and went towards the stove.
The cook looked up and found time for a sympathetic
smile. "Ah! Marie!"

"Give me some soup," Marie said, "before I go upstairs.
I am hungry. It has been a sad occasion."

"It is understood. Poor Marie!" She was asked how her
mother and aunt and sister were, and told to take her bowl
of soup out of the way. Death was always a sad occasion.
The present one, in the hotel, was tragic. Had not Marie
heard? Marie had not heard. Newspapers were seldom read
by any of her family. Now and then she took home *Le Soir
Illustré* and *Week-end*, for them to look at the pictures'

and magazines guests threw into the waste-paper basket. She was sitting down with the bowl of soup in front of her, dipping crusts of rolls into it when they told her, and tears began to pour out of her eyes. She crossed herself and began to sob. She couldn't believe it. It wasn't true. Then Henri in passing, nudged her. "Look out," he said. "Pull yourself together. Madame!"

Marie stood up, and would have made for the door that opened on to the back stairs, but there was not time. Madame De Jonkheere, dressed in her outdoor clothes, gloved and hatted, in black, stood before her, and orders flew like hail. Chamber-maids who took the week-end off to attend a funeral should remember, when they returned, that there was work to be done. The rooms that had been occupied by Lady Fulmer and Mademoiselle had been left untouched since Saturday. One could say they had not been touched since Friday, for the niece of Henri had not done anything except make beds. Those rooms were to be occupied again this evening. They were to be turned out thoroughly, and no skimping, please.

Madame De Jonkheere left the kitchen and went back to the office. Rene was finishing his lunch in the room beyond. She had no appetite, and she couldn't understand how anyone could eat, as Rene was eating, until this distressing affair was ended. Her mother and her husband were eating nothing but soup, and that with no appetite. "Rene!" she called. "Come here!"

"Yes?"

"Bring the luggage down out of three and four."

"But they are not getting the luggage until afterwards. They said so. How much is there?"

"The heavy luggage. They only took one case away on Saturday."

"It would be. I don't know where Jules is."

"Then find him. How can Marie clean those rooms in time, when they are full of luggage?"

"You will be glad, Maman," Rene said, "when these have gone, won't you? When does Madame Ainslie leave?"

"Tomorrow. The original arrangement."

"Then they will all have gone," he said soothingly. "And you will have no reminders."

He went into the hall, paused to light a cigarette, and opening a door into a passage called for Jules. There was no answer. Quite often there wasn't. His quarter-wittedness, Rene reflected, had nothing to do with the war. He came of a family that way. Receiving no answer from his second call he went upstairs; and in the first bedroom Marie, who was busy stripping bed-clothes, asked him, "Have you come for the luggage, Monsieur Rene?" He thought of giving her a little pinch on her behind, then he remembered she had come from a funeral, and it wouldn't be seemly. She wasn't his type, too thick from waist to knee, too short from knee to ankle—a peasant. She had already moved the luggage and stacked it all neatly near the door.

He looked through the open door of the communicating bathroom into the other bedroom. The luggage there was in the position the mother had left it on Saturday, when she and the American vicomtesse had done the packing. They had done it all between them, when the daughter had been taken away from the hotel by the vicomte when the police had finished with them. What a mess people left rooms in! Crumpled tissue paper. Spilt powder. Half-empty jars of face cream. But the mother was a tidy woman, because there was none of this mess in her room. When he had come up for the suit-case she had apologized for the mess in her daughter's room and had pointed to the waste-paper basket. "It hasn't been emptied for days!" Reproachfully, as though they paid enough they should have that service.

He thought, as he stood there, that he would give much to know what had really happened on Friday night, for the police, he felt, had handled the whole case very badly. If he had been them he would have examined other rooms. He liked detective stories, and Lord Peter Wimsey was his ideal. He would have come in these rooms before, if Lady Fulmer had not taken away her key; and he knew his mother would miss the duplicates inside five minutes. He had poked about Madame Ainslie's room, when she was out—but found nothing. Only a letter from America. Was that the gentleman who kept telephoning from London? She went out a lot, and twice he had followed her—as far as Notre Dame and the garden of the Hôtel Arents. And three times le Comte de Fermandois had been to see her, and she had gone out with him to sit by the canal on two occasions. They had put her through it today! Bit by bit. Bit by bit. It all sounded very innocent—if one didn't have certain ideas.

He tried the locks of the trunk. Not that he would really look inside. Still, if they hadn't been locked. . . . The trunk was too heavy for anyone to manage alone. He'd have to go and find Jules. He kicked the overloaded waste-paper basket, and a pile of magazines slid off it. He picked one up and let it drop. Those were Marie's perquisites. She took them home always. The waste-paper basket was lying on its side, where he had kicked it, too full for any of its contents to spill. Only a lipstick container had rolled away across the carpet. Then he noticed that where the basket had been standing there was a round, dark patch, a deep circular stain.

"Rene!" His mother's voice called up the stairs. "*Rene!* We should be leaving now. *Rene!*"

He did not answer. He was on his knees emptying the contents of the waste-paper basket.

"What do you think you are doing?" Madame De Jonkheere had run up the stairs, and she was not only out of breath but in a temper. "Behaving like a common scavenger! When we are due to return to the inquest. Wasting time. The luggage still here. How do you expect Marie to clean these rooms? What kind of example is it, to see you? For what are you looking? Film magazines?"

Rene got slowly to his feet, and smiled. "Regard this," he said. "This dress is not in this condition through being out in the rain." He held out a damp lump of material, which he unfolded; he shook it and from his hands fell what had once been a red dress, now torn and caked with mud and slime. "Uh! It smells of the canal, does it not? And this—also?"

"Put those away," Madame De Jonkheere commanded him, her sense of modesty offended by the sight of feminine underwear in the same condition. "But, I think," she said, when she had control once more, "we should take the dress with us to the court."

.   .   .   .   .   .

Air Chief Marshal Sir Frederick Fulmer had never cared very much for foreigners, but as he walked briskly away from the inquest, dressed in a sober, clerical grey-flannel suit and black tie, he had to admit that on this occasion they had been very fair indeed. He had never cared for foreign countries either, having had enough of what he called overseas to last a lifetime. For his holidays he preferred Frinton, if you wanted the sea, and Gleneagles. But he had had, in the period between the first and second wars, a whole-hearted admiration for the Germans. He worshipped efficiency, and if it had been left to him, he often said, he would have chosen to have the Germans as allies instead of the French. As he walked in the direction of the Hôtel Dierick d'Alsace to pay the bill for his wife and daughter and collect their luggage to take out to Julie de Fermandois's house, he had to admit that Belgian justice—which he sincerely hoped was the last occasion he would ever be an interested party—couldn't have been conducted in a more sympathetic way. In fact, the whole painful proceedings which developed that afternoon, could not have been ended more tactfully.

Striding along he caught sight of himself in the large mirrow of a *patisserie* window; and at any other time he would have been pleased with what he saw. But nothing, he thought, in his whole life had shattered him as this business had done, when his own child, confronted with that sodden piece of material had sobbed out a different story from the one she had told previously. A lovers' quarrel, or a few words of difference—what did it matter, since the outcome was this appalling one? It had been difficult to see exactly what happened, except by leaning on the balcony rail—

fooling, she had called it—she had fallen. And she had not dreamed he was in any difficulty when he told her to leave him. But that wasn't all she had said. It was the rest that was so shattering. Asked why she had not told the truth before, she had confessed she was frightened of her mother, and that it was her mother who had advised her to conceal the truth. Those were one of the classical occasions when you did wish the earth would open and swallow everyone! They had not deemed it necessary to ask Olive to stand up again. The purpose of the inquest had been fulfilled. The verdict was—he supposed, translated— death by misadventure. A heart-attack, the result of over-strain.

Before that, it had seemed there might be another side to the picture. Quite a spicy side too, which in time might have convinced Liz she was well rid of an unsatisfactory young man. But nothing in that, after all. He could have been knocked down with a feather, when he asked who she was at lunch, and the blind fellow said, "She is the widow of an officer no doubt well known to you." So he had had another good look at her in the court, and when poor Liz was faced with the evidence of her folly, tears had streamed out of Mrs. Ainslie's eyes.

When he reached the hotel and was waiting for the car to return for him, and the luggage had been put in the hall, and he had paid the bill and received what seemed both condolences and congratulations from the dark-haired proprietress—nobody could accuse foreigners of not being practical—that it had, after all been solved satisfactorily, he wondered if he should inquire if Mrs. Ainslie was in. But she probably wouldn't want to see him, wouldn't want to talk—not even about Jock, which was what he would have liked to talk to her about, because he hoped she didn't think such men were forgotten. If he talked to her he might, he thought, recapture the feeling of younger and more carefree days, which she must have known with Jock and others, and which he had really never known himself, because he had been too much consumed with ambition and minding his step. For many years Sir Frederick had suffered the delusion that strength of purpose demanded an arrogant and insufferable deportment towards his juniors, but in his maturity and success he had mellowed, and he was a walking contradiction to the old belief that success had an adverse effect upon character and behaviour. And he was, that afternoon, almost pathetically humble and in need of a sympathetic hand to bolster him up. But he left the hotel, and the passing pleasantries of Madame De Jonkheere, in Jean de Fermandois's car feeling that it had been better left as it was. For what could he have said to Jock Ainslie's widow, after all that time? Poor thing, this had probably messed up her holiday, as it had everyone's.

He was relieved to find that both Olive and Elizabeth were not in Julie's drawing-room, and that only Julie herself and Jean were there. He liked Julie; and when Jean poured out a large whisky for him he, temporarily, received a little of the bolstering of which he was so much in need. He was not an unduly sensitive man, but he could not fail to perceive in Jean's deference to his age and position, in the 'sir' that came so frequently in conversation, and in Julie's forced pleasantries that while they were sympathetic they were shocked. They did themselves awfully well here, he had noticed yesterday; and it might be an English house, with those big log fires, the comfortable chairs, and the Scotch. Yes, well, if Jean insisted, he'd have a second one. . . . There was a hell of an evening in front of him, when he must go to that blind fellow's château and discuss tomorrow's funeral—and meet the judge. They'd both had a word with poor Liz, outside afterwards. Decent of the judge. Damn decent. But he was really having the second double Scotch to brace him to go upstairs and face Liz, and then Olive. "Perhaps," he said to Julie, by the door, "Liz didn't know what she was saying."

There was no means of knowing whether either Julie or Jean believed that! And when he reached his daughter's room, and found her standing by the window, still wearing the hat she had worn in the court, he wondered for a moment if it were true. She so seldom wore a hat, he hardly recognized her in one. He had to look at her and look again, and then he took hold of it and lifted it from her head. If she were a boy he could talk straight to her, but she wasn't. He had never had much to do with women; he had never been, what they called in the service, a womanizer. If he had been, would he have been less in a quandary now? Although, romantically speaking, his wife had been a disappointment, he had been faithful to her—even when he was in another country; and when men he knew—senior officers, sometimes —got themselves mixed up, he had only contempt for them. And he wondered why these irrelevant thoughts were running through his head, when he ought to be dealing with that daughter of his, as she ought to be dealt with. But, no— that wasn't the way. Poor kid! But he couldn't say to her, "He'd never have done for you. I knew that all along."

Instead he put a hand on her shoulder and avoided looking at her eyes. He said, "You didn't know what you were saying, did you?" Then as she did not answer, he went on, "It's no good talking about it, Liz. Best to forget. But if you ever get yourself in a mess again, send for me, will you?"

Her lips twisted in a half-smile. "You are always so busy." And as she looked at her father she did not know that he was thinking, 'Curse it! That's true. But it need not be, from now on.' "I can take you," he said, "next time I go to Paris or Washington."

"Just me—alone?" she asked. And she knew that was what he meant. Not her mother. She looked out of the window, where the view of the garden, with the poplars and the barn and the flat fields where the black-and-white cows grazed was the one she had seen from ground-level the day of the party, the day that saw the beginning of everything going wrong. But she knew it had started to go wrong before then—long before then. The difference between them was the difference in their characters, their outlook. He was dead. But she could not weep any more. When he had told her to go, how was she to know? She would never have jumped—she hadn't the courage. If the rail hadn't been unsafe! If Monsieur De Jonkheere had

remembered! If Adrian had told someone else about it!
Then when her mother dragged it out of her that morning,
it had seemed the easy way. Was that, she wondered, what
could be described as a first lesson in life? That there never
was an easy way out of an act of one's own folly and wicked-
ness? She would never love anyone again. But she had
thought that at sixteen, when her mother had found out
about the Polish boy, Witold Sliwinski. But she would
never again bother about anything her mother said. And
she knew she could never write and ask that Mrs. Ainslie
what Adrian had done and talked about in those two
days.

"Just me, alone?" Elizabeth said again. "Just you and
me, on our own, would be very nice." But she was doubtful.
And doubt was in her eyes when she looked at her father
again. "You won't forget, when we get home? You
promise?"

"I promise you," he said gravely. "I promise you,
Liz." And he cleared his throat before he spoke again. "No
need to be frightened, Liz, ever again. You know what
I mean?"

.   .   .   .   .   .

The words a husband and wife spoke to each other that
evening before dinner were only, to a certain extent, a
repetition of words exchanged on other occasions pertaining
to more trivial matters. There were the usual mutual
recriminations. But this time, before the severity of his
expression, the bitterness of his invective, Olive Fulmer's
self-assurance and her confidence began slowly to desert
her, because she was in a position new to her, on the defensive,
and this time, totally at fault. The excuses she began to
make, of worry, distress, concern for their reputations,
began to sound in her own ears as flat and as unconvincing
as they did in his. He knew what he owed to her in the
past, and he knew her now for what she was, and what she
had always been. Having failed to dominate him, she had
dominated and intimidated their daughter. Before her
denial of this, and her obvious distress, he did not soften.

But the tragedy was—if you could use that word in face of the one in which they had all got involved—families had to live together. He could take Liz away with him for short spells, where, as his daughter, she would be made much of, but they'd come back. That was the way it was. He'd chosen this kind of marriage, and at his age, he couldn't change, even if he had the inclination. When he was angry, and he was angry now, he hardened. But he knew it was no use, and he felt his age, and wished they were far from here. Tomorrow, at this time, they would be. With Liz, poor little Liz. . . . She'd get over it, he thought. God! How she'd sobbed in that court! It was a relief to find her so calm, just now in her room. Yes, she'd get over it. She'd meet someone else. . . . Olive would see to that! . . . For that was the way it was, he thought. And how, in spite of all resolutions, and everything that had happened, it always would be.

CHAPTER XIV

In pouring rain the De Jonkheere family, father, mother, and son, watched by Marie and Jules, stood outside the hotel and said good-bye to the last of the English guests of that season. In Monsieur De Jonkheere's hand was a packet of milk chocolate. "For the twins, madame," he said nervously, which brought a tremor into Clare's voice as she thanked him. "I have examined your car for oil and water, madame," said Rene. (*You examined other things that were not your concern! Oh, Rene, why had you to pry and make that discovery?*)

"You will make a return visit, we hope, madame," Madame De Jonkheere said, "with the little girls for a holiday that will not end in the way this has done."

Clare smiled an answer that was polite and in the expected affirmative; but as she drove through the grey streets, and at the Porte glanced back at the towers and roofs, she knew this was her farewell and she would not come that way again. She drove slowly through a drenched countryside and came to the château, where in the avenue the branches of the trees drooped with the heaviness of the rain, and the autumnal leaves shone with brilliant moisture. A woman servant admitted her and conducted her to the library, where a clock told her she was early.

She had not expected to find that room, or any other, empty; and as she waited, alone, her ears anticipated the sound of the children's voices and of their footsteps. She stood by a window and watched the rain descending on to the flagged terrace, forming shallow pools where generations of feet had paced the stones. How forlorn looked the little summer-houses. How empty the lawns that were beginning to be covered with leaves. Today, how seeped, the whole scene, with melancholy! But she would not turn from contemplation of it towards the warmth of the fire until hands drew her back, and their presence brought a longed-for comfort. 'But I am not afraid,' she thought; and turned to face the room which had seen the birth of the libretto, and looked at the table where he had told her the work had been done, where the manuscript was now lying, complete and waiting for the composer. Into this room, then softly illuminated, with the curtains still undrawn so that there was a view of sky slowly darkening the glow of scarlet sunset, she had come to see two men standing side by side, and a wine glass had been put into her hand. . . . And the whole earth she walked on that day was of the substance that dreams were made of. . . . This day, this morning a handful of earth would be picked up and thrown, a handful of Flemish earth. . . .

But still waiting for a sound that would bring her children's hands near to touch her own, she looked up expectantly on hearing movement in the hall. And it was not their hands that drew her to the fire. The servant had entered also, bringing a tray of coffee; and in the action of pouring out a cup, of saying, "Drink this—you are cold," there was no other thought but to minister to a physical need. "Wet, too!" But in helping him off with his black overcoat, in giving him the coffee and standing near him, in silence, while he drank it, a vision of the scene from which he had returned came before her eyes; the scene in which she had believed her presence would have been an intrusion.

It was some little time afterwards, when she had gone from his side, and was sitting across the hearth from him, that she asked in a quiet voice that was once more controlled, "What have you done with Jane and Tilly?"

"I sent them out early," Pierre said. "I thought it was best for them. They knew where I was going this morning. They brought me a bunch of flowers they had picked, which I took and placed with yours and mine. I sent them off to Knocke with Prendergast. They agreed they had some shopping to do, a present they wanted to buy for their grandmother. He has orders what time they are to be back. They shouldn't be long now."

"Oh, good. Because I have to be on the quay with the car at a certain time."

Was she anxious, and eager, Pierre wondered, to be away from here? She who had ministered to him, taking his wet overcoat, putting the cup of hot coffee into his hands, and by her silence sensitive to his thoughts had, in sharing them lightened his own sorrow. Touching that bowed head of grief, knowing that tears were falling that had not fallen the morning Adrian had been found because she could not weep and let her children see her, what words had he said to her that came from his own belief? "Believe, Clare, that there is no death. Only the sense of loss for us who are left." "I do believe!"

In the thought of her going the sense of loss increased, but she was eager to go, he thought, if only to put this experience behind her, perhaps to marry, as she was pledged. So he asked her, lightly, if that was her intention. Although sorrow was her portion now, deep in her heart, there were interests that would fill her world again. And he heard her answer falling as gently and as naturally into his darkness, as her first words to him in the Grand' Place had done. But her explanation made him say, "But you exaggerated it —deliberately? True, the questions were probing, as I feared for you they would be. But that was all."

"Yes. Deliberately," she said. "I knew the first week I was in Bruges that I could never marry him. I knew myself, for the first time, in that matter."

He did not question her further, but spoke to her then of de Castelberg's arrival that afternoon; and he told her that the previous night, when the judge was reading the libretto he had wondered if it was true that children born to a man in the lateness of his physical life sometimes had outstanding mental gifts, and if in the pages of that manuscript there lay an immortality more lasting than a record in the history of English justice. He told her how the judge had asked of him, "Whose children are those I saw outside this morning?" and to repeat what he had said to the judge, that they were Adrian's friends, because immortality lay there also.

They came to speak of Elizabeth, in sadness and bewilderment, in pity. It was easier to dismiss the mother from their thoughts, their consciences. Himself, Pierre said, was not guiltless, if one could think that each one had been as an instrument that contributed, indirectly, to that end.

"He was, Clare, all the time he was working here being drawn away in his mind from that girl. And he began to be a little in love with the character of Marie, searching, until you came, for a living interpretation."

He knew, as he had been speaking, that Clare had risen from her chair; and while he had been speaking he had been thinking that if he were as other men he would let her go, when her children returned, and later on, in England, seek her again. He could write to her—as he would—but if she wrote to him she would know her letters would not be private. But was he as a callow youth, devoid of a sense of fitness, that dressed as he was, having come from the burial of her young lover, he should want to test her feelings towards him? He had learned much from her children of her circumstances, and for their sakes, for security, she would, he felt sure, marry again at some future date. Weighing the advantages against the disadvantages, she might even marry himself. It would be an alien way of life— as a foreigner in a conservative and Catholic community. She was not of his faith. And once he would have thought that an impossible obstacle, even given Papal dispensation. But she would not be, as Julie often was, impatient with its demands on him, or entirely sceptical of its truth. She had her own church, and she would be cut off from it; would miss the comfort of the familiar service, the very feel, real to her, of an English village church. She might marry him out of pity, or loneliness. She would be loyal, having given her word, a sweet companion, bear with his irritability, be understanding of the terror of that returned claustrophobia, a guide in steep places. Did he demand too much when he would only be half-content with that? But to live henceforth in the brightness of her vision, to live as he had never thought he would wish to live again! He remembered how, when he had touched her tightly closed eyelids that compressed her hidden anguish, in her room that morning, and had held her, even in the grief he shared with her, there had been transmitted to him a vision of that face, that form, from the tips of his fingers that were his instrument of sight. If, previously, in hunger he had taken any woman, that woman, nameless, would have been a symbol only, then a discovery beneath his touch that he was betraying what he held sacred.

She was by the window; and when he was beside her she said, "Ought not the children to be back by now?"

"Soon, Clare," he said gently. "I want to thank you for letting me have them here the last few days. They have said they would like to live here, to come back soon. But only, of course, if you came too. I promised to ask you."

"You should not tease them, Pierre. Some day perhaps, when they are older, it would be lovely to bring them to see you, if we ever have another holiday."

"You would not be afraid?"

"Afraid?"

"To come back? To be reminded again?"

"No. Although it is all—here."

"Does it bind us, Clare?" he asked. And he answered for her. "I think it does, but not as a means of escape from our feelings, more as a merging of them."

"I should like to think it does." She hid her face in her hands. She knew if she ever came back, when the twins were older, and herself were older and wiser, she would live again every moment of these past weeks—but live them with a different knowledge, knowing why she had been drawn to Adrian, apart from Jock, in the beginning. For he had been the medium of her first knowledge of Pierre, not only of his sacrifice and courage, but of his personality, his mind, his spirit. That day at Zoute. She had begun to know this, gradually, as one awaking from a drugged sleep, from a dream that had ended in a nightmare, those evenings recently in Bruges when Pierre had brought her news of her children. But what they would say now to each other— and there could not be many minutes left—would only be in the nature of the commonplace to prepare her to face her children calmly and with joy.

"Because," Pierre said, "there is much in that story
Adrian wrote that is close to us. To me, as well as to you."

She lifted her face and looked at him, and she remembered
the day she had read to them in the garden.

"I once," he said, "took up a certain kind of work because
my pride and my conscience, in that order, would not let
me rest. Some of it was routine, but needing steady nerves
and more of a mathematician's brain than any other. But
in that work if I had been unlucky, mine alone would have
been the penalty. I think so. I suppose it was a matter of
luck. But there were a few of our masters who were sometimes lenient to families of men caught in subversive
activities. I risked it, as did others. But the job that landed
me where it did was different. It involved Ghislaine too.
I could have refused. Someone else could have been found.
And if one was being logical and practical one could reason-
ably have said at that stage in the war, with victory for the
Allies in sight, the capture of one airman would not have
brought undue hardship to him, or much loss to the side.
But I was beginning to be bored. I wanted a risk, a different
kind of risk. Robert had got away. I suppose I envied him.
I didn't discount the praise I'd get if it came off, either.
The young people were doing the craziest things daily and
bringing them off. Did I want their admiration, to make
myself one of their number? You could give me the answer.
As Ghislaine could. You have. It is there, in Adrian's manuscript on the table. Where Marie dies—as Ghislaine came to
die in Germany. . . . I wanted, Clare, before you went, to
tell you what you mean to me. Instead, I have told you that."

She had taken his hand, and he felt her lips and her
tears upon it. "That," he said, "is my prerogative. And if it
hasn't loosened the bond between us, Clare, when we meet
again, how shall we meet?"

She could not speak. She could not answer. Not now.
His hand dropped from hers; and they both turned to the
door to meet her children, to be showered with their exuber-
ance, their kisses. But their kisses were in farewell, not
only in greeting. And besides Prendergast, Clare asked,
were there not others whom she should see, and thank for

their care and trouble? She smiled amid the infection o
smiles and laughter round her, when told of the numbe:
who had contributed, both outside and in. But perhaps
Pierre said, if she insisted, there were one or two waitin¡
to say good-bye.

That duty done she hesitated in the hall, with hei
arms round their waists, and disentangled herself. "Go
darlings," she said quietly, "go and get in the car, and wai¹
for me. Just for a few minutes."

    .   .   .   .   .   .

Julie, dressed in the deep black of mourning customary
in the country of her marriage, watched the car bearin¡
her guests away as it went down the drive, and she said tc
Jean, impulsively, "I must go to Pierre." On the departur(
of Olive and Elizabeth with Sir Frederick, when she and
Jean had brought him back from the funeral, she knew
she never wanted to see any of them again. There would
of course, be a bread-and-butter letter from Olive, an
exchange of cards at Christmas, and then a silence unti]
perhaps one day there would be the announcement thaf
poor Elizabeth's heart was mended.

"I must go to him," she said again. "Will you come?"
"No," Jean answered. "You go—alone." She would do
better, he thought, than himself. Pierre was fond of her,
often amused by her. In the dark days after he came back
he seemed to rally quicker in her company, as though her
vitality and her absurdities infused him with a will to live.

Julie pulled off her hat and threw it at Jean as she got
into her car. It was not the same hat, but it was the same
all-enveloping black veil she had last worn on the occasion
of the Requeim Mass for Ghislaine; and the very feel of it
sent memories surging. Her heart felt leaden for Pierre,
and because she had done her best for those poor young
lovers.

Leaving the car at the foot of the steps she hurried up
them to the closed heavy door, and before her hand could
reach the bell the door swung open. She nodded to Prender-

gast and smiled her greeting, and shook the rain off her sleeves. The door was shut behind her, but as she went across the hall he caught up with her. "In the library?" she asked, and went on in that direction.

"Yes, my lady. But if I were you, I would not disturb him."

The old man's eyes were strangely bright and looked strangely knowing. They were watering too. But why was he also smiling? Old servants, she paused to think, as she put her hand on the library door-handle, sometimes took too much upon themselves in their devotion, their loyalty. But she could forgive him, and ignore him. 'What times,' she thought, 'you and I had in the war, when you plodded round Brussels finding your hidden compatriots. We never quite get away in our thoughts from all that do we? It is a curiously tight bond still.' The tears an old man wept were for a young life lost. 'But I shall keep mine back,' she thought, 'from Pierre. I did right to come.' She opened the door. Then she shut it again, very quietly.

"You will not be staying, my lady?" Prendergast asked her a few moments later, when she was near the front door. And Julie shook her head. "But if you were to come back when they are gone. They leave, almost immediately."

She leant against the side of the door for support. "They?" she questioned in bewilderment. "No, I won't stay. I just came to see if there was anything I could do." She could no longer see. 'I'm dreaming,' she thought. 'It can't be.' But she knew it was. She knew that for all her astuteness, her own acknowledged inquisitiveness, events had been gathering under her very eyes, and she had been blind to them. If an old man's tears—like her own—had been for a young life lost, they fell for another reason now. Yet what had she really seen when she opened the library door against an old man's advice? Only a man and a woman standing by the fire. That was all. But the fire-light had been on their faces, and that was enough. No woman looked at a man, as that woman did, as her lips moved, without saying what was in her heart. No man cupped a woman's face in his hands unless the words she had already spoken were what he had been wanting to hear.

Julie dabbed her eyes with a handkerchief. "I'll be back later, perhaps. And I will rely on you not to mention that I have been. I trust you, Prendergast."

The old man smiled. "As you used to say very often. In those other days." He had opened the door, and he looked away from her, out at the rain. "They'll be wondering," he said, "what's up. 'Ad a bit of a wait, after all."

"Who?" And it was then Julie saw the car—not her own—parked across the drive under the trees with its nose towards the avenue, and the faces of two little girls watching her and Prendergast.

Jane and Tilly had seen Julie arrive. They had seen her jump out of the car and run up the steps and disappear inside. They knew who she was—the mother of Gaston and Lucien, who had blue hair and a big jolly laugh. She was all in black today. They knew why. But she had seen them, and she was coming to talk to them. "Hello," they both said. "Have you come to say good-bye to us?" If she were to take as long a time as their mother was taking in saying good-bye she would get awfully wet.

"Yes," Julie said. "Good-bye, Jane, is it? And Tilly?" They heard her laugh her big, jolly laugh, although it was raining on her blue hair, and her curls were changing colour.

"But I expect I shall be seeing you both again."

THE END